Also by Robert Humphreys

SIN, ORGANIZED CHARITY AND THE POOR LAW IN VICTORIAN ENGLAND

No Fixed Abode

A History of Responses to the Roofless and the Rootless in Britain

Robert Humphreys
Department of Economic History
London School of Economics and Political Science

First published in Great Britain 1999 by
MACMILLAN PRESS LTD
Houndmills, Basingstoke, Hampshire RG21 6XS and London
Companies and representatives throughout the world

A catalogue record for this book is available from the British Library.

ISBN 0–333–73846–2

First published in the United States of America 1999 by
ST. MARTIN'S PRESS, INC.,
Scholarly and Reference Division,
175 Fifth Avenue, New York, N.Y. 10010

ISBN 0–312–22563–6

Library of Congress Cataloging-in-Publication Data
Humphreys, Robert, 1928–
No fixed abode : a history of responses to the roofless and the
rootless in Britain / Robert Humphreys.
p.   cm.
Includes bibliographical references.
ISBN 0–312–22563–6 (cloth)
1. Homelessness—Government policy—Great Britain—History.
2. Homeless persons—Government policy—Great Britain—History.
3. Vagrancy—Government policy—Great Britain—History.
4. Homelessness—Law and legislation—Great Britain—History.
I. Title.
HV4545.A3H85   1999
362.5'8'0941—dc21   99–26120
                                                             CIP

This book is printed on paper suitable for recycling and made from fully managed and
sustained forest sources.

10   9   8   7   6   5   4   3   2   1
08   07   06   05   04   03   02   01   00   99

Printed and bound in Great Britain by
Antony Rowe Ltd, Chippenham, Wiltshire

To Harry, Ellen and Sam

Contents

List of Figures

List of Tables

Acknowledgements

Encompassing all the good people I should thank for their support during the writing of this book is not possible. I must however acknowledge the constant belief and fellowship that is always given me so generously from friends and colleagues in the Economic History Department of the LSE. The ready availability of their scholarship has been essential.

I must also recognise the loyal support of the many other friends and family who have continued to have faith in me. To Paul and Adrienne I must offer my thanks for finding the time in their already busy lives to read and comment so constructively on certain chapters. In particular I thank Tricia for her reading, correcting, and organising of the draft script. Also for her complete dependability whenever I needed encouragement.

Of course, the opinions expressed and any remaining faults are entirely mine.

Robert Humphreys

Abbreviations

c.	by Command
CEB	Census Enumerators' Book
CHAR	Campaign for Homeless and Rootless
COS	Charity Organisation Society
CPAG	Child Poverty Action Group
DHSS	Department of Health and Social Security
DoE	Department of the Environment
DRO	Disablement Resettlement Officer
DSS	Department of Social Security
ed(s)	editor(s)
edn	edition
EVA	End Vagrancy Act
GATT	General Agreement on Tariffs and Trade
HMI	Homeless Mentally Ill Initiative
HMSO	His (Her) Majesty's Stationery Office
IBRD	International Bank for Reconstruction and Development
ICs	Instruction Centres
IMF	International Monetary Fund
JP	Justice of the Peace
JVC	Joint Vagrancy Committee
LCC	London County Council
LGB	Local Government Board
MoH	Ministry of Health
NAB	National Assistance Board
OPEC	Organisation of Petroleum Exporting Companies
p(p)	page(s)
PLB	Poor Law Board
PLC	Poor Law Commission
PP	Parliamentary Paper
RCs	Reception Centres
RSI	Rough Sleepers Initiative
SHiL	Single Homeless in London
UAB	Unemployment Assistance Board
UNRRA	United Nations Relief and Rehabilitation Administration

1 Introduction

Nobody knows, or has ever known, how many homeless people there are, and there is no agreement about what in fact homelessness is.[1]

Homeless, wandering, aimless people without roots are to be found in most British towns as the twenty-first century approaches. They huddle for refuge against the cold and rain in nooks and crannies near enough to the passing public to plead in the hope that some may momentarily pause to spare them a few pennies. When the office-workers and shoppers have returned to their homes, the street-dwellers sidle cautiously into their cardboard beds temporarily below the underpass or in the doorways of prestigious department stores. They hope waste heat will muffle them against the cold and that shop-front lights may protect them from roving predators and drunken better-off fun-makers. Their fragile economic resources are exhausted, they are the poorest of the poor, members of a so-called underclass clinging perilously to the fringe of society. When recommending their inclusion as the bottom tier of a proposed new eight-tier social pyramid for Britain, the Economic and Social Research Council explained that socially the position of the underclass 'is obviously the worst of all'.[2] Usually submissive but sometimes truculent, they are mainly scorned and rejected by the more advantaged. Homelessness has increased sharply over the last twenty years with a disturbingly larger proportion of teenagers and young adults. The causes of this undesirable phenomenon are not clear. Are people homeless mainly from economic pressure or because of their own inadequacies? Has the pandering welfare state so eroded individual character as to remove the incentive for the homeless to improve themselves? Or have fault-lines in national economic structures made it impossible for these people to participate in society without further education, positive training and emotional support?

In many ways the plight of the modern-day street homeless is strikingly similar to that of roving vagrants and vagabonds of former times. Through the centuries the number of rootless people and their typology has fluctuated in total and in the varying proportions of them that were hardened petty criminals, social scroungers or genuine bereft innocents. The importance granted by authorities to the problems of the homeless has historically varied. It has depended on changes in

1

demography, the economy, the price of food, the availability of work, natural disasters, disease epidemics, war and the social mood. The homeless poor has always included the young and the old, orphans, widows, people without family or friend and those disabled by accident, war or disease.[3] This volume explains how individual, familial and establishment attitudes have intertwined with economic, ideological and political change to affect the number who were homeless. Repeatedly, when their number increased there were legislative attempts to define and control them. 'Vagrant' has been the word most used by the legislature to describe poor people without a fixed home.[4] Among the many other words used in a derogatory way is 'gypsy'. Gypsies are of course a nomadic people to be found across Europe and other parts of the world. In Britain, as in most countries, they have consistently stood apart from the social mainstream. Because genuine Gypsies travel the country and are not usually wealthy they are viewed as habitual offenders against the law. They are generally shunned by most members of the community and they appear as likely candidates for consideration in a volume dealing with travellers who are poor. However, there is the basic difference that Gypsies tend to be among the most self-sufficient of wandering people if only because their dwelling-place is composite to them and is equally mobile. In spite of this difference it suited the authorities set on applying uniform sanctions against all poor itinerants to include Gypsies in the nebulous catch-all category of vagrant. Nevertheless, because Gypsies were usually not homeless and rarely made use of casual ward, lodging house or hostel, many of the references made in this volume to the travelling poor are not applicable to them. Readers wishing to learn more about the special characteristics of Gypsies are directed elsewhere to one of the many excellent studies already devoted to them.[5]

Addressed in the concluding chapter of this book is the question of how far any explanation of street homelessness through history is justified in focusing on individual character defects while largely ignoring the effect of 'economic booms and slumps, depressed regions, poor housing, schooling, health facilities, occupational opportunities and working conditions'.[6] Do changes in these exogenous circumstances generate social forces which throw light on the causes of street homelessness? The 'structuralist' or 'environmentalist' left-of-centre perspective assumes they do. They are convinced that structural economic factors, social inadequacy and exploitation are major reasons for homelessness which cause people to become trapped in 'ghettoes of poverty'.

Another powerful body of opinion adopts the opposing 'individualistic' view. They contend that the homeless mainly have themselves to blame for their predicament and that it is misleading to envisage them as innocent victims of circumstance. Structural economic factors are rejected other than to recognise that irresponsibly excessive state benefits have been distributed to the detriment of the poor. This is because welfare payments allegedly cocoon the homeless from real privation which has encouraged them to indulge in an indolent anti-social way of life. By the same token, the open-air freedom, the non-commitment to fixed hours, the protracted alcoholic binge within a social group and the feeling of being unburdened by communal responsibility are all seen as being attractive options for the street homeless. With low skills, poor education, uncertain employment (if any), persistent poverty and ghetto dwelling when not tramping, rough sleepers have a high incidence of health problems, both physical and mental.[7] They are seen as indolent people whose willingness to milk the social system has been encouraged by official profligacy. The parasitic demands of the homeless on honest society have allegedly been further stimulated by equally ill-advised or carelessly administered haphazard voluntary gifts. Individualists maintain that the only sure means of rescuing these unwholesome people from the trough of their inadequacies is to sharply curtail both official payments and voluntary gifts. It is argued that the homeless should only be recognised as having rights in a society when they contribute to that society instead of sponging from it. Otherwise, like criminals, their civil rights should be rescinded.

Individualistic views are not new and are strongly founded in history. They were strengthened in the nineteenth century by the belief that the worth of the nation was, in the long run, the accumulated qualities of the people composing it. Britain's greatness was seen to have been built on the strength of character of its citizens. National industrial and economic dominance was the direct result of the energetic application of the entrepreneurial spirit. Personal success incurred diligence, discipline, deference, morality, sobriety and self-reliance. Conformity with social conventions was the responsibility of the individual and essential in the building of an acceptable morality. Poverty resulted from improvidence, insobriety and 'character deficiency'. Individual shortcomings could always be overcome by personal discipline, hard work, and a positive attitude towards self-improvement.

Belief in the paramount importance of individual ethics led the nineteenth-century middle classes to conclude that it was unfair, undesirable and nationally dangerous to allow a lazy residuum to loiter aimlessly in dark corners, occasionally wandering out to disturb honest citizens by their aggressive begging. Allegedly, the influence of this festering group of layabouts spread crime, indecency, illegitimacy and immorality. Societies were formed in London and in provincial towns to repress the malignant mendicity by investigating personal circumstances and infusing Smiles's principles of 'Self-Help' by the withholding of 'promiscuous' charity.[8] The elimination of haphazard voluntary alms combined with a more rigorous interpretation of the Poor Law would, it was alleged, save the ragged 'plague of beggars' from the depths of their personal abyss. Samuel Morley MP, the textile industrialist, dismissed the possibility that the widespread nineteenth-century urban squalor was a contributor to poverty. He explained how in social explanation 'many people begin at the wrong end. They say that people drink because they live in bad dwellings; I say they live in bad dwellings because they drink. It makes all the difference the way you put it. The first essential is not to deal with the habitation, but the habit.'[9]

Dr Thomas Hawksley's rationale in 1869 of forcefully encouraging the poor towards their own moral betterment through a 'system of charity police' was quickly developed by the Charity Organisation Society (COS).[10] They were convinced that the profligacy of 'unwisely administered' charity was doing 'incalculable harm' by seducing the individual from 'the wise and toilsomeness of life'.[11] Lack of work was nothing but a lame excuse used by worthless elements usually destitute from their own fecklessness. Drunkenness, debauchery, and the abandonment of family ethics were seen as the most likely contributors to the indigent person's plight. Good-for-nothing people must be rewarded, as the law required, by workhouse incarceration so that they could benefit morally from deterrent discipline. At a Poor Law Conference in 1881, Mr W. M. Wilkinson provided his 'expert' opinion that tramps were 'perpetuating and increasing the breed and begetting a race which has the very genius of not working within its bones and sinews'. He maintained that if the natural history of this 'nomadic, lowest, seething-class could be written, we should probably find that it is the residuum or dregs of our social system for many centuries'.[12]

The COS banner has again been unfurled in principle on both sides of the Atlantic during the last twenty years. Exponents of their theories ask why modern governments persist with the irresponsibility of undermining individual character by mistakenly supplying universal social benefits. They take up the concept that state welfare provision is largely to blame for the emergence of socially threatening values including: a disregard for family values, single parenting by design, citizenship shortcomings, drug dependency, criminal behaviour, loutishness and an erosion of moral fibre. By succumbing to these temptations the street homeless lose the possibility of developing their own strength of character. Allegedly, people who occupy the streets at night exist in a void without ethical regulation or social restraint. This inadequacy is said to explain the street-dweller's plight in terms of a personal failure to resist the temptation of welfare payments or to accept responsibility for their own well-being.

Sociologists such as Charles Murray who adopt a right-of-centre stance, are not surprised that homeless people, many with an inappropriate family-background, yield to the temptation of accepting social benefits for doing nothing. He relates their shortcomings to inherent genetic weaknesses in 'an underclass' bred by parents who themselves had been discarded by society. Sir Keith Joseph, when UK Secretary of State for Health and Social Security in the early 1970s, proposed that a 'cycle of deprivation' had been transmitted generationally by families bred in poverty. The deviant behaviour of homeless people was attributed to their own broad acceptance that their social values have become warped over generations when their forefathers also suffered low socio-economic status and esteem. Murray and other right-wing strategists concur with the theme that a 'culture of poverty' has been nurtured by years of misguided profligate state welfare policies. Because of the morally destructive nature of welfare 'handouts', a poverty paradox develops once a person believes it to be socially acceptable that they should receive benefit payments. The genuinely disadvantaged, whom welfare was intended to help, are seen to suffer most from severe erosion of their moral fibre and destruction of their self-motivation towards improving themselves. Individualists argue that in the depraved social relationships in which the homeless blissfully wallow, welfare beneficiaries would be derided by their associates should they ever seek a low-paid unpleasant job when state handouts are readily available just by going to collect them. Murray is convinced that these dangerously shallow personal values are 'contaminating the life of entire neighbourhoods'.[13] Such an approach to social problems is predicated on the belief that the best way to lift the street homeless from their nadir is to promote 'a social practice to save, correct, treat or rehabilitate him by the establishment of social control institutions'.[14]

Lawrence Mead is among Social Authoritarians who share the belief that the obligations of citizenship must be enforced. He alleges that without such positive action society will continue to malfunction and suffer the contamination that so concerns Murray and others. Mead is convinced that government welfare programmes for people like the homeless are too permissive in style and content with persistent failure to impose meaningful obligations to match the hand outs. Dependent groups are seen to be shielded from the pressures of functioning with civil responsibility as is required of other citizens. Mead claims that data trends in the USA confirm that social functioning has declined. Between 1960 and 1983, the number receiving family benefits more than tripled, unemployment more than doubled, serious crime nearly quadrupled and there was decline in the academic skills of pre-college students. Mead argues that to reverse these trends it is necessary to invoke public authority. Disadvantaged groups such as the homeless must be mandated to complete social tasks and should not be allowed to shirk low-waged jobs as at present. For the well-being of the nation, they must be made to recognise that the completion of such work is a public obligation akin to paying taxes or obeying the law. An enforced change to a more positive attitude among the poor will, allegedly, also improve them as individuals.[15]

The historical evidence in this volume does not generally support the Murray or the Mead perspectives. Repeatedly there are indications that poverty and its constituent of homelessness arise mainly from structural economic inbalance. Factors bearing on the scale and severity of homelessness nationally include the level of employment, the quality of education and the institutional frameworks which govern the allocation of wealth and income. There are also signs of growing interrelated global, institutional, class-based cultures which increasingly affect the ways poor people are forced to exist throughout our modern world. The 'internationalisation' of industry, symbolised by half of the one hundred wealthiest powers in the world being transnational commercial corporations and not national states, ominously dictates the fate of the poor throughout the world. Decision makers in these vast commercial undertakings are not bound by 'citizenship' morals so much as by the expectations of the shareholder.[16]

HISTORICAL SUMMARY TO VAGRANCY LEGISLATION

Communities have long been alert to a possible danger from some strangers. The transition of this awareness into what became a blanket fear of homeless travellers has not been accidental. It was developed by legislation during the early Middle Ages and then by a stream of Tudor vagrancy laws. Successive statutes habitually portrayed the indigent traveller as someone who constantly verged on criminality. They were seen to be guilty for their own miserable condition and should be made to suffer accordingly for any subsistence relief they might be granted. It was soon recognised as being desirable to control the impoverished itinerant with equal force across the nation as the very rigour of this conformity would militate against mobility. However, uniform control was close to impossible prior to 1834 with 15 635 parishes in England and Wales each separately relieving their own and casual paupers.[17] As officials in each parish levied their own poor rates, there was wild variation in how centrally disseminated edicts were interpreted and applied.

Official concern about the dangers rootless people might bring at any particular period of history can be gauged by the frequency with which pertinent Parliamentary Acts, Bills and Ordinances were proclaimed. Until the nineteenth century, legislative activity was usually in response to direct pressure group action, invariably from the upper echelons of society. More recently, enactments have been prompted by recommendations from the various Royal, Parliamentary or Government Departmental bodies appointed to investigate vagrancy, homelessness and poverty.

It is commonly held that whereas not every Englishman can own a castle, each is expected to acquire a roof over their head. In England, the idea of 'owning one's home is a basic and natural desire'.[18] Definition of what we mean by a home is itself difficult but the campaigning charity Shelter has defined those lacking one as being people 'who live in conditions so bad that a civilized family life is impossible'.[19] Whether or not the particular individual reaches this situation from misfortune or choice, they soon find themselves marooned on the periphery of a society which for most periods in recent centuries has been, at best, largely apathetic to their plight.

Many among the public would settle for the idea that the modern street dweller can be broadly described as either a carefree welfare-grabbing scrounger or a tough drunkard hardened by years of rough living. However, investigations over many years, by a range of researchers, have found that most street homeless are naively drifting in search of work and a more meaningful association with a public that largely ignores their destitution. Street dwellers today are often found to have psychiatric and personality disorders, having been pushed to the margins of an ever more materialistically focused 'developed' world. Until fifty years ago, those who trudged around the country or were recognisably without permanent roots, were dealt with in Britain through a catalogue of 'Vagrancy Acts' which had been augmented repeatedly through the centuries.[20] After the Second World War and coincident with the birth of the Welfare State, the legislative use of the term 'vagrant' was laid aside for a quarter of a century. People previously described in this way benefited from the softer appellation of being 'homeless'. Even then, the vagrancy laws were not scrapped, merely held discreetly in abeyance. As the millennium approached so the moribund legislation was resurrected. The street homeless in particular have had to become alert again to the persistent danger of being charged as vagrants. Many features of twentieth-century street homelessness are characteristic of vagrancy in the past. Sleeping rough, casual work, begging, petty crime, hostels, shelters, common lodging houses, reception centres, soup kitchens, imprisonment profiles and mental instability remain all too common features in the lives of those using our streets as their home.

Medieval vagrants were recognised contemporaneously as having five distinguishing traits: they were poor, able-bodied, without work, rootless and increasingly lawless. Beier claimed that in the sixteenth and early seventeenth century vagrants grew in number as the 'product of profound social dislocations – a huge and growing poverty problem, disastrous economic and demographic shifts'.[21] Although vagabonds, beggars, travelling tradesmen and wanderers had been around since the birth of civilisation, for much of that time they were not subject to the stigmatisation that followed. It was commonly accepted in early times that the provision of alms to the destitute was a Christian duty and that certain pedlars, herbalists, tradesmen, musicians and missionaries depended on mobility for their welfare.[22] Geremek paints much the same picture about responses to the travelling poor on mainland Europe. During the early Middle Ages there was not the persistent humiliation and loss of dignity that begging has more recently incurred. In Europe there was a medieval distinction between the 'shamefaced poor' and other types of pauper. The former term denoted those reduced to poverty after having seen better times. It was 'never applied to the mass of working poor for whom indigence was a normal condition' and for whom the acceptance of charity involved no loss of dignity.[23] The fundamental characteristic expected of the impoverished was that when they needed support they should openly display their gratitude to their donor and offer a prayer for his or her soul. As in most religions, Christian alms were represented as the fruits of a moral notion of the gift and of fortune on the one hand and of sacrifice on the other. It was preached that generosity is an obligation, because 'Nemesis avenges the poor and the gods for the superabundance of happiness and wealth of certain people who should rid themselves of it'.[24]

This volume addresses the social difficulties perceived by British law-makers through history in the fact that some of their countrymen lacked a permanent home. As the industrially structured Mammon started to take a grip, it was considered that because poor travellers were less accountable locally they must form an accompanying potential national threat to social stability should they accumulate. Official attitudes to the homeless in the Middle Ages included simplistic indiscriminate classifications of what has always been a diverse aggregate of individuals. By the sixteenth century, the cumulative effect of 'loosely labelling indigent strangers as criminals and subjecting them to degrading punishments such as public flogging, branding, pillorying and even execution, was to impose an unwelcome stigma on all poor strangers and to reinforce a public and an inbred fear of unattached strangers'.[25] Centuries later a prestigious Government Committee appointed to examine vagrancy still encountered difficulty of definition. They found it impossible to say at what stage a genuine traveller failing to find work should be regarded as a vagrant. Nor could they agree on how much work he needed to accumulate before a so-called vagrant lost that appellation. A fundamental difficulty was that a wide range of poor travellers could well be found side-by-side in a multiplicity of temporary resting places like casual wards, common lodging-houses, shelters, barns and brick works as well as being 'on the road'. The Government Committee noted that another hurdle preventing them defining what they meant by the word 'vagrant' was the huge variation in the total number of poor itinerants dependent on the state of the economy, the weather and seasons of the year.[26]

The difficulty of defining where any particular poor traveller should be fitted along the spectrum between being 'genuinely' homeless and being a hardened professional scrounger is no easier as the twentieth century draws to a close. Take for example the seemingly simple question of where the line can be drawn in contemporary Britain between those with a home and those without. At one extreme of the homelessness spectrum there is broad consensus that those sleeping rough in the streets should be classified as homeless. There is less agreement along the greyer continuum from that extreme. Do the homeless include all the people spending time in hostels, cheap hotels, boarding

houses, cheap bed and breakfasts, squats, crash pads, renting insecure
private premises or staying with friends?[27] When the historic dimension of contemporary expectations and socially specific concepts like
relative deprivation are introduced the scope for indecision as to
which people, now and in former times, should be considered as
homeless is multiplied sharply.[28] This imprecision complicates
attempts at quantitative analysis of the homeless through history.
Nevertheless, data are available which indicate repeatedly that there
was strong legislative and political response to increase in the number
of the itinerant poor and that this numerical escalation was itself
stimulated by economic, social, political or demographic change. The
methodology of bringing legislative cause and effect together with
these exogenous factors has rarely been featured over a protracted
historical period in the literature of vagrancy. This in spite of such
considerations providing the essential backcloth from which to
develop a historically informed picture.

Western democracies depend on market mechanisms to motivate
individuals towards meaningful work. They are then held in employment by both promises of rewards and threats of penalties. Basic to
the modern economic system is a need to constantly improve techniques and products with which to conquer new expanding markets.
Each revision in manpower distribution, created by filling the emerging differently skilled occupations in theory satisfies the requirements
of a variety of dispersed profit-orientated individuals and organisations. The needs of workers as regards their skills, numbers and geographical location are persistently modified in response to these
economic forces. When an economy is strong most workers, motivated
by financial inducement, are assisted by expert training as how best to
absorb the physical, psychological, educational and environmental
changes demanded of them. In periods of economic depression or of
rapid modernisation, more people are left without a job to become
constituents in a national unemployment bank. For those who are
both unemployed and homeless, the opportunity for effective training
and education to equip them for participation in modern society
recedes despairingly in relation to the length of time they remain on
the fringe of that society.

Workers in western democracies have been taught to believe that
the ability and willingness to do a good day's work provides them with
a desirable badge of respectability. So much so that when redundancy
attaches to them the stigma of being without a job, the associated
distress and disorganisation can be psychologically calamitous. In

pre-industrial society such intense trauma was less likely to bear on the honest labourer temporarily without work. Generally, he would not incur stigma as it would probably have resulted from an unwelcome phenomenon like a disastrous harvest for which he could not be blamed. The individual would also be aware of the traditional paternal support mechanisms available to him. Sir Frederic Eden described how on such occasions, the villein, 'if unable to work, was maintained by his lord; as the pauper is now supported by his parish; ... the legislature was not called upon to enact laws, either for the punishment of vagrants, or the relief of the impotent and aged'.[29]

Employment in the industrial era incurs no ongoing irrevocable relationship, as existed between master and rural worker. Now the employee enters into a contract with an employer to receive payment for his labour. When that employer has no more use for him, he is expected to seek his livelihood elsewhere. At times of economic depression in a modern environment of large-scale organisation it can be virtually impossible for the individual to obtain another job. As capitalism developed so governments became increasingly concerned about a possible danger that widespread joblessness may nourish collective civil disturbance. Strikes were the obvious form of demonstration developed from the nineteenth century but there still remained worries about 'crime, mass protests, riots – a disorder that may even threaten to overturn existing social and economic arrangements'.[30]

Early recognition of the state's responsibility for maintaining national stability became apparent during the Tudor dynasty when they advised local authorities to arrange placatory relief for their poor. By the same token, they felt the need to limit any possibility that the relief might become an unjustified temptation for the cunning poor to take what they did not deserve. Relief was steadily to become more stigmatised. From 1834, as part of the New Poor Law's concept of 'less eligibility' poor relief was never allowed to rise much above the meagre level sufficient to prevent starvation. This satisfied economy and made it less likely that an individual would muster excess energy for translation into civil disturbance. Governments have repeatedly made it plain that society expects the destitute to pay for their relief by the completion of a work task.

Social organisation in Britain has tended less to be under public control than its counterparts in many European countries. As regards relieving the indigent this generalisation is less true. For more than four hundred years all who 'cannot obtain food and shelter for themselves or for their nearest dependants, have a right to relief from compulsory rates levied upon the rest of the community'.[31] State involvement in protecting the poor from starvation has become integral with the British heritage. Economic, social, political, cultural and legal factors have intertwined as a backcloth on which, at any particular time, their contemporaries have decided what was the 'appropriate' attitude to the wandering poor. Even then, despite administrators' repeated claims of their success in developing a reasonably respectable and workable Poor Law system, there has consistently been official admission that vagrancy, in all its forms, remained a decidedly more intractable problem.[32]

During the manufacturing era the larger number of people without jobs in depressed phases of the economic cycle has multiplied to disturbing levels. Chronic structural long-term unemployment emerged in the period between the two twentieth-century World Wars to blight the lives of millions of families on a scale never previously envisaged. Although not their original purpose, the welfare provisions introduced after the Second World War helped to placate the workforce when British unemployment leapt over the three million mark early in the 1980s. Since then, a modern-day version of the Poor Law's 'less eligibility' concept has gradually unfolded. In tune with the ideas of Charles Murray and Lawrence Mead, the value of social benefits in Britain has been refined and trimmed in recent years, the strategy being that the unemployed should never be deterred from seeking paid employment no matter how badly paid or superficially unattractive that employment might appear.

For most British people there has been clear improvement in their standard of living over recent centuries. Working-class people are generally decidedly better off in material terms than were their forefathers. Rough sleepers are among the few exceptions. While dependent for their nourishment on handouts, the present-day vagrant poor have scant access to the many twentieth-century domestic innovations which have become part of everyday life for most British people. As a consequence there is little material difference in the lifestyle of the modern street homeless from that of medieval vagabonds or the Victorian residuum. When related to the comfortable living conditions in late twentieth-century society the psychological discomfort of the present-day rough sleeper in his sense of relative deprivation is likely to be worse than was that of his predecessor. Omnipresent media pressure is so pervasive that even those huddled in the damp cold of the urban street cannot fail to absorb the beguiling advertising messages from billboards and from the rejected newspapers serving as their blanket. Their discomfort is compounded with the disconcerting awareness that those just slightly above them on the social scale such as low wage earners lucky enough to have a permanent home, are usually able to enjoy the advantages of a whole range of modern domestic consumer goods.

The social isolation of the street homeless can be demonstrated diagrammatically by locating them in relation to other social groups on a 'grid' system of the type proposed by Mary Douglas, Figure 1.1.[33] Represented at the upper extreme of the vertical participation axis are social groups with strong systematic levels of communication between individuals. The lower pole represents a private insular individual lacking a communicative code with society. The extreme left of the horizontal axis corresponds to a dominating dictatorial group or person. The right extremity would be the location of an individual or small group totally dominated by others in society. To consider some examples, professional groups (P) are likely to be placed in some part of the upper left segment. Providers of a social service (S) are likely to

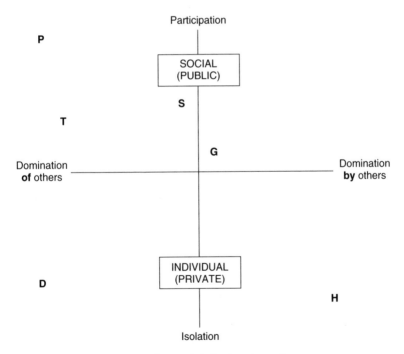

Figure 1.1   The street homeless and their place in society.

be fairly high on the participation axis. They will be inclined to move
to the right on the domination axis and lower on the vertical axis when
acting as individuals. Membership of a trade-union (T) would move
them horizontally leftwards as they are more protected from domination by others. When participating in disruptive industrial action, their
group could increasingly be represented as dominating others. A dem-
agogic dictator would be located in the lower left quadrant by (D) and
would move further away in a south-westerly direction from the inter-
section point as his/her domination isolates them from participation in
society. An integrated group lacking a permanent address, such as
Gypsies (G) would be represented close to the vertical axis because of
their high level of autonomy. As regards participation in society, they
would nestle near to the horizontal axis because although integrated
they are a muted group retaining marked differences with society at
large. The street homeless (H), as an uncoordinated outsider group is
represented in the lower right quadrant. They are well towards the
right extremity of the horizontal axis because of their high depen-
dence on others and well down towards the 'isolation' pole on account
of their tentative unpredictable peripheral association with the
general public. The precise location of the street homeless on such a
diagram is influenced by changing attitudes of government and
society. In the post Second World War Welfare State era the diagram-
matic location of a homeless person would move towards the in-
tersection point. As individualism reasserted itself on British
Governments in the 1980s so the homeless would correspondingly
progress towards a more south-easterly direction. Few, if any, other
social group would be so forlornly isolated.

The problem of the vagrant poor and homelessness in general arises
when individuals and families, usually involuntarily but occasionally
by choice, fail to conform with the commonly accepted characteristic
of social stability in that they lack a permanent home. This volume
monitors legislative response to changes in the number of the vagrant
poor through the centuries. In this way it contributes to the debate as
to why so many homeless people continue to struggle on the fringe of
our flourishing modern capitalist society, much as their predecessors
did in the primitive societal framework of former times. Without the
historical association of economic, social and political factors, it is
easy to forget the past and to seek simplistic explanations based
entirely on the present.[34] Although data on vagrancy and homelessness in their various forms are neither abundant nor precise they form
an essential contribution towards explaining the persistent presence

of so many people in Britain today who lack the dignity of a permanent home.

The essential message from this volume is that time and time again through the centuries the number of homeless people has increased as a direct result of factors such as economic downturn, the cessation of war and climatic catastrophe. The response of those in authority is to clamp down ever harder on the increased numbers 'of no fixed abode' regardless of how valid their reasons may be for having found themselves in their predicament.

2 Early Vagrancy Legislation

Obviously in any state where there are beggars there are also, hidden away somewhere about the place, thieves and pickpockets and temple robbers and all such practitioners of crime .... And the reason for their existence is lack of education, bad upbringing and a bad form of government. Plato[1]

Throughout history, attitudes to the wandering beggar have vacillated between tolerance and repression, the former response being most dominant in early times and the latter gradually taking hold with industrialisation and urbanisation.[2] Most people across Europe were fundamentally poor. There were enormous disparities between them and the few who were fabulously wealthy.

According to Cipolla, the poverty of pre-industrial European societies and the unequal distribution of wealth were 'reflected in the presence of a considerable number of "poor" and "beggars" (the two terms being then used as synonyms)'. Surveys of different countries showed the 'poor', the 'beggars' and the 'wretched' in cities to total between 10 and 20 per cent of the population.[3] With so many people constantly hovering near destitution and with no savings or welfare scheme to support them, their only chance of survival other than breaking the law was the voluntary transfer of essential sustenance through charity. When disasters in the weather or economy struck, all too frequently, there was common awareness that many would be struggling desperately to maintain the narrow balance of life over death. Purse strings were then usually opened by the relatively rich.

Early indications of begging appear in the eighth century BC, when beggars were first mentioned in the Old Testament. An early reference to vagabondage in the British Isles was in the Roman history of *Ammianus Marcellinus* AD 368. It refers to warlike bands of Irish and Scots 'roving over different parts of the country and committing great ravages'. They included rent-paying tribes who had risen against their lords because of the 'exorbitant exactions levied against them to support their prodigal entertainments, exactions which in later times were known under the name of coshering'.[4]

16

Relief to the destitute in Anglo-Saxon Britain was undertaken by the Church. It assumed and accepted the responsibility, individually and collectively, for the care of the impotent poor. To provide assistance for the needy, whether they be sick, widowed, elderly or child was accepted as a fundamental Christian virtue. Gifts were offered, not only for the well-being of those needing assistance but also for the salvation of the charitable. Because almsgiving to the wandering beggar was viewed as a means of washing away one's sin, so the poor itinerant himself became an image of sanctity. Every gift to the needy would contribute through the recipient's prayer to a favourable assessment of earthly deeds when eventually their time of ultimate reckoning arrived. The provision of succour to the poor and the associated self-sacrifice ranked throughout early Christendom on a par with prayer and fasting as outward and visible signs of inward and spiritual grace.[5] Ecclesiastical almsgiving was occasionally augmented by gifts from royalty, nobility or the gentry. Tours of the country or the estates, certain holy days and the funerals of sovereigns and men of great wealth were reasons for liberal alms distribution in Europe as well as in Britain.[6] The Venerable Bede describes how the Anglo-Saxon King Oswald gave Easter food to the poor and employed a servant whose main task was to distribute relief as needed throughout the year. The Kings Alfred and Athelstan are also said to have distributed help to the poor.[7]

Idealistic principles about begging being holy were eventually eroded by more humanistic intrusions. These proposed the concept that since a good Christian contributed his everyday work towards the well-being of society, it was logical that idleness must be anti-social, immoral and fraudulent. As a consequence, even in those early times the King and his nobles recognised the need to keep idle hands occupied. It helped maintain civil order and retained the hierarchical social structure of rulers and ruled, the latter being categorised as part of the land owned by their master. Because of these doubts, Anglo-Saxon legislation alerted contemporaries of possible dangers from harbouring indolent itinerants. King Wihtraed of Kent (AD 690–725) decreed that if 'a shorn man go wandering about for hospitality let it be given him at once, and, unless he have leave, let it not be that any one entertain him longer ... if a man come from afar, or a stranger, go out of the [high]way, and he then neither shout nor blow a horn, he is to be accounted a thief, either to be slain or be redeemed'.[8] Through present-day eyes such laws are stark but were typical of their time. Because they determined each person's lawful place of residence, they were claimed to be protective laws of settlement designed to maintain community peace. An important comparison with what was to follow in later centuries was that the legislation, bleak as it may have been, was not directed primarily against the very poor. In those early days the laws were intended to guard against external threat to communities and as such encompassed rich and poor alike in an epoch when the proximity of adventurous hostile tribes and races was a constant potential danger to the isolated individual or family. Therefore, although the monarch or noble was officially the protector of lower individuals, it became sensible, if only for self-interest, for each freeman to associate himself with some borough or parish and to engage in mutual pledges with others in the same locality. Each individual then reciprocally became responsible for the peace of their community, for tithing, and for the other's safety. In this way, person, family and property were protected. Without this two-way associative responsibility, he might be suspected of being an outlaw to be chased or even slain with impunity. Although these early laws constrained mobility, they also brought security by confining 'every man to some defined and permanent local habitation' at a time when 'various hordes of invaders' attempted to bring the country under subjection. Coode argues that in such an unstable environment a law of 'settled domicile was the indispensable condition of security and progress' and can fairly be recognised as a national and popular law of settlement. It was in no respect a partial compulsory law of removal.⁹ It provided a relatively impartial organisational structure across the community and applicable to all sections of the community. In this way, 'a rude, turbulent, unsettled, and almost lawless people was induced and compelled to adopt the habits of civil life, and to connect themselves with the profitable occupation of the soil in defined localities, practices comparatively unknown to this people previously'. In Saxon times, there was no class of free labourer with 'strong interests to carry their best property, their strength and their skill, to the most favourable market' so that in compelling every person to have a domicile, it did not prevent him from choosing it where he pleased and afforded him with all safe facilities for doing so.¹⁰ In essence, these early settlement laws were aimed at trouble makers. Strangers of good-will such as the travelling jester, able to provide stories, jokes, tricks, acrobatics and news from distant parts, were welcome to the feudal manor as a break in the monotony of life.¹¹

With the same code of security, Saxon peasants lacking a permanent home needed to 'reside with some householder, without whose surety he would not be regarded as a member of the community, nor be entitled to its protection'. The negative side of these early settlement laws was that although they had universal application, they naturally confirmed and strengthened the existing structure between rich and poor. For example, Nicholls maintains that a consequence of these laws was that Anglo-Saxon nobles for the most part spent their time in 'riotous living and in coarse sensual excesses, whilst the great body of occupiers and cultivators of the soil were held in a state of bondage, without the power of removing from the estates on which they may be said to have vegetated'.[12]

King Canute ordained that each householder was responsible for the individuals in his household, whether bonded or free. This responsibility was said to involve elements of both protection and control 'to prevent the growth of vagabondage and violence'. After the Norman invasion, the labouring classes remained serfs or slaves, praedial or domestic, and partly villeins attached to the soil. If anything, the feudal system of bondage became sterner and breaches of the peace were severely punished. William the Conqueror's successors were equally ruthless. They maintained civil order until the barons wrung the Magna Carta out of John in 1215 and provided themselves with the authority to rule all below them with a replica of the regal despotism they themselves had usurped. As a consequence, military chiefs with armed retainers ranged the land and when added to the tougher hardened element of vagrancy created an environment where 'the poor, the aged, and the impotent were encumbrances undeserving of care'.[13] It was from these early years of the thirteenth century that the secular authorities, both national and local, began to show an interest in the way poor relief was provided. The interest was motivated partly by their wish to repress vagrants and partly by their determination to control as many charitable endowments as possible.

In medieval Britain a long journey was never undertaken lightly, but as the maps of Matthew Paris show, a network of highways did exist. The Normans had made the main roads wide enough for two wagons to pass each other and apart from in foul weather they were generally usable. Minor roads were a different story. Constant encroachments caused maddening bottlenecks with surfaces repeatedly falling into 'ruinous disrepair either through neglect or through wilful destruction'.[14] The King and his court, noblemen of lesser rank, administrators of the shires and the courts, all moved on horseback along the same narrow pitted tracks tramped by humble pilgrims, itinerant tradesmen, vagabonds, troubadours and the vagrant poor.[15]

As already noted, although individual freedom may have been constrained by the medieval economy, it did provide a safety net designed
to encapsulate the agricultural worker within a cocoon of 'unfreedom'
within which he could depend on the protection of his liege lord from
the worst excesses of unemployment, sickness and old age.[16] By the
fifteenth century, in most rural areas, access to forest, rivers and
meadows, although regulated, allowed for additional sources of livelihood or grazing, gleaning, picking and gathering. 'A sort of "moral
economy" regulated access to such resources as well as the distribution of its fruits among the needy of a parish.'[17] On the other hand, the
need for 'Lord and labourer' to be a synonym for 'Master and slave'
was fundamental to the economic well-being of the ruling classes so
that any tendency for villeins to stray from their established workplace
should be curbed. This early awareness nurtured the Establishment
view over the succeeding centuries that there was need for ever tighter
legislative constraints on that freedom. It encouraged the development of social stigma which by now was becoming attached to those of
no fixed abode. For poor people able to withstand the hardships and
the uncertainties of tramping, the example of the mendicant friar
showed how to subsist from begging, should work not be available at
home. With the population of England only 5 per cent of what it is
today, there was ample opportunity for personal concealment from
authority for those willing to disregard the dangers and grab the
chance of emancipation by fleeing from their own parish.[18] Travel was,
in principle at least, symbolic of individual independence. Eden
described the bygone relationship between 'landholders and servile
cultivators' and how in difficult times the latter were, in general,
certain of food, since it was 'in the obvious interest' of those who
required their services to provide for their support. But Eden did not
believe this was

> a solid argument against the blessings of liberty. A prisoner under
> the custody of his keeper, may perhaps be confident of receiving his
> bread and water daily; yet, I believe, there are few who would not,
> even with the contingent possibility of starving, prefer a precarious
> chance of subsistence, from their own industry, to the certainty of
> regular meals in gaol ...[19]

As cracks appeared in the feudal traditions whereby the labouring
serf was expected to serve a lifetime obligation to his lord and
manor, a new class of freed labourers emerged. They were intent on

gaining more for themselves and family than the existing social structures permitted. During the late fourteenth century and through the fifteenth century, English exports of wool, representing the larger part of the country's overseas trade, showed a marked transition from being initially dominated by raw material to being mainly in the form of finished cloth by 1500. This is a reasonable indicator of the increasing role of manufacturing in the national economy.[20] Even then, economically and technologically, neither England as a whole, nor its capital London, were exceptional at this time when compared with mainland Europe. For example, London was inferior in international importance to the Italian centres of power, Florence and Venice.[21]

As the shackles of English feudalism slackened a little in the fifteenth century, wages became symbolic of the emancipation of the labouring poor from serfdom. In the labour market this was reflected by the greater numbers of casual labourers moving around the country to better themselves. Organised unionism and collectivism were, of course, not available to aid the labourer's case. In their absence an effective, if precarious, weapon for the individual was the removal of their unappreciated labour to a town or distant estate where work was available. But the chance of freedom from a master's tutelage, which to some was an attractive accompaniment to the emergence of the capitalist economy, left worrying questions unanswered for those who chose a travelling life. It was not clear when or why they could be compelled to return to their place of birth, and under whose auspices such action might be taken?

The industrialising world was to become increasingly baffled by the problem of how to deal with the labouring segments of society when sickness, unemployment or old age left them unprotected against the exigencies of towns bereft of paternal considerations for employees. At times of community strife the landless labourer probably fared better than the villein tied to his precious acres in the common-field. After all, should he be harried in a particular district he could, provided he had the courage, move more easily to another. As tramping labourers wandered across the country looking for employment they joined the hard-core among the fourteenth-century and fifteenth-century travelling community, made up of wandering musicians, travelling shoe-makers, 'pedlars laden with petty wares', begging pilgrims who lived from alms, 'pardoners, strange nomads who sold to the common people the merits of the saints in paradise; mendicant friars and preachers of all sorts'.[22]

Although limited in scope, this emancipation of the labourer was helped by worker shortages as catastrophic pestilences gnawed tragically at Europe's population just as surely as wars savaged the cream of the nation's manhood. England's Hundred Years' War with France, stretching in phases from the 1330s then followed by the Wars of the Roses (1455–85) added to the common people's misery. Ignorance of sanitation nurtured the 'Black Death' in 1349. First, it gained a firm urban foothold before ravaging the countryside and scything the population by more than one third.[23] Workers found themselves in the novel situation of being able to dictate terms for their labour. The new class of free labourers emerged. Those who took to moving around the country to their personal advantage, swelled the numbers tramping. Although wars compounded the effects of the plagues, they also encouraged the English labourers' opportunity to view life from a different perspective and provide the incentive to look elsewhere for work. Many of those who initially left home to fight loyally for King or Lord subsequently cut themselves loose from the manor's social shackles either by accepting the alternatives of urban life or by adopting a more adventurous footloose lifestyle.

As woollen manufacture became sufficiently extensive to prompt some transformation in Britain's economic and social arrangements, sheep-rearing became that much more attractive to entrepreneurial landowners. An export trade in manufactured woollen goods developed in the fourteenth century especially after Edward III encouraged Dutch weavers to immigrate and strengthen indigenous labour with appropriate skills. Landowners moved from raising crops into pasture which had a smaller need for labourers. Some of these rural hands moved with reasonable facility into more urbanised surroundings. Others, steeped for a lifetime in agriculture, found the transition impossible. They turned to the highway in search of other rural localities where their skills might be more appreciated. When the economy was depressed, wanderers had little alternative, if they were not to starve, but to resort to petty theft and when conditions were particularly harsh, robbery with violence. Undesirable as such actions may be, Nicholls points out that they did possess the seed of emancipation as poor travellers were now sampling freedom and sustaining the hope that some would be coerced or reclaimed into becoming good citizens. Previously, as little better than slaves, they were 'irreclaimable and would continue to taint and deteriorate the whole community'.[24]

Fourteenth-century vagrancy legislation was the precursor to later laws in reflecting a new kind of poverty, that of 'masterless men'.

These were people no longer having manorial ties but now subject to the buffetings of the market economy.[25] It is in the gradual movement from feudalism to capitalism that one detects a shift whereby those living on the margins of society gained a degree of mobility and, with it, a loss of economic security. Freedom seemed to count for more than security because as the opportunities for individual initiative increased, so did the number of migrant workers and vagrants. Eden suggested that Dr Johnson's remark on marriage and celibacy about one having many pains, the other no pleasures, may reasonably 'be applied with propriety to freedom and servitude'.[26] During the fourteenth century there was an emerging tendency in the language of legislation and of the judiciary, as well as in the vernacular literature, to see the 'common labourer' not as a wage earner but as an idler and a wanderer. Statutes began to condemn itinerant patterns of employment based on short-time contracts and higher wages rates. They were acknowledged as being 'disruptive of order and wilfully harmful to the organisers of manufacture'.[27] Nevertheless, there are distinct signs that in spite of persistent statutory attempts during Edward III's reign to stifle migratory enterprise in the labouring classes, the lawyers' efforts were often wasted.[28] This was because even for those who had the benefit of a roof over their head, traditional labouring life was exceedingly harsh. Home was often nothing but one primitive mud-walled room with scant furniture and few utensils. Food was rarely more than sufficient to supply energy for mundane daily tasks. Rarely were there enough victuals to guard adequately against the ravages of disease. Life expectancy was below forty years.

Data for southern England, initially compiled by Thorold Rogers, suggest that after a century with little change in basic rates of pay to craftsmen and their labourers, there was an increase during the second half of the fourteenth century and that the higher rates were maintained through the fifteenth century. Also available are data by Peter Bowden for agricultural labourers. This indicates that from the mid fifteenth century, the wage rate of agricultural labourers remained fairly constant over the next fifty years and at a similar value to building labourers. The likely changes in wages for craftsmen and their labourers are illustrated diagrammatically in Figure 2.1.[29]

Within the accuracy of available information, indications are that throughout the early centuries a craftsman received about half as much again as his labourer. Phelps Brown and Hopkins compared the wages data together with an equivalent Index of Prices for a composite unit of consumables from 1280 to 1500. These reinforce the idea

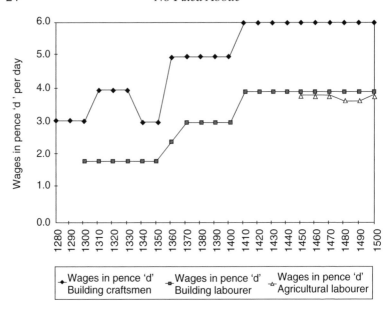

Figure 2.1   Wage rates of building craftsmen, labourers and agricultural labourers, Southern England, 1280–1500.

that worker purchasing power did surge upwards from around the mid fourteenth century and then remained fairly constant through the entire fifteenth century, Figure 2.2.[30]

It is reasonable to assume from Figure 2.2 that a smaller part of building workers' earnings was needed to buy the same essential commodities during the late fourteenth century than had been the case earlier. It would also have helped ease the worker's condition that during the fourteenth century 'rents and interest showed a tendency towards stagnation or reduction'.[31] Even then, labourers, in particular, could not afford to be complacent about the security of their future. There was always the danger from year to year of alarming price fluctuations in those foodstuffs contingent on harvest quality. This is illustrated by Figure 2.3 which plots in greater detail the annual changes in price with the equivalent wage rates over the period 1450–1500. When harvests were below average and because a huge part of the earnings of the very poor still went on food, the violent price fluctuations which occurred continued to have a catastrophic effect on their living condition. The first half of the 1460s well demonstrates

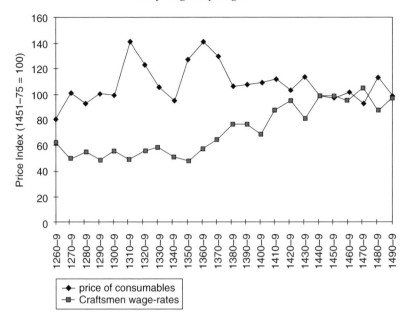

Figure 2.2 Price of composite unit of consumables and equivalent wage rate of building craftsmen, Southern England, 1260–1499.

the dramatic change in fortune for those dependent on wages. The year 1483, well known as a time of bad harvests, was one of those when wage earners temporarily faced a nigh insuperable problem when attempting to purchase food for their family's sustenance. Urban workers who were the more likely to depend mainly on wages for the quality of their life suffered particularly badly.

Nevertheless, in spite of these provisos about the continuing uncertainties for the very poor, the increase in real wages during the second half of the fourteenth century meant that the economic position of the worker did improve generally and that this improvement lasted through much of the following century. This did not suit employers and powerful efforts were made from the mid fourteenth century to contain the unwelcome mobility in the workforce seen as an important contributor to wage rises. Landowners pushed successfully in 1349 to King and Parliament for the Ordinance of Labourers and two years later for the Statute of Labourers. Both laws were ostensibly designed to check the vice of idleness and to constrain mobility which could

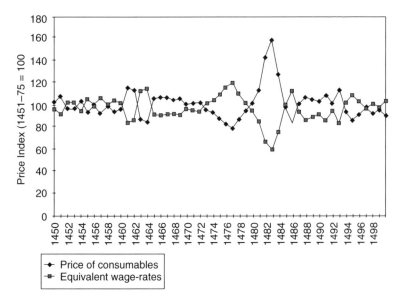

Figure 2.3 Price of composite unit of consumables and equivalent building craftsman wage rate, 1450–1500.

lead to 'inordinate augmentation of wages'. The 1349 ordinance stated:

> Because that many valiant Beggars, as long as they may live of begging, do refuse to labour, giving themselves to Idleness and Vice, and sometimes to Theft and other abominations; none upon the said Pain of Imprisonment, shall under the colour of Pity or Alms, give any thing to such, which may labour, or presume to favour them (towards their desires), so that thereby they may be compelled to labour for their necessary Living.[32]

The 1351 Statute of Labourers generally forbade servants from going

> out of The Town, where he dwelleth in the Winter, to serve the Summer if he may serve the same Town, taking as before is said. Saving that the People of the Counties of Stafford, Lancaster, and Derby, and the people of Craven, and of the Marches of Wales and Scotland, and other Places, may come in time of august, and labour

in other Counties, and safely return, as they were wont to do before the Time.[33]

The Webbs described both laws as determined government attempts 'to bring the labourers back, as nearly as practicable, to the servile conditions of preceding generations'.[34] At a time when serfdom was breaking down, the statutes attempted to provide a kind of substitute slavery. They have been later recognised as attempting to be 'punishments for desertion – labourer's wages were fixed, his place of residence fixed – if he went elsewhere, he must be taken and sent back'.[35] Rubin argues that productive workers remained much in demand while always seeming to 'contain the threat of withdrawal into the world of unproductive independence, the beggar'. He believed it to be a curious and resonant transformation which 'combined worker and ever threatening, menacing sturdy beggar, one which had long-lasting effects on conceptions of poverty and relief'. Employers expressed concern about the broader immorality that once sturdy labourers had sampled vagrant habits they may be tempted to give 'themselves to idleness and vice, and sometime to theft and other abominations'.[36] Landowners' problems raised in the mid century Statutes resurfaced in 1377, the first year of Richard II's reign. Legislation claimed that villeins and land tenants daily withdrew 'their services and customs due to the said Lords'. This was fuel for revolt. With growing commercial activity and the disruption of the pastoral economy, worker mobility increased. The attempts by Richard II to satisfy landowners' claims that tenants and labourers were setting aside established custom and arbitrarily withdrawing their services led to open widespread 'organized tumults, disturbances and insurrections' such as those led by Wat Tyler and Thomas Faringdon in 1381, and, much later, to Jack Cade's march on London in 1460.[37] Rebellions of this nature had to be put down by Parliamentary backed militia. This was often not without turmoil and a compounding of determined worker resentment at the unreasonableness of authority with the urban craftsman no less rebellious than his agrarian counterpart.[38] The force with which constraining legislation was applied remains debatable. However, there can be little doubt that the emerging vagrancy and labour laws were accurate indicators of the employers' determined mood. They persisted in pressurising the civil authorities with their resentment and frustration about the new economic order in which labour was scarce and able to negotiate conditions more favourably to themselves. Rubin claims that by now meaningful social divisions 'were not between town and country, nor between Lords and peasantry, but between employer and wage earner'.[39]

The problems raised in the Statutes of Labourers were rephrased in the 12 Richard II, c. 7 (1388) Act. Concerns about excessive wage-rates were repeated and specifications restricting the labourer to his place of residence tightened. Penalties against absconding labourers already introduced by Edward III in 1360 including, at the discretion of the Justices, burning 'on the forehead with an iron formed to the letter F in token of his falsity' were confirmed as an essential element of the procedures necessary to constrain labour.[40] Coode has expressed the view that in the fourteenth century 'labouring people appear to have caused the legislature continual anxiety and trouble, by their energy in seeking employment wherever the greatest reward was to be got'.[41] This contrasts sharply with what later became the common practice of coupling synonymously the 'indolent' with the penniless traveller. The 1388 Act can be identified as the second clearly distinguishable period in the development of the settlement laws. It prohibited the labourer from leaving his borough without a testimonial and strengthened what were to become a series of attempts over the centuries to control begging within legal limits. The Act assigned geographical limits within which an impotent person might plead for alms and specified punishment for transgression. However, it did introduce an early recognition, if only by implication, that there were circumstances which may possibly justify the provision of relief:

> And that the Beggars impotent to serve, shall abide in the Cities and Towns where they be dwelling at the time of the Proclamation of this statute; and if the People of Cities or other Towns will not or may not suffice to find them, that the said Beggyars shall draw them to other Towns within the Hundreds, Rape, or Wapentake, or to the Towns where they were born, within Forty Days after the Proclamation made, and there shall continually abide during their Lives.[42]

With the steadying of wage rates during the fifteenth century there was an acceptance of the status quo. Confrontation between employer and labourer abated and was signalled by the reduction in pressure by the former on government to produce tougher vagrancy laws. Whereas the Ordinance of Labourers in 1349 initiated fifty years which saw nine new statutes aimed at vagrants and the mobile poor, during the fifty years from 1444 there was no new English vagrancy legislation.[43] The succession of fourteenth-century vagrancy legislation had been sufficient to stabilise mobility and wages, albeit at a higher level. As the fifteenth century proceeded the laws in some localities gradually began to be interpreted with more rigour – especially if applicants for relief had earlier shown the temerity, on their own volition, to ungratefully look outside the parish for work and when this had not materialised they had sent their spouse and children to beg as well as themselves. This harsher attitude was not always applicable. In some towns there were sporadic municipal attempts at collective poor relief. In 1441, Southampton claimed to have provided collectively for 150 people. Some years later Ipswich devoted profits from St James's Fair to relieve lepers. 1474 saw Rye begin regular municipal payments to the impotent.[44] There were also occasional indications by the fifteenth century of difficulties for the poor as the result of agricultural rationalisation, particularly in the form of land enclosure, a concept which would become more widespread in later centuries. Even at this early date there was evidence accompanying wilful destruction of property by landowners and a consequent collapse of economic security for the labourer. The adverse social consequences of such action was recognised and acted upon by the 4 Henry VII, c. 19 (1489) Act. It was promulgated against 'pullying down of townes' … and … 'the evils arising from Waste of Houses, and converting tilled Lands into pasture'. The preamble of the Act told how:

> The Kyng our soveign Lord, havying a singular pleasure above all thinges to avoide such enormitees and myschefes as be hurtfull and prejudiciall to the coen wele of this his londe … daily doth enreace by decolacion and pulling down and wilfull waste of houses and Townes within his realm and leying to pasture londes whiche custumeably have been used to tithe … in some Townes two hundred psones wer occupied and lived by their lawfull labours, nowe ben there occupied two or three herdsmen and the residue fall in ydelness … Owners of Houses let to farm, with Twenty Acres of Land, shall maintain Houses and Buildings thereon necessary for Tillage.[45]

Reflection on the cause and effect of the vagrancy and settlement decrees surveyed in this chapter has confirmed the prompting by landowners and employers keen to conserve whatever they could of the golden days of feudalism by limiting worker mobility. At the same time, for central government, the legislation had the attraction of curbing possible disorder in a potentially violent environment.

In summary, the fourteenth-century laws seem to have been needlessly restrictive, especially when some local authorities applied further constraint with by-laws forbidding able-bodied persons from begging. Behind much of the legislation there was an effort to overcome the alleged innate idleness of travelling people by compelling them to earn their livelihood. Some legislation purposely limited the action of potential donors by preventing the private individual from relieving able-bodied beggars. By restricting alms to people presumed capable of occupying a job, the statutes were attempting to seal another source of potential seepage from the traditional supply of docile, generally predictable labour. The constraining legislation generally acted against the very socio-economic forces requiring a mobile pool of surplus labour which was to become an essential element in the success of the impending industrial revolution.

By the fifteenth century it had become clear that the indiscriminate almsgiving of the medieval Church now required the accompaniment of constraining legislation against vagrancy and mendicancy. Because of their catch-all characteristics the laws maliciously engulfed in their savage penalties the innocent energetic labourer doing nothing more wicked than seeking a lessening of his poverty.[46] It was a trend the law was to follow and develop more strongly in succeeding centuries. In later chapters there is clear indication that for centuries it mattered little to draftsmen steadily strengthening laws restraining the traveller whether they were applied to a rough inveterate crime-bent beggar or to a distraught starving labourer looking anxiously for work.

3 Tudor Response to the Travelling Poor

The tragedy of the tramp is his isolation. Every man's hand is against him: and his history is inevitably written by his enemies.[1]

This chapter examines the condition of the travelling poor during the sixteenth century. After the turmoil of the Hundred Years War and factional friction with the Wars of the Roses, the accession of Henry VII in 1485 initiated the Tudor dynasty. It was an era of relative stability vital for economic advance of the fortunate but throughout the Kingdom poverty remained rife. The world seemed smaller with England constantly gathering new territorial acquisitions. These were to benefit trade greatly in the centuries that followed. The attitudes to religion brought by the Reformation favoured economic development but of most immediate significance was the increase in population from around 1500 after more than a century of decline and stagnation.

The Black Death of 1349 was not, of course, an isolated terror. Nor did the dread of infectious and contagious diseases cease in the fourteenth century. Indeed, a whole series of brutish epidemics stretched well into the seventeenth century. Most feared were those like typhoid fever, typhus, dysentery, influenza and plague, with the latter usually the most lethal. In England between 1351 and 1485 plague struck in 30 different years and between 1543 and 1593 it made 26 annual visits even though it did not succeed in decimating the population as ruthlessly as it had in the previous century. These pestilences, which were more devastating in towns, had put a brake on the process of urbanisation in the fourteenth and fifteenth centuries. When plague was at its worst 'the general impression is that the cities of Europe had a negative demographic balance and that they survived only because of continual inflow from the countryside',[2] a trend which acted against landowners' interests.

The English population at the three-quarter point of the fourteenth century was around 2.2 million. This had probably dropped slightly to 2.1 million by 1430. There was little change until the onset of the sixteenth century when the population then doubled over the next hundred years.[3] The increased availability of labour was vital for the further accumulation of production and urbanisation. It did little to help the labouring classes who remained largely unskilled and under-employed. For those brave or reckless enough to abandon rural pater-nalism there was no certainty of long-term work or of a permanent home. In spite of early signs of proto-industrialism in the sixteenth century, the British economy was to continue being dominated by agriculture for more than two centuries. The same crops had been grown for generations, using the same implements, although wooden ploughs were increasingly now being shod with iron. Emerging indus-tries like textiles, housebuilding, brewing, shipbuilding, mining and glassmaking entailed the continuous supply of large loads of fuel. Textiles were the most profitable. Although the work was largely done at home on rented looms, there were already fulling-mills, for cleans-ing and thickening cloth, possibly employing up to two hundred people.[4]

> Within one room, being large and long
> there stood two hundred looms full strong.
> Two hundred men, the truth is so
> wrought in these rooms all in a row.[5]

Whatever factories did exist, there was no sustained increase in *per capita* income for most of the population. A high incidence of persist-ent poverty remained.[6] The economic activity that developed lacked the constancy of later centuries. Adverse weather retained the poten-tial to throw thousands out of work.

Throughout much of Europe, death rates began to decline in the sixteenth century. As population gradually increased, 'so did tran-siency and beggary' as the demands of a variably expanding economy jostled for a balance with the availability of labour.[7] At times of econ-omic and environmental stress, punishment could not itself immo-bilise the out-of-work labourer motivated by the fear of hunger. Officials recognised the need to provide for relief against starvation as well as continuing the tradition of taking legislative action against mil-itant vagrancy. On the European mainland in the 1520s, Martin Luther advised that begging should be prohibited but that a common chest should be provided for the sick and the aged. His advice was acted upon in a number of German municipalities.[8] Similarly, France, the Netherlands and Switzerland were among European countries where the fluctuating pressures of economic and demographic forces were recognised. It was acknowledged that at a downturn in the economic cycle there was the potential for civil disturbance which initiated a two-pronged approach to the very poor. On the one hand entrenched vagrancy had to be repressed. On the other, there had to be provision against starvation for those judged to be 'deserving'. By the sixteenth century, travellers could be roughly divided into three main groups:

- the better off migrant whose mobility was prompted by the desire to better themselves economically and socially
- the increasing number who moved around to satisfy subsistence needs
- the sturdy rogue who shunned conventional work.[9]

The divisions between the three categories were vague but in sixteenth-century legislation the second and third groups were commonly linked by appellations with a disparaging ring like 'vagrant', 'beggar', 'vagabond' or 'rogue'.[10] This ignored the reality that the majority of the second group were innocents, without a home, trudging from place to place in what was sometimes a vain search for essential nourishment. An early City of London building ordinance, listing wage-rates for workers cleansing and scouring the common ditch, used the term 'vagabond' as a synonym for 'labourer'. Hoskins interprets this, perhaps with some exaggeration, as an indication that in the early parts of the sixteenth century the labouring urban population was 'largely composed of a wandering and homeless crowd of men who would drift from job to job or from place to place'.[11] As the century progressed, 'vagabond' gradually acquired the more pejorative connotations already noted. In particular, vagabond was coupled legislatively with 'rogue' so that 'rogue and vagabond' became indistinguishable terms in the public mind. In an even more encompassing way, 'vagrant' became and remained the catch-all word embracing these and all other poor travellers. It is because the word 'vagrant' has consistently been used in the centuries that followed, both in emerging legislation and in contemporary literature, to embrace any travelling person requiring the means of personal survival, that the practice has been perpetuated in this volume. From what has already been said in earlier chapters, it will be recognised that in spite of the persistently deprecatory connotations created legislatively by the use of 'vagrant' to encompass every poor itinerant, far from all of them freely chose tramping as a style of life other than as a form of escape from extreme personal pressure.

As discussed in Chapter 2, the Christian duty of charity was incumbent upon all Christians according to their means. The early religiously inspired voluntary provision for those in need came haphazardly from a miscellany of community sources – monasteries, fraternities, guilds or from parish initiatives such as town 'stocks', almshouses and church collections. Involvement by the state had mainly been to regulate labour by including them within tough vagrancy legislation.[12] Although relatively benign compared with what was to follow, early sixteenth-century attitudes to out-of-work wandering labourers were still moulded by post Black Death generations of labour shortage which had inculcated the idea that only idlers lacked a job. Urban economies in the early Middle Ages had usually managed to be reasonably prosperous as 'their populations grew only slowly' so that most towns found it possible to support their poor by haphazard charity at times of exceptional distress. But as over-spill from the expanding rural population naturally gravitated towards the towns, local authorities began to have cause for concern during periods when commercial activity slackened.[13]

With the population increase of the sixteenth century and the tendency for people to gravitate towards towns, the problem steadily worsened. Unemployment, underemployment, bad harvests, famine, epidemics, land enclosures, demobilisation of militia, industrialisation, inflation, the dissolution of the monasteries and the decline of great households have all been perceived as contributory factors to the difficulties of the travelling poor. Leonard is of the opinion that 'the greater number of the inhabitants of particular districts, being without resources' contributed incipiently towards riots and the fostering of insurrections.[14] In particular, competition for jobs within the increasing population prevented wages keeping in touch with prices so that workers' real earnings, both urban and rural, declined disturbingly during the century.[15] This became especially acute from 1532–80 when there was the annual 'Tudor' inflation of almost 1.5 per cent.[16] The protracted balance between agricultural labourers' wages and the cost of living that had been sustained through much of the fifteenth century collapsed early in the sixteenth. For decades the cost of living was to shoot ahead of wages so that the disparity widened. C. G. A. Clay suggests that by the end of the century the agricultural labourer's purchasing power was only about 50 per cent of what his forefather had enjoyed a hundred years earlier, Figure 3.1.[17]

Much the same reduction in a worker's ability to buy a range of commodities took place in the building trade. In a similar way, the

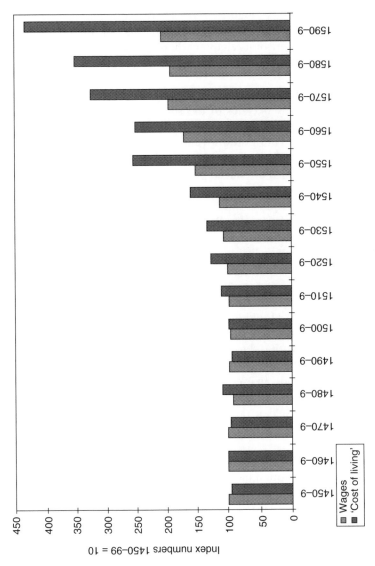

Figure 3.1 Agricultural labourer's cost of living and wages, 1450–1599.

real-wage index for craftsmen collapsed by the mid sixteenth century to about half what it had been 50 years earlier. Then, after some partial recovery, the index value weakened further during the last decade of the century (Figure 3.2).[18] There are good reasons, from Phelps Brown and Hopkins's work, for believing that the relationship established in the previous chapter whereby craftsmen earned about half as much again as did their labourers, remained valid through the sixteenth century.

The nadir in the value of workers' purchasing power was probably reached in the early decades of the seventeenth century.[19] Thorold Rogers described the extraordinarily steep decline in purchasing power during the Tudor stewardship as being part of a continuing oppressive and exploitive campaign against the workers. Another part-explanation for the reduced purchasing power was the sixteenth-century population increase which in true Malthusian form was not matched by an adequate expansion in agricultural production and employment. There was also the complication that as labour transferred into the proto-industrial employment opportunities, their additional spending power increased demand for the limited supply of food with the tendency to push prices up further.[20] Evidence from France, Alsace, Munster, Augsberg, Vienna and Valencia using similar yardsticks on composite units of consumables as applied by Phelps Brown and Hopkins show that wage purchasing power collapsed on the continent in much the same way as in England.[21]

While few doubt that during the sixteenth century the condition of workers worsened considerably, it is reasonable to believe that the raw earnings data provide an excessively pessimistic picture if taken simply as a direct indicator of the fall in wage earners' living standards. Revisionists suggest that the worker's condition may also have been influenced by:

- longer hours being worked as the century progressed
- a bigger proportion of income being provided in kind
- more family-members being employed
- when times were hard, a larger number of labourers relied upon their crofts and gardens than had previously been thought likely.[22]

Even taking on board some revisionism, there remains broad agreement that life under the Tudors was harder for those at the bottom of the social pyramid than it had been for their predecessors. Nor is there much doubt that among the surplus labour looking for jobs in

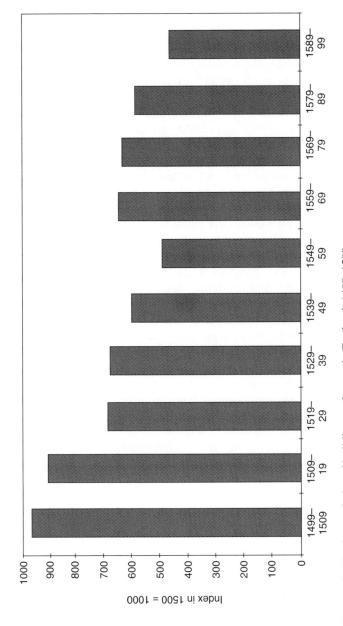

Figure 3.2　Real-wage index of building craftsmen in England, 1499–1599.

the town or elsewhere in the countryside many had to scramble for whatever wages they could. When this failed it was natural that some took 'to the roads or to crime'.[23]

As the purchasing power of wages fell, even the most thrifty were unable to save more than a paltry sum against prolonged family misfortune or the unavoidable occurrence of old age. Workers were left with little recourse but to plead for relief from their betters. Hoskins estimates that two-thirds of the people in provincial towns 'lived below or very near the poverty-line' in the tough 1520s. Rural England was little better, with nearly 60 per cent in the same state. Even critics who argue that Hoskins's data exaggerate the depth of Tudor poverty, accept that those struggling perilously near destitution were around 20 per cent of the population in towns and 10 per cent in rural areas.[24] Even assuming these lower estimates were nearer the truth, there is reason to believe that the sixteenth century had many people wandering around in search of succour and having to resort to begging. With lower real wages it was hardly surprising that even benign workers joined the clamouring travelling throng when harvests were bad and the higher price of corn put it out of their reach.

As demographic and economic change spawned more tramps so came the old fear that insecure itinerants could all too easily accumulate with rebellious intent. Data of vagrant arrests suggests that their contemporary authorities exaggerated the danger of incipient social truculence. Many taken into custody 'seem genuinely to have been unemployed looking for work'.[25] Whether or not official concern about the social dangers of vagrancy was justified, it became an 'immediate and pressing concern of government'. Fearful reports were published of the 'new and terrible problem' of vagrancy which caused the more stable population to live 'in terror of the tramp'.[26] State announcements featured vagrants in high profile among the travelling community and by implication every tramp was operating as a hardened professional beggar. The announcements ignored the reality that many so-called 'vagrants' were innocents who, driven by empty stomachs, lurched from place to place in what were often unfriendly and sometimes dangerous environments. Until limited provision was made in the last quarter of the century, an unemployed man with no reserves to call on had two choices, to beg or to starve.[27] The Privy Council were forced to recognise the plight of the poor and attempted to stabilise the situation by regulating the cost of provisions so 'the worckmen … might live upon theyre wages'.[28] The attempt was in vain for many. There were still those who failed to gain sufficient nourishment and starved in the hedgerows or in the back alleys, as exemplified by the 32 poor folk who expired in the streets of Newcastle upon Tyne following the bad harvest of 1596.[29]

The advance of manufacturing processes and their encouragement for employees to accept seemingly generous wages as their only recompense made the position of working people increasingly precarious. Not only did urbanisation dilute paternalistic philanthropy so that the unemployed poor were in greater danger of penury than ever before but in many trades they were now without the same right to 'bring up their children in honest labour'.[30] Alternate booms and slumps were a feature of the first quarter of the sixteenth century. Even should a man temporarily weather these economic storms there was no guarantee that his original job would again become available to him.[31] There were, of course, no Friendly Societies, Workingmen's Clubs, casual wards or workhouses to help stave off starvation. As the numbers of travellers increased, haphazard traditional voluntary support from Church, Crown and the wealthy became less effectual despite certain charities organising themselves to provide funds for special purposes.[32] Endowed almshouses were developed with ongoing relief for the few fortunate enough to be granted occupancy.[33]

All over Europe, intervention by lay authorities and the compilation of new formulae for dealing with the condition of the poor had been inspired by the Christian Humanism of Erasmus and Juan Luis Vives.[34] Humanist attitudes towards social welfare required that it should be thorough. There was need to combine the three elements of Christian charity, moral reform and involvement of public authority. English vagrancy statutes had undergone little fundamental change during the fifteenth century. Any slight modifications had amounted to little more than tinkering in response to the general move away from serfdom towards a freer commercialised economy. In the changing social climate, the local judiciary often chose not to interpret legislation rigorously. As the tide of travellers showed signs of growth, the dormant vagrancy laws began to be taken from the shelf, dusted down and toughened, particularly as regards punishment.

Eventually, halfway through Elizabeth's reign, central government announced ideas aimed at parishes supporting their needy collectively. As structured action took shape across the country on the relief of poverty so concurrently were the more punitive aspects of vagrancy legislation strengthened. As a backcloth to what became an era of harsher sentencing let us look at some socio-economic trends and whether these may have initiated new vagrancy legislation. Land

enclosures to the exclusion of the agricultural labourer had already
been sampled in the fifteenth century. Tawney has argued that these
were having such an effect that many of those taking to the roads did
so under direct pressures from enclosures introduced by lords of
manors and by their tenant farmers.[35] As the manufacturing processes
for woollen garments developed it became more profitable for landowners and tenants alike to transfer from growing grain into breeding
sheep. Town-dwellers were as eager for the meat as clothiers were for
the wool.[36] Consequently even in localities where the soil had been
cultivated by generations of labouring families they were evicted to
expand sheep-runs on the newly enclosed demesne lands now converted to pasture.[37] Insecure tenants were also dispossessed and their
dwellings demolished.[38] As Thomas More wrote contemporaneously,
'by hook or by crook the poor wretches are compelled to leave their
homes – men and women, husbands and wives, orphans and widows,
parents with little children and a household not rich but numerous'.
They soon had little alternative but to 'steal and be hanged' or 'to
wander or beg'.[39] It was not unusual for the common rights of tenants
to be so curtailed that they lost not only an important subsidiary
source of income but also the means of cultivating their arable holdings. The opportunity to maintain a couple of animals, perhaps a cow
and a pig, meant the difference between 'a precarious economic independence and wretched destitution'. This was especially true in areas
where grazing had been coupled with what had been paternalistic traditions of post-harvest gleaning in the fields and the opportunity to
gather fuel from the hedgerows and coppices.[40] Without these perks,
usually the difference between living and dying, countrymen were
turned adrift to seek an alternative livelihood. This was not easy
because what they discovered was a world where most trades and most
towns were incompatible with their rural ways. Nevertheless, with no
alternative but to tramp afar in the hope of finding a living, they found
themselves adding further to the number of poor travellers.

   With the stagnating population-size of the fourteenth century and
fifteenth century, few people had been without land, even though for
most its extent was pinched. As the population expanded after 1500
holdings became more subdivided and squatting on common land
increased. The 'trend of (land) amalgamation further limited the
chances of gaining a tenancy'.[41] There were now more men without
sufficient land to support their family. Seasons and their weather,
either in excess or dearth, still ruled economies. Inferior harvests
came on average about every four or five years though occasionally

they were bunched together disastrously in a number of succeeding years. There was the persistent worry of becoming engulfed in catastrophic circumstances by the exceptionally poor harvests which came with sufficient frequency to be deeply etched on living memory.[42] It became exceedingly difficult for the agricultural labourer to make ends meet in these circumstances. Deficient crops led to inflated prices of foodstuffs with sharp annual fluctuations (Figure 3.3).[43]

The changes in demography, land ownership, and proto-manufacturing processes added to the tendency for the 'absconding labourer' of the fifteenth century to become the 'destitute mendicant' of the sixteenth. As those thrown out of work looked elsewhere for a job, the numbers tramping the roads increased further when baronial armies were disbanded as the Tudor central administration gained strength.[44] Plagues, both bubonic and pneumonic, remained to compound the general misery. Epidemics not infrequently caused a vicious circle of transience amongst the poor. Labourers attracted by the promise of urban wages found themselves packed into foul densely packed accommodation. When they attempted to flee disease, the concentrated terror added again to the numbers tramping the highway. The dissolution of monasteries between 1536 and 1539 brought more pressure on the domiciled populace to relieve the destitute as religious houses were forced to discharge those mendicants who had depended upon them for sustenance.[45]

The decay of feudalism during the fifteenth century was helped by the steady growth in commerce with a substantial rise in the number of influential merchants. Whereas there had been 169 English merchants operating internationally in the middle of the fourteenth century, there were at least 3000 trading overseas by the start of the sixteenth century.[46] At Westminster, government recognised the vital importance of ensuring that foreign merchants should feel physically secure while trading and transporting their goods across Britain. Any disquiet these gentlemen may have harboured was not likely to be placated by the odd rumour of aggressive marauding bands motivated angrily by hunger. Hall maintains that the possible concerns of foreign merchants about their own safety prompted 'the royal practice of issuing formally executed covenants of safe conduct through the realm'.[47] As the numbers tramping expanded, worry about potential social instability encouraged legislators to re-emphasise that vagrancy statutes should be enforced more rigorously. The idea was to instil national confidence and let commercial travellers know that the state recognised their right to trade in a harmonious environment.

No Fixed Abode

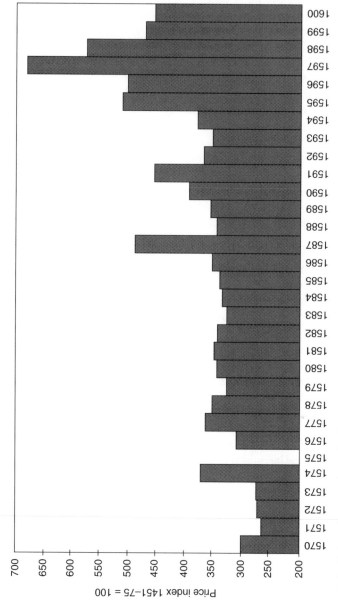

Figure 3.3 Price of composite unit of consumables in Southern England, 1570–1600.

Clearly, price fluctuations of essential commodities had a more profound effect on poorer members of the community than on wealthier people for whom such items occupied a smaller part of their budget. Even workers who traditionally enjoyed reasonably permanent employment had no guarantee of their earnings being inflation proof.[48] In a fascinating book written around 1539 but not printed until 1871, Thomas Starkey wrote of there being no hope for a Common Weal in England if men currently 'blinded with the love of themselves' refused to 'govern themselves soberly by temperate diet' and continued to disregard those without.[49]

It is now instructive to trace the legislation continually introduced by the Tudors in their determination to further repress any tendency towards increased mobility among the poor. Vagrancy legislation up to the late fifteenth century had aimed at geographic and financial constraint of the labourer in addition to the traditional repression of beggars and listed 'imposters', the definitions of which changed with fashion. Early Tudor government signalled their awareness of changing socio-economic circumstances when in 1495 Henry VII authorised the apprehension of all 'idle vagabonds and suspected persons living suspiciously', a concept which gradually crystallised into the infamous 'sus' clauses of the 1824 Vagrancy Act. Local authorities from the sheriff down to the petty constable were ordered to seek out offenders for punishment. Basic penalties prior to expulsion from the vicinity were three days and two nights in the stocks with no nourishment other than bread and water. A repeat of the offence within the same town doubled the punishment.[50] It was required that beggars who were unable to work had to remain in their settlement hundred. In the year 1503 the statute 19 Henry VII, c. 12 tightened the administrative rules further. It compelled local dignitaries including sheriffs, mayors, high constables and petty constables to apply the law more stringently.

There are signs that Henry's legal demands were not always carried into practice with full force. In the late 1520s severe economic depression jolted central authority into yet tougher activity. Real wages were already deteriorating (Figures 3.1 and 3.2) when catastrophe occurred for many with the appalling harvest of 1527, a disaster compounded by the declaration of war the following spring. As the price of wheat shot up, wage-earners were left with few doubts that their rates of pay were determined by the supply and demand for labour and not by the cost of living.[51] England's alliance with France did nothing to alleviate the economic distress because of the related paralysis in the important sale of English cloths to the well-established Flemish markets. Exporters soon stopped placing their usual orders with clothing manufacturers who, in turn, 'ceased to find work for their men'.[52]

The central government feared that food rioting and social truculence would get out of hand and destabilise the country. Every Tudor monarch had to contend with at least one serious rising. Not insignificantly, every sixteenth-century decade from the 1530s onwards saw at least one Act directed towards the relief of the poor and the suppression of vagrancy.[53] The 'whole problem of poverty was taken up with some freshness and originality' in the 22 Henry VIII (1530–1) Act.[54] It was seminal in being the first attempt to distinguish, if hesitatingly, the able-bodied poor from the impotent. The Act alleged that because 'vacabundes and beggars' were continuing to increase daily in 'great and excessyve nombres by the occasyon of ydelnes', more deterrent penalties of additional severity were needed. The preamble blamed begging and the growing numbers travelling the roads 'whereby hath insurged and sprung, and daily insurgeth and springeth, continual thefts, murders, and other heinous offences and great enormities, to the high displeasure of God, the unquietation and damage of the king's people, and to the marvellous disturbance of the common weal'.[55]

The Tudor Establishment hung on to the assumption that work was always available for those who were not too idle to search for it. There was little consideration for the changed relationship between employers and their workforce, nor for the unemployed able-bodied man who genuinely could not find a job. The 1530–1 Act ensured that public humiliation of the able-bodied vagabond was no longer limited to a spell in the stocks. Now, they were 'thoroughly' whipped. It was decreed that any idle man 'hole and myghty in body and able to laboure' who could give no reckoning of how they made their living could be tied to the end of a 'carte naked and be beten wyth Wyppes thoroughe oute the same Market Towne or other place tyll his Body be blody by reason of suche whypping; and after suche punysshement ... the person so punysshed ... shall be enjoyned upon his othe to retourne forthewyth wythout delaye ... to the place where he was borne; or where he last dwelled'.[56]

Dealt with in similar fashion were scholars begging without licence from their University and others using 'dyvers and subtyle craftye and unlawfull games and playes' etc. These were punished by 'whipping at two days together' in the manner 'before rehersed'. Second offenders ran the danger of stigmatic amputation. After being similarly scourged for two days they were 'put upon the pyllory' on the third day from

9 a.m. to 11 a.m. prior to having an ear removed. A third offence warranted extended doses of whipping, pillorying and having the other 'eare cutte of'.[57] It seems likely that these extreme regulations were not often applied to the letter by local justices. However, the mere existence of such laws was a powerful deterrent to mobility for the genuinely destitute person searching for his family's livelihood. For the hardbitten professional vagrant, the harsher laws appeared less awesome. He merely accepted the first tranche of his punishment stoically before swiftly moving on to ply his trade elsewhere. Local magistrates needed to be on their guard against being considered too soft on vagrancy. Neglecting to apply the 22 Henry VIII legislation as prescribed made a local authority liable to a forfeit of 3s.4d. for every 'impotent' beggar and twice the fine for every 'strong' beggar. In partial mitigation of its harshness, the 22nd Henry Act legitimised local begging for people 'compelled to live by alms' through being lame, feeble, blind or old. JPs and other officials could provide each impotent person with a letter authorising them to beg within prescribed geographical limits.

Yet another attempt to restrict the mobility of the poor came five years later with the 27 Henry VIII (1536) Act, drafted by Thomas Cromwell. Those found guilty of vagrancy a third time were decreed to 'have judgement to suffer peynes and execucion of dethe as a felon'.[58] For the first time, repeated vagrancy now counted as a felony and liable to the most final of penalties. What had gradually become clear about Tudor legislation was that whereas earlier law-makers had been prepared to treat the question of vagrancy as an issue mainly concerned with the mobility of labour, an attitudinal change was emerging. There was now the implication that the public should expect vagrants, as a matter of course, to be engaged in some form of criminal activity, if usually petty. Having decided that this assumption was valid it seemed only fair to law-makers that society should take retribution through harsher punishment of offenders.[59] The 1536 Act also contained a more supportive element in making the state responsible for the 'failures and victims of society'. It introduced the concept for later legislators to develop whereby the unemployable poor should be provided for by the weekly collection of alms. Local authorities were urged to ensure that all able-bodied vagrants were set to work. Underlying the statute there remained the stubbornly held persuasion that no person genuinely seeking work could possibly fail to find a job. As a result, 'vagrancy and beggary could be driven from the realm by the application of the criminal law'.[60]

It is likely that sixteenth-century vagrants were dealt with more strictly in the cities than elsewhere. In London, from time to time during the early decades of the sixteenth century, searches were organised for vagabonds and rogues. One such hunt followed the list of Orders prepared in 1517 urging each ward to name its licensed beggars. Totalling over one thousand city-wide, each was given a non-transferrable 'round tin badge' authorising them to beg within a specified area. Each approved beggar was expected, as part of the deal, to exercise restraint when pleading for alms and 'to help to expel and keep out strange vagabonds, on pain of forfeiting their own right to beg'.[61]

In the belief that the penalties against vagrancy in previous Statutes had not been sufficiently tough, early enactments using the authority of the nine-year-old Edward VI in 1547 turned the heat up further with still harsher treatment of the travelling poor. In the First Act, Edward repealed the laws of the previous decade. According to Davies, the 1547 legislation was 'the most savage Act in the grim history of English vagrancy legislation, imposing slavery as a punishment for the refusal to work'.[62] 'Idleness and Vagabundrye' were seen as the 'mother and roote of all theftes Robberyes and all evill actes and other mischiefs'. Save for the lame, impotent, aged or sick, every man or woman loitering without the intention of working was to be arrested. They were then to be marked with a 'V' on the breast using a red hot iron prior to enslavement for two years to his captor or to any such person who could make use of him. It was fully expected that the enslaved individual would need to be induced to work by beating, chaining or other punishments as may become necessary at their master's discretion. An escape attempt during enslavement led to an 'S' being branded on the offender's face. A further attempt led to execution.[63]

The 1547 Act also allowed the children of beggars to be taken from their parents by any person willing to bring the child up in 'some honnest Labour or occupation till he or she come to thage of twentie yeres'. Another novel provision was the removal of 'aged and Impotent and Lame Parsons beggars' not born in the parish nor having lived there for three years. Parish Officers were directed to convey such miscreants on 'horsebacke, Carte or Charret or otherwise as shall seem to their discretions' to the constable in the contiguous parish. The receiving constable then had to convey the vagrant to an appropriate official in his neighbouring parish. This process was to be continued until they eventually arrived at the place 'theie were borne or moste conversant and abyding as is aforesaide'. Once there, they were supposed to be 'kepte and nourished of alms'.[64] Not infrequently, the place of supposed settlement would not accept responsibility for the destitute traveller which meant that his circuit of removal had to continue. This was the case with one poor widow and her six children who, for two years, were sent back from one village to another, both places denying they had any responsibility for them.[65]

It soon became apparent that the enthusiasm of Edward's legislators for punishing vagrants, as displayed in the 1547 Act, outran public sentiment. Few local magistrates were prepared to apply it rigorously. Hoskins has argued that the very fact that such legislation was drafted and passed signified the 'mentality of some of the ruling class' ... in regarding 'the mass of people as slaves, existing to work for only a few'.[66] For Davies, the Act was one of 'sheer incompetence' because of its 'utter failure to institute an effective system of poor relief' and on account of its 'sheer impractibility'.[67] Within three years, sections in the 1547 regulation relating to the punishment of vagabonds and other 'Idle Persons' were repealed and replaced by clauses from the 1531 statute. While making this retreat, the 3 & 4 Edward VI, c. 18 (1549–50) Acts explained that whereas the monarch's early keenness to punish the travelling poor more harshly had been justified as being 'good and holesome', in practice the new statutes had 'not byn putt in dewe execution' because of 'thextremitie of som'.[68]

After the young Edward's death from pulmonary tuberculosis in 1553 he was succeeded by his eldest sister Mary. She generally supported the extreme ideas of the previous administration. However, prompted by the economic depression of the 1550s, the 2 & 3 Philip and Mary, c. 5 (1555) Acts, softened the law to the advantage of the poor. Alms collections were encouraged and there was extension in the scope for licensing beggars. Weekly charitable collections towards the relief of the poor were advocated. Parishioners had to provide an agreed amount through a collector of alms. In parishes with more poor than they were able to relieve, JPs were authorised to licence the poor to beg outside their parish and so within a prescribed 'lymitt, to goo abrode to begg get and receive charitable almes'.[69]

Although the legislature had been forced to step back from Edward's harshest pronouncements, the 25 years from 1547 marked 'a determined effort on the part of the Privy Council to see the laws regarding vagabonds enforced'.[70] Officials in counties, cities and towns were commanded to suppress the growing multitudes of rogues. Official campaigns emphasised the advantages of whipping to deter a class of idler who was allegedly so easily enlisted by zealots into the religious revolts threatening various parts of the country. Where the legislators failed to be effective was that their tough attitude was aimed at the deterrence of criminals. There was little cognisance that many poor sixteenth-century travellers were motivated largely by self-preservation. A survey of 1581 London indicated that most of those accused of begging and vagrancy had travelled long distances. Some had journeyed from Wales, Shropshire, Cheshire, Somerset, Berkshire, Oxfordshire and Essex. Only a few had 'been about London above three or four months' with a minority coming from the more immediate vicinities of Westminster, Southwark, Middlesex and Surrey.[71]

An intriguing point about the sixteenth-century approach to unemployment and mobility was that it was diametrically opposite to the present-day perspective on the subject. In modern Britain, those having the initiative to 'get on their bike' in searching for work at a time of high unemployment were applauded by Conservative Government Ministers. In contrast, the Tudors decried the mobility of unemployed persons seeking work. They drafted their legislation assuming not that the poor traveller was looking for work but that he was avoiding it in such a disorderly manner as to prove a menace to public order.[72] Consequently, those among the destitute who were not prepared to sit on their haunches in anticipation of being saved by neighbourly charity or the parish and searched incautiously for work elsewhere could expect to have their endeavour rewarded with whipping, branding, amputation, imprisonment and even execution. The laws failed to recognise that people were not for the most part beggars by choice. Although it was a fairly lucrative trade, the 'discomforts and pains and penalties attached to it were not slight'.[73] The sad reality fabricated by the Tudor vagrancy laws was that when job-seekers failed to find one, they were often driven into crime. Since begging was forbidden so rigorously there was little alternative but to break the all-encompassing vagrancy laws if they were not to starve.

Much historiographical opinion on sixteenth-century vagrancy and its treatment has been moulded by Thomas Harman, a gentleman of Kent. He wrote disparagingly in the 1560s about the 'abhominable, wicked, and detestable debauch' of the 'rowsey ragged rabblement of rakeshelles' of beggars. They were perceived as being organised cunning and daring thieves so as to be 'often a great hardship to the honest citizens of the poorer classes'.[74] In similar vein William Harrison, writing in 1577, maintained that the trade of professional mendicity had grown and greatly prospered during the previous sixty years. He calculated that their number had grown to about 10 000 beggars and vagabonds 'of one sex and another'.[75] Publications across Europe, even in Catholic countries, referred to 'the deceipts of beggars' based on the 'assumption that idleness is voluntary and wicked'. Those who gave themselves 'wilfully to the trade of begging' must be intent on causing mischief.[76] More recently, A. L. Beier, by averaging the results from various sixteenth-century estimates, suggested that the number of vagrants in England and Wales during the late sixteenth century was between 15 000 and 20 000 out of a population approximating to 3.75 million.[77] On this basis, only about one person in two hundred was said to be a vagrant. As we have seen, many of these would be merely harmless destitutes searching for work. This raises the question as to whether such numbers justified the opprobrium used while creating the catalogue of sixteenth-century punitive enactments directed against them.

It is clear from the wording of the Tudor statutes, as well as from contemporary literature, that central government attempted to enforce on local authorities 'a repressive policy they were disinclined to carry out' on a mobile class of allegedly 'dangerous criminals'. There was little factual evidence of these people causing serious social danger.[78] Much sixteenth-century literature accorded with the harsh legalistic attitudes against vagrants. There were also signs of sympathy for the condition of the labouring classes and some understanding of why occasionally they could be pushed into begging. Henry Arth was one of those who wrote from this sympathetic perspective. He took as his text 'Blessed is he that considereth the poore, The Lorde will deliver him in the time of his trouble'. In weighing the pros and cons of contemporary begging, Arth provides insight on how ideas on the relief of poverty and vagrancy developed in the second half of the sixteenth century. He recognised that 'if any be pinched with penurie the default especially resteth in themselves though some other persons can not be excused'. He also accepted that amongst the poor were those who have 'misspent much good time in idle roguing up and downe, and would not worke' as well as those who had 'beene great wasters in bibbing and belly cheare'. Each of the foregoing were seen to ignore the call of God and his messengers. They should 'leave their evil wayes and serve Him better' so that they could then expect their cry for 'foode' to be heard.[79] But Arth complained with equal fervour about the shortcomings of wealthier people in that 'others (alas) are too hard-hearted, unwilling almost to part with any thing (albeit they richly abound with all things)'. Many among the wealthy were seen as 'poore makers'. Arth detailed ten types of person who 'in all places, are many and grievous' and may be 'tearmed the breeders of the poore', they were:

1. All excessive proude persons in apparell
2. The unmeasurable waisters of meate and drinke
3. The importable oppression of many Landlords
4. The unconscionable extortion of all userers
5. The unsatiable covetousnesse in corne-mongers
6. The wilfull wrangling in law matters
7. The immoderate abuse of gaimming in all Countreys
8. The discharging of servants and apprentices
9. The generall abuse of all Gods benefites
10. The want of execution of good lawes and statutes.[80]

Arth argued that 'concerning the causes of the poore ... the same both proceede partly from themselves through their idleness, etc but more especially from the poore makers ... who if they would forsake their immoderate excesse ... the poor would get daily reliefe thereby'.[81]

MacCaffrey has calculated that more than half the poor in sixteenth-century Exeter lived in 'dire poverty'. Because they had so little to lose there was always the possibility that their desperation would combine in popular revolt.[82] It was much the same across Europe. Stearns argues that in spite of the poverty 'almost surpassing description', the restricted diet created lassitude, not revolutionary energy. Workers' lack of organisation meant that protests were rarely more than individual acts of defiance.[83]

During the last three decades of the sixteenth century laws were enacted which formed the foundation of the Old Poor Law. They specified that each parish was responsible for relieving its poor, whether permanent or casual, able-bodied or non-able-bodied. The emerging trend can be seen in the 14 Act of Elizabeth, c. 5 (1572). This followed in the wake of the Statute of Artificers (1563). It told 'Justices Maiors Sheriffes Baylyffes and other Officers' that through their 'good discretions taxe and assesse all and every the Inhabitauntes'. Each of them must contribute appropriately 'towardes the releef of the said poore People'. Should any person 'obstinatly refuse to give towardes the Helpe and Relief' of the poor they could be imprisoned. At the same time the 1572 Statute re-emphasised the need to apply punitive legislation more vigorously. An even lengthier descriptive list of the travelling people was published. All of them, as a matter of course, could be expected to have criminal intent. Earlier laws had already included a wide miscellany of travellers for legal treatment as vagrants. To these were now added 'all fencers, bearwards, players, and minstrels' not belonging to a nobleman and all unlicensed jugglers, pedlars, tinkers, petty chapmen, common labourers refusing to work, counterfeiters of passports and licenses, scholars begging without written authority from their University, shipmen pretending losses at sea and discharged prisoners begging without authority to pay their gaoler's fees. The 1572 legislation also introduced the concept of the local overseer of the poor. He had the task of punishing a whole miscellany of 'Roges, Vacabonds, or sturdy Beggars' by gaoling, 'grevouslye' whipping, and burning 'throughe the gristle of the right Eare with a hot Yron'. Henry VIII's memory was sustained with the decree that a third vagrancy offence made the culprit a felon who should 'suffer paynes of Death and losse of Land and Goodes' without the benefit of 'Clergye or Sanctuary'.[84] In Middlesex, during the three years following 1572, there were 44 vagabonds branded, eight set to service and five hanged.[85] Despite its harsh edge, the Act recognised that there could be able-bodied persons who were genuinely seeking work away from their own parish and who were not hardened vagrants. The inclusion of this clause makes the 1572 Act a turning point in vagrancy legislation. There was also emphasis on the need for compulsory weekly parish contributions to provide relief for the deserving poor. Parishioners refusing to participate were threatened with a prison committal. For a number of years there was to be somewhat less emphasis on the criminality of vagrancy and more on the need for alternative solutions.

It became more generally accepted that to counter the continued growth in the numbers of travelling poor and the accompanying fear of social disturbance, a more constructive response was needed to deter mendicity. According to Tawney, 'after three generations in which the attempt was made to stamp out vagrancy by police measures of hideous brutality, the momentous admission was made that its cause was economic distress not merely personal idleness'.[86] The whip had few terrors for the man who must either tramp or starve. A defect of the 1572 legislation was that while recognising there were people who were involuntarily unemployed, there was no guidance about how the able-bodied wanderer should be set to work. The 18 Elizabeth, c. 3 (1575–6) Act rectified this omission. It defined how a 'competent store and Stocke of Woole Hempe Flaxe iron or other stufe' should be provided in every city, borough or market town. Houses of Industry should be established so that young people could become accustomed to work rather than wallowing in the pleasures of idleness.[87] At the same time, those who had 'alredye growen up in ydlenes' would no longer have any justification in claiming that work was not available. The establishments were funded partly by compulsory poor rates and partly by voluntary contribution. They provided support for the destitute while coupling stringent labour demands as at Bridewell in London.[88] Bridewell was intended to 'punish sin' and especially sexual misdemeanours. In the year 1560–1 there were 69 vagrants punished there, only 16 per cent of all offenders. Numbers grew steadily. 555 vagrants were punished in 1600–1 which was 62 per cent of all offenders.[89] Bristol, Canterbury, Cambridge, Norwich, St Albans and York were amongst other towns making parallel efforts to Bridewell. Some of these institutions offered little but the demand to complete harsh physical work. Others taught skills such as the making of gloves, silk, lace, pins, bags, felts and tennis balls.[90] Ipswich, where compulsory rates for poor relief were introduced in 1557, also provided a hospital for the poor. This was notable for its compromise between the ideal and the feasible: 'Noe children of this towne shall be p'mitted to begg, and such as shall be admitted thereto shall have badges.'[91] Central government also charged parishes to take the responsibility of raising funds for apprenticing the young poor. Elizabeth's idea of teaching the poor a trade which would equip them for a meaningful place in society was later to receive enthusiastic support from the early Stuarts.

The Acts of 1572 and 1576 together formed the basis of the seminal statutes of 1597–8 and 1601 which have colloquially become designated the 'Old Poor Law'. Frank Aydelotte believed they marked 'the beginning of the end of the old free, merry, vagabond life'.[92] The threat of Houses of Correction for shirkers was, for a while at least, a useful and reasonably effective alternative to whips, stocks, pillories and the gallows. During the later years of the century, events such as the defeat of the Spanish Armada meant that, in spite of the disincentive of able-bodied travellers now facing the danger of having to labour for their relief, numbers tramping were still high and were further augmented by demobilised militia. 'Old soldiers with long service in France or the Netherlands, discharged for wounds or sickness' found it difficult to find employment suited to their disabilities.[93] Although the concerns of the better-off sections of the community about vagrancy were not entirely banished, there were indications that towards the end of Elizabeth's reign poor travellers were being viewed as less of a threat. Signals about this more relaxed tendency include a reduction in orders from the Privy Council concerning vagrants, fewer precepts about them in London, and measures of restraint becoming regular instead of violent and spasmodic. Pamphlet literature showed signs that the 'merry, wicked, resourceful vagabonds of the middle of the century had become merely tame beggars'.[94]

After the fifteenth-century lull in legislation dealing with the travelling poor, the period 1530–98 was, as we have seen, one of renewed activity with 13 proclamations pertinent to our subject. During this period, Acts dealing 'with the vexed problem of vagrancy' had entered the statute book.[95] The 1597–8 Act was prompted by widespread exceptional distress arising from heavy unseasonable rains, poor harvests and escalating grain prices. The social turbulence that had been so feared by Parliaments had already erupted in the form of the 1595 bread riots. 'Widespread dissent then followed general dearth, high prices and increasing unemployment.'[96] The Government was compelled to recognise that by now there were thousands of able-bodied men, both in town and country, anxious to work but without the available opportunity. Crime became a temptation for them. So much so that Sir George More wrote in January 1597 that, it was 'hard in poverty not to sinne'. In the October Parliament of that year, Francis Bacon spoke strongly against the iniquities of enclosures. The depopulation of villages was still continuing 'after a century of preventative legislation' and this had led to growing 'vagabondage, beggary, and honest poverty'.[97] Parliament followed the recommendations of a House of Commons Committee that adequate relief must be provided for destitute cases before they could be expected to abandon mendicity. The various Acts devised by Elizabeth's lawyers came together in the 39 Eliz., c. 3 (1597–8) 'Acte for Punyshment of Rogues, Vagabondes and Sturdy Beggars' and for the 'Reliefe of the Poore'. It was more explicit in its directives to local officials about the collection and distribution of the poor rate and for setting the able-bodied to work. It was now mandatory that overseers of the poor be appointed and empowered to raise 'weekly or otherwise by taxation, from every inhabitant and every occupier of the parish' such sums as were required to set the able-bodied poor to work; to provide 'competent sums of money for the necessary relief of the impotent, old, blind and other poor not able to work; and also for the putting out of children to be apprentices'.[98]

The 39 Elizabeth also had settlement connotations. It listed those who should be publicly flogged before removal to their birth place or last residence. They included:

all persons calling themselves Schollers going about begging'; seamen pretending to have lost their ships or goods; idle persons such as fortune-tellers and those with 'fantasticall Ymagynations'; pretended gatherers of alms for prisons and hospitals; fencers, common players or minstrels; jugglers, tinkers, pedlars and petty chapmen; able bodied wandering persons and labourers refusing to work for current rates of wages and 'not having lyving otherwyse to maynteyne themselves'; discharged prisoners; wanderers pretending losses by fire or otherwise; and 'counterfayte' Egyptians or gypsies.[99]

Most of the people covered by the 1597 legislation were simply displaced. They were usually young, mostly men although a substantial minority were women. Commonly unmarried, there were some whole families on the road. 'Usually they were hustled on their way by villagers who feared and suspected them, or whipped out of parishes by constables enforcing the vagrancy laws'. Too many found a settlement only when 'their bodies were found in barns or under hedges on winter mornings, especially in years of food-shortage, their only memorials being brief anonymous entries in parish registers. One such entry, referred to by Wrightson, related to 'a poor woman which died in a barne at the parsonage whose name we could not learne'.[100]

According to Slack, 'the picturesque or professional rogue appears to have been the exception not the rule'. As we have seen, there were already indications that legislators were attempting to separate from treatment as vagrants those innocently travelling in search of work or improvement.[101] Unfortunately the line between the two was blurred and was to remain so through the centuries that followed. To take an example prompted by the imprecision afforded by the 39 Elizabeth, petty theft or fortune-telling, which could well result in a flogging, might nevertheless have become a necessary means of survival for the genuine work-seeker needing to ward off starvation at times when economic conditions were so dire as to make the chance of gaining permanent employment slim. What is more, commercial advances during the sixteenth century had consolidated the travelling tradesman as a feature in contemporary society with the likes of joiners, cobblers and weavers finding mobility a necessary boost to wage-earning. As with others possessing only more dubious skills such as peddling or ballad-selling, most were only too keen to make an honest living rather than having to turn to crime in order to fend off starvation.

Eventually, the prolonged efforts of the sixteenth-century legislators were brought together in the 1601 Act (43rd of Elizabeth).

Together with its 1597–8 predecessor, this legislation was to greatly influence attitudes and legal processes for nearly three hundred and fifty years until Poor Law institutions were finally dissolved. Late sixteenth-century legislators were beginning to accept that socio-economic factors were important in any worthwhile explanation of why the numbers of displaced persons had increased. Now, it was no longer sufficient to dismiss all itinerant beggars as scheming professionals determined to take advantage of the generosity of the charitable or that others were idle shirkers who dodged physical exertion at every opportunity.

Urbanisation was an important factor leading to Tudor efforts to legally restrain the mobility of the poor. At the outset of the sixteenth century no more than 155 000 English people lived in towns of more than 5000 people. By 1600 the number had more than doubled, a somewhat faster growth than in the population generally.[102] Although the urban centres were a source of attractive wage rates they were, as we have already noted, largely devoid of the traditional rural paternalistic support. When trade and jobs were at a low ebb or after the Tudor inflation had taken hold, unemployed wage-earners were no longer able to buy even subsistence food and needed organised community support. In the countryside things had also changed in ways that multiplied the numbers trudging the road in a desperate search for the means of keeping body and soul together. The enhanced economic advantage of meat and wool production meant that a switch from grain to pasture emphasised to landowners the attractions of enclosure. Many of their workers were stranded without jobs. Furthermore, a gradual rural trend towards a wage economy meant that, as in the urban areas, the allegiance to traditional paternalistic responsibilities had become eroded. Central government had already decided that in these circumstances relief of the impotent poor was more securely funded by the levy of a regular tax than by being left to the whims of haphazard charity.

Tudor vagrancy legislation, taken together with the more general Poor Laws, provided the foundation whereby those who deserved relief were afforded it while those judged to be undeserving were punished. By the end of the sixteenth century, the draftsmen of the legislation created a framework of local responsibility which still permitted some freedom of interpretation. How during the seventeenth and eighteenth centuries the central regimes in succeeding generations each differed in their application and modification of the Tudor laws is the subject of the following chapter.

4 The Travelling Poor in the Seventeenth and Eighteenth Centuries

It is a foul disorder in any commonwealth that there should be suffered rogues, beggars, vagabonds; ... To wander up and down from year to year to this end, to seek and procure bodily maintenance, is no calling, but the life of a beast: and consequently a condition or state or life flat against the rule, that every man should have a particular calling. And therefore the Statute ... [1597] for the restraining of rogues is an excellent statute, and, being in substance the very law of God, is never to be repealed.[1]

Latter-day writers, shocked by the density of urban squalor brought by the growth of manufacture, have woven a mental image of a bygone bucolic age. Allegedly, before the industrial era, labouring people enjoyed a comfortable existence, basked in robust health and had the security of a cosy, if simple, cottage. They are said to have enjoyed the daily pleasure of a nourishing diet made up of untainted food mainly grown in their own garden or smallholding.[2] Nothing could be further from the truth. For most people this idyllic picture of rural life was illusory. The joys that did exist prior to intense industrial urbanisation were mainly restricted to a privileged select minority. Labouring people struggled to exist. For what was usually a short lifespan, they endured in harsh callous surroundings. Their problems were not so obvious, nor have they been as well-publicised, as those associated with the ugly unsanitary manufacturing towns of the industrial age but the pre-industrial economy had its own forms of wretchedness. Apprehension about the future lurked persistently with agricultural labourers who together with their families made up a massive part of the populace. Times were 'brutalising and depressing to the human spirit'.[3] Until the industrial facilities expanded sufficiently in the later eighteenth century, the macro-economy lacked the wider spread of somewhat higher earnings associated with the forests of smoky chimneys and which brought some amelioration of their disadvantages.

Discussion in the previous chapter showed how the 43 Elizabeth, c. 2, Act of 1601 was the culmination of the series of legislative Tudor experiments stretching over three decades, each attempting to deal with poverty. The 43 Act of Elizabeth, colloquially known as 'The Old Poor Law' emphasised that each parish was responsible for its own poor. Local authorities were forced to levy a poor rate on all occupiers of property within the parish boundaries. The mandatory rate had to be collected and distributed correctly on the aged, the infirm and towards apprenticing pauper children to a trade. Parishes also had to set able-bodied relief applicants to complete a task of work.[4] In essence, this meant the impotent could be relieved without payment while the able-bodied must labour for their relief. If the applied labour had been economically productive, the dual policy should have resulted in only those who were in some way mentally or physically disadvantaged becoming a charge on the parish. In practice the process lacked perfection and its application was a constant battle against economic forces.[5] It is particularly pertinent to our considerations that the Old Poor Law also provided further momentum to the already reasonably well-established procedure allowing local officials to rid themselves of destitute strangers considered to be a potential charge on the parish. As we will discover, these tactics were to be refined and strengthened by legislators in succeeding decades. This trend eventually culminated in the crucial settlement and removal laws of 1662. For centuries these militated against the well-being of itinerant poor people. By restricting the mobility of potential workers they can also be seen to have inadvertently hijacked the economic progress of the nation towards modernisation.

The protracted use for more than two centuries of the 43 Elizabeth, with occasional minor tinkering, through to the 'New Poor Law' of 1834, suggests that it was reasonably effective in rationalising relief as well as being adaptable to political, economic and social change. The Elizabethan Poor Law had been drafted with sufficient subtlety to permit a wide range of interpretations. Considerable geographical variation was possible. The early years of the seventeenth century exposed widespread slackness in its application. Local authorities with only limited appreciation of legal matters were not anxious to shoulder the new responsibilities inherent in Elizabeth's Laws, especially when there was rarely much local pressure from influential bodies for them to do so.

In general, the 'lower orders' knew and accepted their place. Most of the population lived in stable poverty. Ignorance encouraged passivity rather than political activism. With the contemporary voting structure, the majority were not only submissive in being 'unwilling to challenge the social and political authority of landed and urban elites, they were unable to do so'.[6] As the pattern of working for a wage gradually increased so the poor were no longer necessarily the help-less victims of misfortune or old age and as such needed to be cared for. Now, there was some expectation that they would perform as responsible individuals and prepare themselves financially for what knocks tomorrow might bring. This theoretical expectation was rarely achievable in practice. The truth was that few wage-earners could earn sufficient when in work to tide them over for more than a short time after they became unemployed. Even those with full-time jobs, such as woollen weavers, constantly dreaded that public demand for garments or blankets might decline. A permanent proletariat was emerging. They needed care when times were bad. Beyond the plight of these people and 'well outside the charitable consideration of the authori-ties' were the vagrant poor. They remained a nagging seemingly intractable problem for the authorities.[7] It continued to be a fact of life that at times when the economy worsened so concurrently did the numbers increase of those turning in desperation to the highway as a means of discovering subsistence.

Within a few months of his accession, James I expressed concern at the growing number of poor people prepared to stray away from their own parishes. He proclaimed that in spite of the best legal endeav-ours of his 'deare Sister deceased, Queen Elizabeth' to repress 'Rogues, Vagabonds, idle and dissolute persons, wherwith this Realm was then much infested' local JPs had connived in their negligence to discharge their new legal powers. James directed attention to the failure of local law officers. They had shirked the banishment of 'incorrigible or dangerous Rogues' to 'Places and partes beyond the Seas' including 'the New found Lande', the East and West Indies, Fraunce, Germanie, Spayne, and the Lowe Countries'.[8] He recom-mended renewed endeavour on the part of local officials to expel such people from our island shores. How rigorously the King's renewed wishes were implemented is not clear, nor, if they were applied, how the intended recipient countries responded. It would hardly have been surprising if rejects were returned from countries over which Britain had no jurisdiction. Such had been the earlier experience of Elizabeth's representatives when attempting to despatch unwanted English Gypsies to Norway. Nevertheless, the seventeenth century growth of the Britain's colonies did provide some 'ready means of ridding this country of the more disorderly elements of the population, moss troopers from the borders, "malignants" and rebels'.[9]

A Circular published in 1608 attempted to stir JPs into more meaningful response to the 1601 Act. This told them they were 'not Justices for their countenaunce onlye!' and that their execution of the law was inadequate.[10] During the following years the Privy Council continued to exhort local officials, with mixed success, to enforce the 43rd Elizabeth more meaningfully both in the repression of vagrants and in relief of the indigent. Economic depression amongst woollen garment makers, coupled with increased prices following the disastrous harvest of 1621–2 sparked outbreaks of worker unrest and prompted wider application of the 1601 statute.[11] Laslett's data from parish registers confirm that in these bleak times an increased proportion of the poor wandered away from their home village. People needed sustenance and, as the last resort before starvation in their new environment, 'sought refuge in the church porch, that half sheltered space in parish life'.[12] Evidence from local sources suggests 'subsistence migration increased dramatically' in the third decade of the seventeenth century. A study of migrant paupers in three Midland parishes included a minority medley of convicted vagabonds, demobilised soldiers and gypsies. More than 60 per cent of the migrants were 'poor travellers' either disabled or searching for work. Their quest had been triggered by the deterioration of England's economic condition in the early 1620s. Numbers tramping were augmented further by the Irish famine of 1628–9.[13]

The continuing hordes of transient poor led the Privy Council to contact local dignitaries repeatedly during the 1630s. They were told to proceed more effectively with laws suppressing unworthy vagrants as well as those relieving the indigent. In 1630, Charles I launched a Commission involving 36 of the principal 'officers of state and nobility'. Its purpose was to put 'in execution the laws for the relief of the poor'.[14] After deliberation, the Commission referred to the 'neglect of dutie' of some JPs. These were instructed 'duely and diligently' to apply the existing law so that 'poore people were better relieved' from both taxation and from charity. A chain of responsibility was established to counter JP laxity. Each had to provide a monthly account of cases to the Sheriffs who in turn sent them to the circuit Judges. Coordinated accounts were then forwarded to the Lord Commissioners.[15]

Charles's involvement in the condition of the poor generally proved beneficial to them. From 1631 to 1640 all facets of the

Elizabethan Poor Law were made operative across the country. Work was provided for the unemployed as well as relief for the impotent. Leonard has claimed that during Charles I's reign 'we had more poor relief in England than we ever had before or since'. Trevelyan has described it as a period showing 'real regard for the interests of the poor'.[16] That is not to say that Charles's Commissioners missed the opportunity of emphasising that 'lazie and idle persons' should be put to work. The continued use of Houses of Correction where rogues and vagabonds should be punished were considered essential. By applying these aspects of the law more rigorously, some local justices succeeded in limiting the numbers of travelling people in their area. But generally there was little change in the number tramping the nation's roads including those 'wandering under the names of soldiers, mariners, glassmen, potmen, pedlars, petty chapmen, conyskinmen, or tinkers'.[17] With the onset of the Civil War, relief to the poor was again curtailed. Many agricultural labourers were cajoled and enticed financially into the army. A period of economic contraction followed with the rising wages under Cromwell contributing, as did the paralysis of the post-war central machinery of government.[18]

A regrettable feature of seventeenth century England was yet further decline in life-expectancy, a criterion commonly accepted by demographers as a measure of living standards.[19] Wrigley and Schofield calculate that from an expectation of life at birth of 39.3 years around the year 1576 there was a shocking fall to 32.3 years during the following one hundred years, that is a reduction of 17.8 per cent. The early 1680s probably incurred further deterioration in the condition of the public even though mortality crises were not apparent.[20] In modern times both Elizabethan and Stuart survival rates would place England amongst the less developed world.[21] Table 4.1 shows that the fall in worker purchasing power that had so blighted the sixteenth century began to bottom out in the 1630s.

The stabilisation of wage rates was influenced by various factors. These included the reduced rate of population growth, the renewed severity of plague outbreaks, disastrous harvests, and the effects of war. Proto-industrial growth also had a steadying effect on wages.[22]

Michael Dalton in the 1635 edition of *The Countrey Justice*, a law book of authority, separated the 'poore by impotency or defect' and the 'poore by casualty' from the 'thriftlesse poore'. The latter he described as:

Table 4.1   Purchasing power of building craftsmen and agricultural labourers in seventeenth-century southern England

	Building craftsmen, index number, 1451–75, = 100	Agricultural labourers, index number, 1450–99, = 100
1600–9	42.5	19.9
1610–9	38.2	44.3
1620–9	42.9	49.5
1630–9	40.2	47.1
1640–9	45.1	50.0
1650–9	47.5	52.0
1660–9	46.7	53.2
1670–9	49.1	54.3
1680–9	54.1	56.1
1690–9	51.3	51.5

Sources: Craftsman data: E. A. Wrigley and R. S. Schofield, *The Population History of England*, 1541–1871 (1981), pp. 642–3. Agricultural Labourer data based on: C. G. A. Clay, *Economic Expansion and Social Change* (1984), pp. 50–2.

1. The riotous and prodigall person, that consumeth all with play or drinking, etc.
2. The dissolute person, as the Strumpet, Pilferer, etc.
3. The slothfull person, that refuseth to work.
4. All such as will wilfully spoile or imbesill their work etc.
5. The Vagabonde that will abide in no service or place.

Dalton recommended that the 'House of Correction is fittest' for those in any of the five categories. 'There such persons being able in body, are to be compelled to labour, that by labour and punishement of their bodies, their forward natures may be bridled; their evil minds betterred, and others their examples terrified' ... and that all such persons sent to the House of Correction, must live there by their 'owne labour and work, without charging the Towne and Countrey, for any allowance or fee to that purpose'. Dalton described a vagabond as 'he which hath neither certaine house, nor stedfast habitation; but liveth idly and loytering'. 'Although he beggeth not' it was now common practice to group the vagabond with the 'Rogue'.[23]

Dalton advised JPs not to license the 'poore to travell' around the country. 'Poore diseased persons' were an exception and should be allowed to visit baths 'for remedy of their griefes'. In addition, the 'Souldier or Mariner' could be given a 'testimonial' assisting them to 'passe the next direct way to their place of birth or dwelling, limiting them therein a convenient time for their passage'.[24]

Based on data from urban vagrancy registers, including those at Salisbury and at Colchester, Paul Slack suggested English vagrants generally travelled in ones and twos. This he contrasted with Irish migrants who tended to move in gangs of 12 or more. Most English vagrants appeared to be young men although females were not an unsubstantial minority.[25] Between 1598 and 1638 the Salisbury register listed 557 passports containing the names of 651 vagrants. All were described as 'wandering'. Unless 'pregnant, disabled, or under the statutory age of seven' they 'were whipped' prior to being passed from constable to constable back to their birthplace or parish of residence.[26] Slack pointed out that vagrancy register data probably accounted for only a small part of the total number of poor people tramping the country.

Land enclosures and their harmful consequences to agricultural labourers mentioned in the previous chapter continued apace in some counties. In Leicestershire, crowds of destitute people, ejected from the land, obstructed the highways and traffic in market towns, according to '*A Petition to Parliament against Enclosure of Land*' (1649).[27] A three-tier system gradually evolved between landowners, tenant farmers and agricultural labourers. The agricultural depressions of the late seventeenth century not only affected the unskilled. More versatile agricultural workers were by now being hired annually. Those who were not out of work for too long usually retained the margin of their existence from common and waste lands 'on which they gathered kindling, grazed animals and hunted game to supplement their meagre wages'.[28] The less fortunate became landless or virtually landless and 'forced by lack of work or home to become vagrants'.[29] Even farmers were occasionally driven by desperation to abandon their farms when unable to satisfy rent demands. They and their families boosted the volume of destitute travellers.[30]

The shortcomings of the labourer's stark existence with so little opportunity for self-improvement mitigated the destabilising stress suffered on leaving their family home and friends to seek improvement elsewhere. In general, the disenchanting factors contributing to why individuals abandoned the relative security of the countryside included unemployment and underemployment, harvest failure, post-war demobilization, disease, parental death, family abuse or personal eviction. The scope of employment in London was tempting as was the potential excitement of flourishing seaports like Liverpool and Bristol. Others seeking a better life were attracted by the level of wages on offer in the expanding mining and manufacturing centres in the North, Midlands and South Wales. But some tramps were individuals with few recent household or kinship ties. Many had personality traits determined or confirmed by experience of a rootless insecure existence in forests, towns or armies. Uncertainty prevailed among the poor in an economy still riddled with seasonal jobs and cyclical underemployment, a situation worsened by the sporadic bad harvest and its accompanying dearth.[31]

The size of towns grew in the seventeenth century, but only slowly. Through to at least the 1660s, a nagging toll on urban population accompanied plague and other infectious diseases which flourished in crowded closely built surroundings. Because burials outstripped births in many towns, urban development was only maintained through the continual inflow of people from the countryside.[32] John Graunt was among the first to make this point with his calculation based on Bills of Mortality from a number of London parishes between 1603 and 1644. It showed there had been 363 935 burials but only 330 747 christenings. Only a supply of 'people from the country' allowed London to grow during the period.[33] Clark concluded that 'physical mobility had a profound and pervasive effect on early modern society'. The growth of many towns depending heavily on their attraction to outsiders.[34] A favourable aspect of internal migration was that it helped to mould favourable demographic profiles in urban communities such as by the correction of regressive age-pyramids.

The dominant 'currents of migration' towards London satisfied Ravenstein's First Law as those Midlanders who drifted to the capital were replaced by others moving from more remote areas.[35] The movement from one locality to another generally occurred 'because people felt that their economic prospects would be better if they went elsewhere'. In the case of the desperately poor this feeling was strengthened by their fear of starvation.[36] Indications are that more prosperous travellers, possibly with a worthwhile trade and the determination to better themselves, were prepared to travel longer distances than was the destitute tramp. This was also often the case with the more robust worldly-wise type of vagrant whose mobility was backed by a thorough knowledge of the national road system. In contrast, movement of destitute migrants driven by subsistence needs was more likely to be more confined in geographical scope. Their initial drift, at least, tended to be to a nearby town where scraps of food might be cadged from the markets. An impression of how localised was mobility was in south-east England is available from the records of those appearing before archdeaconry courts in Sussex. Whereas most defendants between 1580 and 1640 had moved from their birthplace at some time, fewer than one in twenty had shifted more than 40 miles.[37]

Especially attractive to poor travellers were villages which still retained extensive commons in fen, moorland or forest. Newcomers could squat while scratching around to support themselves off the land. Christopher Hill has described how beneath the surface calm of rural England there was a 'seething fluidity' of forest squatters. They included itinerant craftsmen and building labourers, unemployed men and women seeking work, strolling players, minstrels and jugglers, pedlars and quack doctors, Gypsies, vagabonds and tramps. For these people, odds and ends of casual or seasonal work were their best hope. They made footholds wherever newly squatted areas escaped the machinery of the parish. Some travellers used old squats near to where labour had been in demand in the hope that opportunity would again arise.[38] Others left home prepared to look abroad to the New World for the opportunity denied them in their own community. Recruiting officers for the army and navy found some young tramps ready and willing listeners – especially with the temptation of Royal silver used as a conversational precursor.

From time to time urban economies subsided temporarily. They despatched the manufacturing worker back into the jobless cauldron. What made it worse was that geographical concentration of production meant that now there was the likelihood that many in the immediate vicinity would be sharing his plight. Some were then tempted to the road to join the drifting travellers in the hope of finding better things. When the economy went seriously wrong the closure of manufacturing facilities could cause ugly scenes. Around 1629, the unemployed textile workers of Braintree and Bocking, two of the more important Essex centres of production, 'besieged the Quarter Sessions complaining of extreme necessity and disability to maintain themselves and their families'. JPs confirmed that the desperate condition of the contemporary draperies industry threatened 'the livelihood of 30 000 spinners and weavers' in the county.[39] Seventeenth-century urban workers were at a greater danger than their rural peers of facing economic disaster from epidemics. When disease threatened it was usually the better-off who had the means to flee the town quickly. Left in their wake could be a surge of subsistence mobility among the distressed workers who had depended upon them for their livelihood.[40]

In spite of the official pleas for social stability, it is hardly surprising that during the civil troubles of the 1640s, political, economic and social dislocation increased national mobility. Poor harvests in the post-war years lifted the price of grain to a new peak. Some JPs faced with the local realities of destitution became more ready to acknowledge the needs of the destitute, whether impotent or able-bodied. In Cheshire for instance, magistrates laid aside much of their early vigilance against wanderers when faced with a marked increase of the rootless poor that were patently genuine. They adopted a 'comprehensive and firm handling' of the grain trade and its pricing mechanisms.[41]

As discussed in the previous chapter, although Tudor statesmen had no time for idleness amongst the poor, there had been grudging acceptance towards the end of Elizabeth's reign that economic depression could lead to social dislocation. The Stuarts had followed this line of thinking. The Civil War led to the idea that some poor people may have fallen innocently into economic misfortune being buried in the simplistic creed of Puritan legislators. Resurrected was the doctrine whereby the destitute were invariably guilty of their own misfortune. Their lack of moral fortitude was confirmed by the failure of poor people to rectify their own plight. Society's derelict misfits were now seen as deserving little from their betters but pain. In 1647 the indulgent rectitude of those gaining power bred new Ordinances. Stage plays were suppressed; travelling players treated as rogues. Even then, Commonwealth lawmakers soon learned lessons from their predecessors' experience. It was recognised as being impossible to physically confine the travelling poor simply by oppressing them. A 1647 Ordinance therefore attempted a somewhat more constructive approach. It established the London Corporation of the Poor for the 'constant Reliefe and Imployment of the Poore; And the punishment of Vagrants, and other disorderly Persons'. Recommended was the erection of 'one or more Houses of Correction for punishing Rogues, Vagabonds, and Beggers, as they think fit'.[42] The House of Correction theme was accentuated nationally two years later by a Commonwealth Act for the relief and employment of the poor and the punishment of beggars. It offered the choice of work or a flogging.

Justices of the Peace were expected to ensure that physical materials were available with which to occupy relief applicants in labour. The interregnum encouraged public attitudes which placed less emphasis on the obligation of charity and more on the duty of work. Clerical admonitions which had earlier focused on the uncharitable covetousness of the wealthy were redirected against poor people's improvidence and idleness. When their early legislation had little effect in stemming the tide of tramping people the Puritan authorities made a further assault. The Commonwealth, c. 21 (1656) Act was aimed 'against Vagrants, and wandring, idle, dissolute, and disorderly persons'. Allegedly, these people had 'lately shown a great increase' in number.[43] Cromwell's associates then retraced the ineffective steps of their legislative predecessors by attempting to eliminate tramping by extending the scope of local law officers to punish those of no fixed abode. Now, any 'idle, loose or dissolute' person found wandering from their usual place of living or abode and, in the opinion of local law officials lacking sufficient cause for travelling, should be declared a 'Rogue', punishment to be in accord with the 39th Elizabeth. Whether the 'hardening of treatment' of vagrants during the Interregnum indicated a fundamental shift in government policy is not clear. It can be interpreted more 'a function of their rapidly increasing numbers rather than of a new attitude towards them'. Beier has argued that in Warwickshire, at least, 'the JPs of the Interregnum surpassed those of the Personal Rule [of Charles I] by their zealous administration and benevolent attitude towards the poor' and that this 'surely increased their propensity to deal effectively with the problems of the poor'.[44]

The Restoration of the monarchy did nothing to ease the condition of those among the poor who wanted to move from their settlement parish. Charles II quickly made his presence felt by introducing drastic legislation to repress the travelling poor still further. Although the principles of legal settlement and removal were, of course, far from novel, Charles's draftsmen broadened their scope and tightened their severity. Until now constraining legislation had generally been accompanied by efforts to control prices, provide work and where necessary replace paternalistic support with parish relief. Now the balance moved more definitely against the poor traveller. Public attitudes to them remained unyielding. The relief offered by local authorities often lacked semblance of the traditional care provided for the disadvantaged. This firm standpoint was crystallised in 1662 with the seminal 14 Charles II, c. 12 Act of Settlement and Removal.[45]

Regarded historiographically as the second stage in the development of Elizabeth's 1601 Act, it was to become 'a flywheel around which the Poor Law revolved for more than a century and a half'.[46]

Initially the more exacting settlement and removal legislation caused hardly a stir. Neither Parliament nor the public recognised its full portent for the mass of labourers. But soon it was to have far-reaching social impact by formalising and encouraging the early expulsion of destitute visitors from each parish. Exempt from the new legislation were persons occupying property having a rental value of at least ten pounds or who were considered unlikely to become a burden on local ratepayers. Apart from these better-off individuals, possibly totalling one in ten of the population, the 1662 Act decreed that any person whether visitor, job seeker or travelling wage-earner, could be categorised as a beggar. Guilty of nothing other than being without money or a home, such people were victimised.[47] Any of them could be ignominiously removed from the parish in which they were challenged. They need not have committed a crime or even having asked for poor relief.

The 1662 Act encouraged local officers to look anxiously across their boundaries to guard against their neighbouring peers off-loading undesirable individuals or families. It has been seen as a camouflaged reintroduction of the principle of villeinage – an extreme form of parish isolationism. Because it bred suspicion as the cornerstone of interparish relationships, the Act became viewed, by the suffering poor and by enlightened observers alike, as an unnecessary unwelcome intrusion into social harmony. Family values were eroded. As a result of the Act, after losing a job in their depressed settlement parish, men were sorely tempted to collude with their spouse by absconding elsewhere in search of work while leaving his destitute wife and family chargeable to local ratepayers.

A disquieting aspect of the new law was that to qualify for its attention a poor person merely had to be of such appearance that, in the opinion of parish officials, there was a possibility that they might, on some future occasion, apply for parish relief. Hampson has shown that many cases were recorded in Cambridgeshire in which 'honest, industrious labourers, in employment, were judged by the magistrates as being "likely to be chargeable"'.[48] The 1662 Act had broad potential application but among the most likely to be removed were the physically or mentally sick. Also likely to receive the parish officers' attention were newly arrived married men with families who, should they ever find themselves without work, could make a deep hole in the parish coffers. On the other hand, a skilled able-bodied single man could be viewed as a welcome newcomer by a parish plentiful with jobs. Such a newcomer would be especially well received if there was the chance that he might marry a dilatory local wench considered as a possible future drag on the parish, as once married she adopted the settlement characteristics of her migrant husband.

George Coode's Report to the Poor Law Board nearly two hundred years later claimed that the 1662 Act had 'made the parish of settlement a prison' and 'every other parish a hostile fortress'. He alleged that it encouraged the refusal, the restriction or the destruction of habitations while pretending to guarantee everyone a legal home. It denied them a home everywhere else. Too often the Act had left little alternative but 'sordid, compulsory and unprosperous settlement or a vagrant life, for which last it provided the most specious justifications'. The Act was seen to satisfy the 'prevailing desire' to repress the travelling poor estimated to total 30 000. It was designed to 'put down a class whom the community viewed with loathing and a vehement abhorrence'. In doing so, it had wilfully used the common dislike for a relatively small number of people as a pretext for fettering the vast majority of Englishmen.[49] Coode maintained that from 1662, 'the great body of Englishmen had by act of parliament just been imprisoned, each in one fifteen thousandth part of his country'.[50] In Schweinitz's opinion, the seventeenth-century settlement legislation stood for generations of poor people as the 'ultimate on the negative side of the Elizabethan system of assistance by neighbours to neighbours'. The 1662 law combined the principle of forbidding labour movement with that of conveying the majority of Englishmen back to their place of origin.[51] It remained a source of misery for the poor as well as being a persistent irritant, to say the least, for parish officials. Lawyers and medical practitioners could benefit substantially from professional fees they raked from the complex transactions. Typically these amounted to several pounds for the removal of a poor traveller to their place of settlement.[52]

Although the Restoration introduced the inhibiting constraints of the Settlement Acts, it also launched economic concepts that would ease Britain's progress towards being the world's premier industrial nation. The late seventeenth century and the eighteenth century saw development of the Commercial Age's fundamental doctrine that unceasing diligence was the key to individual wealth and worldly success. By the reverse of the same token it seemed self-evident that those suffering economic distress must be guilty of what later the 1834

Poor Law Amendment was to call individual improvidence and vice. Although Restoration legislators refused to believe there could be any reason for poverty which was not rooted in moral failure, there were a few radicals who thought differently. Some nonconformists called for recognition that there were other aspects of responsibility for the poor which all members of society must bear. Prominent among them was John Bellers, a Quaker, who inculcated a new 'supernatural' dimension into the earthly commercial values of enterprise, diligence and thrift.[53] In a period when there was a widening gulf between religion and social ethics, Bellers confronted the prevailing belief that it was reasonable and correct for the individual to make as much personal gain as possible. He insisted that in all commercial transactions it was morally obligatory to take compassionate account of the distressed poor. In an essay presented to the Lords and to the Commons, Bellers argued that 'if there were no Labourers, there would be no Lords. And if the Labourers did not raise more Food and Manufactures than what did subsist themselves, every Gentleman must be a Labourer, and idle Men must starve'.[54] Twice imprisoned for being publicly outspoken, Bellers claimed that 'the Poor without Imployment are as rough Diamonds – their Worth is unknown'. Karl Marx later dubbed him 'a very phenomenon in the history of political economy'.[55]

Renewed Parliamentary concern about the 'disturbed state of the country' showed itself in 1692 with the 4 William & Mary, c. 8 Act 'for encouraging the apprehending of highway Men'. It alleged that roads had lately become 'more infested with Thieves and Robbers than formerly for want of due and sufficient encouragement given to the means used for the discovery and apprehension of such offenders'. The new Act claimed that it had become dangerous in 'many parts of the Nation' for law-abiding citizens to go about their business. Reward was offered to those apprehending a thief or robber with evidence that later led to a conviction. An individual carrying out such an arrest could gain possession of the felon's horse and other goods. Any person who would normally have been castigated as a felon but who exposed and apprehended two other robbers was entitled to a 'gracious pardon' from his own misdemeanours.[56]

The 1692 Act did recognise that the settlement policy introduced thirty years earlier was pressing excessively hard on the labouring classes. A glimmer of hope was offered to the worker yearning for the freedom to move to an occupation elsewhere. He now had two additional ways of acquiring settlement rights away from his birthplace, namely (a) by payment of parish rates in his new surroundings for a year, or (b) by election and service as a parish officer for a year. Furthermore, life became less inhibiting for some young people. They were helped by clarification of earlier ambiguities as to their gaining settlement through completion of an apprenticeship followed by 12 months' formal service and hiring. Married men remained expressly excluded from gaining settlement by hiring.

A few years later, the 8 and 9 William III, c. 30 (1697) Act attempted to clarify the requirement for poor travellers to hold a certificate witnessed, attested, and approved by two magistrates from their parish of settlement. Where appropriate the certificate acknowledged that holders were a settled family. In practice the impact of these certificates in facilitating the flow of labour to burgeoning urban areas was limited. They were used mainly for local movements between more or less contiguous parishes. Those attracted to distant towns by a meaningful job depended more on their ability to earn good wages than on being certificated. Where work was plentiful and wages adequate, parish officers tended not to concern themselves about an influx of welcome labour. The 1697 statute emphasised that 'idle sturdy and disorderly beggars' were excluded from benefiting from the legislation. It introduced the need for all persons receiving parish relief where domiciled with their wives and children to wear a shoulder badge marked with a large 'Roman P' and the first letter of the parish 'whereof such poor person is an inhabitant'. Refusal to wear the badge could lead to their relief allowance being abridged, suspended or withdrawn. The destitute also became eligible for committal to a House of Correction where they were liable to be whipped and serve up to twenty-one days' hard labour. The 1697 Act frequently led to the 'badged' poor being bandied from one parish to the next. This compounded their difficulties in gaining legal entitlement to stay elsewhere.[57] When they had been returned to their settlement parish, not only were the displaced family now stigmatised as paupers but were also exposed to their family and friends as failures without a job, having earlier had the temerity to be dissatisfied with what their own parish had to offer.[58]

Early eighteenth-century newspapers, official documents, treatises and pamphlets abounded with complaints about 'swarms of beggars', 'ballad singers', 'idle people', and 'profligate wretches', 'infesting' the streets of the principal towns, and 'overrunning' the highways connecting them, to the 'manifest discomfort' of the 'respectable citizens'.[59] The 13 Anne, c. 26 (1713) Act established the pattern of eighteenth-century vagrancy legislation. Concentration was now focused on the 'unacceptably high' cost having to be borne by individuals and parishes as a result of the large numbers of parasitic vagrants. The preamble to the Act claimed that many parts of the realm were finding themselves financially oppressed by the habit of conveying vagabonds and beggars from county to county 'who ought not to so' be conveyed. In attempting clarification, the statute provided the following list of persons deemed to be those who, if found wandering and begging, should be punished as such:

All Persons pretending themselves to be Patent Gatherers or Collectors for Prisons Gaols or Hospitals and wandring abroad for that Purpose all Fencers Bearwards Common Players of Interludes Minstrels Juglers all Persons pretending to be Gipsies or wandring in the Habit or Form of counterfeit Egyptians or pretending to have skill in Physiognomy Palmestry or like crafty Science or pretending to tell Fortunes or like phantastical Imaginations or using any subtile craft or unlawful Games or Plays all Persons able in Body who run away and leave their Wives and Children to the parish and not having wherewith otherwise to maintain themselves use Loytring and refuse to work for the usual and common Wages and all other idle Persons wandring abroad and begging (except soldiers, Mariners, or Seafaring Men licensed by some Testimonial or Writing under the Hand and seal of some Justice of the Peace, setting down the Time and Place of his or their Landing and the place to which they are to pass, and limiting the time for such their Passage while they continue in the direct Way to the Place to which they are to pass and during the Time so limited).[60]

Persons apprehending anyone considered to be in one or more of the above categories and found to be wandering or begging or 'misordering him or herself', were entitled to a reward of two shillings. Those found guilty of wandering and begging after obtaining a legal settlement were ordered to be stripped naked to the waist and whipped 'until his or her Body be bloody'. Alternatively they could be sent to a House of Correction 'there to be kept at hard labour'. The offence now being addressed was no longer merely the 'vagrant mode of life'. It was what was viewed as the even more serious situation in which a vagrant was in danger of becoming chargeable to a parish in which he had no right of settlement.[61]

Thirty years later the category of person who could legally be charged as a vagrant was extended still further. 'All persons wandering abroad, and lodging in alehouses, barns, outhouses, or in the open air, not giving a good account of themselves' were added to Anne's 1713 list. The 17 George II, c. 5 (1743–4) Act aimed at making more effectual earlier laws relating to rogues, vagabonds and other idle and disorderly persons, and to Houses of Correction. The length to which the settlement laws could be stretched is illustrated by section 25 of the new legislation. Now, Quarter Sessions were empowered to order a public whipping and six months' imprisonment for any woman wandering or begging who had delivered of a child in a parish to which she did not belong. Another novelty introduced by George II was the idea that after having received their punishment, any male vagrant over the age of 12 years could be sent for service in His Majesty's army or navy. This summary method of recruiting was to be repeated during the remainder of the eighteenth and early nineteenth centuries, when requested by the Privy Council. The rewards initiated in the previous century for 'any person' apprehending vagrants were stepped up. Now there were five shillings for each 'idle and disorderly person' arrested in his own parish and ten shillings for each wandering 'rogue and vagabond apprehended and punished'.[62] The offer of reward often misfired. It encouraged collusion between apprehender and offender.

Chambliss offered the opinion that with George II's vagrancy legislation, the law had been sufficiently reconstructed as to have once more become a useful instrument in the creation of social solidarity. For many years, any changes in the vagrancy laws were merely in the direction of clarifying or expanding the categories covered. Little was introduced to change either the meaning or the impact of the law.[63] Halsbury has noted that in the various statutes:

> elaborate provision is made for the relief and incidental control of destitute wayfarers ... many offenders who are in no ordinary sense of the word vagrants, have been brought under the laws relating to vagrancy, and the great number of the offences coming within the operation of these laws have little or no relation to the subject of poor relief, but are more properly directed towards the prevention of crime, the preservation of good order, and the promotion of social economy.[64]

Although enclosure actions by landowners had by now been processed for centuries the number of enclosed villages increased drastically late in the eighteenth century. Until then, over much of the country, the concept of common land upon which the typical rural labourer could depend economically had remained an integral part of rural life. Even when wages were low and work was slack there was the possibility that a livelihood, a rough one admittedly, could be scratched from the common land. This characteristic of rural England became progressively blurred from 1760 when the urge for landowners to fence off their holdings while at the same time absorbing common land really took off. During the two score years that followed, ten times as many Parliamentary Enclosure Bills were introduced as during the previous 40 years. Collectively they encompassed in excess of three million acres.[65]

The growth in population, the advance of factories and the resulting urbanisation expanded the demand for agricultural products. There was now a more persistent need for wool as raw material for cloth manufacture as well as for meat and dairy products. In addition, there was greater demand for cereals at prices attractive to the farmer. New agricultural techniques benefiting from economies of scale like cross-harrowing added incentive for entrepreneurial landowners to expand their holdings.[66] The Hammonds have described how the developing urban markets stimulated landowners and their tenant farmers to adopt a more businesslike approach.[67] During the eighteenth century the annual wheat harvest in England rose from 29 to 50 million bushels. Unit yields increased by 10 per cent. During the early part of the century almost a quarter of the English crop had been exported. By the 1770s, in spite of the increased production, wheat was being imported.[68] Traditional master–servant relationships which had afforded some protection for the poor in bad times became further eroded. The larger scale cultivation of cereals and a more seasonal need for cropping led to more labourers being hired for specific short periods. Rural communities became more insecure. The younger sons of peasant farmers and those who had lost their farm, had 'to leave and look for employment elsewhere'.[69]

Widespread concern about the persistence with which the itinerant poor were annoying the public was alleged by the Establishment in 1775. The Privy Council's 'special circular' letter to the Lord-Lieutenants of Counties and the Lord Mayor of London urged them to search vigilantly for vagrants. Nation-wide appeals of this nature were used only occasionally. Generally, local officers like JPs and parish constables were left unhindered to apply the Vagrancy Laws 'capriciously, and occasionally even for malicious reasons'. Some years earlier, Horace Walpole had recorded a particularly unsavoury example of how 'a parcel of drunken constables took it into their heads to put the laws in execution'. They collected more than two dozen women and thrust them into St Martin's Round-house overnight with doors and windows closed. Next morning four had been stifled to death. Two died soon afterwards. Many others were 'in a shocking way'.[70]

What became known as Gilbert's Act was the important 22 George III, c. 83 legislation of 1782. It encouraged parishes to unite for greater efficiency and economy. The nomination of 'Guardians of the Poor' was encouraged with their appointment confirmed by two JPs. Guardians were to provide only for the impotent in the poor house. The able-bodied poor were to be catered for elsewhere or hired out for labour. Any deficiency in the wage was to be supplemented from the poor rates to reach subsistence level. JPs were authorised to order outdoor relief and to pressurise guardians 'to provide housing or find employment for a complainant'.[71] The requirement to wear the pauper's badge was removed for those of good character.

Arthur Young's much quoted eighteenth-century sentiments that 'every one but an idiot knows that the lower classes must be kept poor or they will never be industrious', were not at odds with most of his contemporaries. Nevertheless, there was grudging Parliamentary recognition about unreasonable socio-economic pressures imposed on poor travellers by the settlement laws. Widespread food rioting across England in July 1795 indicated frustration and rebellion amongst the poor. The 35 George III Act of 1795 attempted to inject an element of humanity into the parish settlement proceedings. It became illegal for travellers to be removed by parish officers until such time as they had actually applied for relief.[72] Also, the Act required that in the case of sick people the place of settlement should pay any relief granted in the meantime so that those unfit to travel could not be removed forcibly. In spite of these efforts to soften the settlement legislation, critics of eighteenth-century bureaucracy still thought that 'in whatever light these institutions are viewed, ... there is scarcely anything to be perceived but degeneracy and ultimate disappointment'.[73] Throughout the Napoleonic wars and in the years that followed, Whitehall never flagged in their determination to produce legislation. Unfortunately, it did little but tinker with the rules by which poor people might hope to obtain settlement.

Advances in manufacturing technology led to improved productivity in wool spinning and weaving. Traditionally carried out in village homes the skills were increasingly transferred to factories able to benefit from the efficiencies accruing first from water power and later from steam. In the 1790s, in addition to problems brought by enclosures and the transfer of home industries, many rural workers suffered from a succession of inferior harvests. Out of work men had few alternatives if they were to avoid starvation. They could either plead for parish relief, accept the recruiting sergeant's silver or take to the highway in the hope that life was more bearable over the horizon. Recognising that the expansion of industrialisation demanded a greater level of labour mobility, Adam Smith pointed to how the removal of able-bodied labourers and their families from parish to parish was 'a violation of natural liberty'. He attacked the 1662 Act for having inhibited the free market system by unacceptably constraining the mobility of the individual in his search for work. Because of the friction caused to national economic mechanisms, Smith argued that the settlement and removal statutes 'ought to be repealed'.[74] He alleged that there was scarcely a poor Englishman of 40 years of age who had not at some time felt 'most cruelly oppressed' by the legal constraints.

During the two hundred years following 1662, the number of Removal Orders issued nationally implied that, on average, about one or two poor people were removed from the typical parish each year.[75] Even then, this seemingly small number implies an average annual national total of removals exceeding twenty thousand. It leaves little doubt that the Settlement and Removal Acts remained a persistent constraining influence on the mobility of poor people. There can be no questioning the physical aggravated hardship suffered by unfortunate victims forcibly removed from the place where they were then living. One can only conjecture about the psychological pressures that the mere existence of the Act brought to those contemplating looking elsewhere for an economic opportunity to secure a future for themselves and their family. Some have argued that the widely held revulsion at the laws may have led to Adam Smith exaggerating their impact on labour. Certainly, as a practical instrument designed to repress vagrancy the settlement laws achieved only mixed success. Lambert points out that legal loop-holes, when exercised effectively, made it difficult to actually imprison the poor within their parish of birth.[76] What is indisputable is that effort expended on the application of settlement and removal procedures and, when considered appropriate, detecting their legal weaknesses, constructed a costly bureaucratic maze. It created confusion with justices, parish officers and the poor alike. The Acts were repeatedly and widely denounced.

Table 4.2   Estimated population and poor rate in England and Wales at various dates from 1688 to 1801

Year	Estimated population	Total poor rate expenditure	Cost per head of population	
		£	s.	d.
1688	5 500 000	700 000	2	6
1701	5 600 000	900 000	3	2
1714	5 750 000	950 000	3	4
1760	7 000 000	1 250 000	3	6
1776	8 000 000	1 529 780	3	10
1784	8 250 000	2 004 238	5	0
1801	9 172 980	3 750 000	8	3

Source: S. and B. Webb, *English Local Government, 9, English Poor Law History, Part 2/II* (1963), p. 1037.

As the eighteenth century drew to a close there were persistent grumbles from ratepayers about how the total expenditure and the cost per head of population had soared. Table 4.2 illustrates how between 1688 and 1801 the annual Poor Rate expenditure in England and Wales increased from £700 000 to £3 750 000. The cost of rates per head of population had leapt from 2s 6d. to 8s 3d. There had been no abatement in the official position that those who sought work through tramping should be viewed with caution. The appellation 'thief' persisted as a synonym for 'vagrant'. The public were encouraged to believe that poor travellers would pilfer, rob, steal game and spread the two great scourges of pestilence and fire.[77] The Webbs claim that by now it had become habitual for the 'House of Commons, whenever it took a dislike to any irregular course of life, to enact that participants should be deemed rogues and vagabonds. As such, they became subject to all the penalties of the Vagrancy Acts'.[78] Confused local magistrates and guardians were often unaware of or unwilling to delve into the complication of how they might best deal with those who were generally unwelcome visitors. The catch-all processes of the vagrancy legislation inevitably militated against uniform enforcement of the law. The legal disarray and general disaffection with the itinerant poor continued in spite of it now being more generally acknowledged that fluctuations in the number of tramps were usually responses to factors over which an individual had little control. Loss of work, poor harvests and involvement in war were, for those who wanted to see them, recognisable determinants bearing on fluctuation in vagrancy numbers. George III had himself expressed concern, as the American War of Independence closed, about the certainty that 'the number of idle people that this peace will occasion' would be troublesome on the highway.[79] This regal awareness seems to have been conveniently forgotten when the Napoleonic conflicts eventually came to an end. Surprise was then expressed about the large numbers of demobilised militia compounding the vagrancy problem. We will discover in the following chapter that whereas the laws were to be fundamentally redrafted in the 1820s, they continued to weigh persistently against the interests of the poor traveller.

5 Victorian Attitudes

The law in its majestic equality forbids the rich as well as the poor to sleep under bridges, to beg in the streets and to steal bread'.

Anatole France

Alfred Doolittle: 'I am one of the undeserving poor, that's what I am. Think of what that means to a man. It means he is up agen middle class morality all the time. What is middle class morality? Just an excuse for not giving me anything.'[1]

By the beginning of the nineteenth century the vagrancy laws had become exceedingly complex. When coupled with the settlement laws they could become an impenetrable costly legislative jungle for local law officers. Few magistrates were fully aware of the extensive powers at their disposal. Legislation could be interpreted by those with skill so as to cover an exceptionally wide range of travelling people. Should a knowledgeable JP set his mind to it, any poor person moving outside their own parish could be charged with vagrancy on one or another of many pretexts. Flogging was still a possibility. This involved an offender being stripped to the waist and whipped by a constable 'till his body be bloody'. The settlement and removal laws had considerable bearing on much of the confused administration of the poor laws in general and vagrancy law in particular. Half way through the century John Revans was to recall the evidence examined during the 1830s by the Poor Law Commissioners when he was their Secretary. He satisfied himself that 'every one' of the evils of poor law maladministration could be traced directly to the 1662 settlement and removal laws.[2] During the nineteenth century there were to be over 70 Parliamentary Bills relating to aspects of this hated legislation. In the 50 years between 1828 and 1878 there were eight Parliamentary Select Committees, both in the Commons and the Lords, appointed to examine and report on the settlement and removal of the poor. Although weakened by the persistent tinkering, the laws continued to be used into the twentieth century as a means of containing the poor within predictable geographical pockets.

The possibility of becoming part of the workhouse system, either through old age, sickness or disablement, remained a lurking threat for much of the population.[3] Those among the poor who treasured what little local respectability they had were persistently in danger of having to surrender their dignity. By asking for parish support they might be forced to end their days behind the high claustrophobic workhouse walls that they had been taught to recognise as being the ultimate disgrace. Even then, those who were recipients of relief within their own parish were not considered to be the bottom of the social heap. This unenviable position was occupied by the itinerant poor who drifted casually from workhouse to workhouse asking for subsistence. Because of their unpredictability, they were persistently alleged by those in power to threaten social stability. This did nothing to encourage the general public to warm to misplaced poor people. Across society poor travellers were variously viewed with disdain, suspicion and apprehension. The compassionately based response that their medieval predecessors could have expected was less in evidence.

As discussed in the previous chapter, the appearance of the Gilbert Act in 1782 was some indication of the Government's economic realism regarding the condition of the poor and society's responsibility for their well-being. It had signalled the occasional need for inadequate wages to be augmented from the parish chest. During 1802, around a million people, one in nine of England's population, were paupers, in that they received poor relief. Of these, 700 000 were permanently dependent on the parish. They included 300 000 children,

Table 5.1 Population and poor rate in England and Wales at various dates from 1776 to 1834

Year	Estimated population	Total poor rate cost	Cost/head of population		Paupers: population
		£	s.	d.	
1776	8 000 000	1 529 780	3	10	3.8%
1784	8 250 000	2 004 238	5	0	4.8%
1801	9 172 980	3 750 000	8	3	8.1%
1813	10 506 000	6 656 106	12	8	12.7%
1818	11 876 000	7 870 801	13	3	13.2%
1824	12 517 000	5 736 900	9	2	9.2%
1834	14 372 000	6 317 255	9	1	8.8%

Source: S. and B. Webb, *English Local Government, 9, English Poor Law History, Part 2/II* (1963), pp. 1037–8.

165 000 old or disabled people and 200 000 adults incapable of surviving without assistance. There were thousands of workhouses of miscellaneous shape, size and quality scattered across Britain.[4] By 1818 the national poor rate expenditure for England and Wales had leapt to £7 870 801 compared with just over £2m in the wake of the Gilbert Act (Table 5.1). Cost per head of population was now 13s 3d. People benefiting from poor law relief during 1818 numbered 1 567 632. They accounted for more than 13 per cent of the population. National attitudes to poverty and especially to those receiving relief outside of the workhouse had toughened during the Napoleonic conflict. When hostilities ceased the weakness of the economy coupled with the 'alarming' numbers of itinerants made ratepayers even more conscious of Poor Law expenditure. As was to be expected from the national experience after former wars, demobilised militia added to the number of travellers. Some soldiers and sailors were disabled, making it even more difficult for them to find work, a predicament they shared with their civilian counterparts in the cool economic climate. Any benevolence the general public may have embraced earlier regarding the plight of the poor was weakened further.

T. R. Malthus's ideas about the poor being responsible for their own poverty were developed by prominent social theorists. They argued that it was immoral that the public should be expected to support people who lacked the endeavour to even contrive having a roof over their head. Herbert Spencer later combined Malthusian theories with the evolutionary discoveries of Charles Darwin. He proposed that human society was governed by eliminative procedures similar to those applying to lesser animals. Spencer believed that individuals lacking a stable way of life or the means to sustain themselves, as was the case with poor travellers, must suffer from an inherent character flaw. From this he developed the premise that to squander public aid on physically inadequate specimens meddled with nature and long-term must be detrimental to the human race.[5] Spencer's scantily camouflaged agenda being to convince those in authority that such people should be exterminated or, at least, prevented from propagating their inherent weaknesses into succeeding generations. J. M. Fothergill explained the hypothesis with his scenario whereby the physique of those existing in 'town denizens' would become successively more degenerate and warning that by the seventh generation 'they would be tiny objects – manikins merely, a race of dwarfs'.[6]

A House of Commons Select Committee was appointed in response to the mounting opinion that the existing vagrancy laws were confused, inappropriate, and costly. It concluded in May 1821 that there was urgent need for revision and consolidation of legislation 'found to be extremely loose in its definitions and enactments'. The Committee pointed to widespread diverse abuses and frauds such as how the generous reward of ten shillings offered in some counties for the apprehension of a vagrant had turned the practice into a 'regular trade' involving a 'system of collusion between the apprehender and the vagrant'. Commitment to prison was reported as having 'lost its terror' for vagrants. Evidence was unearthed from which it was postulated that far from shrinking from the threat of prison, poor travellers now volunteered for internment. But the Committee's main criticism was lack of uniform response to applicants for relief from locality to locality and how the costly settlement system of passing vagrants to another parish was riddled with 'inefficiency, cozenage and fraud'.[7] The Committee recommended the abolition of the existing legislation. It should be redrafted with the inclusion of stiffer sentences for vagrancy offences.

The following year, the interim 3 George IV, c. 40 Act satisfied some of the concerns of the 1821 Committee. It repealed previous provisions relating to 'idle and disorderly persons, rogues and vagabonds, and other vagrants in England'. An exception was made of those referred to in the earlier 10 George II Act as stage players performing for gain 'in a place where they have no settlement, without letters patent or licence from the Lord Chamberlain'.[8] When the 1822 Vagrancy Bill passed through Parliament it was claimed that during the preceding 300 years, 49 relevant Acts had been passed of which 27 were still in operation. On the Bill's second reading 'it was remarked that £100 000 had been expended' on 'passing vagrants' from parish to parish during 1821 alone. The object of the new legislation was to remove the necessity for such expenditure.[9]

Then followed the seminal 5 George IV, c. 83 (1824) Act 'for more effectual Suppression of Vagrancy and the Punishment of idle and disorderly Persons, and Rogues and Vagabonds, in that part of Great Britain called England'. Earlier laws were repealed and the 1824 legislation was to become the official yardstick on vagrancy to this day. It was 'one of the more important statutes of the nineteenth century' with the basic purpose of 'enforcing ideals of independence, work and family responsibility'.[10] Leigh has described its methodology as 'a mass of punitive legislation of considerable severity, not to say ferocity'.[11]

Like its forerunners, the 1824 Act included catch-all provisions for a wide gallimaufry of homeless and rootless people viewed by ruling

elites as being undesirable misfits. In addition, the law now emphasised the threatening nebulous characteristic of 'suspicion'. It pointed
onerously towards

> every suspected Person or reputed Thief, frequenting any River,
> Canal, or navigable Stream, Dock, or Basin, or any Quay, Wharf or
> Warehouse near or adjoining thereto, or any Street, Highway or
> Avenue leading thereto, or any Place of public Resort, or any
> Avenue leading thereto, or any Street, Highway or Place adjacent
> with Intent to commit a Felony ... [and] ... every Person being
> found in or upon any Dwelling House, Warehouse, Coach house,
> Stable or Outhouse, or any inclosed Yard, Garden or Area, for any
> unlawful Purpose [...] lodging houses, and so on suspected to
> conceal Vagrants may be searched, and suspected persons brought
> before a Justice.[12]

Developing the pattern established under George II, those liable to
be charged with vagrancy under the 1824 Act were classified into one
of three groups. In ascending order of their legal transgression they
were classed as (a) 'idle and disorderly', (b) 'rogues and vagabonds', or
worst of all (c) 'incorrigible rogues'. The likelihood that such aggressive
categorisation would demoralise poor travellers was to be recognised
more than eighty years later by the 1906 LGB Departmental
Committee on Vagrancy. Their report pointed to how such depressing
divisiveness had doggedly remained paramount throughout the nineteenth century when dealing with the itinerant poor. So much so that in
the twentieth century it continued to remain possible that 'persons
committing certain offences shall be deemed to come within one of the
divisions mentioned'. The consequence was that there continued to be
many offenders 'who were in no sense of the word vagrants' brought to
court under some pretext of the vagrancy legislation'.[13]

From 1824 JPs were authorised to punish offenders either on their
own confession or by the evidence on oath of one 'credible' witness.[14]
Sentences ranged from a maximum of one month in a House of
Correction for the 'idle and disorderly' to 12 months' prison with hard
labour for those judged to be 'incorrigible rogues'.[15] If male, the latter
category was still liable for a public flogging. Offenders found guilty of
'sleeping out' in outhouses, unoccupied buildings, and so on without
visible means of subsistence were considered 'idle and disorderly' on
their first offence. A third court appearance could lead to them being
assessed legally as an 'incorrigible rogue'.

Long-term, the 1824 Act was to prove especially useful at times of political tension. It gave the appearance of being comprehensive while in practice being capable of flexible interpretation. This assisted authorities by giving police and magistrates wide discretionary powers to control unsettled persons lacking 'respectable employment'.[16] The new Vagrancy Act went a long way to clarifying the intentions of the interim 1822 legislation. It addressed ratepayers' complaints concerning the financial burden of 'passing' travellers back to their parish of origin as predicated in the 1662 Settlement and Removal Act. The passing system costs were modified to be more equitable. Each parish en route now had to pay its share of the cost of transporting offenders across their boundaries. The 1824 legislation was designed to satisfy parish officials disgruntled at the high removal costs, particularly those located along one of the well defined routes in and out of London or on roads to seasonal places of employment such as the Kent hop-fields. West coast ports of England such as Liverpool and Bristol had also bemoaned their heavy expenditure as unwelcome immigrants were bundled home to Ireland. In the past such places had been regularly burdened with what they saw as unreasonable 'in transit' expenditure. On the well-traversed routes, contractors organised the conveyance of poor people between parishes. There are indications that much of the overall pass system cost arose from crooked pass-masters abusing the system.[17] In addition, habitual travellers themselves became increasingly skilful in exploiting the procedures. Faint-hearted parish officials were intimidated by the holders of forged passes used to gain special benefits by, for example, purporting to be soldiers or sailors and so having the right of relief from every passing parish. It became quite a profitable wheeze for wily travellers to get themselves with their family and belongings conveyed by cart to whatever destination they chose to designate as their place of settlement.

As previously mentioned, the most oppressive edge to the 1824 Act was its emphasis on the extraordinary legal requirement that it was a 'suspicious' person's responsibility to clear themselves of any mistrust levelled against them. The Act's overbearing tone coupled with national economic downturn from the late 1820s, led to there being 15 624 vagrants imprisoned during 1832. This was more than double the 7092 incarcerated in 1825 following a reduction in the number of vagrant prisoners during the first half of the 1820s.

Indications are that as the nineteenth century progressed, fluctuations in the number of travellers applying for casual relief to the Poor Law authorities reflected economic change, Figure 5.1.[18] For example, there is broad agreement that times were tough in the mid 1840s and picked up by mid century, also that trade worsened in the second half of the 1860s to improve for a few years before weakening again in the later 1870s. Prior to the 1842 Poor Law Order, it had been traditional for many of the travelling poor to be given sustenance for consumption outside of the workhouse. By 1880 most casual wayfarers were being retained in the workhouse to complete their work-test. With the same trend continuing, by the turn of the century only one out of every hundred casual applicants were provided with relief without submitting to temporary incarceration. The rest had to accept temporary workhouse confinement and its concomitant labour requirement.

During the 30 years following 1 January 1851 the population of England and Wales increased from 15 382 000 to 25 714 288. As already detected in earlier centuries, it had often become somewhat of a knee-jerk reaction amongst legislators to dampen surges in the number of poor travellers by tightening the vagrancy laws. Invariably, the effect lasted no more than a few years, as was admitted much later by the Local Government Board (LGB) themselves. They noted that traditionally 'when an Act has been passed, or an Order or circular issued by the Central Authority regulating the treatment of vagrants, the number of these persons has fallen, only, however, to rise again gradually until the next Act or Order'.[19]

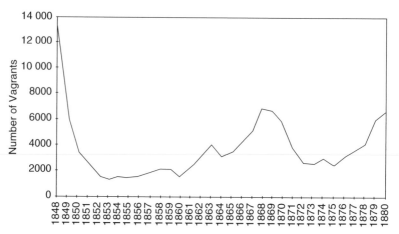

Figure 5.1   Number of vagrants relieved by Poor Law authorities in England and Wales, 1848–80.

Ten years after the 1824 Vagrancy Act the more general Old Poor Law was replaced. The Amendment Act of 1834 launched the 'New Poor Law'. It attempted to focus on the needs of the stable deserving poor while leaving the 1824 Vagrancy Act to address the specific problems set by the wandering poor who because of their unsettled existence continued to be automatically suspected of criminal intent. As legislators before and after them discovered, the division between poverty and vagrancy has invariably been far from clear-cut. Specifically, at that time, the imprecise borderline can be illustrated by typical casual attenders at a Poor Law institution who, when believed to be genuinely searching for work, were subject to the 1834 code but who, when doubts arose, could so easily find themselves shackled by the 1824 vagrancy legislation.

The authorities acknowledged the reasonableness of ratepayers' concerns about rising parish poor rates, alarm at unrest amongst agricultural labourers and the allegedly careless profligate distribution of outdoor poor relief to able-bodied persons. This was ascribed as being a legacy of wartime conditions stretching back to the early years of the century. The Poor Law Commissioners pointed out that the many problems associated with 'the machinery of settlement and removal' could be removed only by the 'entire abolition' of the settlement laws. They then recognised that annulment would be impossible while the distribution of poor relief remained on such a localised basis. Weakly, they confined themselves to meddling with special qualifications such as settlement by apprenticeship and renting. Almost untouched were the main obstacles concerning settlement by parentage, birth and marriage. Redford believed that by this failure 'the Commissioners may fairly be said to have progressed backwards; since the type of settlement they recommended for abolition had originally been introduced to aid mobility'.[20]

The 1834 Amendment itself made little direct reference to vagrants and how associated difficulties should be resolved. Nevertheless, evidence submitted to the Poor Law Commission by the Assistant Commissioners showed that during their deliberations they had identified many of the problems of vagrancy. Their reports suggested that notwithstanding the impact of the 1824 Act, vagrancy had been converted into a profitable trade and that 'the severe and increasing' associated cost burden this brought had little to do with the genuinely destitute. Their 'proof and remedy' for this claim had been accumulated from 'those few districts in which the relief has been such as only the genuine destitute will accept and the resort of vagrants has ceased' or at worst was now only a 'trifling inconvenience'. In line with this approach, the Commission then devised the infamous rule whereby workhouse conditions and facilities should be 'less eligible' than the standard of living of the lowest-paid labourer. The Commissioners were convinced that when the concept of 'less eligibility' had been adopted in what should be the more focused union workhouses and was of an appropriately menial quality, only the genuinely destitute would accept Poor Law relief. As a consequence, they believed, the general problem of undeserving outdoor relief applicants, and the particularly noxious one of casual callers, would 'dissipate' naturally. This proposition has been described as attempting to be 'a deterrent that would drive shirkers to honest toil, promote thrift as a hedge against unemployment or illness, and discourage women from running the risk of extramarital pregnancy'.[21] By amalgamating clusters of contiguous parishes into larger unions, the 1834 Act hoped to make national response more consistent. Again showing weakness and irrationality, they retained the troublesome anomaly whereby the constituent individual parishes remained the financial units chargeable for Poor Law expenditure, this despite the overall responsibility having been transferred to the amalgamated union. In all, the 1834 Act was at fault in failing to deal adequately with casual relief applicants. Union administrators were left in a state of confusion for some years which they were not slow to exploit to their own ends when it suited them. The Poor Law Commission (PLC), as the new central Board became known from 1834, later claimed that it had always been their intention for unions to provide destitute wayfarers with food and shelter, this being a safeguard against criminality, mendicancy and death from starvation. However, the fact that the 1834 Amendment was specific in its principles of segregation but failed to mention casual travelling applicants as a separate pauper classification licensed further local interpretation. Many guardians decided it was not necessary to provide separate workhouse accommodation for casuals. Disarray was widespread for a time as emergent unions made up their own rules. Some shunned destitute travellers entirely while others were decidedly more tolerant.

In 1837, the PLC attempted to clarify their intentions. They stated that no destitute person should be refused a night's accommodation or relief, irrespective of their settlement parish. Workhouse officials were told to distinguish between deserving indigent travellers and 'beggars by profession'. The scheme was that the latter should be dealt with appropriately under the 1824 vagrancy legislation. In 1839, the PLC reinforced their newly found determination that the rights of the poor traveller must be protected by threatening to dismiss Poor Law officers who failed to relieve urgent casual destitution.[22] Vagrants as a class again 'came to be recognized by the Central Authority who from this point issued a series of circulars and orders dealing with them directly or indirectly'.[23]

Most Poor Law institutions started to admit casual applicants into their workhouse complex from the 1840s. Even then a significant minority continued merely to relieve them in kind or provide an admission ticket for a night in a local common lodging house or in a Mendicity Society hostel. Such attempts at economising on local rates misfired in the long-run. Ruses of this type suited the hard-core traveller. He was attracted to any bed that avoided the work-task associated with workhouse casual ward. Up to 1842, in localities where the travelling poor were being received within the workhouse establishment, it was still fairly common practice for them to be accommodated in the able-bodied sections of workhouses. Then, a Commissioners' Instructional Letter required 'casual poor wayfarers and vagrants' be kept in a 'vagrant ward' or other separate ward. It might be presumed that this meant one ward for each sex although this was not stated explicitly.[24] The associated Poor Law Order of 1842 authorised the compulsory detention of vagrants for up to four hours after breakfast on the morning after admission. During this time they had to complete a task of work 'in return for the food and lodging afforded'.[25]

The Poor Law Commissioners maintained the convention of alerting the public to the alleged dangers inherent with many poor wayfarers. They claimed that 'mendicant vagrants' were widely recognised as being persons of 'dissolute character'. As such they could be expected to habitually lead lives of 'laziness and imposture'. Because they were frequently involved in 'intimidation and pilfering' they did not 'possess or deserve the compassion of the public'.[26] Nineteenth-century legislators attempted to assign travellers into two main stereotypes. First was the tough vagrant with little intention of getting a job and ready to turn to crime when necessary. Second was the relatively well-meaning destitute searching for the means of subsistence while suffering incapacity from age, disablement or general inadequacy. Whereas it seemed natural that the tougher element should be treated strictly, the relatively 'deserving' traveller was expected to receive more sympathetic treatment from ratepayers' representatives. This indulgent response acknowledged the danger that an unduly harsh answer from

Poor Law officials to the more deserving applicants might easily deflect them into persistent begging or more serious crime.

Gnawing concern about the travelling population and their need for basic temporary accommodation ensured a flow of pertinent official documents. Evidence, both from Poor Law Inspectors and from local officials, signalled broad concurrence that most itinerants were worthless. This judgement was seen to receive further confirmation with the influx of destitute Irish families fleeing from famine. Vagrants in mid-Victorian Richmond upon Thames became 'overwhelmingly Irish' and were mainly men between the ages of 16 and 59 years.[27] There were allegations that whereas some might have arrived in England to find work, others came with the avowed intention of begging. To discourage the Irish contingent, Mr W. D. Boase was in favour of transferring vagrants entirely to the care of the police. He claimed that although the honest English labourer looking for a job frequently lacked 'settled habits of industry or pride of self-dependence', they were 'physically superior', wore better clothing (generally the grey frieze) and were 'less disgustingly filthy and invested with vermin' than the Irish who were committed to begging.[28] The Earl of Donoughmore, guardian of the Clogheen Union in Ireland, disagreed vehemently. He ridiculed the idea that many poor people left Ireland with the express purpose of begging. Donoughmore believed that the destitute would have 'a much better chance in Ireland than he had in England'. He claimed that 'even the very poorest in Ireland' gave to beggars.[29] Irish people looking for a job as well as food were prepared to travel extensively. Many were attracted to the industrialising areas while others moved around offering themselves casually as construction navvies or seeking seasonal agricultural employment.

We have noted how indecisively workhouse accommodation for casuals was dealt with in the 1834 Amendment. This was but one example of an ambiguity which contributed to the failure of Commissioners' efforts to concentrate decision-making in Whitehall. Another factor was that the central administrators lacked the legal punch to force local guardians into interpreting official documents strictly in accord with their wishes. This weakness was considerably reduced shortly after Whitehall acquired additional power as the Poor Law Commission was translated into the Poor Law Board (PLB) with Charles Buller as its new President in 1848. He introduced the Poor Law Union Charges (No. 2) Bill which embodied the main provisions of W. H. Bodkin's preceding Poor Removal Amendment (No.2) Bill. Both pieces of legislation nudged towards an acceptance that the cost of dealing with destitute persons should be borne by the Poor Law Union and not by the individual parish.

In a PLB Minute of 4 August 1848, Buller claimed to have received nation-wide representations from people concerned about the 'continual and rapid increase of vagrancy'. He accepted that this was partly due to temporary exceptional distress but was certain that the main reason was the 'regular provision of food and lodging' at workhouses. This allegedly irresponsible extravagance diminished the 'privations of a vagrant life, and tempt[ed] a resort to it' on the part of those who otherwise may have thought twice about taking to the road. Buller impressed on guardians 'the absolute necessity of discriminating by inquiry and investigation between real and simulated destitution'. Responsibility for dealing rigorously with casual applicants was placed squarely with guardians. They were reminded of being the representatives of 'those who suffer from the evil' and must realise that the remedy lies 'principally in their own vigilance and energy'. Buller urged national uniformity in the rigorous detailed examination of relief applicants. Persistence with the incontrovertible principle of law granting relief to the genuinely destitute was still required. Equally there was the attempt to prohibit the profligate 'misapplication' by guardians of public funds to pretenders.[30] Buller's Bill did remove one of the anomalies inherited from 1834 by adding vagrants to the union common charge. The further recommendation that contributions of the parishes towards the union costs should be assessed on the rateable value of each parish, rather than with reference to past Poor Law payments, was defeated by the land-owning lobby as had previous attempts at change.[31]

Buller also advised the use of police constables as auxiliary relieving officers to scrutinise the claims of all travellers applying for casual Poor Law relief. As the 1905–9 Royal Commission on the Poor Laws later remarked, the 'vagrant appears to be always sensitive to Circulars from Headquarters'.[32] For some years Buller's deterrent strategy proved effective and contributed to a sharp decrease in the number of casuals relieved. The national vagrancy total on Poor Law relief dropped dramatically from 13 714 on 1 July 1848 to 5662 twelve months later and to 1484 casuals by 1 July 1853. Although helped by a fall in Irish immigration, there is ample corroboratory evidence from local level about the more stringent police response yielding success. After increasing 'so materially' in the 1840s it had reduced to its 'ordinary average' by the 1850s.[33] PLB Inspector G. Piggott noted that in Dorking (Surrey) whereas in the 1840s vagrant numbers in some years exceeded 2500, 'the number so relieved in the year 1851 was only 50 and these chiefly infirm wayfarers or women with children'.[34] In the same year the Dorking guardians informed the Poor Law Board that the 'number of paupers relieved in the 6th week of the Quarter ended Lady Day 1851' were 144 workhouse inmates and 571 outdoor recipients but no vagrants.[35] The 1851 Dorking Census Enumerators' Books provide clues as to what happened to some of the travellers deterred from using workhouse facilities. Whereas on census day there were no occupants in the local workhouse casual wards, there were eight 'vagrants' and nine 'Itinerate musicians' spending the night at an 'Inn and cheap lodging house' nearby. Although generally adversely critical of workhouse accommodation at Dorking it is hardly surprising that Mr Piggott's inspection was on this occasion able to report 'there are sufficient Vagrant wards'.[36] Elsewhere, other PLB Inspectors confirmed a sharp drop in casual numbers around mid century. Mr H. B. Furnell who inspected the PLB District comprising Derbyshire, Nottinghamshire, Lincolnshire, Staffordshire, and the East Riding of Yorkshire, reported a massive decrease in the number of casuals. The total number of 83 750 vagrants relieved in his District during the six months ending Michaelmas 1848 had dropped to 16 208 in the equivalent half-year of 1849. Furnell attributed this mainly to the prompt action of magistrates in dealing with 'a most pernicious and formidable abuse'. He was confident that an 'important check' had been given to the 'intolerable grievance of vagrancy'.[37]

From 1853 onwards there was further evidence that harsh vagrancy legislation was only 'evanescent'.[38] The number of casual Poor Law applicants again began to turn upwards nationally. A PLB Circular dated 30 November 1857 summarised responses to the travelling poor in the nine years since Buller's Minute. It reported little change in systemising the relief and in testing the authenticity of the 'destitute houseless poor'. The means of classification and reception were found to be 'generally defective'. 'Good and bad, young and old, clean and dirty, disorderly and deserving persons' continued to be crowded together. It was proposed that several Metropolitan unions and parishes should combine into six asylum districts. The PLB informed guardians that such administrative streamlining would bring overall financial benefit. They should not be deterred by initial higher interim costs.[39] The fear of civil disturbance based on the allegation that the offspring of the growing army of travelling people had potential for a hereditary class of criminals culminated in the Industrial Schools Act (1857). Any child above the age of seven and below fourteen charged with vagrancy could be sent for 'remedial care' to a certified industrial establishment. The parent or guardian of the child became liable for the weekly cost of their maintenance which was not expected to exceed three shillings.[40]

By the 1860s, police enthusiasm about receiving casual applicants, injected by Buller's legislation, had waned, not least because of the vermin that vagrants introduced into police cells. Constables and senior officers campaigned for discontinuation of their own involvement. Some members among the Poor Law Board Inspectorate were themselves becoming disenchanted with the idea of using the police as vagrancy reception agents. Mr R. B. Cane reported on 27 November 1865 his doubts about the 'successful treatment of vagrancy' being dependent upon the 'intervention of the police'. He believed that the biggest 'check' on increased vagrancy numbers was the imposition of 'work'.[41] Cane claimed that the response from casual applicants to the employment of police officers as assistant relieving officers was by 'no means of a uniform character' and often less than favourable. Some guardians had been inclined to abandon the use of constables from the mid 1860s after finding no 'marked result ensued'. Cane believed that a long-term reduction in vagrancy would come only from a nationally uniform control system applied with 'judicious firmness'. Essential for success were 'similar vagrant wards, treatment, diet, and work repayment' under a watchful Master's eyes. He was convinced that nothing was 'more distasteful to the habitual mendicant and vagrant than Labour'. Only after 'oakum picking' had been 'exclusively adopted by the majority' of unions was there likely to be a marked decrease in the number of casuals.[42] But not all Cane's colleagues concurred with his doubts about the use of police officers. A PLB Circular of 1868 was still advising the use of 'some person clothed in the authority of a constable as an assistant relieving officer'. This was said to be generally 'the most expedient course' towards a 'sound and vigilant discrimination' between the truly 'destitute wayfarer' and the 'professional tramp'. By now not only were distinctive wards being advocated but the desirability of 'separate accommodation for each individual' was entering the agenda.[43]

Victorians were convinced by seemingly sound moral reasons that those without a settled way of life should be viewed with caution and anxiety. In particular, it seemed reasonable in an era when decision makers in Britain propagated the Smilesian virtues of thrift, diligence and respectability that any individual lacking even the stability of a humble cottage must be guilty of self-indulgence and depravity.[44]

There was also the premise that individuals, especially those who were poor, naturally felt drawn to a cluster of temptations like laziness, restlessness, improvidence and irresponsibility, and that these must be continually repressed.[45] As a consequence, people who acceded to these enticements were perceived as a threat to the physical and moral health of the community, not least because they allegedly distributed disease and crime across the country. Together they were seen to form a 'great mass of rough, unmoral and uneducated' potential and could form a dangerous anarchical weapon during times of political tension. England accepted the cogency of Smiles's epistles as secular interpretations of the religiously inspired work ethic. The heavenly rewards promised by the Church were now paraded as earthly morals guaranteed to improve an individual's character, wealth and life-style. Spencer's hypothesis regarding the survival of the fittest in human society seemed to be confirmed by the daily indications that the rich did rather well out of life whereas nature 'understandably' rejected the indigent poor. Meanwhile, there were local innovative attempts to rid themselves of rootless people. Some parish officials threatened arrest unless travellers evacuated themselves promptly from the parish. Others went to the expense of employing a 'beggar poker' who 'armed with a painted pole about five feet long, warned the beggars to move on and, if it were necessary, escorted them like a guard of honour to the side of the town'.[46]

Eventually, persistent PLB focus on the unfairness of parish chargeability provided the opportunity for reform in the 1860s. Much of the progress can be attributed to C. P. Villiers, appointed PLB President in 1859 with a seat in the Cabinet. His involvement with Poor Law affairs stretched back to his secretarial work for the 1832–4 Royal Commission. The winter following his PLB appointment was particularly bitter. Widespread fears about the inability of local Poor Law officials to deal unaided with the exceptional distress gave sensible power to Villiers' elbow for change. He argued that the 1834 legislation had inadvertently encouraged landed proprietors to maintain close parishes and by driving away the poor had overburdened nearby open ones. This was unfair both to the parish and to the poor.[47] Villiers' persistence culminated in the 28 and 29 Victoria, Union Chargeability Act (1865). This removed the legal anomaly of parish rating and union management by making poor rates and administration coincident within the union. The new Act also ended the ludicrous situation whereby the destitute poor were chased from parish to parish within the same union. Acrimonious and costly legal battles over pauper removals were not uncommon. Within two years, a further Metropolitan Poor Act dictated the need for uniform charge-ability for the casual poor throughout London. According to Caplan, prior to this time 'every winter in the poorer metropolitan parishes, homeless destitute persons died on the streets' because certain parishes claimed their inability to make adequate relief provision as the result of inequitable charging across the city.[48]

Reports by Poor Law Inspectors in 1866 still exposed lack of national conformity in the treatment of casual applicants. Eighty-six unions remained without a casual ward. Others had 'quite unsuitable accommodation'. 195 unions imposed no work task. It was clear that Buller's policy of 1848 making guardians responsible for discriminating between casual applicants had not always been applied diligently. One reason was that local officers were not prepared to accept responsibility for the possible consequences of refusing relief to genuine applicants. Therefore, no matter what the quality of their case, casuals were responded to in similar fashion by any one union. The 1866 Inspectors' reports also showed there to be little common ground between unions across the country as regards the diet provided, the task enforced or the period of retention imposed on casuals.[49]

Although the possibility of economic factors contributing to the changing numbers tramping the roads had long been incontrovertible, the idea was still largely kept under wraps by the authorities. The likelihood of a causal connection between unemployment and the travelling population remained shelved throughout most of the century. Contemporaries were encouraged to view nineteenth-century poor wayfarers as having three determining characteristics. They were of repulsive nature, of 'evil disposition' and were destitute. This last characteristic did little to disincline some ratepayers from retaining the entrenched opinion that most wayfarers held covert assets which rendered them undeserving of help. Impartial investigation, admittedly rare, showed such opinion to be misplaced. The majority of wayfarers were devoid of support and frequently of failing health.[50]

Industrial and urban expansion sponsored a miscellany of shelters, lodging-houses and refuges opened as private initiatives. Often they satisfied the need for temporary accommodation of rail-building navvies and other building workers. Travellers deterred from applying for Poor Law relief at the workhouse could also apply for a night's stay. Alternatively, if they had a few pennies, they might choose to stay at one of the more traditional common lodging houses still featured in most towns. Despite their filth, foul smell and overcrowding, lodging houses could usually be relied on to provide warmth, if only by the proximity of other bodies. There was the added attraction of a yarn with old cronies away from the restrictive prying of the parish constable, workhouse officer or moralising hostel superintendent. Although the Common Lodging Houses Acts of 1851 and 1853, launched by the Earl of Shaftesbury, had required local authorities to inspect and enforce minimum standards of sanitation, most premises remained overcrowded and unhygienic. The 1875 Public Health Act made a further attempt to apply higher minimum sanitary standards to common lodging-houses. Local authorities were made responsible for ensuring that keepers of common lodging-houses (a) restricted the number of lodgers, (b) separated the sexes, (c) promoted cleanliness and ventilation, and (d) took precautions against the spread of infectious disease. The new rules were not applied uniformly. Common lodging houses offered little attraction to decent women. Of more appeal to the destitute female traveller, who didn't mind being sermonised, were charitable refuges providing short-term food and austere shelter. Mendicity Societies, some with a long tradition, developed the refuge concept as an overt sign of Christian pity. By the 1860s and 1870s the haphazard profligacy of some such organisations became the butt of criticism from crusading charity rationalisers.

Workhouse casual wards remained generally available if purposely uninviting with their sparse allowance of food and rudimentary sleeping accommodation. 'Beds' were sometimes nothing but a common platform of bare boards covered with a single blanket separated from each other by a plank on edge. Workhouse relief retained the disadvantage to many travellers of incurring the need to complete hours of unpaid restrictive physical toil.[51] The common diet for casuals throughout the 1850s and most of the 1860s was 5 ounces (oz) of bread on the evening of admission and a further 5 oz with one and a half pints of porridge next morning. Children, the aged and the infirm had 'modified diets'. Vagrants accepted for more than one night might be switched to the more varied inmate diet. When in 1868 the PLB made another push towards workhouse conformity, they circulated an enhanced 'proposed dietary' for wayfarers. Now they were entitled to each receive 8 oz of bread or alternatively 6 oz of bread and one pint of gruel in the evening. Breakfast was stunningly similar with the recommendation that half be held back until satisfactory completion of 'the task of work'.[52] It is doubtful whether even this enhanced fare provided sufficient energy for casuals to fulfil their allotted workhouse task let alone satisfy any subsequent employment opportunities. The scant sustenance provided by the authorities coupled with what too frequently was unhygienic ward accommodation helped to sustain the conventional concerns that casual paupers were likely contributors to epidemics of infectious or contagious disease.[53]

Some wards in the late 1860s were still being described in official reports as 'disgraceful'. In places relief was 'practically refused with the effect of driving men to commit crimes for the purpose of getting into prison'.[54] 'Tearing up' had become a common workhouse occurrence 'owing to the filthy state of the Vagrants clothing'. Furthermore, there was a widespread demand that vagrants be bathed, their clothes disinfected, and that they should be housed in 'harsh but clinically clean sleeping quarters'. The 1868 PLB Circular suggested that:

- a register of applicants for admission should be maintained
- vagrants should be searched and bathed
- they should be made to perform a work-test of not more than four hours, and
- a uniform dietary should be adopted.[55]

This regime had the temporary effect of reducing casual wards applicants from a national total of 7020 on New Year's Day 1869 to 5430 twelve months later.

One of the early 'Special Committees' set up by the emergent Charity Organisation Society (COS) addressed vagrancy and mendicity, subjects which they were never to tire of examining. They concluded that existing charitable night refuges, free dormitories, public soup-kitchens, and the 'innumerable doles of bread, groceries, coal, and so on' were 'most mischievous' in that they tended to promote vagrancy.[56] 'Detailed and lively stories' of attempted fraud by vagrants which had allegedly been successfully thwarted by COS vigilance began to absorb a disproportionately large space in their propaganda. Even Charles Loch, COS General Secretary, who himself lacked nothing in his determination to deter mendicants, found the need to publicly criticise a colleague who was 'altogether too detective' in his attitude to vagrancy.[57] At Brighton, the local COS was developed from the long established Brighton, Hove and Preston Mendicity Society, already committed to repressing mendicity by applying relief in a 'careful systematic manner'. Members were required to 'exercise some of the highest attributes of human character' in tackling with responsible firmness the problems of the poor.[58] During the calendar quarter ending 24 June 1872 the Brighton COS 'decided' upon a total of

610 vagrancy cases. 53 were dismissed as 'not requiring relief, ineligible, or undeserving'; 15 were 'referred to the Poor Law, and to associated or private charity'; 19 were 'assisted by the Society'; and '523 were relieved with bread'.[59]

COS provincial reports claimed that the majority of tramps applying to them for relief could be assured of sustenance even though this usually meant little more than a pennyworth of bread 'to be consumed on the premises'. Birmingham COS seemed more magnanimous than most. In the 12 months 1879–80 they relieved 518 tramps with 'bread and grocery', provided 22 with a 'night's lodging', 'forwarded' 25 home 'by railway', gave 12 'special donations' and 'refused' only eight applicants.[60] Derby COS were much less generous. Whereas 'about 2000' tramps applied for relief to Derby COS during their formative year of 1879, for 'very good reasons only 358 .... had bread given to them'. The vast majority of those favoured with relief were men. 187 were said to be 'labourers', 15 were 'fitters and turners', 11 were 'carpenters and joiners', 11 were 'painters, glaziers, gas fitters and plumbers' and 10 were bricklayers. 33 other 'occupations' were claimed by the tramp influx but none of these added to double figures. Unlike much of the information provided in other parts of the country, it is noteworthy that not one of the tramps relieved by Derby COS in 1879 claimed to have been a member of the armed forces. Of the 16 tramps at Derby who were not men, nine were 'women with their husbands' and seven 'children with their parents'.[61]

The two kitchens of the Liverpool Central Relief Society (CRS) distributed 45 372 quarts of soup during the year ending 31 October 1880. Of these, 11 447 quarts were 'distributed gratuitously' through the police to cases of 'urgent distress'. The remainder was sold at one halfpenny per quart either directly to the poor or with CRS tickets sold to the wealthier public for passing on to the needy. The 12-month total cost of making the soup was £190 3s 10d. Of this £98 3s 9d went on ingredients, £33 15s 0d in wages, £18 11s 3d for coal and £39 13s 10d 'by repairs, utensils, advertising and so on'.[62] A correspondent to the *Liverpool Lantern* described the tribulations suffered by the wife of an unemployed 'sober industrious' man. She had attempted to obtain CRS soup for her family alongside 'scores of others' only to find the supply 'expended' for the day. Next morning the same woman had been more successful. The soup she received was described by the *Lantern's* correspondent as 'a sort of lumpy material of a bluish-yellow tinge', looking 'very much like bill-stickers' paste'. The soup put the writer 'in mind of the stuff that my Uncle Sandy used to feed to his pigs'. The difference was that the pig food had a 'richer and more palatable appearance' because of the 'good bran and potato peelings boiled in it'.[63]

It was reported both at Oxford and at Brighton that many more vagrants had needed to be 'dealt with' in 1879–80 than in the previous year. Oxford Anti Mendicity Society and COS reported 1674 vagrants during the year, an increase of 629. Brighton COS served 'no less than 4360 persons' with 'bread in the office' to be 'consumed on the spot'. This 'remarkable feature' of having to relieve 'a very great increase' in the number of wayfarers was 'in spite of the enforcement of a more stringent rule in the administration of this kind of relief'.[64] It involved 960 more 'wayfarers' than the previous year and was accounted for 'alone' by the 'great depression of trade and agriculture' then being suffered. Table 5.2 compares the number of vagrants relieved during 1878–9 and 1879–80 by the Poor Law authorities with those assisted by the COS at Brighton. It will be noted that in spite of the increase in the number of tramps helped by the COS during the second 12 months, the local casual ward continued to be the main tramp-relieving agency in Brighton. They provided assistance to 15 726 applicants in 1879–80, an increase of 4031 over the previous year.[65] It is also apparent from Table 5.2 that whereas through the summer and early autumn months the COS found it necessary to relieve very few tramps, the numbers helped by the Poor Law authorities remained high.

Nineteenth-century Mendicity Societies and other groups reported begging letters as being a prominent means by which the indolent imposed themselves on the public. Investigation by Oxford COS was said to expose how in the cases of the many tramps applying to them for help 'almost every story sifted by them proved ... to be absolutely fictitious'.[66] A flavour of these begging letters, as published by provincial COSs and the kind of response they evoked is informative:

Dear Madam, Please to excuse me from trobling you to-day after your kindness to me; but I am lieing on my death-bed, and I have not a friend in this world to help me; and if you can assist me a little to get a pair of sheets and a sleeping-gown I would feel very much oblidge to you, as we dont know when the hour might come. The doctor was hear last night, and he said I will not recover. The children is going into the poor-house on tuesday, and I dont think I will be spared till then. Dear Madam, this will be the last time I will ever write to you.' The lady to whom the letter was addressed sent it for guidance to the Edinburgh Association for Improving the Condition

Table 5.2   Vagrants/wayfarers relieved by 'the parish' and by Brighton COS
during 1878–9 and 1879–80

| Month | 1878–9 | | 1879–90 | |
	Parish	COS	Parish	COS
October	848	20	1 899	318
November	1 090	278	1 169	584
December	681	275	992	481
January	1 044	396	1 234	708
February	988	443	1 238	596
March	1 058	592	1 352	611
April	851	360	1 602	533
May	1 279	545	1 798	394
June	912	415	1 198	33
July	822	32	1 236	49
August	1 147	33	1 412	30
September	975	11	596	23
Total	11 695	3 400	15 726	4 360
Increase			4 031	960

Source: 9th *Annual Report, Brighton COS* (1880), p. 8.

of the Poor who advised her not to supply the sheets or sleeping-gown. This was because the Association's investigation had apparently found the statements untrue in that the writer was not yet dead although 'the doctor said she would not recover'.[67]

This involves a young man who had lost his left leg and was found by an officer of Leeds COS presenting a 'begging petition in which it stated that he had lost his leg by a fall down granary steps at Pontefract, and that he required £10.10s. to purchase a cork leg. It was ascertained that he lost his leg when twelve years of age by falling off an apple tree that he was robbing, and that for the last six or seven years he had lived by begging for a cork leg, and that he had served two terms of imprisonment for that offence. He was sent to three months' imprisonment.[68]

Reports from charities attempting to organize voluntary disbursements related to the treatment of poor itinerants usually included reference to how their investigation or previous knowledge had exposed the applicant's unworthiness. The following examples are typical:

A woman applied for assistance to a lady, case sent for investigation. Applicant is a tramping beggar, well known to the Society, and quite unworthy of charity. It is, perhaps, well to know that nearly all foreign beggars ask for assistance to proceed to London, or some large town at a distance from Brighton to see their Consul, with a view to being sent to their homes, which is the last thing they think of doing. Reported to Sender.[69]

The (COS) Agent saw a woman begging, and, knowing her to be an imposter, and given to drink, had her brought before the Bench, and she was sentenced to 14 days imprisonment.[70]

Man going about obtaining money by begging under false pretences and lies; was found to be an idle vagabond who had procured money from many people, chiefly ladies; was prosecuted by this Society and sentenced by the justices to one month's imprisonment.[71]

In 1879 a Parliamentary Select Committee enquired into how the settlement and removal laws were being applied, particularly with regard to dispatching migrants back to Ireland. They concluded that the number of Irish paupers in Britain had 'largely diminished'.[72] Irish wage rates had doubled after of the traumatic diminution in the population from the pre-famine 1845 total of over eight million to a mere 5 400 000 in 1871. In the interim years, socio-economic opportunity in Ireland had been transformed.

Local Government Board (LGB) Inspector John Lambert addressed the Salisbury Literary and Scientific Institution in 1868. He was convinced that so long as the public persisted in bestowing indiscriminate alms to able-bodied beggars there was no hope of mendicity being repressed. Any relief must be uniformly administered and offered only to the genuinely destitute. At the same time, Lambert was against repressive punishment as this would 'assuredly prove unavailing'. He clashed with most of his peers when pointing to how it was counter-productive to treat vagrancy as a disease. Vagrancy was 'but a symptom of something wrong, either in the character of the individual, the condition of society, or the institutions of the State'.[73]

When the more powerful LGB replaced the Poor Law Board in 1871, it acted quickly under the Presidency of James Stansfeld through the Pauper Inmates Discharge and Regulations Acts 34 and 35 Victoria of that year. Guardians were provided with more power to incarcerate casuals until they had completed their morning's work. Introducing the Bill, Lord Kimberley referred to a resurrected proposal that the relief of vagrants should entirely be in police hands. He 'intimated that though he thought this change might have great advantages he had decided against the proposals on the grounds that it might take the police from their other duties'. Kimberley also realised that it could lead to 'considerable expense in the building of separate sets of wards in connection with police stations'.[74] To discourage the London homeless from moving between casual wards all metropolitan workhouses were henceforth defined as one institution. Casual paupers then were in an 'anomalous position' in being 'totally distinct from the ordinary paupers'.

The concept of a uniform response system for paupers generally that had pervaded the central authorities' general thinking since 1834 was now applied with renewed vigour to casual applicants. The perceived failure in the system 'hitherto adopted in the relief of this class of pauper' had made it necessary for the emergent LGB to provide 'increased power of detention to the guardians'.[75] The 1871 Act strengthened recommendations of the PLB Circular three years earlier. Included was the control of casual admittance, the drying and disinfecting of their clothes, a forced bath in water of 'suitable temperature', dietary advice, approved sleeping accommodation in separate cells, beds or compartments to dilute the chance of riot, together with details of the labour task each casual must undertake before leaving. Male applicants were to be 'cleansed' on admittance in bath water. In many places this was changed only infrequently. After a 'strip search' the stoving method used to purify their clothes often left them with scorch marks providing clear indication to the public at large that the wearer was a vagrant.[76] Such procedures were intended to deter all but the genuinely destitute. The 5th section of the 1871 Act insisted that a casual pauper could not discharge himself from the casual ward: (a) before 11 a.m. on the day following his admission, nor before he had performed the work prescribed, and (b) if he had been admitted into the casual ward of the same union on more than two occasions during one month, before 9 a.m. on the third day after his admission. In his pamphlet *Honour all Men*, W. H. Syme wrote of the 'undiscerning spirit of insensate persecution' meted out to vagrants. He claimed they were 'locked up the long day in bare, miserably cramped cells ... constrained to lie, some in darkness, and all in the corrupting idleness of solitary confinement'.[77]

The 1871 Acts were glaringly irrational. Their avowed aim of inculcating an attitude of self-help amongst casuals was negated in that their late-morning discharge made it virtually impossible for them to find worthwhile employment that day. For some years the LGB were undeterred by the occasional criticism that did surface. Soon they were reporting that casuals were being dealt with reasonably satisfactorily in 'wards set aside for the purpose in 572 of the 645 unions'. They remained 'highly' disapproving of the practices applied in the remaining 73 unions. Most London workhouses had responded to LGB pressure for tighter administration in dealing with casuals. Some constructed new wards on a 'cellular' plan. This was seen to have the advantage over the traditional 'associated ward' of isolating casuals from their peers and preventing the 'interchange of intelligence' for 'evading the operation of the law'.[78] Elsewhere in the country facilities for casuals remained largely unchanged.

A few unions persisted with the procedure rejected by the central authorities whereby casual applicants for parish relief were despatched to a local lodging-house for the night. The LGB commented scathingly that this meant they were subject to 'no control, had no task of work to perform' and were at liberty to leave the next morning at whatever hour they chose.[79] Even where unions did have separate casual wards the provision was not 'in all cases satisfactory' with various unacceptable measures used to deter wayfarers. They were frequently housed in the oldest, least weatherproof parts of the buildings with only the bare minimum of bedding and heating. The detention of casuals over two nights made it necessary for the emergent LGB to prescribe a dietary for vagrants which included a midday meal. This caused interminable difficulties in many workhouses.

As might have been expected from earlier experience subsequent to the implementation of new rigorous legislation, the 1871 Act deterred poor travellers from applying to workhouses for a while. By the beginning of 1875 the national daily average had fallen to 2235. This was less than half the number in 1870. Table 5.3 shows how, in line with the LGB's 'crusade against outdoor relief', which was also initiated by the 1871 Act, the number of casual paupers dropped markedly for a few years. Then as the impact of the legislation faded and as the economy weakened, the number of itinerants rose again in the later seventies. By the beginning of 1880 they had grown nationally to a total of 5914, more than when the crusade began. In one Surrey workhouse, for example, occupants of the casual ward had

Table 5.3   Number of vagrants and paupers relieved by the Poor Law compared with the population of England and Wales, 1870–80

Date 1870–80	Population, millions	Vagrants in workhouse	Vagrants relieved outside	Paupers in workhouse	Relieved outside	Vagrants, total
1.1.70	22.224	4147	1283	169 471	915 727	5430
1.7.70		5513	1117	144 594	843 663	
1.1.71	22.501	2784	951	168 071	917 890	3735
1.7.71		3440	853	141 552	832 051	
1.1.72	22.789	2562	816	156 795	824 600	3378
1.7.72		1987	385	134 506	742 764	
1.1.73	23.096	2565	462	154 171	736 446	3027
1.7.73		2154	331	135 135	687 586	
1.1.74	23.409	2721	368	152 279	680 483	3089
1.7.74		3006	293	137 944	646 404	
1.1.75	23.725	1944	291	155 655	662 557	2235
1.7.75		2850	352	134 238	612 268	
1.1.76	24.045	2999	295	151 930	601 419	3294
1.7.76		3028	339	138 201	569 641	
1.1.77	24.370	3830	343	161 021	571 982	4173
1.7.77		2940	383	147 017	563 158	
1.1.78	24.700	4546	562	171 421	576 583	5108
1.7.78		3306	326	154 162	571 879	
1.1.79	25.033	4196	458	179 541	625 691	4654
1.7.79		6938	727	166 983	605 388	
1.1.80	25.371	5347	567	194 651	649 387	5914
1.7.80		7041	701	172 458	600 249	

Source: *30ᵗʰ Annual Report of Local Government Board*, Appendix E, pp. 356–9, PP 1901 [c. 746], XXV.

reached such a level that the overspill had to be bedded on straw. This prompted strong objections from the LGB on the grounds of 'fire, infection, harbour of vermin, and so on'.[80]

    The proportion of casual applicants claiming to have once been members of the armed forces varied markedly with place and time. In the 1850s, one workhouse Master had alleged that 'nine-tenths of vagrants' had served in the Army and Navy as 10 to 12-year enlisted men. Numbers applying to casual wards were later augmented by shortservice ex-soldiers who, as part of a scheme to reduce the armed forces, were discharged in their mid twenties. They took to tramping when finding it difficult to get a job. Half the vagrants applying at Kingston upon Thames claimed past Army service.[81] In contrast, some institutions aimed at relieving the poor traveller had no ex-servicemen applying to them over long periods.[82] Where they felt the need to apply, it is unlikely that the systemised unwelcoming responses of some Poor Law officials and other anti-mendicity agencies were deterrents to penniless demobbed servicemen. Their previous tough military training and harsh experiences helped to soften psychologically the coarseness of some of the hospitality on offer. For the officials responding to applicants for occasional relief there remained the fundamental difficulty of assessing whether or not the growing number of late nineteenth-century travellers were mainly 'undeserving' or 'deserving'. Some of the increase was attributable to out-of-work agricultural labourers hit by the agrarian depressions of the 1870s.[83]

As the self-proclaimed moral leader of the world, the British Establishment was anxious to show how they were treating poor itinerants with favourable fair firmness in comparison with their counterparts overseas. They were also not averse to implying that there might be certain advantages in adopting some elements of the foreigners' tougher approach. A series of reports published by the LGB in 1875 referred to the 'Poor Laws in Foreign Countries'. They claimed that under the poor law systems of nearly all European countries there was provision for the 'suppression or punishment of vagrancy'. Moreover, the overseas procedures allegedly retained a 'good deal of the rigorous and repressive character of the older enactments that they are intended to replace'. Although 'modified in accordance with the more humane spirit of a later age ... they seemed to belong less to the annals of poor law than of criminal legislation'. Andrew Doyle, the LGB Inspector charged with the coordination of these overseas reports concluded that:

- in Belgium the 'much more severe legislation' of 1866 had seemingly 'already borne good fruits' in repressing vagrants
- in German states there was said to be 'legislation of repression' with accompanying 'police regulations generally very harsh in character'
- in Austria the law on vagrancy was reported to be 'extremely severe'
- in Denmark convicted beggars were 'imprisoned for Fifteen days on bread and water' while vagrants got thirty days, and

- in Sweden new legislation provided for 'punishment of vagrancy and mendicity by hard labour for not less than one month ... and conveyance to their place of settlement'.[84]

Mr J. J. Henley reported that vagrancy in parts of the USA had 'become serious' during the 1870s. Tramps without visible means of support, had previously travelled from one locality to another causing 'little more than annoyance'. Now they had allegedly 'become dangerous, threatening the peace of society'. A Bill was introduced to the New York Assembly in 1877 designed to provide 'a treatment of vagrants of great severity'.[85]

The impression that overseas policies for the repression of vagrancy were more rigorous than that in the UK had the complicity of officialdom. Those attending Poor Law Conferences revelled in the idea that methods used by foreign countries to repress the vagrant persistently involved the police and imprisonment. Such ideas featured regularly in papers dealing with the seemingly intractable problem of how to 'relieve' the poor traveller.[86] W. M. Wilkinson described the contemporary handling of vagrants as merely being repressive and not industrial or educational. He referred glowingly to the reformative systems in continental Europe and instanced those in Paris, Ommerschaus in Holland and Hohnstein in Switzerland where vagrants were allegedly retained for long periods so as to gradually habituate them to work.[87]

Although the oppressive character of continental and USA laws were repeatedly emphasised by the LGB, they themselves well knew that the poor traveller could expect much the same fare in the UK. Prison sentences were continually being meted out by magistrates to those judged to have transgressed the British catch-all vagrancy laws. George Brine, referred to at a Poor Law Conference in 1881 as the 'acknowledged king of the beggars', apparently had the 'proud boast ... that he had been in every gaol and workhouse in England ... only for offences committed against the Vagrant Acts'.[88] The LGB also admitted, if with less emphasis, that in practice not all overseas regulations treated vagrants harshly. For example, although Russia, Poland and Portugal each had legislation against vagrancy and mendicancy, they were enforced only rarely and with notable tolerance.[89]

Part of the official drive to repress UK vagrancy involved the tactic of ensuring that pleasantries never filtered into their reception. Workhouse officers were advised to inform applicants immediately that they were bound to complete a rigorous work task in return for any relief. Male vagrants retained in custody for a single night had commonly to break around two hundredweight of stone, the precise weight being dependent on the stone's nature. Local officers could alternatively direct them to pick one pound of unbeaten oakum or two pounds of beaten oakum. As an alternative, it suited some guardians to demand the completion of other commensurate tasks such as digging, wood-cutting or corn-grinding. Female casuals had to pick half a pound of unbeaten or a pound of beaten oakum when not required to work for three hours washing, scrubbing and cleaning of the workhouse.[90] For casual paupers detained for more than one night the tasks were stepped up. For each entire day detained, men had to break around seven hundredweight of stone or, if it suited the authorities better, pick seven pounds of unbeaten or four pounds of beaten oakum. By 1886, Joseph Chamberlain's seminal Circular condemned such work as being degrading. Local authorities were urged to replace unpleasant task work with employment directed to the public good and which did not incur the stigma of pauperism.

When Sir Luke Fildes's sombre portrayal of *Applicants for Admission to the Casual Ward* was exhibited at the Royal Academy in 1874 it provoked debate as to whether an artist ought to paint such scenes of wretchedness.[91] The School of Social Realism among British artists in the late nineteenth century ventured to illustrate conditions of life across strata of society shunned by others as being suitable subjects. *Hard Times 1885* by Hubert von Herkomer was a product of this School. It depicted an out of work agricultural labourer with his wife and two children tramping in search of employment in the depth of the great agricultural depression of the 1880s. The utter despair and hopelessness of their situation permeates von Herkomer's canvas. Artists' attempts to make a broader public aware of working-class struggles eventually withered as the subjects were not popular with middle-class buyers.

The LGB continued to be exercised by the problem of determining a period of detention for casuals which optimised between punishment and personal motivation. The Casual Poor Act (1882) followed by the LGB General Order dated 18 December of the same year attempted to progress the escalating casual numbers now described as 'any destitute wayfarer or wanderer'. The 1882 Act extended the minimum detention period to two nights but allowed casuals to leave at 9 a.m. on the third day provided they had completed the prescribed work. Travellers admitted more than once during the same calendar month into any casual ward of the same union had his period of detention extended. He was not entitled to discharge himself before 9 a.m. of the fourth day after his admission although he could be removed at any time during that time by a workhouse union officer or by a police constable.[92] Not surprisingly, following the 1882 Act the number of casual applicants dropped for a few years before turning up again from 1886. Within ten years the number of casuals in workhouses had more than doubled. This contrasts with overall pauper numbers which had numerically remained fairly constant at around the 800 000 mark for England and Wales for the last quarter of the century. On the evening of New Year's Day 1870, almost 5 per cent of the people in England and Wales were receiving Poor Law relief. By the end of the century the increase in population, tougher laws and economic progress meant that only 2.5 per cent were receiving Poor Law benefits. In contrast, the number of casual applicants and their proportion of paupers in general, had increased over the same period after a temporary numerical downturn following the 1871 legislation (Table 5.4).[93]

Table 5.4   Number of vagrants relieved on the night of 1 January by the Poor Law authorities in England and Wales, 1850–1900

Date 1 January	Population, millions	Pauper total	Vagrants	Paupers per 1000 population	Vagrants/ paupers per cent
1850	14.947	882 711	3717	59.1	0.42
1855	17.019	841 636	1556	49.5	0.18
1860	19.686	845 594	1542	43.0	0.18
1865	20.884	975 764	3339	46.7	0.34
1870	22.224	1 085 198	5430	48.8	0.64
1875	23.725	818 212	2235	34.5	0.27
1880	25.371	844 038	5914	33.0	0.70
1885	26.922	789 021	4866	29.3	0.62
1890	18.448	793 465	5701	27.9	0.72
1895	30.052	827 759	8810	27.5	1.23
1900	31.743	807 595	5579	25.4	1.22

Sources: 1850 and 1855 data from *11th Annual Report of Poor Law Board*; 1865 to 1900 data from *30th Annual Report of Local Government Boards*, Appendix E; also *LGB Departmental Report on Vagrancy*, Appendix V, PP 1906, CIII [c. 2892], p. 20.

Even the earlier discharge time of 9 a.m. was found to be impractical for genuine work-seekers. Eventually, in 1892, yet another LGB General Order eased the life of casuals 'desirous of seeking work'. Those completing their work task satisfactorily during the previous day now could claim discharge on the second day after admission at 5.30 a.m. in summer and 6.30 a.m. in winter.[94] Long before this sensible change was introduced officially, guardians were already bending the rules as they thought fit in ways that were traditional with many aspects of the Poor Law.[95] As early as 1886, half the unions in England and Wales were not detaining casuals for a second day. This had the attraction of cutting costs while ridding themselves quickly of unwanted human burdens.

An LGB Circular in 1896 again repeated the clarion call for conformity. It claimed that 'strict admission' sharply reduced the number of applicants. Again, as had become the pattern subsequent to previous restrictive edicts, the rise in the numbers of casuals was eventually stemmed. Even then, almost ten thousand vagrants were relieved on the first day of the new century. This was much larger than the period prior to 1894 and compares with the 2235 vagrants relieved by the Poor Law a quarter of a century earlier. As we will see in the next chapter, and as has invariably been the case in post-war histories, the homeless numbers again moved upwards as the end of the South African War was shadowed by economic depression.

A persistent feature of the many attempts through the nineteenth century to repress vagrancy was that, apart from casual applicants for poor relief, there was a dearth of worthwhile official data related to the total number of people tramping around the country. Research on the social composition of nineteenth century urban slums has demonstrated the closeness of neighbourhood support. This in turn has fostered ideas of limited mobility and the spacial concept of the 'urban village'. Despite this, 'there existed shiftless substrata of tramps and vagrants who moved from place to place and lodging-house to lodging-house'. They passed 'through the community but were not part of it'.[96]

As in earlier times, changes in the vagrancy laws during the nineteenth century were typically presaged by an official announcement of an alleged dangerous threat to public security from the increase in vagrancy. Rarely had it been possible, or even attempted, for lawmakers to bother about supporting their allegations with reliable quantitative information. The Poor Law authorities were themselves well aware that those occupying casual wards on any night were not

likely to form the majority of the travelling homeless. Therefore with
the realisation that much of the evidence provided in this chapter is
from Poor Law statistics, the reader may doubt whether the portrayal
is a reasonably accurate impression of trend changes in vagrancy
numbers overall. Any such disquiet should be mitigated by recognition that fluctuations in Poor Law numbers through the nineteenth
century largely mirrored the same economic, social and political
factors that caused change in the total number of poor itinerants.
Confirmation of this comes from contemporary reports. They repeatedly spoke of casual ward occupancy being a reflection of vagrancy
overall. The police authorities estimated that the total numbers of
travelling people lacking a permanent roof in England and Wales on
1 April in the years 1867 and 1868 were 32 528 and 36 179 respectively. These figures were said to include vagrants in casual wards
which at the beginning of the years in question were 5027 in 1867 and
6129 in 1868 or about one-sixth of the Police total.[97] This proportion
tended to be used by the Local Government Board in their occasional
attempt to calculate the total number living off the roads during the
nineteenth century. Later calculations moved to favouring a factor of
between one-fifth and one-quarter. For example, Admiral Christian
in evidence to the 1906 LGB Departmental Committee on vagrancy
considered it likely that those in a casual ward on any one night were
about one-fourth of the homeless total. Taking what limited information they had into account, the Departmental Committee assumed
that around the turn of the century in years of industrial activity the
number of travelling poor was probably between 30 000 or 40 000.
Equally, it was accepted that at times of economic depression, there
may be as many as 70 000 or 80 000 tramping without a fixed abode.
Between these limits it was thought that the number of vagrants was
'affected by the conditions of trade, weather and economic circumstances'.[98] When these assessments of the total number of travellers
are compared with the Departmental Committee's calculation of 'permanent' vagrant numbers, there is the implication that at least one-
third of all vagrants in good times and nearly two-thirds in bad times
were genuinely unemployed men wandering expectantly from casual
job to casual job. In recent centuries there were always the caravan-
dwelling Gypsies and tinkers moving around the country but, as discussed in Chapter 1, they were most unlikely to seek help from Poor
Law authorities unless the medical facilities of the workhouse
infirmary was needed. As regards the number of poor itinerants in
Scotland, when requesting public support to 'check the fearful evil of

vagrancy', Glasgow Charity Organisation Society estimated that during 1879 there were between 50 000 and 60 000 vagrants north of the border.[99]

William Booth's solution for removing poverty from Britain featured labour colonies. They were seen as necessary elements within the spectrum of broad corrective support for the underprivileged.[100] Although their ideas had an authoritarian ring, Booth's Salvation Army saw the destitute as deserving of better things.[101] By the end of the century his Christian Soldiers were providing refuges for the homeless with a national total of around 14 000 beds even though much of the accommodation was primitive. The beds were provided with the accompanying fervent hope that visitors would seize the opportunity for their religious salvation. Would-be organisers of relief decried what they saw as the Salvation Army's misplaced confused benevolence. The COS featured among Victorian voluntary institutions which tackled the homeless problem with a more methodical rigour. While avoiding overt religious association they pointed to the moral dangers confronting the poor resulting from the widespread obduracy among most charities against thoroughly investigating the integrity of relief applicants.[102] The result of what was seen by the COS as irresponsible slackness in charitable distributions allegedly needlessly submerged an individual's character in a 'pauperism direction'.[103]

For decades a substantial minority of Poor Law guardians urged that they should be permitted to administer improved relief to wayfarers travelling in search of work or with other praiseworthy objectives.[104] They attempted to develop regional systems whereby travellers with honest intentions might be encouraged to take a predetermined route between casual wards. Way-leave tickets were provided for exchange at specified places for midday bread and occasionally a piece of cheese. Later in the day, a bed might be guaranteed to genuine travellers. There was even the possibility that the need to perform their assigned task would be waived.[105] These procedures were aimed at providing the traveller with some short-term security. For the authorities they provided a natural control mechanism fabricated on a framework of threat to the traveller that a prison sentence for vagrancy awaited any individual's attempt to defeat the system. Fourteen days in gaol was meted out to those found guilty of vagrancy while benefiting from the way-leave procedure. The schemes varied in detail but the Berkshire system was typical. Established in August 1871, it involved pass-books containing personal details of the traveller and specifying his final destination. Relief stations were created at police constables' houses between workhouses.

Other schemes mainly sponsored by voluntary subscription were launched with mixed success in some southern and midland English counties. Similar procedures to those in Berkshire were tried in Gloucestershire from 1866, Cumberland and Westmorland (1867), Dorset (1870), Hants (1870), Kent (1871), Wiltshire (1871), North Wales (1884), West Sussex (1906) and East Sussex (1909).[106] In the way-leave systems attempted in Herefordshire, Worcestershire and Ayrshire poor travellers could receive midday bread from mendicity societies en route.[107] All the schemes presupposed that only a man genuinely seeking work would walk the twenty miles or so a day needed to satisfy the predetermined schedule. They were aimed 'not at diminishing vagrancy, but only at lessening its accompanying evil of mendicancy'.[108] Counties experimenting with the various way-leave schemes claimed that they had brought not only a reduction in the number of vagrants relieved in Poor Law unions but also a decrease in cottage robberies and petty larceny. Other counties were less enthusiastic. They argued that policies conducted by charities were counterproductive. They had the tendency to drive 'professional' vagrants away from casual wards and encourage them to beg from the public for the few pence required for an overnight stay at a local lodging house.[109] As a consequence the way-leave ticket system failed to receive the complete backing of the Government. It was not developed nationally. The influential J. J. Henley was certain that way-leave tickets were undesirable. He claimed that they provided working men with 'an inducement to be lodged and fed, at the public expense, when travelling on their own business through the country'.[110] Way-leave procedures also had the weakness of providing little assistance for the many who were genuinely seeking work but could not predict their route in the way prescribed. Nor were all guardians necessarily keen on incurring the additional cost of the workhouse-based schemes.

As the twentieth century approached some politicians and civil servants were finding the 1834 Amendment an embarrassing reflection on an unenlightened era. Economic depression as a cause of unemployment was now being more readily accepted as a social hurdle beyond an individual's control. Poverty rather than pauperism was beginning to be the problem tackled by social investigators. The changing attitudes prompted a succession of minor administrative Poor Law reforms. In 1894, for example, it became permissible for workhouse officials to distribute dry tea, milk and sugar to allow women to make their own afternoon tea. In 1897 the employment of trained nurses was being mooted for the care of the sick poor.[111] The same year saw an LGB General Order providing for an improved diet for children under the age of seven years by 'giving them milk'.[112]

Destitution and how it might affect the numbers of casual applicants for relief remained an intractable conundrum for the authorities. Minor modifications to official policy, each attempting to control the problems as they arose, bore little fruit. Government ministers seem to have lost confidence in attempting new fundamental solutions. Guardians remained highly selective in applying some snippets of the advice Whitehall offered while disregarding others with the same dumb insolence exercised by their predecessors.[113] Lack of uniformity in local administration remained a permanent characteristic of the nineteenth-century Poor Law. When local workhouses responded harshly to casual applicants they wandered elsewhere, often sleeping in the open, to the alarm of local householders. Where regimes were relatively soft, 'multitudes came into the casual wards, burdening ratepayers'.[114]

London and the larger cities contained many homeless people who scratched what existence they could from the streets. Individuals who found themselves forced to indulge in the workhouse fare found the casuals' diet did not provide sufficient nourishment for an active life. Many who may initially have honestly searched for work rapidly degenerated in health and confidence. Rejected by society they became hard-core vagrants devoid of hope. 'Charity and the casual wards kept them barely alive and at the end their bodies would be sent, unidentified, to the anatomy schools.'[115]

Middle-class attitudes to social problems tended to modify in the later decades of Victoria's reign. Idealist campaigns made inroads into classic economic doctrines. T. H. Green, Henry Sidgwick and Alfred Marshall were among those causing a paradigm shift in the dominant philosophy taught in British Universities. The traditional assumption that it was natural for there always to be lower social classes was refuted.[116] Although a reforming zeal encompassed individuals and organisations of varied persuasion and motivation, their broad focus on poverty and homelessness brought the problems into the public domain.[117] There was less support for the 1850s practice of using the words 'residuum', 'refuse' and 'offal' as synonyms for both the sewage waste of the sanitary problem and the human waste that constituted the social problem.[118] In spite of the modified thought processes the problems of poverty and vagrancy continued unabated. The dawning decade of the twentieth century saw a Royal Commission and Government Departmental Committees appointed to resolve the ongoing difficulties. Their successes and failures are discussed in the next chapter.

6 Vagrancy around the World Wars

Those who have work, how can they know
The bitter times you undergo.
Each morn you 'wake, only to roam
In search of work to keep a home.[1]

At the beginning of the twentieth century Government was having to accept the likelihood that without positive socio-economic action there would always be some hard core of itinerant poor. Their acceptance was coupled with the comforting, if mistaken, belief that the numbers involved would never be large and would comprise but a few entrenched eccentrics. A few reformist Edwardians considered that the treatment of casuals in workhouses remained shameful in its general lack of care. They suggested society should abandon its 'undiscerning spirit of insensate persecution' and accept responsibility for the 'ruin' of those human lives provided with only a 'meagre and pernicious education ... unemployment ... the blight of slum environment ... the insidious attractiveness of sparkling ale saloons' which together bred 'utter hopelessness'.[2] Any idea that vagrancy numbers would remain small quickly evaporated when, within a few years, workhouse casual wards reached unprecedented occupancy levels. It had been recognised that the war in South Africa and a period of good trade were 'no doubt largely responsible for the low vagrancy figures reached in 1900'.[3] When, in the early years of the century these contributory factors no longer applied, it did not stop Whitehall alleging, shortly after figures started to rise, that the reason for the phenomenon was that local Poor Law officials were not applying the rules regarding casual applicants with sufficient rigour. Laxity of administration was still seen to be providing unwarranted comforts to idle layabouts. Guardians were said to be compounding the difficulties of increased applicant numbers through being mistakenly tempted to economise by not detaining repeat casuals for more than one night.[4] Vagrancy loomed again as 'the most intractable problem confronting Poor Law administrators'. Official concern reached such a pitch by July 1904 that a Departmental Committee was appointed by the

President of the Local Government Board (LGB) to examine the whole subject of vagrancy. As had earlier investigators, they soon recognised that 'vagrancy' was a 'very elastic' term. They found it quite impossible to say at what stage a workman genuinely tramping in search of work and failing to find it should be regarded as a vagrant. As a consequence of this time-honoured dilemma, the Committee tamely concluded that vagrants could be found in many localities, namely: on the road, in casual wards, common lodging-houses, charitable shelters and prisons, in addition to other peripheral resorts such as barns, brick-works, haystacks, viaduct arches and so on. Lack of 'trustworthy' vagrancy statistics was blamed by the Committee for their inability to come up with more definite conclusions, let alone solutions. Few Committee members disagreed that casual wards contained a minority of those wandering around the country without a home or other assets. They were also aware that when circumstances were considered appropriate by the authorities any of the poor homeless could be charged under vagrancy legislation.

In their 1906 Report the LGB Departmental Committee expressed the opinion that the 'real cause of vagrancy' was 'indiscriminate dole-giving'. Without this there would be 'little necessity for casual wards or labour colonies' for the itinerant poor. It was believed that 'idle vagrancy, ceasing to be a profitable profession, would come to an end'. The Report stated that, in the past, those who had attended casual wards had often been infested with vermin and a large proportion suffered 'itch and other skin diseases'. It was claimed that more recently, now that casual ward applicants had been forced to take a bath, they had a 'much higher standard of cleanliness', had 'sound boots' and were 'well nourished'. But in most respects the characteristics of tramps had apparently not changed for the better. They were reported as continuing to live an 'unsocial and wretched sort of existence' with 'no object in life' and little hope for an improved future. Allegedly, tramps attending casual wards were still likely to be leading an existence that could be 'truly said' to be 'poor, nasty, mean, solitary, brutish'. Even then, the Committee had no doubt that 'the class of people who frequent the charitable shelter or habitually sleep out' was 'still lower'. The man who slept in his clothes at a shelter, or passed the night on a staircase, was 'often verminous and always filthy'.[5]

The LGB Departmental Committee recommended that the casual ward system should be further strengthened. They regurgitated the thesis that control would be better transferred from Union officials to the police. This toughening attitude included the recommendation that 'certified' labour colonies should be established in which habitual vagrants could be compulsorily detained for periods of 'at least six months'.[6] This proposal failed to gain parliamentary approval. Like much of their work, it became subsumed within the activities of the parallel more powerful 1905–9 Royal Commission on the Poor Laws and the Relief of Distress. Undeterred by their lack of parliamentary support, the LGB pushed on by implementing less contentious Committee recommendations not requiring new legislation. These included:

- the phasing out of short-term prison sentences for minor vagrancy
- annual licensing and stricter supervision of common lodging-houses
- local authority regulation of voluntary bodies providing food and shelter to the destitute
- increased powers to prevent sleeping out, and
- the reception of children and women casuals in the main body of the workhouse rather than in casual wards.

This last recommendation was initiated by evidence to the Committee indicating that some casual wards were 'the most horrid places a man could go into'. Common lodging houses were mentioned as being 'often very filthy'. In such places 'a man would get a more comfortable bed as far as the softness of it went' but it would be 'generally infested with vermin'. Mr J. Howe offered his opinion in evidence that both casual wards and common lodging houses 'ought to be swept off the face of the earth'. Neither were fit 'for human beings to go into'.[7]

The later LGB *Metropolitan Poor Law Inspectors' Advisory Committee's Report on the Homeless Poor* (1914) described how after the Boer War ended in 1901, many homeless persons had flocked to London. They 'swelled the ranks of those destitute persons who collected nightly' in areas centring on the Thames Embankment. This locality was seen to have the attraction of shelter afforded under the approaches to the river bridges. The proximity of theatres and restaurants also provided the opportunity of earning a few pennies by fetching cabs and carriages for patrons. Other havens from bad weather populated by street dwellers at night-time were the staircases and landings of nearby common lodging houses 'in which they would have slept the night had they the few pence required to pay for a bed'. These lodging houses were especially numerous in Whitechapel where in particular streets, men and women, often with children, 'took advantage of the open door of a tenement house'. Members of the

Local Government Board Committee emphasised that there could be 'no question that their condition of destitution is extreme'.[8]

Colonel Gerard Clark calculated that in 1910 there were 'at least 1500 men and women collected on the Embankment' nightly hoping for charitable assistance. He considered it a 'scandal' that these people were not being helped more effectively. Clark recommended 'a system of labour homes or colonies' to serve as 'moral' infirmaries where their characters would be developed by keeping them at work.[9] Charles Loch, General Secretary of the Charity Organisation Society accepted that a man without work had the 'choice of two evils'. Either he entered his local workhouse or tramped elsewhere in search of employment. On balance Loch believed it better for the man to 'go on the road and make his effort' because this was 'the bravest thing to do'.[10] Many unemployed men took to the road who were 'neither vagrants or professional tramps' simply because this was the most obvious way of looking for work when local contacts had failed.[11]

The LGB Advisory Committee were displeased that official responses to casual workhouse applicants often remained dependent on the whim of a local administrator in spite of it being the basic tenor of the New Poor Law that there should be national conformity. The Committee's Report again emphasised the perceived need for an improved and uniform standard in casual wards. Formation of joint vagrancy committees (JVCs) were encouraged to develop cooperation between contiguous Poor Law unions. The purpose was to rationalise casual relief administration regionally in the belief that eventually it would lead to the creation of a nation-wide culture. This was to turn out to be a slow process stretching over two decades. Nevertheless, by 1 April 1930, prior to the Poor Law Act of that year, a total of 32 JVCs had been formed in England and Wales, representing most unions in 45 counties.[12]

The number of poor travellers using the Poor Law casual wards nationally on the nights of 1 January and 1 July in each of the years 1900–18 is shown in Figure 6.1.[13] The figures show that occupancy rose through the first decade of the century from an average of less than five thousand for the night counts of 1 January 1900 and 1 July 1900 to consistently approach ten thousand in each of the years 1909, 1910 and 1911. From then occupancy of the wards dropped steadily so that by the end of the war there were fewer than one thousand five hundred casuals on the average night.

Also shown over the same period is the yearly mean percentage of unemployed members of certain trade unions. It is readily accepted that the unskilled unemployed, that is the working-class element most likely to be using Poor Law wards, were unlikely be strongly represented in the trade union data. Equally, it is reasonable to suppose that fluctuations in the availability of work signalled by them would broadly reflect the general state of the job market. As a consequence, they provide circumstantial evidence about the employment opportunities of those lacking skills. The broad similarity in pattern of the data sets for casual ward occupancy and unemployment over the first 18 years of the twentieth century is apparent from Figure 6.1.

Prompted by a letter to the national press from Charles Loch expressing concern about the number of destitute persons sleeping on the Embankment, a Special Advisory Committee was formed in 1912 at a meeting convened by London's Lord Mayor. Represented were Government departments, local authorities and charitable agencies concerned with the capital's homeless. The LGB echoed the comments of their nineteenth-century predecessors in pointing out that much of the difficulty associated with vagrants arose from lack of uniformity in administrative response to casual ward applicants. To resolve the inconsistencies the control of 24 of London's casual wards

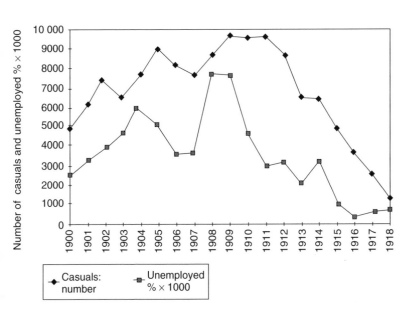

Figure 6.1 Number of casuals relieved and unemployment, 1900–18.

was transferred on 1 April 1912 from the several Boards of guardians to the Metropolitan Asylums Board. The remaining wards were closed. The Lord Mayor's Committee devised a special scheme to deal with homeless persons in the City centre whereby deputed police officers were on duty between 10 p.m. and 2 a.m. They distributed tickets to homeless persons, directing them to the Asylums Board Office on Waterloo Pier for interview by the officer in charge. Guided by the principle that only habitual vagrants should be dealt with in casual wards, all other applicants were directed to an appropriate voluntary agency. These included the Church Army, Dr Barnado's, the Salvation Army and lesser known charities. This type of hostel accommodation was likely to be relatively clean but tramps found them 'far drearier than the worst of the common lodging houses'.[14] The charitably funded shelters usually had specific aims. These included the rescue of 'young women', destitute children, young servants, young women 'in business', 'upper class' servants, 'inebriates', clerks and discharged prisoners. The nature of relief provided in the voluntary hostels normally consisted of food and a bed though some merely provided a 'sitting up rest'. The period homeless travellers could stay varied from one night to a number of months. Some shelters were free, others charged a few pennies or alternatively required the fulfilment of specified work. The average monthly number of tickets issued by the police and details of their use for the period 1912–14 is shown in Table 6.1. The data generally indicate a steady decline in the number relieved by both the official and voluntary sectors. A striking divergence from this trend were the figures for August 1914, the month Britain declared war on Germany. The number of tickets issued by the police in that month temporarily rose to 1773 from the 993 of July. This was explained by the large numbers going to London to 'join the colours' but having 'no money for a bed until they were actually enlisted'. Further, those men who applied but were rejected by the military authorities as medically unfit found themselves stranded.[15] Homeless numbers then rapidly subsided again. It is noticeable from the more detailed data that almost without exception, from February 1913, the number of persons directed to charitable agencies, month by month, exceeded those sent to casual wards. In other words, those considered by the Asylums Board Officer as not being habitual vagrants and possessing the ability 'to make a fresh start in life' if 'afforded the opportunity' made up most of the applicants.[16] Furthermore, it appeared that a substantial proportion of those initially directed to the casual wards were found not to 'have

Table 6.1 Monthly number of tickets issued by the police to the Metropolitan homeless during 1912, 1913 and 1914; also where shelter was offered and the extent to which the offer was accepted

	1912 Nov/ Dec	1913 1st quarter	1913 2nd quarter	1913 3rd quarter	1913 4th quarter	1914 1st quarter	1914 2nd quarter	1914 3rd quarter	1914 4th quarter
Tickets issued by police:	2298	1423	1130	1330	1339	1110	1060	1264	453
Tickets presented at Asylum Board Office by:									
Men	1955	1285	993	1134	1224	1032	925	1114	362
Women	64	30	27	34	28	19	30	49	21
Tickets issued by Asylum Board Office towards help from:									
Charities	462	596	576	612	718	597	526	636	190
Casual wards	1558	717	443	506	533	453	429	531	193
Total tickets not used:	1037	413	308	435	372	303	361	402	169
Tickets issued by the police not used:	43%	28%	27%	32%	28%	27%	34%	34%	37%
Tickets issued towards casual wards:	77%	55%	43%	45%	43%	45%	45%	46%	50%

Data are monthly average for each of the seasonal quarters tabled. Because the ticket scheme did not start until November 1912, the monthly average tabled for that year is for November and December.

Source: Report of Metropolitan Poor Law Inspectors' Advisory Committee on the Homeless Poor, Appendix B, pp. 11–12, PP 1914–16 [c. 7840], XXXII.

become habituated to a vagrant life'. About 600 such persons were redirected from casual wards to voluntary agencies during 1914 'with every hope of success attending their efforts'.[17]

The Special Advisory Committee congratulated themselves in 1914 on their rehabation scheme being a 'gratifying success'. In proof of their claim they had 'numerous examples' of what had been achieved. They believed that the following typified the successful 'nature of this side of the work':

A young man came from the provinces hoping to improve his position. After two months' work he lost his job by his own fault. Casual work at the docks failed and gradually sinking lower he drifted on to the streets. Here he was directed by a police constable to apply at the office at Waterloo Pier and was sent to one of the Church Army Homes. In the Home he worked well and was finally sent back to his employer in the provinces.

A soldier on furlough while awaiting his discharge got drunk in London on his way from Aldershot to the provinces and was robbed of his money and railway warrant. Thus stranded he betook himself to the Embankment, where he was passed to the Salvation Army. His story was proved to be accurate, he was given money and forwarded to his destination.

A civil servant became ill and in consequence of a medical report was given a gratuity and left the service. He lost in business all he had derived from the gratuity and eventually found himself on the streets. He was sent through the Waterloo Pier Office to the 'Morning Post' Embankment Home, the managers of which obtained for him a good situation at a well-known caterer's.

A man formerly employed as a chauffeur tramped to London with the object of enlisting in the Army. As he had no reference with him, he was unable to do so. He found himself stranded on the streets when he was sent by the Police to the Waterloo Pier Office. There he was forwarded to the Willow Street Mission who were able to set him on his feet again.[18]

A series of official surveys investigated the extent of London homelessness in the period 1910–14. They provided data on those who had spent the night in shelters without beds, those sleeping rough on the streets, those in free lodging houses or hostels supplied by voluntary

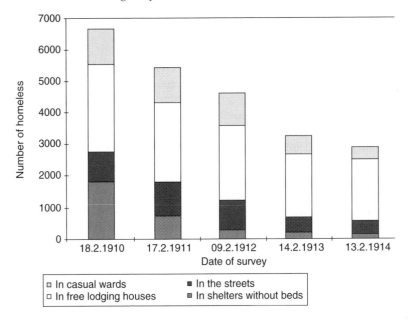

Figure 6.2 Homeless people and their mode of shelter, 1910–14.

agencies and those in Poor Law casual wards (Figure 6.2).[19] The surveys showed that the overall nightly number of London homeless needing relief fell from an average of 6644 in February 1910 to 2881 four years later. The data provides further circumstantial justification for the use of Poor Law data as a surrogate for changing trends in those making up the total number of destitute people lacking a fixed abode. Not surprisingly, the biggest reduction in the use of alternative shelters was where occupants were expected to spend the night sitting upwards, often on a hard bench.

Whereas 1778 homeless people had the need to endure this experience in 1910, there were only 106 prepared to accept the ordeal four years later. It will be noted that the numbers in all categories of homeless temporary accommodation dropped markedly as the war approached. The type retaining most popularity were 'free lodging houses', that is, charitable hostels.

When casual ward numbers showed a steady decline in the years immediately preceding the 1914–18 hostilities the LGB believed a major contributory factor was favourable movement in the labour market. Other aids to the downward trend were claimed to be:

- improved administration largely resulting from their metropolitan ticket scheme
- provision of old age pensions
- the implementation of the National Insurance Act, and
- the introduction of Labour Exchanges.[20]

The LGB explained that the advent of war was the further crucial factor contributing to the 'abnormal decline' in London applications from a normal 1025 applications for casual relief in September 1914 to only 282 in the December of that year.[21] As with earlier wars, those itinerants who had been dubbed 'unemployable' were quickly found a useful place in society working in support of the national effort. Reservists and other able-bodied among the homeless were rapidly enlisted into the colours. Other territorials, already in employment at the outbreak of war were transferred to military service. This left vacancies for others who would otherwise have been without a job. A large amount of labour was absorbed by the War Office in building accommodation for the troops and in the construction of mushrooming armament factories.

When the opportunity arrived for escape from life on the road, most people grabbed it. Tramping in the twentieth century was not an easy life. As Patrick MacGill discovered, it was hard to obtain constant employment. 'A farmer kept me for a fortnight, a drainer for a week, a road mender a day and after that it was the road, the eternal, soul-killing road again.'[22] The way-ticket systems discussed in the previous chapter continued to suffer mixed responses in the period prior to 1914. Although the concept had previously gained only grudging approval from central officialdom, it did receive enthusiastic support from some witnesses to the 1906 Departmental Committee. Wider use of way-leaves was recommended whereby a genuine work-seeker should be provided with a ticket. They would then be entitled to lodging, supper and breakfast in casual wards on a specified route. The right to leave early next morning was also granted to those who had shown willing by completing a relatively small set task. Lunchtime sustenance of bread and cheese was also recommended.[23] The passing of men 'genuinely seeking work' around the country from one workhouse to the next was approved. The proviso was that they could confirm their identity with an unemployment insurance card. The 1909 Poor Law Royal Commission Report was only lukewarm about the idea of way-tickets. They observed that as pieces of paper they could be bought cheaply on London's black market. Attempts to launch a refurbished scheme nationally were not successful.[24]

Despite Victorian dilution of the long-standing settlement and removal laws, they continued to cause significant social friction by inhibiting the unhindered movement of poor people. As late as the year 1907 'upwards of 12 000 persons' were forcibly removed from one parish to another in England and Wales.[25] Reformers described how Poor Law authorities, when finding casual applicants 'ragged and unkempt', first imposed 'degrading ... punitive, excessive and unremunerative' labour tasks on them. Then they hounded them 'from town to town and county to county, without the smallest attempt at remedial measures'.[26] Fashionably retained among the Victorian and Edwardian propertied classes was the idea that most poor people inherited a predisposition to travel from workhouse to workhouse because of the freedom of spirit it brought. As a consequence, it was alleged that those who succumbed to such attractions must be involved in a form of self-indulgence.[27]

Competing attitudes to destitution and its removal appeared in the two reports circulated by the two opposing cliques within the 1906–9 Commission. Both camps agreed that the existing mixed workhouse system had glaring faults. The Majority Report recommended that they should be replaced by 'public assistance authorities' but that basically the Poor Law system should remain. It was to be another twenty years before the idea of public assistance committees was implemented. The Minority of Commissioners published their separate report condemning the contemporary procedures as being intrinsically bad. They advocated the abolition of the Poor Law system and recommended that the state should organise to prevent rather than palliate destitution. Specialised unstigmatised municipal services responding separately to the differing needs of various categories of disadvantage were recommended.[28]

Table 6.2 shows how, for the years 1904–13, homeless men and women in the capital spent their night in casual wards as against in sit-up shelters and sleeping rough on the streets. When considered together with Figure 6.2 there is the implication that by 1913 the idea of spending a night on a London street or even 'sitting up', as unpopular as that proved, was preferred by both destitute men and women to occupying a casual ward bed. The Poor Law Inspectors were quick to claim that this resulted directly from the unified approach gained by the previously mentioned transfer in February 1913 of casual ward administration to the Asylums Board.[29] The ratio of poor homeless women to men was larger in London than was the national average. Homeless children hovered annually around 1 per cent of the adult total.[30] How many early twentieth-century vagrants

Table 6.2   Homeless men and women in London and their mode of shelter, 1904–13

Survey date	Sleeping in streets and sitting up in shelters		In Poor Law casual wards	
	Men	Women	Men	Women
29.2.1904	1563	184	1034	175
17.2.1905	1869	312	926	210
08.2.1907	1998	402	963	197
15.1.1909	1895	170	1001	184
18.2.1910	2510	220	928	173
17.2.1911	1462	321	962	129
09.2.1912	978	213	900	132
14.2.1913	522	127	493	52
24.10.1913	551	141	352	46

Report of the Metropolitan Poor Law Guardians' Advisory Committee on the Homeless Poor, p. 9, PP 1914 [c. 7307], XLIV.

were mentally unstable is unknown. The 1908 Royal Commission on the Feeble-minded were not able to detect an 'excess' of mental defectives amongst vagrants but accepted that many of those discharged from mental institutions could eventually do nothing but wander aimlessly between prison, workhouse and temporary shelter.[31]

During the First World War the Minister of Reconstruction appointed a committee under the chairmanship of Sir Donald Maclean which included on its agenda how best to rehabilitate any post-war itinerant unemployed and vagrants. Recommendations included:

- detention colonies for confirmed vagrants similar to the disregarded recommendation of the 1904–6 Departmental Committee
- voluntary labour colonies for genuine work-seekers, and
- pro-active work-finding Labour Exchanges.

Maclean believed that if all large cities could be persuaded to establish municipal lodging houses, the problem of vagrancy would rapidly dissolve. His Committee proposed that any destitute wayfarer unable to pay for his lodging would be referred to a newly formed local authority Home Assistance Committee to which all the existing functions of Poor Law institutions would then be transferred.[32] But apart from pursuing the perceived need to urge the wider formation of JVCs to rationalise response to the needy, the post-war government generally shirked Maclean's proposals.[33] Amongst the ideas laid aside were his resurrected concepts of detention and labour colonies brewing since the nineteenth century. This despite some cross-party support claiming that similar establishments on the continent had produced favourable results. Some of these enthusiasts for colonies formed the Vagrancy Reform Society to promote the concept of enforced detention but the effort proved little more than a damp squib. More popular post-war were lower profile reformative establishments run by voluntary agencies. The Salvation Army, the Church Army, the Christian Service Union and the 'Morning Post' Embankment Home were among those persisting after the war with their chosen mission. In various guises they attempted to promote the opportunity for casuals to improve their condition of life. Each establishment allowed men to leave at will.

From 1920 casual ward numbers multiplied rapidly. During the next 12 months, difficulties brought by the sharp economic depression with unemployment approaching 17 per cent were compounded by the social instability of disillusioned ex-servicemen. Figure 6.3 relates the number of unemployed with those receiving relief as casuals in England and Wales between the two World Wars.[34] The similarities between the two data sets are apparent. Well-intentioned attempts immediately in the wake of the first of these wars to place demobbed militia in meaningful jobs were swamped by the deluge of 1920–1 unemployment. In an attempt to tackle the problem, the 1911 National (Unemployment) Insurance Scheme was extended in 1921 to cover a wider range of occupations. At the same time, Parliament demanded a stricter interpretation of the 'not genuinely seeking work rule'. The intention was to force men to seek work further afield. Should their search end in failure, as was common, the unemployed person needed to beg a note from the would-be employers who had refused them a job to 'prove' they had been genuine work-seekers.

Despite recommendations aimed at the improvement and rationalisation of conditions, many casual wards remained 'most unsatisfactory'.[35] Sleeping, washing, toilet and medical facilities were all the subject of widely based condemnation. Even then, the stubbornly fabricated inhospitality failed to deter the needy thousands who nightly claimed admission to one or the other workhouse during the 1920s.[36] At the cessation of hostilities there had only been around one

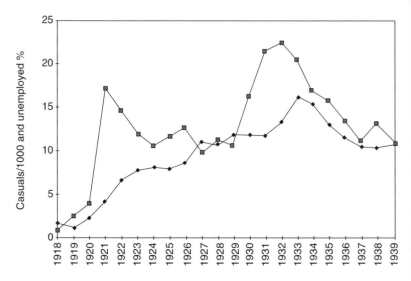

Figure 6.3   Casuals receiving Poor Law relief and number unemployed, 1918–39.

thousand casuals on Poor Law relief in England and Wales but numbers grew steadily. By the night of 31 March 1930, there were 13 296 poor travellers needing to accept Poor Law facilities. In the years that followed the situation worsened further. There were few nights during the late 1920s or throughout the entire decade of the 1930s when the occupancy of casual wards fell below the 9000 level. Although these numbers were themselves disturbing, few doubted that they were but indicative of a greater number of desperate people unable to establish a settled way of living. By accepting the assumption made by the 1906 LGB Departmental Committee that those occupying casual wards were roughly 20 per cent or 25 per cent of the 'whole moving stream' then, for more than ten years leading up to the Second World War, it was common for about 40 000 poor persons in England and Wales to be wandering around the country without a permanent home.[37] When compared with casual ward attenders pre-war, more were now younger able-bodied men. The authorities accepted that most were looking desperately for work. Although the number tramping the road had risen alarmingly, they were of course only a small fraction of Britain's unemployed who hovered stubbornly above the two million mark throughout the first half of the 1930s.[38]

Neville Chamberlain had worked assiduously on reforming local government throughout the 1920s. Nevertheless, it was not until 1930 that the Poor Law Act of that year finally followed the basic 'public assistance' recommendation of the 1909 Poor Law Report. The 642 Poor Law unions were abolished and the responsibilities of their Boards of Guardians transferred to the administrative counties and to the county boroughs. The local authorities were directed to appoint Public Assistance Committees to supervise the administration of the Poor Law in their locality. A Ministry of Health (MoH) Departmental Committee preceding the 1930 Poor Law Act attempted to separate the needs of various categories of destitute traveller. It was accepted as being inappropriate that they should be housed in a single institution. Resettlement hostels were recommended for capable able-bodied men. Less able people were to be referred to specific outside agencies. These included hospitals for the sick and diverse voluntary organisations such as those specialising in the care of women and the training of unemployed unskilled youngsters.

A special investigation initiated by the MoH Committee into the mental condition of casual ward occupants built on the work of the 1908 Royal Commission on the Feeble-minded. It indicated that 15.7 per cent of casuals were feeble minded, 5.4 per cent insane and 5.7 per cent suffered from a psychoneurotic condition. The Committee believed these statistics taken from various localities were 'fairly representative of the country as a whole'. Even then, they considered themselves unable to provide guidance on the form of appropriate response to mentally disadvantaged applicants other than suggesting they should be offered institutional treatment under the Mental Deficiency Acts.[39] This process reaped little improvement. Some years later, the problems of young wayfarers were diagnosed at a COS Conference. It was reported that most lads seeking help from voluntary missions suffered from 'some form of neurosis' which often brought 'a rapid deterioration and shattered morale'.[40]

An interesting aspect of the data for casual ward occupants in England and Wales on certain years between 1910–30 which puzzled the authorities was the persistent annual tendency in the periods both before and after the hostilities for a low December occupancy to increase steadily to reach its peak around June (Table 6.3). By July numbers had dropped and were as low or even lower than in December. Then numbers usually rose again to remain until early

Table 6.3 Number of casuals relieved in England and Wales on an average Friday in certain years 1910–30 inclusive. Figures are in thousands

Year	Month											
	Apr	May	Jun	Jul	Aug	Sep	Oct	Nov	Dec	Jan	Feb	Mar
1910	13.5	13.3	13.4	10.3	10.6	11.8	12.2	11.6	10.6	11.1	11.4	12.0
1914	8.9	8.8	7.2	5.5	7.6	7.5	7.8	7.9	7.3	7.3	8.3	8.7
1919	1.6	1.5	1.4	1.3	1.2	1.2	1.1	1.1	1.1	1.1	1.1	1.2
1928	11.5	12.1	11.6	10.4	10.9	10.6	9.6	10.6	10.5	10.5	11.4	12.0
1929	12.2	12.5	12.1	9.9	11.3	11.5	10.6	11.2	10.5	10.7	11.0	11.1
1930	11.8	12.1	11.1	9.2	10.8	10.6	9.8	10.6	10.5	10.9	11.5	11.8

Source: Report of Departmental Committee on Relief of Casual Poor, Appendix V, PP 1929–30, XVII.

September before dropping suddenly in October, rising again in November and falling through December. The MoH accepted that seasonal employment went 'some way' to explaining these fluctuations in numbers relieved but were quite unable to explain the changes in the 'existence of the whole body of casuals'.[41]

In 1928 the MoH investigated the 'constituent elements of the casual ward population' in London and certain provincial unions. The age distribution and gender of casuals was again compiled for the same unions in 1930 (Table 6.4). These data 'confirmed the impression' that 'a certain proportion of working men' had not thereto been provided for by the 'machinery available for the relief of unemployment and were not the type for whom the casual ward is or could be suitable'.[42] It will be noted that as regards both men and women, well over half the casual ward occupants were aged 40 years or more. This contrasted with the impression gained in the immediate post-war years when there were indications of a younger element taking to tramping in search of work. There is the possibility that a good

Table 6.4 Age distribution of men, women and children in certain casual wards on 10 February 1928 and 14 February 1930

Date	Male age groups					
	16–21	21–30	30–40	40–60	Over 60	Total
10 Feb 28	76	376	512	1129	379	2472
14 Feb 30	57	290	491	1112	374	2324

Date	Female age groups					
	16–21	21–30	30–40	40–60	Over 60	Total
10 Feb 28	1	5	23	56	25	110
14 Feb 30	1	7	28	65	18	119

	1928	1930
Infants under 3	2	3
Boys under 16	1	None
Girls under 16	1	2

number of those taking to the post-war highway remained disillusioned with what was supposed to be a more stable society but which could not provide them with work. Faced with chronic long-term unemployment they found themselves unable to get off the tramping treadmill. It is not unlikely that some of the men and women who were out of work were tramping as a result of their home and belongings being repossessed and they themselves evicted.[43] This all too frequent process resembled the rural proletarianisation of former times associated with land closures when, as we have seen in earlier chapters, poor families lost their bit of England and their cottage. They were similarly dispersed to become transients in search of a firmer social foundation.

Over the six-month period 1 October 1927 to 1 March 1928 an in-depth analysis of the 'whole number' of casuals relieved in a large provincial union was added to the data. The Committee warned that this evidence should to be regarded with some caution since it depended 'either upon the uncorroborated statements of the casuals themselves or upon the personal bias of the officers making the returns'. Nevertheless, indications were that:

- 22 per cent of the men were 'undoubtedly seeking work'
- 29 per cent were 'temporarily unemployed persons possibly seeking work'
- 28 per cent were 'undoubtedly habitual vagrants', and
- 21 per cent were 'possibly habitual vagrants'.

Out of a total of 8876 persons passing through the provincial union during the same six months, 7559 (85 per cent) described themselves as labourers. The remaining 1317 casuals were distributed between 74 occupations. Featured among these were; 295 seamen and sailors, 150 painters, 79 grooms, 78 porters, 77 stokers, 75 fitters, 65 clerks, 59 firemen, 57 cooks, 40 tailors, 37 bootmakers, 25 bricklayers and 22 carpenters. Nine said they had 'no occupation'. Almost one half of those interviewed were aged between 40 and 50 years.[44]

The MoH Departmental Committee conceded that 'as a general rule it must be true that long periods of industrial depression swell the number of casuals'. It was all the more surprising then that the Committee found themselves unable to trace any direct link between the Ministry of Labour weekly unemployment statistics and the number of casuals relieved pre-war, post-war or at the end of the 1920s. Using the same data, neither William Beveridge nor the Webbs found difficulty in detecting definite correlation between vagrancy and unemployment.[45]

Some casual attenders had taken to the road to avoid the humiliation of 'signing on' at a Labour Exchange. For someone like Joe Loftus who prided himself on independence they were frequently degrading places: 'Dreary, dismal, gloomy, dirty and hopeless, painted a typically standard olive drab with clerical staff to match.' With little knowledge of life or work outside the dole office, their main concern, it seemed, was to 'pay out as little as possible, not even your entitlement, to keep you at arms length by humiliation and assuming you guilty of wilful idleness before you even opened your mouth'.[46]

The 'ideal' scenario described by the Ministry of Health in 1930 as to how casual applicants should be received by local authorities provided modern 'procedures' were 'perfectly observed' was still acutely reminiscent of the nineteenth century. This applied to sleeping accommodation, clothing, cleanliness, diet and attitude. But the reality was all too often even more unpalatable. The MoH admitted that in practice casual wards were all too 'frequently' inferior to their 'ideal'. Many 'clearly' fell short of 'perfect world' standards while in a 'certain number' conditions were 'infamous and intolerable'. In at least one casual ward there were no baths, no night clothes and each man had to bed down directly on to a dirty dusty wooden floor in his own clothes. In another location, sleeping accommodation consisted of a shed which 'on a decent farm would not be considered fit for an animal of any value'. Committee members visited wards where two men were 'locked in a small cell that was built for one person and kept there in darkness for 12 or 13 hours'. Other casual wards had no heating. Many had no day rooms or where they did exist were 'crowded almost to suffocation'. 'In a large number' of places the official regulations were persistently spurned with the use of dirty towels, blankets and sheets together with uncomfortable or inadequate beds or hammocks. Occupants' complaints about the food they had been offered exposed inadequacy, monotony and lack of vegetables. Gruel was sometimes the only liquid on offer. Meals served without a fork, spoon or knife were not uncommon. Tasks were found to be not so much excessive as 'frequently so trivial or so useless' as to be degrading. Work in some wards was said to be 'a farce' with inmates 'simply being bored stiff, waiting and waiting and waiting' to get out. The MoH brushed aside locally sponsored excuses that the many divergences from official recommendations served as effective deterrents to vagrancy. The ministry pointed to 'the curious fact' that, for instance, lack of bathing facilities were a positive incentive to the habitual casual. Central government claimed that far from attracting other men to a life of vagrancy, a general raising in the standard of accommodation and treatment would raise self-respect. It would become easier for casuals 'to regain their proper places in the life and work of the community'.[47]

In England and Wales casuals continued to receive their occasional night's lodging in one of the 300 Poor Law wards still functioning prior to the Second World War. Older wards were commonly situated close to the other parts of the institution. Some had a separate entrance from the public road. The newer ones occasionally stood at a distance from the main buildings. George Orwell described how 'spikes' in the 1920s and the 1930s often looked 'much like a prison' with their 'rows of tiny barred windows and a high wall and iron gates'. They consisted 'simply of a bathroom and lavatory and, for the rest, long double rows of store cells'. Seen in the mass the inmates appeared to Orwell as 'a disgusting sight; nothing villainous or danger-ous, but a graceless, mangy crew, nearly all ragged and palpably underfed'.[48]

Although there continued to be many shortcomings, the 1930s did also bring improvement in some areas. According to a later National Assistance Board (NAB) report, the best of the modern wards were beginning to be 'admirably designed and equipped'. So much so that when after the Second World War some wards were closed, 'hospitals and other authorities' were eager to acquire them for their own use. Responses to the inter-war travelling poor in Scotland differed from the rest of Britain. In some places it was the policy to refer casuals to 'model lodging houses'. In others they used casual shelters consisting of rooms in (or an outbuilding to) a cottage which the caretaker of the casual shelter occupied rent-free as part of his remuneration. Elsewhere, provision for casuals in Scotland was made at the local Poor House. Occasionally accommodation was in a building such as a gatehouse separate from the main wards and not so clearly part of the establishment as were the more typical casual wards.[49]

The concept of compulsory detention of habitual vagrants as advo-cated by the 1906 LGB Departmental Report and supported by Maclean, had again been laid aside in the 1930 MoH Report. Although the latter realised 'it would be difficult', they recommended remedial measures to combine the benefits of voluntary efforts focusing on a person's physical and spiritual fitness with the facilities available at Ministry of Labour centres. The idea was that the seemingly permanently unemployed could be better trained to take up what work was 'reasonably in sight'.[50] In marked contrast to Government ideas in the 1980s, allegedly based on traditional precedence which demanded more mobility on the part of the unemployed, the Ministry of Labour emphasised in 1930 that men were not expected, 'still less encouraged', to walk the country in search of work. On the contrary, one of the chief purposes of Employment Exchanges was said to be the removal of the need for unemployed persons to tramp about looking for work.[51]

The voluntary organisations committed to assisting a range of poor homeless people towards a more secure lifestyle were developed further in the 1930s. As an example, the Wayfarers' Benevolent Society established in 1916 had opened fifteen hostels by 1933 specifically to help young men 'regain their feet'.[52] Well-meaning as they were, charitable efforts were still found inadequate to satisfy the national need. Their efforts were augmented in 1934 when the centrally administered Unemployment Assistance Board (UAB) superseded local Public Assistance Committees in being responsible for the cost of maintaining and training the unemployed. The UAB was designed to promote the welfare of unemployed applicants by providing such assistance as may be found necessary to speedily get them to work. In reality, the newly formed Instruction Centres (ICs) were less vocational training centres and more part of a regime to tone-up 'physical and mental condition' with the idea of inculcating habits of punctuality and decency. As the UAB itself put it, 'the able-bodied poor are set to work, though in more recent years this phrase has been replaced by the euphemism of training'.[53]

W. J. Smart, writing in the late 1930s, pinpointed six reasons why many people were still homeless, namely:

- prolonged unemployment
- drunkenness
- 'borderline mental deficiency'
- 'domestic maladjustments'
- inappropriate early environment ('little children being born and reared in places unfit for dogs'), and
- heredity.[54]

George Cuttle reviewed the responses of Poor Law officials and others to the plight of the poor in mid Essex during the 50 years prior to the setting up of the UAB in 1934. Like many before him, Cuttle floundered in his attempt to separate 'vagrants' as a group from others applying for casual relief such as the 'homeless', 'irregulars' and those 'sleeping rough'. As ever, the dividing lines between the various groups were found to be amorphous. Nevertheless, Cuttle had no doubt that vagrancy remained a problem 'of the first importance' requiring urgent attention by people better qualified to deal with it than were local guardians. Whereas Cuttle was against begging and believed all 'allied methods of appealing for alms should be dealt with strictly by the police', he stressed the amorphous divisions between poor travellers and emphasised the public suspicion with which most of them were unfairly viewed. He wondered whether punishment may not have too frequently fallen on 'the wrong shoulders'. Cuttle cited examples of past incidents to illustrate the cynicism of local Poor Law officials:

> A man in June, 1904, was charged with refusing to break stones; he had broken 1 cwt instead of four. He pleaded guilty; after the evidence and the statement that he had been quite civil, he added that he had had no food for three days before entering, and had never before been in the Union-House; the Chairman of the Bench had said, 'You don't look like an ordinary Casual'. He was sent back to finish his task.

> In March, 1908, a man aged 74 came in from Romford on a Saturday; he was given a draught for his cough, and his allowance of bread and water, and discharged on Sunday morning; he crossed the road and collapsed, was brought back and died shortly. He was in the last stage of bronchitis and heart disease.'

Cuttle explained that 'the point of these incidents is supplied by the answer to the first man; he had said nothing about his hunger because he thought 'they wouldn't believe him'.[55] When the economy in some regions of Britain improved during the 1930s, there was irritation amongst the better-off about the large number of people still sleeping rough and begging charitable support. Some in the wealthier parts of Britain refused to recognise that unemployment in the nation as a whole remained cruelly high. In fact, numbers occupying casual wards had kept on rising from 1930 to the peak reached on 27 May 1932. On that night, 16 911 persons slept in Poor Law casual wards in England and Wales, the highest number ever recorded.[56] Occupancy numbers subsided a little from the mid 1930s but in the years up to the outbreak of the Second World War there were consistently more than 10 000 finding it necessary to occupy Poor Law premises temporarily.

Those whom George Cuttle classified as sleeping rough were usually homeless. Although they included law-breakers, most were 'without offence'. Their numbers were swollen by the regular 'practice of turning able-bodied men of varying degrees of physical and mental capacity out of the workhouse' which was 'only mentioned occasionally' in guardians' reports. 'Strangers, even if not known vagrants, were not looked on with favour'. Those found guilty of sleeping rough frequently found themselves committed to prison and doing hard labour after being hauled before the magistrate for transgressing vagrancy legislation. To take some typical examples:

- 'a wire worker of Huntingdon found in a malting in December 1900 was given ten days' hard labour'
- 'a labourer of "no fixed abode", who broke a window as he was "starving and had nowhere to sleep" was given seven days' hard labour; he asked the Mayor to make it a month, but the Mayor said, "Nonsense, an able-bodied man like you can get work"'
- 'in July 1906, an old soldier aged 56, who had been in the House, and for some time sleeping "rough", hanged himself in an outhouse .....'
- 'in August 1912, for sleeping in a stable, a man was given 14 days' hard labour'.

But for many farmers the need of certain people to sleep rough continued to be recognised as their normal way of living.[57]

The Vagrancy Act (1935) was one of the few pieces of legislation that can be interpreted as having the intention of diminishing pressure on those without a fixed abode. It was intended to prevent undue hounding of the homeless by abolishing 'sleeping out' as an offence. Repealed was the threatening catch-all phrase from earlier legislation whereby a 'person wandering abroad' could be considered as having committed an offence if 'they did not have any visible means of subsistence'. Even then, the replacement clause did not sweep away all the legal cobwebs. It retained nineteenth-century connotations that the travelling poor were incipiently guilty of some offence or other. A homeless person could still be judged vagrant and 'deemed a rogue and vagabond' should he 'appear to be likely' to cause 'damage to property, infection with vermin, or other offensive consequence'.[58] Nevertheless the new Act did help reduce vagrancy convictions to a level which remained roughly constant up to 1939.

It is clear that prior to the Second World War, many people incapable of gaining permanent employment or of making a settled existence for themselves continued to find it necessary to drift around the country scratching an existence as well as they could. Some started out with the commendable idea of providing a service to the public using skills like peddling, kitchen-knife sharpening or boot repairing. Unfortunately, maintaining a livelihood in this way was precarious. All too often they also found themselves having to join those who tramped without much idea about how to subsist without resorting to begging. Destitute travellers continued to emerge from diverse backgrounds. Few received guidance let alone positive support as to how they might rehabilitate themselves in society. Most remained untouched by government training schemes. Some tramps in the 1920s and 1930s traced their restlessness back to an earlier association with the sea. Others had started wandering confused by the mental disarray with which they had been infected in the Flanders trenches. At least this group had the mixed blessing of their disability rendering them no longer fit to share the horrors of the Second World War which lay in wait for their younger tramping compatriots. Some poor travellers had formerly been proud apprentice-served tradesmen. When thrown out of work they had chosen to take their destiny in their own hands by seeking work elsewhere rather than join their mates in organised job and hunger marches to London. No matter what their background, all categories of itinerant shared the need to decide from a variety of unattractive alternatives where they would seek shelter for the night. Always they had the doubtful consolation of knowing that as a back-stop they had the statutory right of a bed in a Poor Law casual ward. This is assuming they had not knowingly or unwittingly strayed into one of the lurking minefields of vagrancy legislation.

Prior to the Second World War, citizens in the more prosperous regions of Britain had increasingly become a consumer-orientated society. More than ever before, a settled way of life had become essential for any person wishing to participate fully in the benefits of modern society. For secure comfortably situated observers of the social scene, only individuals with the strength of character to establish themselves with a fixed abode deserved the recognition of their respectability. They alone had the right to enjoy the material comforts of industrialised 'civilisation'. Individuals lacking the guts needed to get a home of their own had earned no such right. Chapter 7 examines the efforts of British Governments and voluntary organisations after the Second World War to rehabilitate the poor itinerant within a welfare state established with the concept that every individual had the basic right of food, education, health and a home.

7 Homelessness and the Welfare State

… any permanent, regular, administrative system whose aim will be to provide for the needs of the poor, will breed more miseries than it can cure, will deprave the population that it wants to help and comfort …[1]

'When I use a word, Humpty Dumpty said in a rather scornful tone, it means just what I choose it to mean – neither more or less.'[2]

During the second half of the twentieth century there has been an increased tendency, by both governments and the general public, to describe as 'homeless' those without a settled way of life who formerly had been collectively known as 'vagrants'. It has become common practice to identify homeless families or individuals by the type of temporary accommodation they occupy. This includes that of sleeping on our streets. Prior to the 1939–45 war the alternative temporary beds available for the homeless included casual wards, common lodging houses, hostels and night shelters. Since the war, reception centres which soon replaced the casual wards and a particularly cheap type of bed and breakfast 'hotel' have been added to the list. Such an identification scheme for homeless persons is bizarre bearing in mind that a characteristic of their condition is that they are destined to keep moving around and are unlikely to occupy any one type of accommodation for long.[3]

Shortly after the cessation of hostilities in 1945, the Ministry of Health (MoH) under the incoming Labour Government published plans for the eradication of destitution.[4] Circular 136/46 followed the pattern of the 1930 MoH Departmental Report. This in turn had echoed the Minority recommendation of the 1905–9 Royal Commission regarding the need to specify special needs for various categories of homeless person. 'Methods of disposing of seven categories' of men were defined:

1. those in work but lacking shelter were to be provided with temporary accommodation
2. those desiring work were to be sent to the placing officer of the local employment exchange

137

3. the disabled were to be sent to the Disablement Resettlement Officer
4. those disabled persons considered by the Medical Officer to be capable of work after medical treatment were to be sent to the 'appropriate agency'
5. young persons requiring 'mental or moral rehabilitation' were to be restored to their families or sent to a 'voluntary hostel'
6. the 'hard core' of habitual vagrants would receive suitable treatment or when necessary dealt with firmly to 'discourage the spread of idle vagabondage' and
7. those incapable of work and unsuitable for training were to be encouraged to enter an institution.[5]

During the 1939–45 war the authorities had been too preoccupied to publish regular data on Poor Law casual attenders. While hostilities were in progress, 'care of the homeless' took on a new connotation with focus on preparations for how persons displaced from their homes by bombing could best be billeted. An extraordinary wartime nation-wide emergency strategy was designed to care for the possible homeless victims of enemy action. It was claimed officially on 31 March 1943 that 12 132 'first time' and 9311 'second time' rest centres existed in England and Wales. Should they ever be needed they were said to be capable of accommodating a total of 2 360 000 persons. On the same theme, 'Help your Neighbour' pacts between households were encouraged.[6]

These exogenous threats to the stability of British society subsided towards the cessation of hostilities. Government then again turned to consider the destitute traveller problem that had been so intractable during the twenty years prior to the conflict. In spite of property destroyed by enemy action, there were few people in Britain immediately in the aftermath of the war who felt the need to apply for relief at Poor Law casual wards. On the last Friday of June 1945 there was a total of only 340 casuals in England and Wales. Then, year by year, the number of casuals steadily advanced with 744, 1134 and 1306 counted on the last Friday in June in 1946, 1947 and 1948 respectively.[7] An HMSO publication, *Persons in Receipt of Poor Relief* provided further information about the men, women and children relieved in the post-war years as Poor Law casuals in England and Wales. On 1 January 1947, they totalled 1545, compared with the 1192 counted on 1 May 1946 (Table 7.1). The thirty destitute travellers reported as being relieved 'otherwise' had been boarded in

Table 7.1   Number of casual men, women and children in receipt of poor relief in England and Wales on the night of 1 January 1947

	Admin. County of London	Other English counties	English county boroughs	Wales	Total	Relieved in instit'ns	Relieved 'otherwise'
Men	416	532	537	26	1485	1456	29
Women	–	26	27	–	53	52	1
Children	7	–	4	7	7	–	
Total	416	565	564	30	1545	1515	30

Source: *Persons in Receipt of Poor Relief (England and Wales)*, (HMSO, 1947), PP 1947–8, XXII, pp. 21 and 33.

common lodging houses in 'places where no casual ward was available'.[8]

As part of a new 'comprehensive' welfare approach to social problems and with the firm intention of consolidating the wartime reduction in the numbers of 'hard core' travellers, the MoH recommended a system of hostels for training and rehabilitation for 'persons without a settled way of living'. Compared with the inter-war years they were of course a small group and still officially perceived as being unfortunate people on society's periphery. Not only were they seen as being socially disadvantaged but also suffering some personal 'inadequacy' such as a difficulty 'to fit in with society and co-operate with people helping them'.[9] Welfare enthusiasts were confident that the 'small-scale' casual problem would soon dissolve further as the few remaining habitual work-shy, anti-social types were 'given suitable treatment'. With UK unemployment seemingly permanently erased with the help of demand management of a burgeoning economy, there were good reasons for believing that the inter-war spectre of needing to care for huge numbers of destitute homeless would never again materialise. After all, in the new welfare-conscious era the aged, the sick and otherwise disadvantaged groups would naturally be cared for by appropriate health and social practitioners.

The Poor Law authorities were abolished on 5 July 1948 when the newly appointed National Assistance Board (NAB) took responsibility for the implementation of MoH Circular 136/46. The remaining Poor

Law facilities for casuals were redesignated 'reception centres' (RCs) under Part 2 of the new National Assistance Act. Part 3 of the Act obliged local authorities to care for persons 'in urgent need' by establishing hostels, the expectation being that they would be required for only a short period. As regards their responsibilities towards young people, most local authorities interpreted the Act as applying entirely to those with dependent children. Now that there was full employment they were not prepared to accept that a 'homeless single person' could genuinely be 'in urgent need' and largely left them to their own devices. Under the Act, travelling people became entitled to welfare payments, even when outside the National Insurance scheme. This, together with the greatly improved job opportunities, seemed to explain why neither street homelessness nor begging were in much evidence. Official confidence remained high that before long only the minuscule number besotted with the travelling life would remain and that they would prefer to use reception centres. With the Labour Government's commitment to quickly rectifying what housing shortages did exist, there were cogent reasons for believing that a permanent home would soon be available for everyone.

Wartime closure of casual wards had meant that only 215 remained out of the 371 wards operational in 1939. In spite of the post-war upward trend in the numbers using the facilities, the total was still small compared with pre-war. They continued to be phased out and by the end of 1958 there were only 60 reception centres (Table 7.2). Of these all but four were administered on the Board's behalf by local authorities reimbursed for approved expenditure on 'persons without

Table 7.2   Number of reception centres functioning in England and Wales before 5 July 1948, on 5 July 1948 and on 31 December 1958

Location	4.7.1948	5.7.1948	31.12.1958
In hospital premises	193	70	19
In local authority premises	138	105	32
In casual shelters	40	40	4
In Crown premises	nil	nil	5
Total	371	215	60

Source: *Report of the National Assistance Board for 1958*, PP 1958–59 [c. 781], VIII, p. 28.

a settled way of living'. Accommodation was either in local authority premises or in refurbished former Poor Law institutions taken over by the new hospital authorities in 1948. In little over ten years the number of localities using hospital premises had been reduced to nineteen.

The 1948 National Assistance Act was intended to encourage casuals to stay at the reception centres when in ill-health or, when fit and able-bodied, until 'constructive' assistance could be offered them.[10] The persistent difficulty remained of determining the classification of people who did continue to use the centres. Most were found to be neither hardened vagrants nor were they capable of looking after themselves. In an effort to resettle able-bodied itinerants, case-work methodology was used to determine each casual's background, personal problems, skills and qualifications.[11] People who were found mentally or physically disadvantaged were then supported by appropriate local authority services. Although they had been launched with a well-intentioned new image, reception centres retained some deterrent characteristics from the workhouses. Occupants continued to be referred to as casuals. The doors opened at 4 p.m. after which each new applicant was forced to take a bath or shower. As in the past, at the authorities' discretion their 'wet or verminous clothing' was removed for disinfection and drying. Menus remained stunningly boring. After spending the night in their dormitory, casuals normally had to complete some traditional task work.

The 1950 NAB report accepted that the numerical trend for persons living 'without a settled way of life' had been upward from the end of the war to November 1949. However, they detected hopeful signs that the ascending trend was tailing off. As proof they pointed to the average number of unsettled people for December 1949 being less than that for the previous year.[12] A further survey of reception centres conducted by local authorities in England and Wales on the night of 23 January 1950 reported that 2302 men, 91 women and 12 children were being accommodated. In Scotland there were 88 men, 13 women and three children in receipt of a bed for the night. Of the men in England and Wales, 411 were under 30 years of age, 484 were from 30 to 39, 562 from 40 to 49, 709 from 50 to 64, and 136 were aged 65 or over. Rather more than 600 of the men, that is more than 25 per cent and mostly from the older age groups, had some mental or physical disability. Nevertheless, the majority of the reception centre users were able-bodied men of working age and said to be in the prime of life. Of the 2166 under 65 in England and Wales, 1750 had no trade or special skill. Only 325 of the total of 2302 men, that is around 14 per cent, were described as tramps of the 'old kind'. As many as 700 men gave the appearance of spending their time touring around reception centres in a limited geographical area. Indeed, 1416 of the men admitted having previously attended other centres. Unhappy home conditions or the 'lack of parents to give them anchorage' provided explanation of the unsettled life of many younger men.[13]

The number of casuals claiming relief in reception centres during the first half of the 1950s was still small compared with pre-war. Seasonal influences are apparent from the monthly data 1948–56 (Table 7.3). June and July persistently featured as low-occupancy months, presumably because improved weather increased the comparative attractions of sleeping rough.

NAB reports in the 1950s confirmed earlier patterns that about half of the occupants in reception centres were in 'robust health'. Around a quarter of them suffered physical or mental disability. The 1952 NAB report emphasised the gross inaccuracy of some picturesque impressions of reception centre attenders. They were found to be nothing like the romantic story-book tramp of old, walking with his belongings slung over his shoulder, living and enjoying an open-air life free from responsibility, content to do an odd job or beg a meal when necessary. In reality, reception centre users were usually found to be people with an 'unhappy or unwise' upbringing. Their weakness or 'indiscipline' of character could frequently be traced back to adverse circumstances earlier in life. Irregularity was the abiding feature of whatever employment they had managed to find in the previous twelve months. Efforts to place casuals in gainful employment through the local Ministry of Labour offices, seemed generally 'to be wasted'.[14]

Some early NAB reports have been described as 'catalogues of despair'.[15] This was because they recognised the persistent failure to resettle men speedily enough and feared that staff efforts were sometimes squandered. On occasions, many months after their apparent reclamation, some men found themselves unable to resist the call of the road.[16] In 1953 the NAB reiterated their policy about encouraging casuals to stay at a centre while efforts were made to get them to take work and settle down to 'normal' life.[17] Casuals were said to be hesitant about staying too long at any one centre because of the greater risk of being offered employment. Each knew that should he turn the job down he could face a charge under section 51 of the National Assistance Act for failing to maintain himself.[18] Reception centre inmates also ran the risk of being prosecuted for 'contravening the

Table 7.3 Average nightly number of casuals accommodated in reception centres month by month in England and Wales, 1948–56

Year	Jan	Feb	Mar	Apr	May	June	July	Aug	Sept	Oct	Nov	Dec
1948							1454	1731	1808	2040	2304	2368
1949	2482	2617	2551	2494	2376	2060	2019	2089	2200	2412	2459	2367
1950	2501	2487	2476	2499	2476	2174	2184	2246	2257	2254	1342	2239
1951	2351	2332	2264	2204	2152	1975	1863	1991	2043	2063	2192	2106
1952	2190	2232	2353	2382	2282	2084	1985	2168	2320	2335	1476	2233
1953	2392	2465	2544	2598	2385	2202	2143	2222	2188	2276	2384	2300
1954	2426	2402	2355	2295	2142	1957	1742	1836	1776	1830	1881	1784
1955	1859	1841	1810	1779	1751	1584	1422	1558	1606	1705	1773	1749
1956	1822	1929	1866	1949	1848	1733	1626	1828	1775	1857	1913	1819

Source: National Assistance Board Reports for 1954, 1955, 1956 and 1957.

regulations' which in the majority of cases was NAB-speak for failing to complete the task of work allocated them.

In spite of some disappointment about their failures, the NAB also described 'encouraging' cases. Each was intended to show how casuals had been rehabilitated into society. Most had first come to the attention of the NAB when undernourished, in poor health, devoid of familial love, lacking in skills or after having served time in prison. The caring diligence of reception centre staff featured in examples of how in some cases the NAB tactics had successfully nurtured a positive attitude. They claimed that if the improved frame of mind could be maintained, in what were often sadly disillusioned cases, it would greatly improve the well-being both of the individual and of society. Some of the examples that follow of 'persons without a settled way of life' are a curtailed form of the published case-study but the general NAB message is maintained:

1. W., aged 21, came from a bad home in Dawlish; his parents had turned him out 3 years previously. When admitted to Exeter Reception Centre he was undersized and delicate. He could not recall ever 'sleeping in a bed'. This was thought to be possibly partly due to him being a 'chronic asthmatic'. The Superintendent at Exeter Centre arranged for him to attend hospital 'as an out-patient for breathing exercises'. Eventually he was well enough to earn sufficient to pay for his local lodgings. He provided 'entire satisfaction' to his employer. He often visited the Superintendent and his wife who continue to 'take a close interest in his well-being'.

2. R., aged 41, was first admitted three years previously, in 1950, to the Board's directly administered Reception Centre at Kelvedon. He had spent half his life on the road and had been 'convicted many times for larceny'. He held a job down for nine months. Then he left and was sentenced to 6 months' imprisonment for theft. After release he eventually returned to the Kelvedon Centre. He was found residential work at a hostel sufficiently close for his progress to be monitored weekly by a member of the RC Advisory Committee. Although occasionally showing 'a fit of pique', R. 'remained happy and contented' for most of 1953 before moving to a similar post in another hostel.

3. M. first came to the notice of the Board's officers three years previously in 1950. Then about 20 years old, he was sentenced to 14 days' imprisonment for defrauding the Board. His mother had

been certified under the Mental Deficiency Acts which had resulted in M. spending the first 14 years of his life at a children's home. The Superintendent of the Ipswich Reception Centre recognised he was 'sub-normal intelligence' but had a willingness for work. He was now 'doing well' in an agricultural job near Bishop Auckland earning sufficient to keep himself. 'The Warden at Ferryhill' was keeping 'in touch'.[19]

4. A man had spent 18 years tramping the roads. At the age of 59, he had been admitted extremely unkempt to a Centre in September 1950, that is five years previously. He was cleaned up, provided with clothing and found employment as a labourer. His wages were, he said, the first he had handled for 11 years. Lodgings were found for him after the usual settling-in period and he remained there until the landlady died. The Reception Centre officer then helped him to get fresh lodgings. He had remained there in the same job for the last five years.[20]

The National Assistance Board reported in 1954 that 9396 casuals had been placed in jobs directly from reception centres during the year. This relatively 'large' number was attributed to the 'full employment conditions' of the time and to 'much patient effort by officials'.[21] The NAB were at pains to point out that the number of casuals actually involved in the job placement figure was 'of course, very much smaller' than the number they had quoted. This was said to be because casuals characteristically stayed in employment for only a short period, often not beyond the first pay-day.[22] Guarded optimism began to feature in NAB reports when the number of casuals occupying official premises subsided in the late 1950s (Figure 7.1). The same public relations script was followed that had been prepared by the Poor Law authorities a century earlier with the NAB treating it as a sign of their success when able to report low occupancy figures. Equally, they were proud to reflect in their 1956 report 'the popularity of reception centres on Christmas Day when most centres provided special meals. 2079 casuals were relieved on the night of 25–26 December 1955, which was 330 above the monthly average for December.[23]

Photographs published by the NAB in 1958 aimed at illustrating the favourable changes for the casual poor within the reception centres they controlled. Victorian brick-built wards with their individual 'typical cells' had largely been replaced by timber-clad 'war-time buildings' with corrugated sheet roofs where casuals shared dormitories.[24] People struggling without a settled way of life continued to be

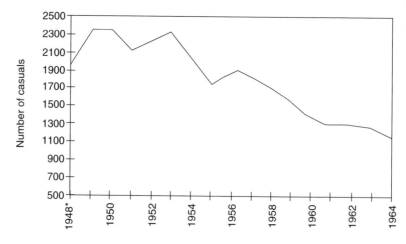

Figure 7.1 Average nightly number of casuals in reception centres, England and Wales, 1948–64.

* The average nightly number for 1948 is for months July to December inclusive.

portrayed less as doing so by choice than as a residual problem from personal inadequacy. Officials still under the spell of post-war welfare-state euphoria remained set on identifying and rectifying individual problems at an early stage. In an increasing proportion of cases mental instability was found to be 'the cause of a man taking to the life of a vagrant'.[25]

A London County Council (LCC) survey in the early 1960s emphasised that it had become conventional to use the term 'homelessness' to describe the condition of those who for centuries had been viewed by the law and many members of the public as 'vagrants'. The elimination of the need for anyone in the UK to have an unsettled lifestyle still seemed a realistic target. The LCC pointed to how one of their more recent surveys had discovered only six people sleeping rough in central London. They concluded that any other poor itinerants there may have been must have used their social security payments for lodging-house beds which effectively was keeping them off the streets. The numbers occupying casual wards had remained quite small.

Any complacency in official circles was soon shaken when shock media reports during the spring and summer of 1962 alleged that about 1000 'of the vagrant type' were sleeping rough in central

London, notably around the main railway termini. The NAB described the reports as mischievously misleading and claimed that even should they contain some element of truth, rough sleeping could no longer result from lack of available temporary accommodation. This was because the vast Camberwell male reception centre had vacancies, as did the centre for women at Southwark.[26] In 1963 an LCC survey re-established official confidence with its conclusion that on a typical night 'only' around 120 people slept rough on the capital's streets. The media claims of the previous year were again dismissed as being wildly exaggerative. Others remained uneasy that the official figures were far from telling the whole story.

The NAB pointed out in 1964 that the 1200 or so people who used the remaining 23 official reception centres on an average night was 'a very small number compared with the nearly two million people' receiving 'ordinary cash assistance' of various kinds. Nevertheless they acknowledged a need for continued concern if only because 'the number of different persons over a full year' needing assistance must be 'considerably more than the nightly figure'. They admitted ominously that 'when note was taken of those living in common lodging-houses' whose clientele partly overlapped with reception centre users, the number of 'unsettled people' could well be increasing.[27] This possibility was confirmed by a special 1966 NAB report on *Homeless Single Persons* which implied strongly that the number of homeless people was on the increase. It noted that almost one third of the 27 000 or so people in lodging houses or hostels providing accommodation either wholly or partly for homeless single persons claimed they occasionally had to sleep rough. They also calculated that a total of around '13 500 persons, almost all of whom were men, from time to time slept rough or used reception centres'.[28] Rose believes these were 'certainly underestimates' as many down-and-outs were adept at concealing themselves.[29]

By 1966 the NAB were painting a more complex canvas. Records of individuals regarding their employment, income, social circumstances and health patterns suggested 'strongly' that many men in lodging-houses, hostels, reception centres or sleeping rough had 'problems ordinarily recognized as requiring help from community services'. Most of these individuals were aged 40 or over, male and single. Many had strayed into an unsettled life 'following the disturbance in personal relationships, such as the breakdown of a marriage or the death of a parent or wife'. Answers to a questionnaire prepared for reception centre users and for people seeking assistance at the Board's local offices indicated that shortage of money was the main reason for sleeping rough. Almost 30 per cent of rough sleepers slept out in preference to alternative temporary accommodation that might be available. More than 60 per cent had no close relatives or had not been in touch with relatives for more than a year. 57 per cent of those aged under 60 were unemployed, 90 per cent had at some time in the past applied for public assistance, 21 per cent sometimes used reception centres, 41 per cent occasionally used lodging-houses, 9 per cent had been in prison during the previous two months and about 20 per cent felt in need of help and advice.[30]

NAB pen-pictures 'of some persons known to sleep rough' in 1966 included:

A man aged 60 was known to have done no regular work since 1931 when he left his wife the day after their marriage. It was not known what he did before then. Since then he had wandered the country, living by doing odd jobs such as putting coal into coal-houses for private householders. He regularly returned to one area to live in an old hen coop. He had never paid national insurance and never applied for national assistance. Efforts had been made, particularly by a doctor whose practice was local to the hen coop, to persuade him to move into a hostel or home. But he flatly refused to change his way of life. He was a well-known character in the area and regarded as a harmless person who 'never caused any trouble'.

Aged 54, a man had earlier served over 16 years in the Army. He had been discharged at the end of the 1939–45 war after being a prisoner-of-war in Germany for five years. He then wandered about Britain for some years, mostly sleeping out but sometimes using lodging-houses. He applied for national assistance all over the country, moving quickly from one place to another. On at least three occasions he was admitted to hospital for psychiatric treatment. For the past year, however, he had settled down in a hut on a relative's allotment and refused to move from it. All efforts to persuade him to move or to persuade him to obtain work had been unsuccessful. An assistance allowance was being paid to him, and another relative provided his meals.

A man of 50, of subnormal intelligence, had slept out in a small town for years. He slept in the middle of a large rhododendron bush, or in a park shelter, or when it was very cold, in the railway sheds. Physically he was in excellent health and kept himself clean.

He was well known and well liked in the locality, in which some of his relatives lived. He received a weekly assistance allowance but refused to move into any form of accommodation. 'He appeared to be very contented with his lot and to enjoy his popularity as a local figure.'[31]

Although they were not without problems, for some years the Part 3 proposals of the 1948 Act had worked reasonably well. But, as we have seen, in defiance of full employment and improved national affluence, reception centres remained uncomfortably popular relative to the figures immediately post-war. Their attractiveness became less surprising from the mid 1960s with a relentless growth in the numbers having to accept temporary accommodation from local authorities (Table 7.4). Long-term homeless families now featured among the occupants. With them came greater official readiness to reintroduce the Victorians' habit of blaming the needy for their own predicament. More echoes of

Table 7.4   Homeless persons in temporary accommodation supplied by local authorities during 1966–72 in Greater London and in the rest of England and Wales

	1966	*1969*	*1970*	*1972*
Greater London:				
Families including men	1 085	1 652	1 868	1 989
Families excluding men	509	700	952	989
Rest of England and Wales:				
Families including men	578	1 326	1 481	1 776
Families excluding men	386	526	625	694
Total persons in England and Wales:				
men, 16 years and over	1 935	3 347	3 740	4 170
women, 16 years and over	2 787	4 545	5 298	5 764
children under 5 years	4 081	5 822	6 397	6 121
children 5 years and over	4 228	7 775	8 848	9 799
Total persons	13 031	21 489	24 283	25 854

Temporary accommodation provided under Sections 21(1),(b) and 26 of *National Assistance Act 1948* and Section 1 of *Children and Young Persons Act 1963* (all local authorities).

Source: *Annual Social Trends* (HMSO), 1971 and 1973.

Poor Law attitudes by officials were heard in various cases exposed by the media. It was claimed that in some localities husband and wife had been heartlessly and needlessly kept apart. Mothers with young children were expected to have found somewhere more permanent within three months, otherwise they too became liable for eviction at which time their offspring would be taken into care.

Using tactics resonant of the 'less eligibility' clauses in the 1834 Poor Law Amendment, local authorities began to ensure that Part 3 accommodation was uncomfortably austere even when compared with the worst type of privately rented room. Newspaper articles and Jeremy Sandford's TV play *Cathy Come Home* attracted public attention to the indecent squalid overcrowding of some 'Part 3' hostels. This climate of public disquiet led to the founding of the housing campaign Shelter. In the 1970s the charity Crisis at Christmas (now Crisis) was also established to distribute blankets and to supply nourishment to down-and-outs over the festive season.[32]

Causes and effects of increased homelessness remained just as indefinable. Often the immediate cause given at the initial interview obscured the deep-seated reason why families and individuals were distressed. Family tensions seemed to be featuring ever more strongly. The following factors were all found to be exacerbating the situation:

- the 1960s 'baby boom'
- a fashionable willingness to accept 'unmarried mothers'
- an increased tendency for youngsters to leave the parental home at a younger age, and
- an increased divorce rate.

Drake and others argued that an amalgam of economic, social and personal processes encouraged homelessness at different social levels, including those of the individual, the family, the social group and of society as a whole. 'Housing and labour market factors, migration, demographic and socio-cultural factors interact(ed) to create the preconditions of ... homelessness in the mismatch of housing ... job supply and demand.'[33] Another contributory factor was growth in inner-city profit-seeking developments like office blocks and shopping centres, together with infrastructure improvements favourable to the business community. These developments caused accelerated demolition of what had been low-cost accommodation including cheap lodging houses. The building of decent affordable accommodation failed to match the bulldozers' destruction. As the private rented sector in the domestic sector shrank so the remaining landlords adopted policies which excluded low-income families. Single people and childless couples had greatest difficulty in finding accommodation with local authority allocation policies stacked against them. Drake's report, sections of which the Government found unacceptable, refuted the officially inspired hoary image of the homeless person. They were not necessarily middle-aged, disease-ridden alcoholics who had chosen to sleep rough or live in hostels or lodging houses. Drake identified three categories of person among the single homeless other than the commonly featured middle-aged dosser, namely:

- the young
- the elderly, and
- the victim of technological change.

People in each of these categories were found to have suffered severe personal difficulties before becoming locked into a downward spiral of homelessness involving medical, penal and rehabilitative institutions, refuges and the street.[34] Persons lacking a fixed abode were rarely found to be villains or wastrels cunningly sidestepping the rigours of modern living. Most were immature, unskilled and of low intelligence. Many were suffering some amalgam of physical disability, mental inadequacy, unemployment or debt.

The 1976 *Home Office Working Party Report on Vagrancy and Street Offences* had recommended the abolition of the offence 'sleeping rough' as described in the 1935 Amendment of Section 4 of the 1824 Vagrancy Act. A new offence of 'causing a nuisance by sleeping rough' was introduced. It combined the 1935 provision guarding against infection by vermin or other offensive consequences with a more general offence of lodging in circumstances such as to cause a nuisance in a public place or without the consent of the owner or occupier on private premises or land. Fortune-telling and peddling were repealed as vagrancy offences. Charges previously brought under the heading 'begging' were replaced by a new offence related to the 'concept of persistence'. The infamous 'suspected persons' clause of the 1824 Act was restricted to a person whose antecedent conduct in a public place revealed his intent to commit an 'arrestable' offence.[35] To prevent unsuitable persons from gaining additional state assistance, Section 25 of the Supplementary Benefits Act (1976) provided that those who persistently refused to maintain themselves and accepted benefits were guilty of an offence liable to three months' imprisonment or £100 fine or both.[36] This provision, in association with the availability of reception centre facilities, was aimed at motivating 'reclaimable' people towards a more settled way of life.

As noted in Chapter 5, the structure of the 1824 Act had derived from the use of the criminal law to repress those able-bodied itinerants suspected of possessing propensities to vagrancy. They were stigmatised as 'rogues, vagabonds and sturdy beggars'. The NAB from their inception had of course tended to lay aside the tradition of calling a person of no fixed abode a 'vagrant'. The appellation 'homeless single person' had been intended to identify and categorise itinerant people, whether single or effectively single, who made use of accommodation provided for transients. The approach has been likened to a 'flag of convenience' denoting not only the single homeless but a disparate body of people including:

- the tough traveller
- the casual labourer
- the itinerant navvy
- the mentally ill
- the physically disabled, and
- the old age pensioner with no family connections.

However, neither the term 'vagrant' nor the 1824 Act were expunged entirely from the legal vocabulary and it is noteworthy that its use had crept back into circulation in the title of the Home Office Working Party of 1976. For those who were homeless the nineteenth-century legislation had remained a lurking unpublicised threat. When considered appropriate the vagrancy statutes could easily be brought out of the locker ready with the traditional pejorative connotations to encompass 'persons from whom' it was believed, criminal conduct might 'be anticipated'.[37] In this way, ideas of a modern breed of social misfit were contrived as being part of an 'undeserving poor'. This procedure had close parallels with the Victorian attacks on 'the residuum, the submerged tenth and the dangerous classes'.[38] During the late 1980s, as the numbers 'sleeping out' increased, so did the use of dormant Vagrancy Acts. 573 people were prosecuted nationally in 1988 under the 1824 legislation. 500 of these were by the Metropolitan Police. Prosecutions shot up again the following year when 1396 vagrancy charges were brought in four out of the 14 Central London Magistrates Courts. Young people produced the biggest surge in numbers. The campaigning organisation End Vagrancy Act (EVA) claimed that this was because of:

- inadequate protection for mentally disturbed people under the Care in the Community programme
- new restrictions in the social security system, and
- contraction in the amount of available accommodation.

EVA contended that growth in the number sleeping rough was not the only reason for the increased use of vagrancy legislation. It was identified as being a conscious attempt to 'tidy up' particular areas of London.[39]

The enlarged responsibilities given to local authorities in the 1948 National Assistance Act regarding homeless people were in practice often interpreted as being applicable only in an emergency. They were rarely viewed as involving a genuine pressure on the authorities to provide long-term housing. Applications from homeless people were therefore normally dealt with by local welfare or social services departments. A Shelter survey in 1972 described how local authorities had supplied temporary accommodation which included old warehouses, disused police stations, army camps and decrepit tenements. Families had been cajoled to share sparse rudimentary facilities. Others had been forced to sleep in dormitories, cubicles, and police cells.[40]

The Housing (Homeless Persons) Act 1977, later to become Part III of the Housing Act 1985 was more specific about the responses expected from local authorities to homeless applicants for assistance. The 1977 Act was the first to provide homeless people with the right to a home. 'Homelessness' was defined as the lack of accommodation which could be occupied by the applicant together with any person(s) who normally resided with him or her. A person locked out of accommodation or forced to leave because of violence was classified as homeless; so were those who ordinarily resided in mobile homes or in houseboats with no place to park or moor.[41] Crucially, the Act transferred the responsibility for providing permanent accommodation for the homeless from local authority welfare departments to their housing departments. Authorities now had to satisfy a framework of the statutory duties designed to secure housing for certain homeless people 'in priority need'. Included were:

- those with dependent children or pregnant
- those with mental or physical disability

- old age pensioners
- frail people approaching retirement age, and
- those homeless from an emergency like fire or flood.[42]

It was accepted that people were homeless not only because of emergency or personal crises but because of the long-term failure of many local authorities to provide accommodation. 'Reasonable preference' had now to be given to homeless persons in allocating council houses. Housing departments must do one of four things for 'priority need' applicants, namely:

1. provide advice and appropriate assistance
2. take reasonable steps to avert homelessness
3. provide advice and temporary accommodation, or
4. provide permanent accommodation.[43]

The 1977 legislation undoubtedly represented a softening in government policy towards those homeless assessed as being in priority need. Persons not so categorised could still expect little help in finding accommodation.[44] Criticism of the Act ranged from those who saw it as a 'scroungers charter' to those who, like Lord Soper, described the retained concept of 'intentional homelessness' as 'gobbledygook'. Others pointed to what they described as its categorisational divisiveness. Some critics saw it as a return to Victorian notions of the undeserving and deserving poor.[45] Shelter provided illustrations of the many unfortunate people who fell outside the Act's 'priority need' groups and were therefore considered to be undeserving. These 'single homeless' included:

- families with children over 16 years
- battered women without children or with offspring over 16 years
- childless couples
- those under retirement age who had a handicap or disability which legally was considered insufficient to render them vulnerable
- young people aged 16 to 18 years (including those coming out of care), and
- anyone else under official retirement age.

Thompson provided case-study illustrations of homeless people excluded by the 1977 Act. She typified:

A mother aged 47 years and her daughter, aged 18 years, were homeless but found not to be in priority need. Although provided with temporary accommodation by their authority for a short period this was subsequently withdrawn and they were left literally homeless. Advice workers managed to find them a room in a hostel for women which they share with one other person. Facilities are shared with several others. No long term permanent housing options exist for them. The local authority wrote them explaining that 'present housing shortages are such that it is unlikely you will receive an offer of housing'.

Ms B was a young girl of 17 years. She left home and went to stay with a friend when she could no longer bear sexual abuse from her father. This had been going on for five years. When Ms B went to the council and applied as homeless, the council demanded evidence of proof that her father had sexually assaulted her before taking any action. 'Evidence' in practice could have meant Ms B going through the trauma of seeking to have her father arrested, in order to prove her case of need to the housing authority. It was only after a local advice and the social services department intervened that the housing authority accepted responsibility for Ms B, placing her in temporary accommodation awaiting rehousing in another borough.[46]

Unemployment in Britain, already high from the world recession sparked by the 1973 OPEC action, increased starkly from 1979. Government spending cuts meant that well over three million people were soon without a job or prospects. With local authority house-building programmes savaged as part of the Government economies, there was a dramatic worsening in the homelessness problem. A continuing difficulty for the authorities was defining 'single homeless'. By now it was a term increasingly being used synonymously with the more derogatory hereto outdated descriptions of 'vagrant, dosser or tramp'.[47] Local authorities, particularly in south-east England, found themselves forced to lodge the homeless in costly, often unsuitable, bed and breakfast (B&B) accommodation. Department of Health and Social Security (DHSS) expenditure on B&Bs rocketed nationally. From £52 million in 1979 it shot up to £380 million in 1984. Accompanying this huge escalation was the widespread official embarrassment that B&Bs all too often offered the lowest quality of living at the highest cost.[48]

For people under 26, board and lodging allowances were reduced in the 1980s with the period for which they received benefit restricted to a few weeks in any one locality. Young people were expected to be motivated by the Government's procedures and disregard the reality of nation-wide high unemployment by 'getting on their bike' and discovering work elsewhere. Memories from history began to appear on Britain's streets with the resurgence of soup kitchens catering for the hungry homeless.

The Audit Commission's *Report on Housing the Homeless* (1989) recommended local authorities to use measures which may achieve better standards of accommodation at lower cost than were B&Bs. Ideas included more low-level lettings for the homeless and reduction of the vacancy period between lettings.[49] These recommendations were in the face of evidence suggesting that the number of households accepted as homeless by local authorities in England had grown from 21 388 in 1973 to over 100 000 by 1985 and still rising (Table 7.5). Partial blame for the increase was put on changed recording procedures. Another explanation was that since 1977 local authorities had been forced to accept responsibility for a wider range of homeless people. But no manipulation or reinterpretation of the data could disguise the massive underlying upward trend.

Table 7.5 Homeless households provided with accommodation by local authorities shown in intervals of three years, 1973–94

Year	Accepted as being of 'priority need'	Other homeless found accommodation by local authorities	Total homeless households
1973			21 388
1976			33 720
1979			56 000
1982	72 373	6 000	78 373
1985	102 000	9 000	111 000
1988	123 600	12 600	136 200
1991	160 900	9 600	170 500
1994	135 300	8 300	143 600

Sources: (a) 1973 and 1982 data for England and Wales, 1976 for England only, and 1985, 1988, 1991 and 1994 data for Great Britain. Data from annual publication *Social Trends* (HMSO), and (b) 'priority need' as defined in the *Housing Act 1977*.

In the population as a whole, the number of one-person households had greatly increased since the Second World War. In 1961 they had been only 11 per cent of households. By 1987 single households were 25 per cent of the total and still rising. Demographic changes like longevity, higher divorce rates and marital separations had each contributed to the number of single-person households. Other factors involved personal misfortunes like abusive family background, educational inadequacy, poor health, unemployment and low insecure income. Those larger hostels that remained for single homeless people were now being viewed as having retained an unacceptable aura of institutionalisation. They were seen to be too large and too impersonal, even of forbidding appearance. Residents had scant privacy and little choice as to when they might eat or even watch TV. Through not being required to shop, to cook or to participate in the myriad of other everyday tasks that make up modern living, residents had progressively become deskilled and worldly naive. Because large hostels provided no security of tenure they reinforced a transient lifestyle on those staying there. Once trapped in such a 'circuit of homelessness' it became increasingly difficult to gain access to mainstream housing.[50] Tony Wilkinson has described his own humiliating encounters with some reception centre staff who considered it their duty to shame the poor and 'frighten them out of destitution'. He had to endure squalor and violence. In one of the larger hostels staff padlocked fire doors even though they were aware drunks habitually smoked in bed.[51]

Under pressure from the Campaign for the Homeless and Rootless (CHAR), Government looked towards Housing Associations and to charities with hostel accommodation such as the Salvation Army, the Simon Community, the Cyrenians and St Mungo's. The small hostels operated by such organisations were seen to be more attractive and advantageous to the homeless than had been the impersonal reception centres. The few that remained were renamed 'resettlement units' with the intention of soon phasing them out as part of the new 'care in the community programme'. Initially, there was general acceptance for what on paper appeared to be an imaginative and encouraging approach. Soon there was disenchantment. Stern criticism of the concept pointed to such inadequate funding that the theoretical scheme had scarcely been put into practice. Commentators now decried deinstitutionalisation as having been nothing but a cynical cost-cutting exercise. Vulnerable members of the community were repeatedly being found floundering in the uncertainties of bureaucratic confusion.[52] Inadequate alternative accommodation led to human tragedies and financial scandals. Stories about corrupt landlords featured regularly in the news media. Stories were rife about offensive overcrowding, lack of sanitation, vermin, glue-sniffing, prostitution and personal intimidation. People suffering from a miscellany of emotional or physical handicaps were being forced to accept inappropriate accommodation whether provided commercially, charitably or by the local authority.[53] The modern vagrant's life under the guise of street homelessness may have had certain differences from that of his predecessors but it had remained, for the authorities, a frustrating intractable problem but not one that featured highly among their spending priorities.

Modifications to the social security structure in 1985 and again in 1988 further eroded benefits to the homeless and in particular to youngsters.[54] Sixteen and seventeen year olds, other than certain exceptionally vulnerable groups, lost entitlement to income support from September 1988. It was replaced with a youth training offer.[55] From 1989, people living in board and lodging accommodation could no longer claim a DHSS allowance to offset the high costs. They now received only income support at the ordinary rate with nothing additional for food and heating bills.

The high unemployment levels of the 1980s and 1990s reinforced earlier indications that homelessness was linked with joblessness. This was especially apparent with school leavers and young people generally. The DoE's 1977–80 survey had shown 44 per cent unemployment amongst the homeless aged under 25 years. Ten years later, research at London's Centrepoint hostel revealed 87 per cent of their clients were out of work with 42 per cent never having had a full-time job. Evidence of this kind cut no ice with Whitehall. By 1989 there were 5000 fewer beds available for the homeless than there had been 10 years earlier.[56] More and more people were sleeping rough, squatting, or living in grubby dilapidated 'hotels'. DoE data show that the number of households accepted as homeless annually had increased unrelentingly through the 1980s (Table 7.6).[57]

By 1991 there were 170 500 homeless households. Numbers then improved while remaining embarrassingly high. Haggling continued about why so many more people remained homeless but few questioned that an increased number of youngsters had found themselves trapped in a Catch-22 situation. Many were unable to obtain work without a fixed address but were unable to secure a home without a job.[58] The great majority (80 to 85 per cent) of households officially accepted as

Table 7.6 Homeless households found accommodation by local authorities. Reasons for homelessness shown as percentage of total number

	England 1975	England 1976	GB 1981	GB 1986	GB 1989	England, Wales, North Ireland 1994
Parents/relatives/friends no longer able/willing to accommodate, %	29	26	42	40	44	33
Breakdown of relationship with partner, %	11	12	17	20	20	21
Court Order/mortgage default or rent arrears, %	11	11	11	13	12	10
Loss of private rented dwelling/loss of service tenancy/other reasons, %	49	51	30	27	24	36
Total households found accommodation in thousands	34	34	83	118	147	143

Notes: 1975 and 1976 data for England; 1981, 1986 and 1989 for Great Britain; 1994 data percentages for England, Wales and Northern Ireland but 1994 total of households is for Britain.

Sources: *Social Trends* publications.

homeless were either families with young children or with a pregnancy. Most of the parents were themselves young. A broadly accepted guideline statistic is that the grand total of homeless persons is roughly three times the number of homeless households. Using this assumption, during the early 1990s in excess of half a million adults and children were officially being recognised as homeless in England and Wales.

Campaigners for the homeless complained repeatedly that access to the limited amount of new accommodation was mainly by referral and targeted at specific groups. Greve has argued that in the 1990s 'structural factors' involving the housing market, employment opportunities, wage levels and demographic change all contributed directly and indirectly to homelessness. Consequently, people were 'unable to find or retain housing at rents or prices they can afford and with security of tenure'.[59]

The uneven distribution of homelessness across the country was illustrated in a 1982–3 survey by the Chartered Institute of Public Finance and Accountancy. This covered 350 out of the 401 local authorities in England and Wales. It showed that in spite of the growing seriousness of the problem, the average annual net expenditure on attempts to rectify homelessness totalled £578 per thousand of the population, that is less than 60p per person or around one penny per week. Reflecting the uneven spread of homelessness across the country, net expenditure per thousand population was £3737 in Inner London boroughs compared with £315 for English non-metropolitan districts. There were more than six acceptances of homeless households per thousand households in Inner London. Elsewhere in England there were fewer than two registered homeless households for every thousand.[60]

To counter the charge that legislative restrictions had contributed to the increase in the number of homeless single people, the Department of the Environment (DoE) surveyed single homelessness in the early 1990s. They investigated 1853 people across England. Interviewees were living either in hostels or B&B accommodation provided for the single homeless, or were sleeping rough. They were getting what nourishment they could from day centres, soup kitchens and from begging. Most were unemployed men, many long-term. A substantial number had lost what experience they ever might have had of meaningful paid employment. Nearly half of the interviewees were still 'looking for work'. Studies of homelessness in the 1990s, such as that by Hutson and Liddiard and that by Crane, provided insights into contemporary problems suffered by young people:

Gareth (24) explained 'people won't employ you if you haven't got an address, so you've got to have an address before you can get employed. It's one big circle you know. You've got to have an address to get employed and you can't get an address unless you've got the money to move in'.

Robert (24) pointed out that 'when you go through life and you get a bit of work here and a job there, it's very complicated. The DSS (Benefits Agency) runs it as if it's simple – you're either working or you're not. It's not like that. All you end up doing is full-time unemployment'.

Stewart (21) when asked where he had been living in the previous few months, answered, 'On the streets basically ... I'd nip on the buses and sleep on there and I'd get kicked off there at four in the morning. I'd just be wandering around. I was in a hell of a state like, rundown'.

Gaynor (24) when asked what was the hardest thing about sleeping rough replied: 'Not being able to have a wash and clean clothes, going without food, getting attacked and things like that, ... I mean I got raped'.

'I walked into B&B with my partner but walked out a single parent. It causes it. When we were in B&B we didn't have a job – no one will give you a job without a proper address. Since I've got a little part-time address. I can get a bank account. I can do anything I want because I've got an address. That's the most important thing for someone to have'.[61]

Critics pointed to how the health of rough-sleepers was being aggravated by their living conditions. Many were not receiving treatment even though they had access to a doctor.[62] Government concern was sufficient to prompt the DoE to allocate nearly £100 million for expenditure spread over the three years 1990–3 on a rough-sleepers initiative (RSI). It was intended to eliminate the need for people to sleep rough. Funding was included for advice and for outreach work. New emergency hostel places became available with a range of temporary and permanent accommodation. This was being provided for 'several thousand homeless people, most of whom had a history of rough sleeping'. The DoE claimed that the initiative brought 'a significant reduction' in the number of people sleeping rough in central London. At the end of the three-year trial in 1993 the RSI was continued for a similar period. This was 'both to offer help to the remaining people sleeping rough and to provide for the continuing flow of newly homeless people'. It was accepted that some of those still sleeping rough needed psychiatric help and specialised accommodation if they were to have a real chance of being successfully resettled.[63] The campaigning group *Single Homelessness in London* (*SHiL*) analysed RSI data and information about the 1990 Department of Health Homeless Mentally Ill (HMI) initiative. Both schemes had brought improvement but much remained to be done.

National homelessness figures from Shelter for 1994 suggested that, although the RSI had brought some reduction from the 1991 peak, the plight of Britain's homeless people remained appalling. The 146 119 households still accepted by local authorities as being homeless represented around 419 400 individuals. Even these stunning figures were not themselves all-embracing. They failed to include the tens of thousands of single homeless not accepted as being priority cases. SHiL claimed that in 1995 there were still 45 000 single homeless in London alone. These included those in temporary accommodation as well as the number sleeping out. In addition there were the 'hidden' homeless including at least 32 000 single people in need of permanent accommodation but temporarily sponging space from friends or relatives. SHiL were concerned that from 1995–6 the supply of RSI move-on housing would diminish. They identified the need for more well-equipped long-stay hostels capable of providing specialist care and high levels of support to people who had got into the habit of sleeping out.[64] The RSI was again repeated for a further three years from 1996. With the most recent extension, there was the specific innovation of money becoming available to improve the condition of provincial rough-sleepers. The Simon Community's head count on the morning of 1 November 1997 revealed 1748 rough-sleepers in Central London, including those in shelters, an increase of 215 on figures collected on 21 March 1997. People actually sleeping on the London streets were said to number 358 on 1 November 1997, an increase of 77 over the previous March.[65]

It is clear that the homelessness expressed by the nocturnal occupation of urban streets is but an indicator, akin to an iceberg's tip, of a much more deepseated malaise of poverty and despair in modern Britain. As the millennium approaches the world's 'developed' societies share the dilemma of why embarrassingly large numbers of dispossessed people seem to be an inherent adjunct of an economic system which abandons them while increasing the growing material wealth of the majority. Jeanne Moore claimed that in the mid 1990s London had a shanty town as large as might be expected in notorious Latin American cities, but it is hidden. She pointed to the media's misleading obsession of focusing merely on the more extreme types of homeless typified by those living rough on the streets. This camouflaged the plight of the greater number of people existing in hostels, shelters and other temporary accommodation who also lacked a secure lifestyle.[66]

Rossi's study of social conditions in the USA provides typical profiles of the homeless. They showed that only very few were not suffering from either endemic unemployment, underemployment, chronic mental illness, alcoholism or poor health.[67] Many had brushed with the criminal justice system and were struggling to gain minimal levels of social support. The street homeless make up a substantial part of the so-called 'underclass'. This term has been used for years by sociologists like Giddens and Runciman to describe marginalised minorities in western societies. As discussed in the introductory chapter to this volume the appellation 'underclass' has more recently been adopted with a more pejorative slant by a group of social theorists serving a different political agenda. During the 1980s and 1990s, as the number of people sleeping on the streets of western democracies has escalated so Charles Murray and others have described what they allege is a pathological manifestation of a dependency culture nurtured by misguided profligate welfare policies.[68] It is seen as being quite understandable for young men and women to seek public welfare benefits whenever they are available. At the same time it is argued that when youngsters do accept these benefits they are not exercising the same moral righteousness expected by their forebears. According to this right-wing social perspective, the people who wallow easily in acceptance of social benefits lose sight of the fact that such gifts erode the responsibilities of parenthood because welfare handouts fail to encourage an enduring relationship with a companion of the opposite sex. Abandoned women with children allegedly become self-reliant, domineering and mutually supportive. Without an adult male figure they are unable to protect their children from the seemingly alluring street life that promises short-term excitement while disguising the likely concomitant long-term misery.[69] Murray and his supporters contend that persons without a permanent home struggle for so long at a miserable socio-economic level that their chance of participation in the labour market becomes shattered. The physical existence of the street homeless becomes dependent on their receiving external material assistance for which they can offer no payment other than, at best, gratitude. This individualistic perspective points to how most street dwellers show indications of having rejected western culture including its association with the intrinsic value of hard work, lawfulness and the nurturing of a conventional nuclear family. As people reject their social responsibilities, the less they are willing to study or work and the more they become side-tracked by society's mainstream. Prolonged state dependency allegedly creates a culture of social isolation, geographic concentration and eccentric behaviour bred on an attitude of submissive expectation. Destigmatisation of social benefit payments has meant that it has become socially acceptable in poor communities to be without a job. The street homeless are therefore seen to be enticed by free social provision to act on misleading incentives and on what eventually are self-defeating values and degrading beliefs.[70]

British governments in the 1990s have clearly been influenced by the foregoing hypotheses. This has led them to the understanding that welfare payments involve the great danger of creating a breed of scroungers. Despite widespread opposition from charitable organisations formed to assist derelict people, the Government pushed ahead with the 1996 Housing Bill. Local authorities in England and Wales were no longer bound to give homeless households priority on their housing list. Instead the homeless were directed to 'suitable' private sector accommodation rather than the local authorities themselves having to provide social housing. A Shelter report claimed to expose the hazards of the new Bill. It alleged that the private rented sector had provided 'the most expensive housing, in the worst condition, with least security and often with unscrupulous landlords'. According to Shelter, if homeless households were not given priority when social housing was allocated they would continue to experience the problems associated with homelessness such as debt, insecurity, poor health, difficulty in finding work, disrupted education and so on.[71] The result would therefore be counterproductive towards any plan to make homeless people socially responsible and financially independent.

British governments during the closing decades of the twentieth century have been comfortable in the knowledge that many members of the public are content to brand the homeless as social parasites. Honest citizens are also not discouraged from harbouring the suspicion that rough-sleepers turn to criminality immediately the need arises. Prosecutions for begging in London increased fourfold in the five years to 1994. Overwhelmingly, those who were arrested were homeless. Even the resurrection of the 1824 Vagrancy Act, with its catch-all provisions, was not considered by John Major's Government to be an adequate control mechanism for rough-sleepers. The 1994 Criminal Justice and Public Order Act was introduced to criminalise many of the activities associated with homelessness such as travelling and squatting.[72] This legislation faced strong opposition in both Houses of Parliament. An alliance of outside bodies protested against its infringement of human rights. Nevertheless, the Act received the Royal Assent in November 1994 relatively unscathed. *The Spectator* considered the new legislation to be repressive and unacceptable.[73] In the Parliamentary election year 1997, the New Labour leader Tony Blair showed signs of empathising with Tory initiatives. He favoured 'zero tolerance' policing, was proud that he never gave to beggars and believed it appropriate to be intolerant of street dwellers.[74]

While politicians present a common front in their resolve not to be soft on social scroungers, miserable conditions are still being endured in British common lodging houses, bedsitters, local authority and privately run hostels. Sleeping on the streets is broadly recognised as an overt indicator of destitution accompanied by obvious dangers to public health and personal well-being. Less obvious are the threats and disadvantages posed by living in an illegal squat, being crowded with a number of strangers into a badly equipped old hostel, or trying to bring up children in a cramped B&B hotel.[75] Unless those involved are suffering some form of mental affliction or other handicap that makes them feel socially inadequate, it is difficult to believe that they can find such conditions other than distressing.[76] However, the homeless continue to be widely dismissed socially as being undeserving of sympathy let alone support. Many among the public remain convinced that the plight of the homeless is generally rooted in their own irresponsible behaviour. Greve discounts such thinking as present-day 'myths' used by the 'prejudiced' in their attempts to explain away modern-day homelessness. He contends that it is bizarre for people to mistakenly harbour the idea that thousands of pleasure-bent young people flood constantly towards London and the south-east. The suggestion that teenage girls intentionally become pregnant to jump the council housing queue is similarly disregarded.[77]

Tory policies on the homeless in the 1990s have been based on the strategy of attempting to induce in them a more responsible personal commitment by the curtailment of what they considered to have been profligate welfare payments. Specific homeless groups, like single parents and the young, have been pinpointed as those whose participation in society would improve subsequent to their being taught to recognise and obey the dictates of authority. The tactic is to methodically inculcate in them the idea that their receipt of welfare benefits does not exempt them from accepting social responsibility and as such they are no different from other members of society. Consequently, much in the way of the Wisconsin model of workfare advocated by Lawrence Mead, claimants for benefit will not be permitted to shirk unpopular lowly paid jobs said to be essential for the efficient functioning of the community.[78] In being made to re-engage with the work process, those who as street homeless are social outcasts will, so it is argued, be better equipped to establish themselves in society. While in opposition New Labour raised few objections to the Conservative Government's procedures. Some considered that this was merely an electoral tactic aimed at gaining middle-class approval, but once in power Labour's New Deal retained strong similarities. It pledged to get young people off benefits and into work and was clearly influenced by the workfare model. 18 to 24 year olds unemployed for six months while in receipt of the Jobseeker's allowance would lose their benefit if they failed to take up one of four options;

- substantial employment with a company
- up to 12 months full-time study
- six months with an environmental task force, or
- six months voluntary sector work.

In his 1998 New Year message Prime Minister Blair billed his New Deal as the most radical reform of the Welfare State since the Second World War. When taken in conjunction with the Government's promised repeal of the offensive clauses in the 1996 Housing Act there are hopeful signs of better times ahead for Britain's homeless. If Labour's 'war against poverty' results in a return to the virtual elimination of homelessness as experienced fifty years ago Blair's New Deal will justifiably be heralded as a great social advance.

8 Conclusion

It is not to die, or even to die of hunger, that makes a man wretched; many men have died; all men must die ... but it is to live miserable we know not why; to work sore and yet gain nothing; to be heart-worn, weary yet isolated, unrelated, girt in with a cold universal laissez-faire.
Thomas Carlyle.[1]

The involvement of governments in the condition of the homeless, or the vagrant poor as they have usually been pejoratively described in history, has varied from occasional sympathetic support to the more familiar response of punitive legislative action. We have seen how repeatedly through the centuries emergent disciplinary laws were directed against the vagrant poor and phased closely with an increase in their number. This increase has itself similarly been strongly related to wider social, economic, political or demographic changes. There is clear indication that official responses to people without resources or a home have been neither haphazard nor accidental. As a matter of routine, governments have legislated to constrain the spatial movement of a diverse range of people usually sharing the characteristic of being homeless but bundled together for legal purposes under the catch-all appellation 'vagrant'.

Regardless of who through history has initiated the investigation into the types of person described as vagrant, they invariably show that most share the misfortune of having no fixed abode but are not hardened villains. They are inclined to be people without a job or prospects.[2] Often they are distraught, hungry, poorly educated, lacking in skills and although demotivated keen for the opportunity to improve themselves. Nevertheless, through history when owing to factors outside of their control the number of poor itinerants increased, central government has responded promptly and repressively. The factors which at that particular time were causing more of their citizens to wander around poverty-stricken without a permanent base were laid aside. From the Middle Ages it became more and more common for the legislature to blame the numerical escalation squarely on the itinerants themselves. This official attitude was made more publicly palatable by first concentrating on the unpleasant aspects of the hardened traveller minority who had brushed with the law. Then attention was drawn to how, influenced by the minority, the larger numbers of itinerants might collectively imperil public order and even become a financial burden on ratepayers. This fabricated threat to the stability of the state was then routinely made the excuse for ever harsher legislation. The foregoing repressive sequence has occurred again and again in British history. The legislature have repeatedly attempted to control the mobility of very poor people while doing little to alleviate their distress. Time after time, the blocking of perceived loopholes in existing statutes has dampened vagrancy growth and often reduced their number for a while. With equal certainty, after a few years, additional social, economic, political or population pressures have again forced the vagrancy numbers upwards.

Early medieval vagrancy legislation was ostensibly introduced to limit the spread of virulent diseases. There was also the less publicised reason that job opportunities for workers surviving the epidemics were enhanced by mobility. Such was typically the case in the aftermath of plague. The Black Death in the late 1340s, a particularly serious visit of the bubonic pestilence, so decimated the working population in some parishes as to change the employer:employee relationship in the latter's favour. Labourers found themselves in a rare position of strength. They were able to bargain about both wages and work conditions. If their master would not heed their demands they could now venture to another plague-savaged locality where a labourless employer might be more amenable to them. The landowners' need to stamp out this uncommon and, for them, unacceptable situation prompted the Statute of Labourers (1351). This bound workers geographically more tightly to their own parish and economically to a lower wage than they might have gained by moving elsewhere. Additional legislation, such as that sanctioned by Edward III and another by his successor Richard II tightened the confinement of the labourer. Spatial limits were imposed on impotent people pleading for alms. Painful physical punishments were administered, particularly to the able-bodied traveller asking others for help towards his subsistence. The second half of the fourteenth century introduced a battery of another eight similarly restrictive laws. Taken together they proved adequate for the next hundred years to satisfy landowners' and other employers' needs for constraining the movement of labour.

In 1495 early Tudor government through Henry VII signalled additional sharpening of the vagrancy laws. The end of the Wars of the Roses had cast redundant retainers on to an unresponsive labour market. With their widened horizons and unwanted military skills they were not easily absorbed into the local economy from which they had originated. 'Destitute of service' many turned to vagrancy rather than starve.[3] By restricting labour mobility and begging by idle vagabonds and similar 'suspected' persons, the 1495 legislation was a precursor of the sentiments eventually formulated in the 1824 Vagrancy Act.

Tudor and most succeeding dynasties persistently amplified constraining statutes when factors like a downturn in the economy or a poor harvest prompted labourers to look outside their parish for work. Each emergent law assumed that any man honestly seeking work could always find it within his own parish. Therefore, by implication, anyone even contemplating employment elsewhere must potentially be a rogue or a vagabond. Henry VIII acted strongly against what was seen as the threat from a growing number of idle vagabonds and beggars. Henry's firmness became the touchstone for his successors whenever they considered it appropriate to again dampen vagrancy numbers and to limit the general mobility of the poor.

Increasingly, under the blanket designation 'vagrant', it became customary to place the onus on penniless travellers for the 'continual thefts, murders and other heinous offences' allegedly increasing to such a dangerous level as to jeopardise the security of the nation. Integral to what became the standard form of legal package was an intensification of deterrent penalties. During the sixteenth century this included public humiliation, flogging, stigmatic amputation and imprisonment. Between 1530 and 1597 there were 13 new statutes involving vagrancy. These culminated in the 39 Elizabeth Act (1597). This law and its confirming legislation four years later, applied to an even more multifarious range of traveller all bundled legislatively together. Rogues, vagabonds and vagrants were however consistently maintained as the principal foci for public attention. Like many of its predecessors, Elizabeth's 39th Act was said to be initiated by the perceived threat that the increased number of mobile poor would endanger public order. As on other occasions, the expansion of the itinerant population was related to widespread work shortage, escalating grain prices, exceptional distress from poor crops and militia discarded after the Spanish wars. A further wave of economic depression during the 1620s in the proto-industries together with price inflation reflecting disastrous harvests found Privy Councillors exhorting local officials towards more rigorous application of Elizabeth's legislation. Cromwell's Civil War victory led to redundant soldiers from both armies tramping the nation's roads. They joined the distraught agricultural labourers already cast adrift by adverse harvests. The

Commonwealth legislature responded, as had their predecessors, with restrictive ordinances. Now they were against 'wandering, idle, dissolute' people.

Restoration of the Monarchy brought no abatement of pressure on the vagrant. Charles II was quick to introduce the seminal 1662 Settlement and Removal Acts. He used the excuse that they merely corrected the Puritan inability to prevent the labourer from straying outside his settlement parish. With the 1662 legislation constraint on the mobility of the ordinary Englishman intensified. No longer were the majority of citizens permitted to seek work elsewhere without the risk of being treated as a vagrant, being punished and then ignominiously shipped 'home'. Various adjustments to the settlement and removal legislation followed incessantly. Most merely further clouded the geographical horizons of the common people and many repressed them by ever more 'effectual punishment'. Late seventeenth-century and eighteenth-century statutes were characteristically preceded by reflections on the anticipated social dangers from increased vagrancy. Forgotten in typical fashion were the deficient harvests which instigated George III's Act of 1792. It recommended that all rogues, vagabonds and vagrants, three designations the local magistrate could expand upon elastically to include whichever poor stranger he chose, should be whipped or sent to a House of Correction before despatch back to where they legally belonged. Repressive law makers were activated yet again when the economic slump after the Napoleonic Wars meant a throng of unemployed civilian tramps and Irish immigrants were predictably boosted by discarded soldiers and sailors.

Disquiet about the vagrant poor whom ratepayers had been conditioned to condemn as work-shy loafers, culminated in the crucial 5 George IV Act of 1824. It called for the more effective suppression of vagrancy and for the punishment of all idle and disorderly persons, rogues and vagabonds. The Act militated against a wide range of homeless and rootless people, now billed by the authorities as potentially dangerous misfits. The mere 'suspicion' that any may harbour criminal intent was now sufficient to have them criminally charged as a vagrant. When in the 1880s economic decline prompted a resurgence of tramping, the Casual Poor Act of 1882 was on cue to intensify life's difficulties for travellers using Poor Law casual wards. It extended their minimum workhouse detention to two nights.

Early in the twentieth century, government concern about the increased number of wayfarers flooding the roads after the South

African wars led to the LGB Departmental Committee being formed in 1904 charged with examining all aspects of vagrancy. Their recommendations two years later helped to stem the rate of increase but it took the improved economy and military recruitment prior to the First World War before traveller numbers really plummeted. After the war, tramping as a lifestyle expanded rapidly, fuelled by a collapsed economy and discarded militia. Massive unemployment in the 1920s and 1930s popularised Poor Law casual wards and packed charitable hostels. Then, following the established pattern, the Second World War saw 'vagrancy' numbers evaporate when the nation called.

The end of hostilities in 1945 heralded an exception to the sequence by which Britain's roads might have been expected to be deluged with disillusioned ex-servicemen. This break with the past was helped by a relatively sound economy, a more watchful and enlightened electorate, a better-educated workforce, an increased welfare consciousness and an acute awareness of promises made to returning heroes that the unemployment miseries of the 1920s and 1930s would not be repeated. Globally, lessons had been learned between the World Wars from the moribund condition of the international economy. Widespread autarky had brought prolonged seemingly irremovable domestic strife across many countries until preparations for 1939–45 hostilities increased employment. There was also a feeling among the Allies that without strong western economies, communism could sweep from the Soviet Union across Europe once fascism had been vanquished. Imaginative action was taken to stimulate global multilateral trade. New international institutions like the IMF, IBRD and GATT facilitated post-war reconstruction. Millions of dollars were poured into Europe by the USA from July 1945, first through UNRRA and then with Marshall Aid. The demand for labour in Britain was soon insatiable indigenously. Empire immigrants were welcomed, mainly from the West Indies. For more than twenty years after 1945, sleeping rough seemed to have been banished as a relic of history.

Then from the 1970s, public attitudes were methodically averted from the possible advantages they might have accrued from welfare statism. The potential benefits of returning to laissez-faire policies were broadcast. Government found it easier to disregard the high level of homelessness and street dwelling which thirty years earlier would have registered with the public as being morally unacceptable. Decline in manufacturing industry, reduction in the availability of manual jobs, erosion of the apprentice system and a widening gap between rich and poor, all contributed to there being hundreds of thousands of people in Britain classified as homeless during the 1980s. Many more also lacked a permanent abode but failed to meet the official criteria for homelessness.

As outlined in the introductory chapter, there are basically two competing explanatory models as to why throughout our history there have remained people at the bottom of the social scale grouped for official convenience under derogatory terms like vagrant, street dweller and underclass. One model assumes failure of the individual and weakness in their character as being the main cause. The second spotlights unfairness in national economic structure and in society's deficiency in supplying to the underprivileged a suitable education, employment and home. The first model, based on the inherent character of the human being, explains the condition of today's homeless, much as they would vagrants of the past, in terms of their adaptive weaknesses. These include; citizenship shortcomings, criminal attitudes, disregard of family values, genetic debilities, loutish irresponsibility, drug dependency, single parenting by design, inadequate or negligent parenting, idleness and willingness to depend on hand-outs, whether from state or charity. In contrast, the structuralist or environmentalist perspective blames the plight of the homeless on factors like; social deprivation, ecological bias, environmental distortions, ethnic divisions, ghettoes, illiteracy, limited education, inadequate social services, low pay, poor housing, poor security rights, disablement, unemployment, part-time work and inner city decline. Because the debate between individualism and environmentalism remains vibrant it is useful to examine briefly the reasoning behind both models in attempting to explain why today there are again such disturbingly high numbers of people 'of no fixed abode' in a wealthy democracy like Britain.

To explain the condition of the homeless, individualists point to weaknesses in a person's character. They describe the well-intentioned though mistaken diligence with which western governments have scrupulously supplied the poor with their bodily needs. They explain how even the lowest level of social benefits now provided to the poor ensures that no British citizen need suffer ill-health from deficient diet or from adverse climate. Life for today's street homeless is seen to be incomparably softer than the subsistence poverty still suffered by the teeming millions of undernourished people in lesser developed countries. The contrast can be seen as having provided western governments with an excuse for their own domestic inadequacies. Their own constituents are fed the comforting knowledge that the material value of western social welfare is far beyond the wildest dreams of the average worker in peaceful 1990s India let alone any one of the miserable hordes of homeless refugees regularly drifting across Africa.

As the end of the twentieth century approaches, street dwellers have found public attitudes hardened against them. During the last two decades moral principles akin to those of Victorian Mendicity Societies resurfaced in Britain and the USA, encouraged by right-wing social theorists. On both sides of the Atlantic politicians have applauded Charles Murray's affirmation that the work ethic has been savaged by the careless irresponsibility of state welfare.[4] President Reagan supported such concepts wholeheartedly. He explained to the American public that the homeless were in their predicament 'largely by choice'.[5] The street homeless were seen not as passive victims of faulty economic structures but as active agents logically pursuing their own best interests. This undesirable situation has allegedly been reached in a social climate swamped by sweat-free assistance provided by a misguided state and by equally mischievously advised voluntary sources. Welfare payments are said to have undermined the motivating ethic of self-help and nurtured a culture of poverty. Government provision of social benefits is perceived as having provided not a social safety-net but a dangerous snare to further erode the homeless person's shattered morals. The style of life to which the long-term homeless are subjected is seen to be self-perpetuating. In a society where jobs are often dull, badly paid and difficult to obtain, it is easier to hang around with equally demotivated peers knowing that state welfare will preserve your idleness and strengthen your disregard for your dependants.

Conservative governments in Britain have concurred with these ideas. They did not want their grassroots supporters to believe that they fostered undue sympathy, let alone misguided feather-bedding, for homeless individuals who lacked the guts to make a success of their own lives. Politicians and right-wing sociologists conducted a chorus glorifying the idea that state assistance has poisoned the moral fibre of the nation. Hard work and adherence to 'family values' would be the essential elements in any strategy to get the 'underclass' to rehabilitate themselves in society. The readiness to cast the street homeless as 'undeserving' resurfaced. In 1994, the Prime Minister John Major believed street dwellers to be offensive 'eyesores'. David Willetts, Conservative MP and 'thinker' was impressed by American research suggesting that job prospects depended more on church membership than on education or economic status.[6]

There were also ominous signs for the homeless that should they gain power the Labour Party would perpetuate the attitudes of the Conservative administration. In 1995 Shadow Home Secretary Jack Straw expressed little sympathy for street dwellers and was particularly disenchanted by the 'aggressive begging by squeegee merchants, winos and addicts'.[7] Frank Field, Labour MP, former Director of the Child Poverty Action Group (CPAG) and Social Security Minister in the 1998 New Labour Government has readily acknowledged unfairness in the nation's economic structures. At the same time he points accusingly at a new generation of 'benefit cheats', including those among the homeless who are rotting the moral fibre of the nation.

Adherence to individualistic views explains why late twentieth-century governments have cared little for homeless families generally and still less for street dwellers. This disregard explains why many citizens today find it easy to ignore the miserable human flotsam occupying our urban pavements. Nagging worries a passerby may have about being oblivious to a street dweller who may genuinely need help are corrected by tabloid outpourings. They depict the homeless as layabouts with stories of how they make fortunes from begging and selling *The Big Issue*. Any public concerns about the condition of destitute people are mollified by comforting allegations that those in poverty largely revel in their condition. They are routinely rebuked and ostracised for being dirty, smelly, lazy, socially undesirable, a financial burden on society, a blot on the environment and a disturbance to social equilibrium. The homeless poor are bracketed with devious work-dodgers enjoying a carefree life while the employed majority endure the personal stresses of modern employment structures. The spread of these attitudes serves the same purpose for the modern legislature as did the crude coupling in bygone times of the innocent work-searching labourer with the hardened vagrant. The reality that the number of homeless people changes because of overpowering exogenous socio-economic factors is largely spurned.

Structuralists and environmentalists reject individualistic attitudes including what they see as their misleading comparisons between our modern-day rough-sleepers and the poverty-stricken in less-developed countries. While appalled that wealthy nations do so little to improve the condition of those experiencing desperate poverty in poorer countries overseas, they claim that the plight of Britain's street homeless can be assessed only in relation to the social environment in which they find themselves. Poverty, it is argued, must be viewed as a condition shaped by a particular economic, social and spatial context.

Rapid technological advance has encouraged new expectations and aspirations for people in the industrialised world. It has heightened mankind's potential and for most westerners has made for a more comfortable and longer healthier life. However, much of this qualitative improvement is only available to those able to participate in a contemporary society which excludes the homeless poor by disinterest. In the environmentalist view, a country that makes technological progress without the commensurate educational and social advance of all its citizens guarantees divisive sectional impoverishment. Harrington has pointed to how 'one bowl of rice in a society where all other people have half a bowl may well be a sign of achievement and intelligence; it may spur a person to act and fulfil his human potential. To have five bowls of rice in a society where the majority have a decent balanced diet, is a tragedy'.[8] Psychologically based explanations of extreme poverty have been developed which take account of the disadvantaged individual's own perspective on his society without necessarily blaming the person for their condition. Moore offers a 'place theory' in which the heterogeneity of Britain's homeless population and an individual's experience is considered 'within a particular physical and social context'.[9] Psychosomatically induced distress and illness among today's vagrant poor is compounded by the relentless ubiquitous advertising of domestic comforts enjoyed by most westerners.

Decision makers in industrialised nations are criticised for their insensitivity to the suffering of those at the base of the social pyramid. Late twentieth-century individualistic interpretations of poverty and its causes are viewed as cynical, peripheral, judgemental and ill-advised. Many recent policies aimed at determining what is best for the homeless are denounced for their mistaken tendency to place unwarranted emphasis on physiological needs to the exclusion of the educational, social and psychological. Officially constructed poverty-lines tend to reflect class-biased subjective judgements as to what are 'necessary' contemporary human requirements and which other elements of modern living are 'unnecessary' luxuries. By the failure to include opinions of the poor in such formulations they are seen as a modern version of the historical tradition whereby ruling classes consistently projected their mores and values selectively downwards regardless of how unsuitable they were for the recipients.

Structuralists dismiss the concept which condemns street dwellers to be part of a permanent underclass with inherent generationally transmitted inadequacies. The very idea is seen as a heartless illusion. They point to how a useful role in the structure of society is quickly found for such people whenever there is a labour demand from the national economy or from the armed forces. Whereas it is agreed that self-reliance is a commendable personal characteristic to be encouraged from each citizen, the point is made that people at the bottom of the social ladder like the street homeless usually lack adequate education, employment or a home. Without these attributes it is much more difficult to nurture and develop confidence in one's own ability.

Charities working for the homeless empathise with structuralist explanations of their condition. In the hope of engendering favourable public response, Shelter, Centrepoint, CHAR, Crisis, St Mungo's and The Big Issue Foundation publish pen-pictures of typical contemporary street and hostel dwellers with explanations of why they are in such a state of desperation. These personal dossiers of individual hardship add weight to earlier studies. They demonstrate that most of today's rough-sleepers would welcome the opportunity for personal advancement. Unfortunately, they lack the essential educational grounding and the modern skill requirements that potential employers need. These are unlikely to be acquired without specific positive professional guidance. As a result of the Conservative Government's illusion of benefits from the de-institutionalisation of psychiatric units, an unusually high proportion of today's street dwellers suffer forms of mental illness likely to shatter self-confidence and deepen depressive tendencies.

The inherent social injustice of competitive western democracies is perceived by structuralists as being the root cause of homelessness. They see it as shameful for there to be widespread complacency in western governments about their failure to provide a decent life for each of their citizens. They challenge the soundness of a society in which a favoured majority grows materially richer while a substantial minority remain progress-immune. Townsend showed that in the ten years to 1989 the real annual income of the average UK household increased from £10 561 to £13 084 at that year's prices. The average income of the richest 20 per cent increased from £20 138 to £28 124 or by £7986. At the lower end of the spectrum average real income dropped from £3442 to £3282 or by £160.[10] Since then the gap between rich and poor has widened. Although encouraging economic trends over much of the 1990s have banished the spectre of unemployment for many, the ignominy of being without a job remains stubbornly real for those at the bottom of the social pile. As the rich have progressively got richer so they have become anaesthetised to the privations of the poor. Occasionally, while on their way to some pleasant social engagement, they inadvertently stumble over a pathetic rough sleeper. Only then are they for a short while subject to an annoying short-term reminder that some of their fellow countrymen are failing to cope with present-day living. In general the better-off manage to keep themselves economically, socially and geographically aloof.

Those with well-paid jobs and a home contrive not to be affected by the claims of the Child Poverty Action Group that factors leading to the widening poverty gap include unemployment, low pay, mean welfare benefits, increased longevity and the greater numbers of lone parents.[11] Social inequality in Britain was addressed by an ecumenical Christian group chaired by Bishop Sheppard of Liverpool. Their report published in April 1997 rounded on the unwillingness of the main political parties to confront and resolve the basic social issues like unemployment, wealth inequality, poverty and homelessness. The report pointed to the 'wickedness' of an ever more prosperous majority failing to accept responsibility for the increased number living in dire poverty.[12] For such sentiments to be adopted by Parliament there would need to be a fundamental change in the official response to social problems. Time and again the woeful cry has echoed from Westminster about lack of the money with which to improve the condition of what parliamentarians on both sides of the House have no embarrassment in labelling as the 'underclass'. One thing is certain, without the political will, sufficient money will never become available to make meaningful change.

This volume has suggested that a number of social-contact features are shared by street dwellers, whether in history or today. They include:

- sleeping rough
- casual poorly paid work
- begging
- unpredictable mobility
- petty crime
- imprisonment profiles
- mental instability
- soup kitchens
- hostels

- shelters, and
- common lodging houses.

As in the past, modern governments continue to conflate homelessness, begging and crime. To each of the three conditions they attach the traditional aura of stigmatisation. Vagrancy Acts, long dormant, have been reactivated in the closing decades of the twentieth century to provide a legal ambush for any homeless person who strays marginally from the expected mode of contemporary behaviour. The Criminal Justice and Public Order Act (1994) specifically updated nuances of the potential criminalisation of homelessness. It strengthened the impression that no homeless person should be greatly surprised at finding themselves facing the charge of being a crime-orientated vagrant.

The Conservative Government's stand-off position to the street homelessness problem indulged the excuse that individual difficulty is now better served with the personal caring touch of charity. This is founded neither on the evidence of history nor on the abilities of contemporary voluntary support groups. Charitable organisations supporting the homeless persistently admit their financial inadequacy. They agree that together they can do little more than apply a temporary tourniquet to mollify the extreme effects of structural social problems which metaphorically require corrective surgery, a blood transfusion and intensive care. Historiography abounds with examples of how the availability of the voluntary gift is unpredictable and inadequate to serve other than small sections of the community, and then temporarily. Charity is rarely able to do more than satisfy the immediate needs of the desperately distressed.

This volume has traced changes in vagrancy laws through many centuries. Time and again, legislation has emerged from the central Establishment deploring a recent massive increase in the number of poor people resorting to a nomadic existence. The legislature's focus has persistently been on the imperative of controlling the threat arising from the activities of the potentially unruly homeless masses. Always the official spotlight falls on how allegedly the rootless poor could collectively disturb and even disrupt the tranquillity of more 'civilised' society. Consistently the homeless are suspected of, but seldom protected from, society's worst excesses. Fortunately for the well-being of the community as a whole, in the past the danger of riot from below has generally been greatly exaggerated in Britain. But it may be that the Establishment's long-term alleged apprehension about poverty-motivated social disturbance may at last be justified unless the widening gap between the 'haves' and the 'have-nots' is narrowed. Those who bear a disproportionate share of the social burden and the risks of economic change, but enjoy few if any of the benefits, may not be prepared to passively accept their miserable fate indefinitely.

By calling on the virtue of Victorian values, recent British Governments have thought fit to marginalise and stigmatise this deprived, mainly helpless, group. Largely ignored by the legislature have been the economic, social, demographic and political factors which caused the increased numbers to tramp and beg and sleep ragged in some public corner. Rarely have meaningful efforts been made to rectify the itinerant's predicament by rehabilitating them into society through the basic human rights of education, employment, health care and a permanent home. Shortly after New Labour's success in the 1997 UK Parliamentary election, charities supporting the homeless jointly published a ten-point 'battle plan' for central Government to address if it was serious about ending the causes of the crisis.[13] The recommendations were for them to:

1. take homelessness seriously
2. build more homes
3. fill Britain's empty buildings
4. deal with the causes
5. guarantee the right to a permanent home
6. make housing affordable
7. take action locally
8. fund more training
9. target young people, and
10. give homeless people the right to vote.

The fact that Labour has in the past governed Britain at a time when street homelessness was all but eliminated may have acted as a spur to Mr Blair's administration. Early indications from Housing Minister Hilary Strong were encouraging. She is committed to the repeal of 'offensive' sections of the Housing Act 1996 and to the reintroduction of regulations giving homeless families and individuals priority access to social housing.[14] The setting up of a Social Exclusion Unit in December 1997 with the reduction in the numbers sleeping rough as one of its main tasks suggests that the emergent Government at least recognises that there is a problem. Their Task Force is committed to tackling the root causes of poverty rather than the consequences of social inequality. During 1998 the Labour Government funded initiatives designed to satisfy their commitment to provide every street dweller with the opportunity for safe warm shelter. But the closure of a well-established St Mungo hostel towards the end of that year, apparently through lack of financial support, indicated that problems for the homeless are far from over. Those of no fixed abode must hope that the heralded New Deal of New Labour will bring them a brighter future for the new millennium.

Notes

CHAPTER 1   INTRODUCTION

1. John Greve and others, *Homelessness in London* (1971), p. 55.
2. 'Constructing Classes', Report by Economic and Social Research Council (December 1997).
3. Miri Rubin, 'The Poor', in Rosemary Horrox (ed.), *Fifteenth-Century Attitudes* (Cambridge 1994), p. 169.
4. Descriptions of the roofless and rootless show that over the centuries many words or phrases, most of them derogatory, have been applied to them by contemporaries. They include: debased, degenerate, depraved, deviant, disadvantaged, dishonest, the bottom of the social pyramid, characterless, dangerous class, disposable element of society, disreputable, dosser, drifter, drop-out, drug addict, drunkard, feckless, gypsy, homeless, hooligan, hustler, idle able-bodied, incompetent mothers, itinerant, lapilli (Kirk Mann), loafer, proletariat, malingerer, marginalised, mentally inadequate, migrant, outsider, pauper, physically inadequate, rag-picker, relative surplus population, reserve army (of unemployed), residuum, rough, roofless, rough-sleeper, roughs, social scavenger, socially inadequate, street dweller, subnormal (*New Survey of London*, vol. 1, p. 23), tramp, traveller, underclass, undeserving, unemployable, unemployed, unmarried mothers, unrespectable, unworthy, vagabond, vagrant, wastrel, welfare cripple.
5. For example: H. Woodcock, *The Gypsies, Being a Brief account of Their History* (1865); George K. Behlmer, 'The Gypsy Problem in Victorian England', *Victorian Studies*, 28, 2 (1984–5), pp. 231–43; and Raphael Samuel, 'Comers and Goers', in H. J. Dyos and M. Wolff, *The Victorian City* (1976), pp. 123–60.
6. Peter Archard, 'Vagrancy – A Literature Review'; in Tim Cook and G. Braithwaite, *Vagrancy: some new perspectives* (1979), p. 14.
7. C. Cottingham, *Poverty and the Urban Underclass* (1982), p. 3.
8. Samuel Smiles, *Self-Help with Illustrations of Conduct and Perseverance* (1859).
9. I. C. Bradley, *Enlightened Entrepreneurs* (1987), p. 51.
10. Thomas Hawksley, *The Charities of London and Some Errors in their Administration* (1869), p. 16.
11. C. S. Loch, *The Charities Register and Digest* (1890), pp. iv–v.
12. W. M. Wilkinson, 'The Vagrant', *Poor Law Conferences* (1881), p. 323.
13. Charles Murray, 'The Emerging British Underclass' in Ruth Lister (ed.), *Charles Murray and the Underclass* (1996), p. 25.
14. Peter Archard, as previously quoted, pp. 12–13.
15. Lawrence M. Mead, *Beyond Entitlement: the Social obligations of Citizenship* (New York, 1986), pp. 1, 7, 8, 82 and 84.

16.   Peter Townsend, *The International Analysis of Poverty* (1993), pp. 101–6.
17.   *First Annual Report, Poor Law Commissioners*, PP 1835, XXXV.107, [*c*. 500], p. 6.
18.   'Housing Policy: A Consultative Document', *Department of the Environment* (1977), p. 50.
19.   'The Grief Report', Shelter (1972), p. 9.
20.   An early appearance of the word 'vagrant' in an English statute was in 1547, 1st ed.VI, c. 3, where it was used synonymously with 'vagabond' and 'loiterer'.
21.   A. L. Beier, *Masterless Men* (1985), p. 3.
22.   J. J. Jusserand, *English Wayfaring Life in the Middle Ages* (*XIVth Century*), 8th edn (1891), pp. 29–30.
23.   Bronislaw Geremek, *Poverty* (1994), pp. 40–1.
24.   Marcel Mauss, *The Gift* (1990), p. 18.
25.   Joan M. Crouse, *The Homeless Transient in the Great Depression* (1986), pp. 12–13.
26.   *Report of the Departmental Committee on Vagrancy*, vol. 1, pp. 1906 (c2852), CIII.1, p. 16.
27.   Sophie Watson, *Housing and Homelessness* (1986), p. 9.
28.   W. G. Runciman, *Relative Deprivation and Social Justice* (1966).
29.   F. M. Eden, *The State of the Poor*, vol. I (1797), p. 59.
30.   Frances F. Piven and others, *Regulating the Poor* (1972), p. 7.
31.   E. M. Leonard, *The Early History of English Poor Relief* (1965), p. 1.
32.   Rachel Vorspan, 'Vagrancy and the New Poor Law ...', *English History Review*, 92 (1977), p. 59.
33.   David Sibley, *Outsiders in Urban Societies* (Oxford, 1981), pp. 47–9.
34.   William J. Chambliss, 'A Sociological Analysis of the Law of Vagrancy', *Social Problems*, 12 (1964), pp. 67–8.

CHAPTER 2   EARLY VAGRANCY LEGISLATION

1.   Plato, *The Republic* (1987), p. 308.
2.   Irene Glasser, *Homelessness in Global Perspective* (1994), p. 15.
3.   Carlo M. Cipolla, *Before the Industrial Revolution, European Society and Economy, 1000–1700* (1981), pp. 13 and 15.
4.   C. J. Ribton-Turner, *A History of Vagrants and Vagrancy ...* (1887), p. 3.
5.   S. and B. Webb, *English Local Government: English Poor Law History: Part I, The Old Poor Law* (1927 edn), p. 1.
6.   Bronislaw Geremek, *Poverty* (1994), pp. 36–7.
7.   E. M. Leonard, *The Early History of English Poor Relief* (1965), pp. 2–3; Thomas Fuller, *The Church History of Britain from the Birth of Jesus Christ until the Year MDCXLVIII*, Book II (1655), p. 126.
8.   C. J. Ribton-Turner, as previously quoted, p. 7.
9.   George Coode, *Report to the PLB on the Law of Settlement and Removal of the Poor*, PP 1851 [c. 675], XXVI.1, pp. 9–10.
10.   As note 9.
11.   C. I. Cohen and others, *Old Men of the Bowery* (1989), p. 41.

12. George Nicholls, *English Poor Law*, vol. I (1898), pp. 13–14 and 16.
13. As note 12, pp. 21–2.
14. Christopher Hibbert, *The English* (1987), p. 63.
15. Doris M. Stenton, *English Society in the Early Middle Ages* (1964), p. 252.
16. Karl de Schweinitz, *England's Road to Social Security* (Perpetua edn, 1975), p. 2.
17. Miri Rubin, 'The Poor', in Rosemary Horrox (ed.), *Fifteenth-century attitudes* (1994), p. 170.
18. D. C. Coleman, *Economy of England, 1450–1750* (1977), p. 20; Karl de Schweinitz, as previously quoted, p. 4.
19. F. M. Eden, *The State of the Poor* (1797), p. 57; cited in Karl de Schweinitz, as previously quoted, p. 2.
20. A. R. Bridbury, *Economic Growth: England in the Later Middle Ages* (1962), p. 32.
21. D. C. Coleman, as previously quoted, p. 49.
22. J. J. Jusserand, *English Wayfaring Life in the Middle Ages (XIVth Century)*, 8th edn (1891), pp. 29–30.
23. John Lambert, *Vagrancy Laws and Vagrants* (1868), pp. 3–4.
24. George Nicholls, as previously quoted, p. 32.
25. A. L. Beier, *Masterless Men* (1985), p. 12.
26. F. M. Eden, as previously quoted, p. 3.
27. Miri Rubin, as previously quoted, p. 173.
28. George Coode, as previously quoted, p. 12.
29. Henry Phelps Brown and Sheila V. Hopkins, 'Seven Centuries of Building Wages', in their, *A Perspective of Wages and Prices* (1981), pp. 3–4; and Peter Bowden, 'Statistical Appendix' in Joan Thirsk (ed.), *Agricultural History of England and Wales, IV (1500–1640)* (1967), p. 865.
30. Henry Phelps Brown and Sheila V. Hopkins, as previously quoted, pp. 28–9.
31. Carlo M. Cipolla, as previously quoted, pp. 216–17.
32. 23 Edward III, c. 5–7 (1349), *Statutes of the Realm*, vol. I (1810), p. 308.
33. 25 Edward III, Stat. 2, c. 2–5 (1350–1), *Statutes of the Realm*, as above, p. 312.
34. S. and B. Webb, *English Local Government: English Poor Law History: Part I, The Old Poor Law* (1927 edn), p. 25.
35. *Report of the Departmental Committee on the Relief of the Casual Poor*, Appendix 1, PP 1929–30 [c. 3640], XVII.121, citing Stephen's 'History of the Criminal Law'.
36. Miri Rubin, as previously quoted, p. 175.
37. Keith Feiling, *A History of England* (Book Club edn, 1975), pp. 257–60; S. and B. Webb, as previously quoted, pp. 27–8.
38. C. Oman, *The Great Revolt of 1381* (1906), pp. 8–9, 5.
39. Miri Rubin, as previously quoted, p. 175.
40. 12 Richard II, c. 7 (1388), *Statutes of the Realm*, vol. II (1816), p. 58.
41. George Coode, as previously quoted, p. 11.
42. *Statutes of the Realm*, II (1816), p. 58.
43. C. J. Ribton-Turner, as previously quoted, pp. 176–7.

44. Philip O'Connor, *Britain in the Sixties: Vagrancy* (1963), p. 42.
45. 4 Henry VII, c. 19 (1488–9), *Statutes of the Realm, II* (1816), p. 542.
46. S. and B. Webb, as previously quoted, pp. 28–9.

CHAPTER 3   TUDOR RESPONSE TO THE TRAVELLING POOR

1. R. H. Tawney, *The Agrarian Problem in the Sixteenth Century* (New York: Torch-book, 1967), p. 275.
2. Carlo M. Cipolla, as previously quoted, pp. 160–5.
3. Julian Cornwall, 'English Population in the Sixteenth Century', *Economic History Review*, 23 (1970), p. 44.
4. Christopher Hibbert, *The English* (1987), pp. 173–4.
5. G. M. Trevelyan, *English Social History* (1946), p. 137.
6. L. A. Clarkson, *The Pre-industrial Economy in England 1500–1750* (1971), pp. 9–10.
7. Frances F. Piven, *Regulating the Poor* (1972), p. 8.
8. S. and B. Webb, *English Local Government, 8, English Poor Law History* (1929; repr. 1963), pp. 31–2.
9. Peter Clark, 'The migrant in Kentish towns 1580–1640', in Peter Clark and Paul Slack (eds), *Crisis and Order in English Towns 1500–1700* (1972), p. 138.
10. See note 4 of Chapter 1.
11. W. G. Hoskins, *The Age of Plunder, King Henry's England 1500–1547* (1976), p. 112.
12. Paul Slack, *The English Poor Law, 1531–1782* (Cambridge 1995), p. 6.
13. C. G. A. Clay, *Economic Expansion and Social Change, England 1500–1700*, vol. I (1984), pp. 216–17.
14. E. M. Leonard, *The Early History of Poor Relief*, (1965), p. 61; D. M. Palliser, *The Age of Elizabeth* (1992), pp. 139–45.
15. E. A. Wrigley and R. S. Schofield, *The Population History of England, 1541–1871. A Reconstruction* (1981), Appendix 9, pp. 638–44.
16. H. Phelps Brown and S. V. Hopkins, 'Seven Centuries of the Price of Consumables', in H. Phelps Brown and S. V. Hopkins, *A Perspective of Wages and Prices* (1981), p. 10; also R. B. Outhwaite, *Inflation in Tudor and Early Stuart England* (1969).
17. C. G. A. Clay, *Economic Expansion and Social Change in England, 1500–1700*, vol. 1 (1984), p. 50.
18. E. A. Wrigley and R. Schofield, *The Population History of England*, Appendix 9 (1981), pp. 638–44. Others have pointed out that in the 50 years from around 1510 to 1560 the price of provisions more than doubled whereas the rise in wages increased by only about 50 per cent; E. M. Leonard, *The Early History of Poor Relief* (1965), p. 16. Also refer to P. Bowden, 'Statistical Appendix', in Joan Thirsk, *The Agrarian History of England and Wales, IV, 1500–1640* (Cambridge 1967), p. 865. Also, H. Phelps Brown and Sheila Hopkins, 'Seven Centuries of Building Wages', in Phelps Brown and Hopkins, *A Perspective of Wages*

and Prices (1981), pp. 1–12. As explained in the previous chapter, the composite commodity used to calculate purchasing power can be looked upon as a package always containing the same sized bags full of bread-stuffs, meat, cloth and so on. The precise contents of each bag were varied from period to period depending on the best evidence available from contemporary sources.

19. P. Bowden, 'Agricultural Prices, Farm Profits, and Rents', in Joan Thirsk (ed.), *The Agricultural History of England and Wales, IV, 1500–1640* (1967), p. 865.

20. H. Phelps Brown and S. V. Hopkins, 'Wage-rates and Prices: Evidence for Population Pressure in the Sixteenth Century', in H. Phelps Brown and S. V. Hopkins, *A Perspective of Wages and Prices* (1981), p. 61.

21. H. Phelps Brown and S. V. Hopkins, 'Builders' Wage-rates, Prices and Population: some Further Evidence', in H. Phelps Brown and S. V. Hopkins, *A Perspective of Wages and Prices* (1981), pp. 78–98.

22. A. L. Beier, 'Poverty and progress in early modern England', in A. L. Beier and others (eds), *The First Modern Society* (Cambridge 1989), p. 227.

23. H. Phelps Brown and S. V. Hopkins, 'Wages and Prices: Evidence for Population Pressure in the Sixteenth Century', in H. Phelps Brown and S. V. Hopkins, *A Perspective of Wages and Prices* (1981), p. 67.

24. A. L. Beier, as previously quoted, p. 203; W. G. Hoskins, *Provincial England* (1965), p. 84; W. G. Hoskins, *The Age of Plunder* (1976), p. 32; J. F. Pound, *Poverty and Vagrancy in Tudor England* (1986), pp. viii–xii.

25. D. M. Palliser, *The Age of Elizabeth* (1992), p. 143.

26. W. K. Jordan, *Philanthropy in England 1480–1660* (1959), p. 78; R. H. Tawney, as previously quoted, p. 268.

27. John Pound, *Poverty and Vagrancy in Tudor England* (1986), p. 79.

28. E. M. Leonard, *The Early History of English Poor Relief* (1965), p. 52.

29. A. L. Rowse, *The England of Elizabeth* (1950), p. 399.

30. B. Kirkman Gray, *A History of English Philanthropy* (1967), p. 5.

31. John Pound, as previously quoted, p. 5.

32. W. K. Jordan, as previously quoted, pp. 369–71.

33. D. M. Palliser, as previously quoted, p. 148.

34. Paul Slack, *The English Poor Law, 1531–1782* (Cambridge 1995), p. 6.

35. R. H. Tawney, as previously quoted, pp. 269–80.

36. Keith Feiling, *A History of England* (Book Club, 1975), p. 510.

37. John Pound, *Poverty and Vagrancy in Tudor England* (1986), pp. 5–10.

38. James A. Williamson, *The Tudor Age*, 3rd edn (1964), p. 3.

39. Thomas More, 'Utopia', Book 1; cited in E. Surtz and J. H. Hexter, *The Complete Works of St. Thomas More, Volume 4* (Yale 1965), p. 67.

40. C. G. A. Clay, *Economic Expansion and Social Change, England 1500–1700*, vol. I (1984), p. 220.

41. D. B. Grigg, *Population Growth and Agrarian Change: an Historical Perspective* (Cambridge 1980), p. 89.

42. W. G. Hoskins, 'Harvest Fluctuations and English Economic History, 1480–1619', *Agricultural History Review*, xii (1964).

43. H. Phelps Brown and S. V. Hopkins, 'Seven Centuries of the Prices of Consumables' in H. Phelps Brown and S. V. Hopkins, *A Perspective of Wages and Prices* (1981), p. 29.

44. Philip O'Connor, *Britain in the Sixties, Vagrancy* (1963), p. 42.

45. C. J. Ribton-Turner, *A History of Vagrants and Vagrancy ...* (1887), p. 83.

46. E. P. Cheyney, *An Introduction to the Industrial and Social History of England* (New York 1920), p. 139.

47. Jerome Hall, *Theft, Law and Society* (Boston 1935), p. 336.

48. John Pound, as previously quoted, p. 14.

49. Thomas Starkey, 'The Nature of the Common Weal'; in C. H. Williams (ed.), *English Historical Documents 1485–1558* (1967), p. 302.

50. 11 Henry VII, c. 2 (1495); Ribton-Turner, as previously quoted, p. 67.

51. J. E. Thorold Rogers, *A History of Agriculture and Prices in England: ... 1259–1793*, vol. III (1882), p. 95.

52. E. M. Leonard, as previously quoted, p. 48.

53. John Pound, *Poverty and vagrancy in Tudor England* (1986), pp. 78–9.

54. W. K. Jordan, as previously quoted, p. 84.

55. George Nicholls, *English Poor Law* (1898), p. 115.

56. 22 Henry VIII, c. 12 (1530–1), *Statutes of the Realm*, vol. III (1817), p. 329.

57. As note 56, p. 330.

58. 27 Henry VIII, c. 25 (1535–6), *Statutes of the Realm*, vol. III (1817), p. 560.

59. William J. Chambliss, 'A Sociological Analysis of the Law of Vagrancy', *Social problems*, 12 (1964), pp. 73–4.

60. W. K. Jordan, as previously quoted, p. 85.

61. Frank Aydelotte, *Elizabethan Rogues and Vagabonds* (Oxford, 1913), p. 62.

62. C. S. L. Davies, 'Slavery and Protector Somerset; the Vagrancy Act of 1547', *EHR*, 2nd series, XIX, no. 3 (1966), p. 533.

63. 1 Edward VI, c. 3 (1547), *Statutes of the Realm*, vol. IV (1819), pp. 5–6; George Nicholls, as previously quoted, pp. 129–30.

64. As note 63, pp. 7–8.

65. Christopher Hibbert, *The English* (1989), p. 182.

66. W. G. Hoskins, *The Age of Plunder*, as previously quoted, p. 106.

67. C. S. L. Davies, as previously quoted, p. 549. The ferocity of the punishments meted out during the Tudor period was not peculiar to vagrants and should be taken within the context of the times. Whipping was a punishment applicable at common law to most minor criminals and it was a customary notion that all larcenies exceeding one shilling should be punished by death. *Report of the Departmental Committee on the Relief of the Casual Poor*, Appendix 1, Ministry of Health, PP 1929–30 [c. 3640], XVII.121, p. 54.

68. C. J. Ribton-Turner, as previously quoted, p. 94.

69. 2 & 3 Phil. and Mary, c. 5 (1555), *Statutes of the Realm*, vol. IV (1819), p. 281.

70. Frank Aydelotte, as previously quoted, p. 63.
71. C. J. Ribton-Turner, as previously quoted, p. 120.
72. R. H. Tawney, as previously quoted, p. 271.
73. B. Kirkman Gray, as previously quoted, p. 5.
74. E. M. Leonard, as previously quoted, p. 12, citing Thomas Harman, *Caueat or Warening for Common Cursetors*, 2nd edn, 1567.
75. William Harrison, *Description of England*, vol. 1 (1887), p. 59.
76. Christopher Hill, *Society and Puritanism in Pre-Revolutionary England* (1991), pp. 263–4.
77. A. L. Beier, 'Vagrants and the Social Order in Elizabethan England', *Past and Present*, 64, August 1974, p. 5.
78. *Report of the Departmental Committee on the Relief of the Casual Poor*, Appendix 1, Ministry of Health, PP 1929–30 [c. 3640], XVII.121, p. 55.
79. Henry Arth, *Provision for the Poore now in Penurie, out of the Store-House of Goods Plenty, Explained by H.A.* (1597).
80. Henry Arth, as above (brackets in original), p. C2.
81. Henry Arth, as above, pages D3 and D3 reverse.
82. W. T. MacCaffrey, *Exeter, 1540–1640* (1958), pp. 94–5, 116–17.
83. Peter N. Stearns, *European Society in Upheaval* (1975), p. 53.
84. 14 Eliz., c. 5 (1572), *Statutes of the Realm*, vol. IV (1819), pp. 591, 593, 594.
85. Clayton Roberts and David Roberts, *A History of England*, Volume 1 (1991).
86. R. H. Tawney, *Religion and the Rise of Capitalism* (1966), p. 260.
87. *Statutes of the Realm*, vol. IV, Part I (1819), p. 611.
88. E. M. Leonard, as previously quoted, pp. 31–4, 65–6.
89. Paul Slack, *Poverty and Policy in Tudor and Stuart England* (1988), p. 93.
90. Philip O'Connor, as previously quoted, p. 45.
91. Philip O'Connor, as note 90, pp. 43–4.
92. Frank Aydelotte, as previously quoted, p. 69.
93. James A. Williamson, *The Tudor Age*, 3rd edn (1964), p. 422.
94. Frank Aydelotte, as previously quoted, pp. 74–5.
95. W. K. Jordan, as previously quoted p. 89.
96. John Pound, *Poverty and Vagrancy in Tudor England* (1986), pp. 48–50.
97. G. E. Aylmer, 'Unbelief in seventeenth-century England', in D. Pennington and K.Thomas (eds), *Puritans and Revolutionaries* (1978), p. 33; and James A. Williamson, *The Tudor Age*, 3rd edn (1964), p. 422.
98. C. J. Ribton-Turner, as previously quoted, p. 128.
99. *Statutes of the Realm*, vol. IV, Part II (1819), p. 899. Anthropologists have claimed that by the middle of the sixteenth century, vagrants were describing themselves as 'egyptians', later shortened to 'gypsies', in order to capitalise on and exploit an exotic identity to gain earnings as fortune-tellers and dancers: Irene Glasser, *Homelessness in Global Perspective* (1994), p. 11
100. Keith Wrightson, *English Society 1580–1680* (1982), p. 142; also, Paul Slack, *Poverty and Policy in Tudor and Stuart England* (1988), p. 97.

101. Paul Slack, 'Vagrants and Vagrancy in England, 1598–1664', *Economic History Review*, 2nd series, 27 (1974), p. 364.
102. D. B. Grigg, as previously quoted, pp. 94–5.

CHAPTER 4   THE TRAVELLING POOR IN THE SEVENTEENTH AND EIGHTEENTH CENTURIES

1. William Perkins, *A Treatise of Callings, Workes*, I (1612), p. 755. Cited by Christopher Hill, *Society and Puritanism* ... (1991), p. 251.
2. F. Engels, *The Condition of the Working Class in England* (1845; Stanford, 1968), pp. 9–12.
3. L. A. Clarkson, *The Pre-Industrial Economy in England 1500–1750* (1971), p. 238.
4. M. E. Rose, *The English Poor Law, 1780–1930* (1971), pp. 11–12. As noted in the previous chapter, the 39 Eliz. c. 3 (1597) Act had for the first time provided for the appointment of overseers of the poor in each parish empowered, with the consent of the justices, to raise taxes so that they could respond competently to the needs of the poor.
5. Philip Styles, 'The evolution of the Law of settlement', *University of Birmingham Historical Journal*, IX, no. 1 (1963), p. 43.
6. Ann Hughes, *The Causes of the English Civil War* (1991), p. 67.
7. Keith Wrightson, *English Society 1580–1680* (1982), p. 141.
8. C. J. Ribton-Turner, *A History of Vagrants* and Vagrancy ... (1887), pp. 132–3.
9. *Report of the Departmental Committee on the Relief of the Casual Poor*, Appendix 1, Ministry of Health, PP 1929–30 [c. 3640], XVII.121, p. 56.
10. Philip O'Connor, *Britain in the Sixties, Vagrancy* (1963), p. 45.
11. E. M. Leonard, *The Early History of English Poor Relief* (1965), p. 246.
12. Peter Laslett, *The World We Have Lost – Further Explored* (Cambridge, 1983), p. 148.
13. J. Kent, 'Population Mobility and Alms', *Local Population Studies*, no. 27 (1981), pp. 36–8; for further details of local data refer to A. L. Beier, 'Poverty and progress in early modern England', A. L. Beier and others (eds), *The First Modern Society* (1989), pp. 231–6.
14. C. J. Ribton-Turner, as previously quoted, pp. 150–1; Philip O'Connor, as previously quoted, p. 46.
15. N. J. Smith, *Poverty in England 1601–1936* (Newton Abbot 1972), p. 83.
16. E. M. Leonard, as previously quoted, pp. 132, 266; G. M. Trevelyan, *English Social History* (1942), pp. 170–1; J. S. Morrill, *Cheshire 1630–1660* (1974), p. 247.
17. C. J. Ribton-Turner, as previously quoted, p. 154.
18. Frances F. Piven and others, *Regulating the Poor* (1972), pp. 16–17.
19. A. L. Beier (1989), as previously quoted, p. 230.
20. E. A. Wrigley and R. S. Schofield, *The Population History of England, 1541–1871* (1981), pp. 208–9.
21. A. L. Beier (1989), as previously quoted, pp. 230–1.

22. H. Phelps Brown and S. V. Hopkins, 'Wages and Prices: Evidence for Population Pressure in the Sixteenth Century', in H. Phelps Brown and S. V. Hopkins, *A Perspective on Wages and Prices* (1981), p. 67.

23. Michael Dalton, *The Countrey Justice* (1635), pp. 101 and 123.

24. As note 23, pp. 101–2.

25. Paul A. Slack, 'Vagrants and Vagrancy in England, 1598–1664', *Economic History Review*, 2nd series, 27 (1974), pp. 361–79.

26. As note 25, p. 361.

27. Cited in N. J. Smith, as previously quoted, pp. 12–13.

28. Frances F. Piven and others, as previously quoted, p. 17.

29. Ann Hughes, *The Causes of the English Civil War* (1991), p. 131.

30. C. G. A. Clay, *Economic Expansion and Social Change, England 1500–1700*, vol. I (1984), p. 93.

31. D. C. Coleman, 'Labour in the English Economy of the Seventeenth Century', *Economic History Review*, 2nd series, VIII (1955–6), pp. 280–95.

32. Carlo M. Cipolla, *Before the Industrial Revolution: European Society and Economy, 1000–1700* (1981 edn), p. 164.

33. C. H. Hull (ed.), *The Economic Writings of Sir William Petty together with the Observations upon the Bills of Mortality by John Graunt* (1963), pp. 369–70.

34. Peter Clark, 'Migration in England during the late Seventeenth and early Eighteenth Centuries', *Past and Present*, 83 (May 1979), p. 57.

35. E. A. Wrigley, 'A simple model of London's importance in changing English Society and Economy 1650–1750', in John Patten, *Pre-industrial England* (1979), pp. 191–217; E. G. Ravenstein, 'The Laws of Migration', *Journal of the Royal Statistical Society*, XLVIII, part II (June 1885), p. 198.

36. C. G. Clay, *Economic Expansion and Social Change, England 1500–1700*, vol. I (1984), p. 189.

37. Peter Clark, 'The migrant in Kentish towns 1580–1640', Peter Clark and Paul Slack (eds), *Crisis and Order in English Towns, 1500–1700* (1972) pp. 138–44; Paul A. Slack (1974), as previously quoted, p. 368.

38. Christopher Hill, *The World Turned Upside Down* (1987), pp. 48–9.

39. B. Supple, *Commercial Crisis and Change in England, 1600–1642* (1959), pp. 103–4; E. M. Leonard, as previously quoted, pp. 47–9.

40. Paul Slack, 'Poverty and politics in Salisbury 1597–1666', Peter Clark and Paul Slack (eds), *Crisis and Order in English Towns, 1500–1700* (1972), p. 170.

41. J. S. Morrill, *Cheshire 1630–1660* (1974), pp. 248, 251.

42. C. H. Firth and R. S. Rait, *Acts and Ordinances of the Interregnum*, vol. I, pp. 1042–5.

43. R. H. Tawney, *Religion and the Rise of Capitalism* (Pelican, 1966), p. 263; C. J. Ribton-Turner, as previously quoted, pp. 161–2.

44. A. L. Beier, 'Poor Relief in Warwickshire, 1630–1660', *Past and Present*, 35 (1966), pp. 99–100.

45. 14 Charles II, c. 12 (1662), *Statutes of the Realm*, vol. V (1819), pp. 401–5.

46. E. M. Hampson, *Treatment of Poverty in Cambridgeshire; 1597–1834* (1934), p. 125.

47. Joan M. Crouse, *The Homeless Transient in the Great Depression* (1986), p. 14.

48. E. M. Hampson, as previously quoted, p. 138.

49. George Coode, *Report to the PLB on the Law of Settlement and Removal of the Poor*, dated 5 August 1851, PP 1851 [c. 675], XXVI.I, p. 188 and p. 30.

50. As note 49, p. 16.

51. Karl de Schweinitz, *England's Road to Social Security* (1975), pp. 39–40.

52. E. M. Hampson, as previously quoted, p. 137.

53. R. H. Tawney (1966), as previously quoted, pp. 269–70.

54. George Clarke, *John Bellers; His Life, Times and Writings* (1987), pp. 238–44.

55. John Bellers' Dedication to Robert Earl of Oxford reprinted in A. Ruth Fry, *John Bellers 1654–1725, Quaker, Economist and Social Reformer* (1933), p. 124; and John Bellers, *The Quaker Tapestry*, Panel E2.

56. 4 William & Mary, c. 8 (1692), *Statutes of the Realm*, vol. VI (1819), pp. 390–1.

57. C. J. Ribton-Turner, as previously quoted, pp. 173–6.

58. Dorothy Marshall, *The English Poor in the Eighteenth Century* (1926), pp. 175–80.

59. S. and B. Webb, *English Local Government: English Poor Law History: Part I: The Old Poor Law* (1927), p. 357.

60. 13 Anne, c. 26 (1713), *Statutes of the Realm*, vol. IX (1822), pp. 976–82.

61. *Report of the Departmental Committee on the Relief of the Casual Poor*, Appendix 1, Ministry of Health, PP 1929–30 [c. 3640], XVII.121, p. 56.

62. S. and B. Webb (1927), as previously quoted, pp. 367–9 and 169–73.

63. William J. Chambliss, 'A Sociological Analysis of the Law of Vagrancy', *Social Problems*, 12 (1964), p. 74.

64. H. S. G. Halsbury, Earl of, *The Laws of England* (1912), pp. 606–7.

65. J. L. and B. Hammond, *The Village Labourer*, 4th edn (1936), p. 17.

66. Frances F. Piven and others, as previously quoted, pp. 17–18.

67. J. L. and Barbara Hammond, *The Village Labourer*, 2 vols (1948).

68. R. B. Jones, *Economic and Social History of England, 1770–1970* (1971), p. 23.

69. C. G. A. Clay, *Economic Expansion and Social Change, England 1500–1700*, vol. I (1984), p. 98.

70. *Letters of Horace Walpole to Sir H. Mann*, July 1742, cited by S. and B. Webb, *English Local Government: English Poor Law History, Part I; The Old Poor Law* (1927), pp. 366–7.

71. Paul Slack, *The English Poor Law, 1531–1782* (1995), p. 56.

72. Arthur Young, *Eastern Tour*, vol. IV (1771), p. 361.

73. Philip O'Connor, as previously quoted, p. 48.

74. Adam Smith, *The Wealth of Nations*, vol. I (1776; 5th edn 1930), pp. 142 and p. 435.

75. S. and B. Webb, as previously quoted, pp. 334–42.

76. John Lambert, *Vagrancy Laws and Vagrants* (1868), p. 18.

77. Dorothy Marshall, as previously quoted (1926), p. 230.
78. S. and B. Webb, as previously quoted, p. 352.
79. Clive Emsley, *Crime and Society in England, 1750–1900* (1987), p. 28.

CHAPTER 5   VICTORIAN ATTITUDES

1. Anatole France, *Le Lys rouge* (1894), p. 94; G. B. Shaw, *Pygmalion* (Penguin, 1957), p. 58.
2. John Revans, Reports to the PLB on the Laws of Settlement and Removal of the Poor (1850), p. 94, PP 1850 [c. 1152], XXVII.229.
3. George Bourne, *Memoirs of a Surrey Labourer* (First published 1907; Breslich & Foss, 1983).
4. Bernard A. Cook, 'Poverty' in Sally Mitchell (Ed), *Victorian Britain* (1988), p. 624.
5. H. Spencer, 'The Coming Slavery', *Contemporary Review,* vol. XLV, April 1884.
6. J. M. Fothergill, *The Town Dweller, His Needs and His Wants* (1985), p. 113. This attitude was disowned by the Local Government Board early in the twentieth century. They found 'no information to show that the often repeated statement that tramps breed tramps has much foundation in fact'; *Report of the LGB Departmental Committee on Vagrancy,* Chapter III, PP 1906, CIII [c. 2852], p. 26.
7. *Select Committee on existing laws relating to Vagrants,* pp. 3–4, PP 1821, [c. 543], IV.121.
8. C. J. Ribton-Turner, *A History of Vagrants and Vagrancy* (1887), pp. 683 and 681.
9. *Report of the Departmental Committee on the Relief of the Casual Poor,* Ministry of Health (July 1930), PP 1929–30 [c. 3640], XVII.121, Appendix 1, p. 57.
10. David Jones, *Crime, Protest, Community and Police in Nineteenth Century Britain* (1982), p. 198.
11. Leonard Leigh, 'Vagrancy and the Criminal Law', in Tim Cook (ed.), *Vagrancy* (1979), p. 97.
12. 'Vagrancy Act', 5 George IV, c. 83 (1824), Section 4, *Statutes at Large,* 23, 4 Geo.IV to 5 Geo.IV, pp. 781 and 783.
13. *Report of the LGB Departmental Committee on Vagrancy,* Volume I, PP 1906 [c. 2852], CIII, pp. 7–8.
14. George Nicholls, *A History of the English Poor Law* (1898) p. 196.
15. Offences covered a vast range but could broadly be divided under three headings: 1. those of the kind created by Tudor legislation and committed by persons of a 'disreputable mode of life, such as begging, trading as a pedlar without a licence, telling fortunes, or sleeping in outhouses, unoccupied buildings, and so on., without visible means of subsistence'; 2. offences against the poor law such as leaving wife and family chargeable to the poor rate, non-completion of a workhouse task or damaging property of the guardians; and 3. offences by 'professional criminals' such as being found in possession of housebreaking implements or a

gun or other offensive weapon with 'felonious intent' or being found on any enclosed premises for 'an unlawful purpose', or frequenting public places for the 'purposes of felony'. *Report of the Departmental Committee on Relief of the Casual Poor*, Appendix 1, p. 57, Ministry of Health (July 1930), PP. 1929–30, [c. 3640], XVII.121.

16. David Jones, *Crime, Protest, Community and Police in Nineteenth Century Britain* (1982), p. 198.

17. Dorothy Marshall, *The English Poor in the Eighteenth Century* (1926), p. 244; Lionel Rose, *Rogues and Vagabonds* (1988), p. 10.

18. Data used in Figure 5.1 based on those in the *11th Annual Report of the PLB*, Appendix 33, PP 1859, IX, [c. 2500], pp. 196–9; also *22nd Annual Report of the PLB*, Appendix D, PP 1870, XXXV, [c. 123], pp. 286–7; also *30th Annual Report of the LGB*, Appendix E, PP 1901, XXV, [c. 746], pp. 356–9.

19. *Report of the LGB Department Committee on Vagrancy, Volume I*, as quoted previously, p. 14.

20. A. Redford, *Labour Migration in England, 1800–50* (1926), pp. 84–5.

21. Mark Neuman, 'Poor Law', in Sally Mitchell (ed), *Victorian Britain* (1988), p. 613.

22. *5th Annual Report, PLC*, PP 1839, XX.I [c. 239], pp. 52–3.

23. *Report of the Departmental Committee on the Relief of the Casual Poor*, Appendix 1, Ministry of Health (July 1930), PP 1929–30, [c. 3640], XVII.121, p. 59.

24. S. and B. Webb, *English Poor Law Policy* (1929; reprint 1963), p. 64.

25. S. and B. Webb, *English Local Government, 8, English Poor Law History, 2/1*, (1929; reprint 1963), p. 404.

26. *PRO MH 10/9, 15 February 1841.*

27. Simon Fowler, 'Vagrancy in Mid-Victorian Richmond, Surrey', *Local Historian*, 21 (1991), p. 67.

28. C. J. Ribton-Turner, as previously quoted, p. 269; *Report of the LGB Departmental Committee on Vagrancy, Volume I*, PP 1906 [c. 2852], CIII, p. 10.

29. C. J. Ribton-Turner, as previously quoted, p. 279.

30. *First Annual Report Poor Law Board*, Appendix A No. 7 (1848).

31. Maurice Caplan, *International Review of Social History, XXIIII* (1978), p. 278.

32. *Royal Commission on the Poor Laws and the Relief of Distress*, PP 1909, XXXVII, p. 569.

33. *Second Annual Report of the Poor Law Board*, PP 1850 [c. 1142], XXVII, p. 11.

34. PRO MH 12/12222, 15 January 1852.

35. As note 34, 9 April 1851.

36. As note 34, 16 January 1851.

37. *Second Annual Report of the Poor Law Board*, Appendix 13, as previously quoted, pp. 96 and 98.

38. *Royal Commission on the Poor Laws and the Relief of Distress*, as previously quoted, p. 569.

39. *Eleventh Annual Report, Poor Law Board*, PP 1859 [c. 2500], IX, p. 31.

40. C. J. Ribton-Turner, as previously quoted, pp. 184–6.

41. *18th Annual Report Poor Law Board,* PP(1866) [c. 3700], XXXVIII, pp. 116 and 105 (Cane's emphasis).

42. As note 41, pp. 113–14 and 106,

43. *21st Annual Report Poor Law Board,* PP (1868–9) [c. 4197], XXVIII.I. pp. 74–5.

44. David Jones, as previously quoted, p. 178. See also Samuel Smiles, *Self-Help with Illustrations of Conduct and Perseverance (1859).*

45. Rachel Vorspan, 'Vagrancy and the New Poor Law ... ', *English History Review,* 92 (1977), p. 73. Of course, the idea that the homeless wanderer was attracted by idleness is debatable. Much evidence suggests that life on the streets has always been extremely time-consuming with the simplest of subsistence and personal maintenance tasks requiring the expenditure of much time and effort. Julia Wardhaugh, 'Homeless in Chinatown', *Sociology,* vol. 30, no. 4, November 1996, p. 707.

46. Margaret K. Kohler, *Memories of Old Dorking* (1977), p. 41.

47. Maurice Caplan, 'The New Poor Law and the Struggle for Union Chargeability', *International Review of Social History,* XXIII (1978), pp. 285–91.

48. Maurice Caplan, as note 47, pp. 267–300.

49. *Report of the Departmental Committee on the Relief of the Casual Poor,* Appendix 1, PP 1929–30, [c. 3640], XVII.121, pp. 62–3.

50. David Jones, as previously quoted, p. 180.

51. M. E. Rose, *The English Poor Law, 1780–1930* (1971), p. 194.

52. *21st Annual Report Poor Law Board, as previously quoted,* p. 76.

53. Simon Fowler, as previously quoted, p. 68.

54. *PRO MH32/46, 20 March 1882.*

55. M. A. Crowther, *The Workhouse System, 1834–1929* (1983).

56. *Charity Organisation Reporter* (1872), p. 127.

57. M. Rooff, *A Hundred Years of Family Welfare* (1972), pp. 56–7.

58. *Charity Organisation Reporter* (1872), p. 177.

59. As note 58, p. 172.

60. *Eleventh Annual Report, Birmingham COS* (1880), p. 8.

61. *First Annual Report, Derby COS* (1880), pp. 8, 9 and 13.

62. *17th Annual Report, Liverpool CRS,* (1879–80), pp. 8 and 30–1. There is a slight discrepancy in the CRS report. On p. 31 the total amount of soup distributed through the year is quoted as being 45 018 quarts. This contrasts with the cited amount taken from p. 8 of the CRS report.

63. *Liverpool Lantern,* 1 March 1879, p. 323.

64. *Ninth Annual Report, Brighton COS* (1880), p. 1. Note that the large increase in wayfarer numbers discussed in the COS report should be considered against the knowledge that the previous year had seen a decrease of 606 in wayfarer numbers. *Annual Report, Oxford Anti Mendicity Society and COS* (1880), p. 14.

65. *Ninth Annual Report, Brighton COS* (1880), pp. 3, 5 and 8.

66. *Charity Organisation Reporter,* 7 July 1875, p. 104.

67. *Thirteenth Annual Report, Edinburgh Association for Improving the Condition of the Poor* (1880), p. 5.

68. *Ninth Annual Report, Leeds COS* (1880), p. 12.

69. *Twelfth Annual Report, Brighton COS* (1883), p. 26.

70. As note 69, p. 27.
71. *Ninth Annual Report, Walsall COS* (1884), p. 7.
72. C. J. Ribton-Turner, as previously quoted, p. 305.
73. John Lambert, *Vagrancy Laws and Vagrants* (1868), p. 46.
74. *Report of the Departmental Committee on the Relief of the Casual Poor*, Appendix 1, p. 64, Ministry of Health (July 1930), PP 1929–30 [c. 3640], XVII.121.
75. *First Report, Local Government Board, 1871–2*, no. 18, 'Vagrancy – Circular Letter from the LGB to Boards of Guardians', PP 1872 [c. 516], XXVIII, pp. 54–63.
76. Glen Mathews, *Midland History*, 11/12 (1986–7), p. 107.
77. W. H. Syme, *Honour all Men* (1904), pp. 4–5.
78. *Fifth Annual Report of Local Government Board*, PP 1876 [c. 1585], XXXI, p. xxxiii.
79. *First Annual Report of Local Government Board* (1871–2), as previously quoted, p. 56.
80. Comments by J. J. Henley, Poor Law Inspector: PRO, MH12/12229, 22 June 1881. In the 1840s, 'straw and rags' were provided for vagrants' bedding by at least one Home Counties workhouse, Simon Fowler, as previously quoted, p. 67. Similar treatment is reported from the Midlands in 1888 when women and children at Worcester workhouse were 'merely littered down on bags of straw', Glen Mathews, as previously quoted, p. 107.
81. PRO, MH 12/12222, 16 January 1851.
82. *First Annual Report, Derby COS* (1880), pp. 8, 9 and 13.
83. *Dorking (Surrey) Census Enumerators' Book, 1881.*
84. Andrew Doyle, *Reports on Poor Laws in Foreign Countries*, PP 1875 [c. 1255], LXV, pp. 64–8.
85. J. J. Henley, *Report on the Poor Laws of certain of the United States*, PP 1877 [c. 1868], XXXVII, pp. 37–8.
86. For example A. H. C. Brown, 'Relief of Vagrants', *Poor Law Conferences* (1881), pp. 281–2.
87. W. M. Wilkinson, 'The Vagrant', *Poor Law Conferences* (1881), pp. 325–6.
88. W. C. P. Purton, 'Relief of Vagrants', *Poor Law Conferences* (1881), p. 5.
89. Andrew Doyle, *Reports on Poor Laws in Foreign Countries*, PP 1875, [c. 1255], LXV, pp. 68.
90. Although oakum-picking was prohibited in prisons from 1896 as being too degrading for female convicts, it was still being demanded in some rural workhouses during the 1920s. S. and B. Webb, *English Local Government, 8; English Poor Law History, Part 2* (1929; repr. 1963), p. 415.
91. *Gallery Guide to Art Treasures of England Exhibition*, Royal Academy, 22 January–13 April 1998.
92. 'Casual Paupers Regulations Order, 18th December 1882', in W. G. Glen, *The General Orders relating to the Poor Law* (1898), p. 1051.
93. Prior to 1 January 1896, the number of casual paupers relieved during the day and the night respectively were not required to be distinguished

in the annual pauperism returns. Special Parliamentary Return No. 432, Session 2, 1895 suggests that ordinary returns prior to that date in many unions represented the night count only. When available, data for any time during the 24-hour period indicated a total of only about 10 per cent in excess of the night count. For later years the disparity between the two sets of data increased with the day and night figure commonly in excess of 50 per cent more than the night only total. For example, the number relieved at any time on the day or during the night of 1 January 1900 totalled 9841 in comparison with the night-only total of 5579. Refer to *LGB Departmental Committee on Vagrancy,* Appendix V, PP 1906 [c. 2892], CIII, p. 20.

94. *Twenty-second Annual Report LGB,* PP 1893–4 [c. 7180], XLIII.I, pp. 14–5.
95. *Sixteenth Annual Report LGB,* PP 1887 [c. 5131], XXXVI.1, p. 70.
96. Carl Chinn, *Poverty Amidst Prosperity: the Urban Poor in England, 1834–1914* (1995), p. 134.
97. *Twenty-second Annual Report of Poor Law Board,* PP 1870 [c. 123], XXXV.1, pp. xxx–xxxii. Also refer to PRO, MH32/46, 25 February 1882. Surveys carried out by Worcestershire police in the 1880s suggested that only between 10 per cent and 39 per cent of wayfarers applied to workhouses for relief and leads to the conclusion that there were many more *bona fide* work-seekers than the authorities generally were prepared to accept; Glen Mathews, as previously quoted (1986–7), pp. 102 and 105; The Webbs estimated between 10 per cent and 20 per cent of vagrants used casual wards, S. and B. Webb, *History of English Local Government; English Poor Law History Part 2,* as previously quoted, p. 403.
98. *Report of Departmental Committee on Vagrancy,* PP 1906 [c. 2852], CIII, p. 22.
99. *Seventh Annual Report, Glasgow COS* (1880), p. 17.
100. William Booth, *In Darkest England: and the Way Out* (1890).
101. Rider Haggard, *Regeneration* (1910).
102. D. Owen, *English Philanthropy, 1660–1960* (1965), p. 243;
103. Miss Tillard, 'The Relief of the Homeless', *Charity Organisation Review,* vol. VII (1891), pp. 29–31.
104. *Ninth Annual Report, Poor Law Board* (1866–7), p. 22, PP 1867, [c. 3870], XXXIV.I.
105. *Twenty First Annual Report PLB,* p. 75; PP 1868–9 [c. 4197], XXXVIII.I.
106. 'Statistics prepared for the Special Committee of the COS on Vagrancy and Mendicity', issued with the *Charity Organisation Reporter,* 17 April 1872; Rachel Vorspan, 'Vagrancy and the New Poor Law ... ', *English History Review,* 92 (1977), p. 70.
107. C. J. Ribton-Turner, *A History of Vagrants and Vagrancy ...* (1887), pp. 318–31.
108. Rachel Vorspan, as previously quoted, p. 70; and S. and B. Webb, as note 97, as previously quoted, pp. 412–13
109. Glen Mathews, as previously quoted, p. 108.
110. *PRO, MH 32/46, 20 March 1882.*
111. John Leach and John Wing, *Helping Destitute Men* (1980), p. 4.

112. *Report of the Departmental Committee on Vagrancy*, vol. I, PP 1906 [c. 2852], CIII, p. 15.
113. S. and B. Webb, as note 97, p. 414.
114. Mark Neuman, 'Beggars and Vagrants', in Sally Mitchell (ed.), *Victorian Britain* (1988), p. 71.
115. M. A. Crowther, *The Workhouse System 1834–1929* (1983), p. 249.
116. G. H. Sabine, *A History of Political Theory* (1963), p. 737; Melvin Richter, *The Politics of Conscience: T. H. Green and his Age* (1964), pp. 269–70; Alfred Marshall, *Principles of Economics* 2nd edn. (1891), p. 3.
117. Sophie Watson, *Housing and Homelessness* (1986), p. 35.
118. Gertrude Himmelfarb, *The Idea of Poverty* (Trowbridge, 1985), p. 358.

CHAPTER 6   VAGRANCY AROUND THE WORLD WARS

1. Jonathan Davies, 'The Unemployed', *Montgomeryshire Express and Radnor Times*, 16 January 1937.
2. W. H. Syme, *Honour all Men* (1904), pp. 5–6.
3. *Report of the LGB Departmental Committee on Vagrancy*, chapter III, PP 1906 [c. 2852], CIII, p. 23.
4. M. A. Crowther, *The Workhouse System, 1834–1929* (1983), p. 255.
5. *Report of the LGB Departmental Committee on Vagrancy*, as previously quoted, p. 26.
6. Report of the LGB Department Committee on Vagrancy, vol. I, PP 1906 [c. 2852], CIII, pp. 121 and 118–10
7. J. Howe, *Minutes of Evidence to LGB Departmental Committee on Vagrancy*, vol. II, PP 1906 [c. 2891], CIII, paras 2097–2100.
8. *Report of the Metropolitan Poor Law Inspectors' Advisory Committee on the Homeless Poor*, PP 1914 [c. 7307], XLIV, p. 6.
9. G. Clark, '"Ins-and-outs" and Tramps, the Detention of', *Poor Law Conferences, 1910–11*, pp. 627–8
10. C. S. Loch, *Minutes of Evidence, 1904–6 LGB Departmental Committee on Vagrancy*, vol. II, as previously quoted, paras 8838–9.
11. John Burnett, *Idle Hands* (1994), p. 161.
12. *Report of the Departmental Committee on the Relief of the Casual Poor*, Ministry of Health, PP 1929–30 [c. 3640], XVII.121, pp. 7–9.
13. As mentioned in the previous chapter, Poor Law data on the occupancy of casual wards had prior to 1 January 1896 generally concerned the number relieved on a particular night. Occasionally, attendance checks had been made over a 24-hour period, which indicated that the disparity with the night data was small. Subsequently, the gap between the two data sets widened but how many of those counted during the day were different individuals from those spending a night was found by the Local Government Board impossible to quantify because of the potential for double counting. During the first decade of the twentieth century such checks as were made suggested about 75 per cent more occupancy than did the regular 'night only' surveys. The 1909 LGB Report warned against undue credence being given to the inflated

figures. They drew attention to the number included 'twice over' by the same itinerant person benefiting from more than one union during the period. The LGB concluded that the night count was the more accurate and meaningful. Refer to *LGB Report*, PP 1909 [c. 234.1], LXXV, pp. iii–iv; also *LGB Departmental Report on Vagrancy*, PP 1906 [c. 2892], CIII, p. 20. Data for casual ward occupancy in later years shown in Figure 6.1 are from LGB annual reports. Unemployment data from *British Labour Statistics: Historical Abstracts, 1886–1968* (1971), p. 305.

14. George Orwell, *Down and Out in Paris and London* (Penguin, 1989), p. 157.

15. *Report of the Metropolitan Poor Law Inspectors' Advisory Committee on the Homeless Poor*, PP 1914–16 [c. 7840], XXXII, p. 6.

16. As note 8 above, p. 8

17. As note 15 above, p. 7.

18. As note 8 above, p. 10.

19. As note 17 above, p. 7.

20. As note 8 above, p. 10.

21. As note 15 above, p. 6.

22. Patrick McGill, *Children of the Dead End* (1915; 1980 edn), p. 114.

23. *Report of the LGB Departmental Committee on Vagrancy*, vol. I, PP 1906 [c. 2852], CIII, p. 118.

24. John Stewart, *Of No Fixed Abode* (1975), p. 145.

25. *Majority Report of the Royal Commission on the Poor Laws and the Relief of Distress* (1909), XXXVII, vol. 1, Part VIII – chapter 2, p. 124.

26. W. H. Syme, *Honour all Men* (1904), p. 3.

27. Rachel Vorspan, 'Vagrancy and the New Poor Law in Late-Victorian and Edwardian England', *English History Review*, 92 (1977), p. 73.

28. John Leach and John Wing, *Helping Destitute Men* (1980), p. 4.

29. As note 15 above, p. 7.

30. As note 15 above, p. 9.

31. *Report of the Royal Commission on the Care and Control of the Feebleminded*, PP 1908 [c. 4202], XXXIX, pp. 132–3.

32. *Report of the Departmental Committee on the Relief of the Casual Poor*, Ministry of Health, PP 1929–30 [c. 3640], XVII.121, pp. 7–8.

33. Lionel Rose, *Rogues and Vagabonds* (1988), p. 152.

34. Data used for unemployment are from the official statistics based on National Insurance returns: *HMSO British Labour Statistics: Historical Abstract, 1886–1968* (1971), p. 306. Other estimates have attempted to include the entire workforce, for example: C. H. Feinstein, *National Income, Expenditure and Output of the United Kingdom (1855–1965)* (1972), p. T128. Alternative estimates such as this have been subject to much debate, centring on factors such as the inability to take adequately into account those who in depressed times do not sign on for benefits and so on (for a multiplicity of reasons) but who would certainly accept a job should one become available. Poor Law data for England and Wales are from *LGB Annual Reports*.

35. *Report of the Departmental Committee on the Relief of the Casual Poor*, Ministry of Health, PP 1929–30, as previously quoted, p. 9.

36. Lionel Rose, as previously quoted, pp. 155–61.

37.   S. and B. Webb, *English Local Government, English Poor Law History*, part 2/1 (1929; repr. 1963), p. 946.

38.   B. R. Mitchell and P. Deane, *Abstract of British Historical Statistics* (1962), p. 66.

39.   *Report of the Departmental Committee on the Relief of the Casual Poor*, PP 1929–30, as previously quoted, pp. 16, 40, 50 and Appendix III.

40.   *Charity Organisation Quarterly*, vol. XI, April 1937, no. 2, p. 151.

41.   *Report of Departmental Committee on Relief of the Casual Poor*, PP 1929–30, as previously quoted, Appendix V.

42.   *Report of the Departmental Committee on the Relief of the Casual Poor*, as previously quoted, p. 15.

43.   A similar situation existed in 1930s USA, see Kathryn M. Neckerman, '"Underclass", Family Patterns', in Michael B. Katz (ed), *The 'Underclass' Debate* (Princeton, 1993), p. 204.

44.   *Report of the Departmental Committee on the Relief of the Casual Poor*, as previously quoted, pp. 13–15.

45.   *Report of the Departmental Committee on the Relief of the Casual Poor*, as previously quoted, pp. 13 and 99; W. H. Beveridge, *Unemployment: a Problem of Industry* (New edn, 1930), p. 12; S.and B. Webb, as previously quoted, p. 403.

46.   Joe Loftus, 'Lee Side', in John Burnett, *Idle Hands* (1994), p. 261.

47.   *Report of the Departmental Committee on the Relief of the Casual Poor*, as previously quoted, pp. 18–20 and 25–7.

48.   George Orwell, *Down and Out in Paris and London* (Penguin, 1989), pp. 144–6.

49.   *Reception Centres for persons without a settled way of living*, National Assistance Board Report (1952), p. 8.

50.   *Report of the Departmental Committee on the Relief of the Casual Poor*, as previously quoted, pp. 28–9, 44–7.

51.   As note 50, p. 23.

52.   John Stewart, as previously quoted, p. 145.

53.   UAB memo 281, AST 7/314, Public Record Office cited by Noel Whiteside, *Bad Times* (1991), p. 102.

54.   W. J. Smart, *Christ and the Homeless Poor* (1938), pp. 204–16.

55.   George Cuttle, *The Legacy of the Rural Guardians* (Cambridge 1934), pp. 287, 265 and 282.

56.   *Reception Centres for persons without a settled way of living*, as previously quoted, p. 5.

57.   G. Cuttle, as previously quoted, pp. 239, 240, 246 and 247.

58.   'Vagrancy Act', 6 June 1935, 25 George V, Chapter 20, *Public Acts and Measures*, 25 and 26 George V (1934–5), pp. 195–6.

CHAPTER 7   HOMELESSNESS AND THE WELFARE STATE

1.   De Tocqueville, 'Memoir on Pauperism' (1835) cited in S. Danziger and P. Gottschalk, 'The Poverty of Losing Ground', *Challenge,* May/June 1985, p. 32.

2. Lewis Carroll, *Through the Looking Glass*.
3. John Stewart, *Of No Fixed Abode* (1975), pp. 2–3.
4. *Public Assistance, Vagrancy*, Ministry of Health Circular 136/46, June 1946.
5. Suzanne M. Wood, 'Camberwell Reception Centre: a consideration of the need for health and social services of homeless, single men', *Journal of Social Policy*, 5, 4 (1976), p. 390.
6. *Summary Report of the Ministry of Health*, PP 1942–43 [c. 6468], IV, p. 27.
7. *Reception Centres for Persons without a Settled Way of Living*, National Assistance Board Report (1952), p. 5.
8. *Persons in Receipt of Poor Relief*, pp. 21 and 33 (HMSO, 1947), PP 1947–48, XXII.
9. John Leach and John Wing, *Helping Destitute Men* (1980), p. 6.
10. The 1952 NAB Report on *Reception Centres for persons without a settled way of living*, pp. 6–7, confirmed that 'more than a quarter' of the casuals interviewed had been at the same centre for a month or more.
11. Suzanne M. Wood, 'Camberwell Reception Centre...', as previously quoted, p. 391; John Stewart, as previously quoted, p. 56.
12. *1949 National Assistance Board Report*, p. 29.
13. *1950 National Assistance Board Report*, pp. 29–30.
14. *Reception Centres for Persons without a Settled Way of Living*, National Assistance Board, (1952), pp. 5–8.
15. John Stewart, as previously quoted, p. 147.
16. *1953 National Assistance Board Report*, p. 24.
17. As noted 16.
18. As noted 16.
19. As noted 16, pp. 24–6.
20. *1955 National Assistance Board Report*, p. 33.
21. *1954 National Assistance Board Report*, p. 20.
22. *1959 National Assistance Board Report*, p. 31.
23. *1956 National Assistance Board Report*, p. 19.
24. This is indication of the changing official attitudes in responding to casual applicants. It will be recalled from Chapter 5 how from the 1870s the use of individual cells was a cornerstone of LGB strategy in 'dealing more competently' with casuals.
25. *1959 National Assistance Board Report*, p. 32.
26. *1962 National Assistance Board Report*, p. 49.
27. *1964 National Assistance Board Report*, pp. 45–6.
28. *Report on Homeless Single Persons*, National Assistance Board (1966), pp. 169–70.
29. Lionel Rose, *Rogues and Vagabonds* (1988), p. 179.
30. *Report on Homeless Single Persons* (1966), as previously quoted, pp. 177, 172, 173 and 174.
31. *Report on Homeless Single Persons*, Appendix XII (1966), as previously quoted, pp. 245–6.
32. Lionel Rose, as previously quoted, pp. 180, 184–5.
33. Madeline Drake and others, *Single and Homeless*, DoE (1981), p. 12.
34. As note 33, pp. 15–17.

35. *Report of the Working Party on Vagrancy and Street Offences*, Home Office (1976), pp. 24–5.
36. Leonard Leigh, 'Vagrancy and the Criminal Law' in Tim Cook (ed.) *Vagrancy* (1979), p. 113–14.
37. As note 33, p. 95.
38. Paul Q. Watchman and others, *Homelessness and the Law* (1983), p. 9.
39. *EVA Campaign Briefing Paper* (June 1990), pp. 2, 3 and 4.
40. Shelter, *The Grief Report* (1972).
41. Lorraine Thompson, *An Act of Compromise* (1988), p. 9.
42. Maureen Crane, *Elderly Homeless People Sleeping on the Streets of London* (1993), p. 8.
43. Paul Q.Watchman and others, as previously quoted, p. 33.
44. John Greve and others, *Homelessness in Britain* (1990), p. 29.
45. *Hansard*, 385 HL Official Report (15 July 1977), col. 1157.
46. Lorraine Thompson, as previously quoted, pp. 55 and 59.
47. Madeline Drake and others, as previously quoted, p. 9.
48. Lionel Rose, as previously quoted, p. 182.
49. Audit Commission, *Housing the Homeless: the Local Authority Role* (1989), p. 2.
50. Jill Vincent and others, *Homeless Single Men* (1995), p. 2.
51. Tony Wilkinson, *Down and Out* (1981), p. 8.
52. Bob Hudson, 'Unsettling the Unsettled', *Housing*, October 1985, vol. 21, no. 10.
53. Lionel Rose, as previously quoted, pp. 191–3.
54. For example, the *1985 Board and Lodging Regulations,* the *Social Security Act 1986* and the *Social Security Act 1988;* John Greve and others, *Homelessness in Britain* (1990), p. 16.
55. Isobel Anderson and others, *Single Homeless People* (1993), pp. 1 and 2.
56. *Guardian Education*, 5 March 1996, p. 10.
57. For further discussion: Angela Evans, *Alternatives to Bed and Breakfast* (1991).
58. Rosy Thornton, *The New Homeless* (1990), p. 9.
59. John Greve and others, as quoted previously, pp. 8 and 16.
60. *Social Trends* (1985), p. 129.
61. The first four of these examples are from Susan Hutson and Mark Liddiard, *Youth Homelessness* (1994), pp. 128–30; the fifth from H. Crane, *Speaking from Experience: Working with Homeless Families* (1990), p. 40.
62. Isobel Anderson and others, as previously quoted, pp. ix, x, and 12.
63. Geoffrey Randall and Susan Brown, *The Rough Sleepers Initiative: an Evaluation*, Department of the Environment (1993), p. v.
64. SHiL *Building on Initiatives*, Single Homelessness in London (1996), pp. 5 and 8.
65. *The Big Issue*, no. 259, 17 November 1997, p. 8.
66. Jeanne Moore and others, *The Faces of Homelessness in London* (1995), pp. 1 and 38.
67. Peter H. Rossi, *Down and Out in America* (1989), p. 177.
68. Charles Murray, *The Emerging British Underclass* (1990).

69. Paul E. Peterson, 'The Urban Underclass and the Poverty Paradox', in C. Jenks and others (eds), *The Urban Underclass* (1991), p. 12.
70. J. D. Greenstone, 'Culture, Rationality and the Underclass', in Christopher Jenks and others (eds), *The Urban Underclass* (1991), p. 399.
71. Shelter, *Housing Bill and Benefit Changes* (1996), pp. 1 and 2.
72. Julia Wardhaugh, 'Homeless in Chinatown ...', *Sociology*, vol. 30, No. 4, November 1996, p. 702.
73. Derek Hawes and Barbara Perez, *The Gypsy and the State*, 2nd edn. (1996), pp. 126–47.
74. *The Big Issue*, no. 215, 13–19 January 1997, p. 4.
75. Evidence for London's rough sleepers in 1996 suggested that (a) 74 out of a population of 365 rough sleepers in central London died during the year, (b) the average age of rough sleepers dying from natural causes was 46 years, (c) they were 35 times more likely to kill themselves than were the general population, (d) rough sleepers were four times more likely to die of unnatural causes like accidents, assaults, drug or alcohol poisoning. Crisis, *Still Dying for a Home* (1996)
76. For example: Tim Cook, *Vagrant Alcoholics* (1975); D. Brandon, *Homeless* (1974); Tony Wilkinson, as previously quoted; *The Times*, 23 September 1973.
77. John Greve and others, as previously quoted, p. 17.
78. Lawrence M. Mead, *From Welfare to Work* (1997).

CHAPTER 8 CONCLUSION

1. Thomas Carlyle, *Past and Present*, p. 203.
2. R. Vorspan, 'Vagrancy and the New Poor Law in Late-Victorian and Edwardian England', *English History Review*, 92 (1977), p. 60; *Report of the Departmental Committee on Vagrancy*, vol. 1, PP 1906, CIII [c. 2852], pp. 24–5; Glen Mathews, 'The Search for a Cure for Vagrancy in Worcestershire, 1870–1920', *Midland History*, 11/12 (1986–7), pp. 105–6; S. and B. Webb, *History of Local Government, English Poor Law History*, part II (1963 edn), pp. 403, 947.
3. John Pound, *Poverty and Vagrancy in Tudor England* (1986), p. 2.
4. Charles Murray, 'The Emerging British Underclass', in Ruth Lister (ed.), *Charles Murray and the Underclass* (1996), pp. 40–1.
5. Cited by E. L. Bassuk, 'The homeless problem', *Scientific American,* 251 (1984), pp. 40–5.
6. Barry Hugill, 'Britain's Exclusion Zone', *The Observer,* 13 April 1997.
7. Julia Wardhaugh, 'Homeless in Chinatown ...', *Sociology*, vol. 30, No. 4, November 1996, p. 701.
8. Michael Harrington, *The Other America* (1962), p. 178.
9. Jeanne Moore and others, *The Faces of Homelessness in London* (1995), p. 10.
10. Peter Townsend, *The International Analysis of Poverty* (1993), p. 195; also see *Income and Wealth* (Joseph Rowntree Foundation 1995).

11. C. Oppenheim, *Poverty: the Facts* (CPAG 1990), p. 91.
12. David S. Sheppard (Chairman), 'Unemployment and the Future of Work', *Christian Ecumenical Churches Report,* April 1997.
13. *The Big Issue*, no. 231, 5–11 May 1997.
14. Shelter: *News Release,* 22 May 1997.

Bibliography

London publication unless otherwise stated.

Principal 'Vagrancy' Statutes – chronologically listed

Wihtraed (AD 690–725), C. J. Ribton-Turner, *The History of Vagrants and Vagrancy* (1887), p. 3.

Canute (AD 1017–35), C. J. Ribton-Turner, as above, p. 7.

23 Edward III [c. 5–7], 1349, 'Ordinance of Labourers', *Statutes of the Realm,* I (1810), p. 308.

25 Edward III, Stat.2 [c. 2–5], 1350–1, 'Statute of Labourers', *Statutes of the Realm,* I (1810), p. 312.

12 Richard II [c. 7], 1388, *Statutes of the Realm,* II (1816), p. 58.

4 Henry VII [c. 19], 1489, *Statutes of the Realm,* II (1816), p. 542.

11 Henry VII [c. 2], 1495, *Statutes of the Realm,* II (1816), p. 574.

22 Henry VIII [c. 12], 1495, *Statutes of the Realm,* III (1817), p. 329.

27 Henry VIII [c. 25], 1535–6, *Statutes of the Realm,* III (1817), p. 560.

1 Edward VI [c. 3], 1547, *Statutes of the Realm,* IV (1819), pp. 5–6.

2 & 3 Phil. and Mary [c. 5], 1555, *Statutes of the Realm,* IV (1819), p. 281.

14 Elizabeth [c. 5], 1572, *Statutes of the Realm,* IV (1819), pp. 591–4.

18 Elizabeth, [c. 3], 1575–6, *Statutes of the Realm,* IV (1819), p. 611.

39 Elizabeth [c. 3], 1597, *Statutes of the Realm,* IV (1819), p. 899.

Commonwealth [c. 21], 1656, C. H. Firth and R. S. Rait, *Acts and Ordinances of the Interregnum,* I, pp. 1042–5.

14 Charles II [c. 12], 1662, *Statutes of the Realm,* V (1819), pp. 401–5.

4 William and Mary [c. 8], 1692, *Statutes of the Realm,* VI (1819), pp. 390–1.

13 Anne [c. 26], 1713, *Statutes of the Realm,* IX (1822), pp. 976–82.

5 George IV [c. 83], 1824, Section 4, *Statutes at Large,* 23, 4 Geo. 4 to 5 Geo. 4, p. 781 and 783.

45 and 46 Victoria [c. 36], 1882, W. G. Glen, *The General Orders Relating to the Poor Law* (1898), p. 1051.

25 and 26 George V, 1934–5, *Public Acts and Measures,* pp. 195–6.

Parliamentary Papers (PPs) – chronologically listed

Report of Select Committee on existing Laws relating to Vagrants, PP 1821 [c. 543], IV.121.

First Annual Report of Poor Law Commissioners, PP1835 [c. 500], XXXV.107.

5th Annual Report of Poor Law Commissioners, PP 1839 [c. 239], XX.I.

2nd Annual Report of Poor Law Board, PP 1850 [c. 1142], XXVII.

John Revans, *Reports to the Poor Law Board on the Laws of Settlement and Removal of the Poor,* PP 1850 [c. 1152], XXVII.229.

George Coode, *Report of the Poor Law Board on the Law of Settlement and Removal of the Poor,* PP 1851 [c. 675], XXVI.1.

11th Annual Report of the Poor Law Board, App. 33, PP 1859 [c. 2500], IX.

18th Annual Report of the Poor Law Board, PP 1866 [c. 3700], XXXVIII.

21st Annual Report of the Poor Law Board, PP 1868–9 [c. 4197], XXVIII.I.

22nd Annual Report of the Poor Law Board, App. D, PP 1870 [c. 123], XXXV.

1st Report of the Local Government Board, PP 1872 [c. 516], XXVIII.

Andrew Doyle, *Reports on Poor Laws in Foreign Countries,* PP 1875 [c. 1255], LXV.

5th Annual Report of the Local Government Board, PP 1876 [c. 1585], XXXI.

J. J. Henley, *Report on the Poor Laws of certain of the United States,* PP 1877 [c. 1868], XXXVII.

16th Annual Report of the Local Government Board, PP 1887 [c. 5131], XXXVI.1.

22nd Annual Report of the Local Government Board, PP 1893–4 [c. 7180], XLIII.1.

30th Annual Report of the Poor Law Board, App. E, PP 1901 [c. 746], XXV.

Report of the LGB Departmental Committee on Vagrancy, vol.1, PP 1906 [c. 2852], CIII.1.

Report of the Royal Commission on the Care and Control of the Feeble-minded, PP 1908 [c. 4202], XXXIX.

Report of Royal Commission on the Poor Laws and the Relief of Distress, PP 1909 [c. 4499] XXXVII.

Report of the Metropolitan Poor law Inspectors' Advisory Committee on the Homeless Poor, PP 1914 [c. 7307], XLIV; also PP 1914–16 [c. 7840], XXXII.

Report of the LGB Departmental Committee on the Relief of the Casual Poor, Appendix 1, PP 1929–30 [c. 3640], XVII.121.

Report of the Ministry of Health, PP 1942–3 [c. 6468], IV.

Hansard, 385 HL Official Report (15 July 1977).

Reports, Pamphlets and Papers – chronologically listed

PRO, *MH 12/12222,* 16 January 1851.

PRO, *MH 12/12222,* 15 January 1852.

Charity Organisation Reporter, 17th April 1872.

Charity Organisation Reporter, 7th July 1875.

The Liverpool Lantern, 1st March 1879.

17th Annual Report, Liverpool Central Relief Society (1879–80).

9th and 12th Annual Reports, Brighton Charity Organisation Society (1880 and 1883 respectively).

11th Annual Report, Birmingham Charity Organisation Society (1880).

1st Annual Report, Derby Charity Organisation Society (1880).

13th Annual Report, Edinburgh Association for Improving the Condition of the Poor (1880).

9th Annual Report, Leeds Charity Organisation Society (1880).

Dorking (Surrey) *Census Enumerators' Book* (1881).

PRO, *MH 12/12229,* 22nd June 1881.

PRO, *MH32/46,* 25 February and 20 March 1882.

9th Annual Report, Walsall Charity Organisation Society (1884).

Charity Organisation Quarterly, vol. XI, April 1937.

Public Assistance, Vagrancy (Ministry of Health Circular 136/46, June 1946).
Report on Persons in Receipt of Poor Relief (HMSO 1947).
Annual Reports of the National Assistance Board.
Report on Reception Centres for Persons Without a Settled Way of Living (National Assistance Board 1952).
Report on Homeless Single Persons (National Assistance Board 1966).
British Labour Statistics: Historical Abstract, 1886–1968 (HMSO 1971).
The Grief Report (Shelter 1972).
Report of the Working Party on Vagrancy and Street Offences (HMSO 1976).
'Housing Policy: A Consultative Document', Department of the Environment (1977).
M. Drake and others, *Single and Homeless*, DoE (HMSO 1981).
Housing the Homeless: the Local Authority Role (Audit Commission 1989).
EVA Campaign Briefing Paper (June 1990).
Isobel Anderson and others, *Single Homeless People* (HMSO 1993).
Income and Wealth (Joseph Rowntree Foundation 1995).
Geoffrey Randall and Susan Brown, *The Rough Sleepers Initiative: an Evaluation* (HMSO 1993).
Single Homeless in London, Building on Initiatives (SHiL 1996).
Housing Bill and Benefit Changes (Shelter 1996).
Still Dying for a Home (Crisis 1996).
'Unemployment and the Future of Work', *Christian Ecumenical Churches Report* (April 1997).
The Big Issue (13 January, 5 May and 17 November 1997).
'Constructing Classes', *Report by Economic and Social Research Council* (December 1997).

Nineteenth Century and Earlier Publications – alphabetically listed

Henry Arth, *Provision for the Poore now in Penuries, out of the Store-House of Goods plenty, Explained by H.A.* (1597).
William Booth, *In Darkest England and the Way Out* (1890).
A. H. C. Brown, 'Relief of Vagrants', *Poor Law Conferences* (1881).
Thomas Carlyle, *Past and Present* (1843).
George Coode, *Report to the Poor Law Board on the Law of Settlement and Removal of the Poor, dated 5 August 1851,* PP 1851 [c. 675], XXVI.I.
Michael Dalton, *The Countrey Justice* (1635).
F. M. Eden, *The State of the Poor* (1797).
F. Engels, *The Condition of the Working Class in England* (1845; Stanford 1968 edn).
Thomas Fuller, *The Church History of Britain from the Birth of Jesus Christ until the Year MDCXLVIII, Book II* (1655)
Thomas Harman, *Cauaet or Warening for Common Cursetors*, 2nd edn (1567).
William Harrison, *Description of England, Vol. 1* (1887).
Thomas Hawksley, *The Charities of London and Some Errors in their Administration* (1869).
J. J. Jusserand, *English Wayfaring Life in the Middle Ages (XIVth Century)* 8th edn (1891).

John Lambert, *Vagrancy Laws and Vagrants* (1868).

C. S. Loch, *The Charities Register and Digest* (1890).

Alfred Marshall, *Principles of Economics*, 2nd edn (1891).

George Nicholls, *English Poor Law, Vol. I* (1898).

William Perkins, *A Treatise of Callings, Workes, I* (1612).

W. C. P. Purton, 'Relief of Vagrants', *Poor Law Conferences* (1881).

E. G. Ravenstein, 'The Laws of Migration', *Journal of the Royal Statistical Society, XLVIII*, part II, June 1885.

J. E. Thorold Rogers, *A History of Agriculture and Prices in England: 1259–1793, Vol. III* (Oxford 1882).

Miss Tillard, 'The Relief of the Homeless', *Charity Organisation Review*, vol. VII (1891).

Samuel Smiles, *Self-Help with Illustrations of Conduct and Perseverance* (1859).

Herbert Spencer, 'Coming Slavery', *Contemporary Review*, vol. XLV (April 1884).

Thomas Starkey, 'The Nature of the Common Weal', in C. H. Williams (ed.), *English Historical Documents, 1485–1558* (1967).

Alexis de Tocqueville, *Memoir on Pauperism* (1835).

C. J. Ribton-Turner, *A History of Vagrants and Vagrancy and Beggars and Begging* (1887).

W. M. Wilkinson, 'The Vagrant', *Poor Law Conferences* (1881).

H. Woodcock, *The Gypsies, Being a Brief Account of their History* (1865).

Arthur Young, *Eastern Tour, Vol. IV* (1771).

Twentieth Century Publications and Editions – alphabetically listed

Peter Archard, 'Vagrancy – A Literature Review' in Tim Cook and G. Braithwaite, *Vagrancy: Some New Perspectives* (1979).

Frank Aydelotte, *Elizabethan Rogues and Vagabonds* (1913).

G. E. Aylmer, 'Unbelief in seventeenth-century England', in D. Pennington and K. Thomas (eds), *Puritans and Revolutionaries* (1978).

E. L. Bassuk, 'The homeless problem', *Scientific American*, 251 (1984).

George K. Behlmer, 'The Gypsy problem in Victorian England', *Victorian Studies, 28, 2* (1984–5).

A. L. Beier, 'Poor relief in Warwickshire (1630–1660)', *Past and Present*, 35, December 1966.

A. L. Beier, 'Vagrants and social order in Elizabethan England', *Past and Present*, 64, August 1974.

A. L. Beier, *Masterless Men* (1985).

A. L. Beier, 'Poverty and Progress in early modern England', in A. L. Beier and others (eds), *The First Modern Society* (1989).

John Bellars, *The Quaker Tapestry, Panel E2*.

William Beveridge, *Unemployment: a Problem of Industry* (New edn, 1930).

George Bourne, *Memoirs of a Surrey Labourer* (1983 edn).

P. Bowden, 'Agricultural Prices, Farm Profits and Rents', in Joan Thirsk (1967).

I. C. Bradley, *Enlightened Entrepreneurs* (1987).

A. R. Bridbury, *Economic Growth: England in the Later Middle Ages* (1962).

Henry Phelps Brown and Sheila V. Hopkins, *A Perspective of Wages and Prices* (1981).

John Burnett, *Idle Hands* (1994).

M. Caplan, 'The New Poor Law and the struggle for Union Chargeability', *International Review of Social History,* XXIII (1978).

William J. Chambliss, 'A Sociological Analysis of the Law of Vagrancy', *Social Problems* 12 (1964).

E. P. Cheyney, *An Introduction to the Industrial and Social History of England* (New York 1920).

Carl Chinn, *Poverty amidst prosperity: The urban poor in England 1834–1914* (1995)

Carlo M. Cipolla, *Before the Industrial Revolution, European Society and Economy 1000–1700* (1981).

G. Clark, '"Ins-and-outs" and Tramps, the Detention of', *Poor Law Conferences* (1910–11).

Peter Clark, 'The migrant in Kentish towns 1580–1640', in Peter Clark and Paul Slack (eds), *Crisis and Order in English Towns 1500–1700* (1972).

Peter Clark, 'Migration in England during the Seventeenth and early Eighteenth Centuries', *Past and Present 83,* May 1979).

L. A. Clarkson, *The Pre-industrial Economy in England 1500–1750* (1971).

C. G. A. Clay, *Economic Expansion and Social Change, England 1500–1700,* vols I and II (1984).

D. C. Coleman, 'Labour in the English Economy of the Seventeenth Century', *Economic History Review, 2nd Series, VIII* (1955–6).

D. C. Coleman, *Economy of England (1450–1750)* (1977).

C. I. Cohen and others, *Old Men of the Bowery* (New York 1989).

Philip O'Connor, *Britain in the Sixties: Vagrancy* (1963).

Bernard A. Cook, 'Poverty', in Sally Mitchell (ed.), *Victorian Britain* (1988).

Tim Cook, *Vagrant Alcoholics* (1975).

C. Cottingham, *Poverty and the Urban Underclass* (Lexington 1982).

Julian Cornwall, 'English Population in the Sixteenth Century', *Economic History Review, 23* (1970).

Maureen Crane, *Elderly Homeless People Sleeping on the Streets of London* (1993).

Joan M.Crouse, *The Homeless Transient in the Great Depression* (New York 1986).

M. A. Crowther, *The Workhouse System, 1834–1929* (1983).

George Cuttle, *The Legacy of the Rural Guardians* (Cambridge 1934).

C. S. L. Davies, 'Slavery and Protector Somerset; the Vagrancy Act of 1547', *Economic History Review,* 2nd series, XIX, no. 3 (1966).

Clive Emsley, *Crime and Society in England, (1750–1900)* (1987).

Angela Evans, *Alternatives to Bed and Breakfast* (1991).

C. H. Feinstein, *National Income, Expenditure and Output of the United Kingdom, 1855–1965* (1972).

Keith Feiling, *A History of England* (Book Club edn, 1975).

J. M. Fothergill, *The Town Dweller, His Needs and His Wants* (New York 1985).

Simon Fowler, 'Vagrancy in mid-Victorian Richmond, Surrey', *Local Historian,* 21 (1991).

A. Ruth Fry, *John Bellers 1654–1725, Quaker, Economist and Social Reformer* (1933).

Bronislaw Geremek, *Poverty* (1994).

A. Giddens, *The Class Structue of the Advanced Societies* (1973).

Irene Glasser, *Homelessness in Global Perspective* (1994).

B. Kirkman Gray, *A History of English Philanthropy* (1967).

John Greve and others, *Homelessness in London* (1971).

John Greve and others, *Homelessness in Britain* (1990).

D. B. Grigg, *Population Growth and Agrarian Change: a Historical Perspective* (1980).

Rider Haggard, *Regeneration* (1910).

Jerome Hall, *Theft, Law and Society* (Boston 1935).

H. S. G. Halsbury Earl of, *The Laws of England* (1912).

J. L. and B. Hammond, *The Village Labourer*, 4th edn (1936).

E. M. Hampson, *Treatment of Poverty in Cambridgeshire; 1597–1834* (1934).

Michael Harrington, *The Other America* (1962).

Derek Hawes and Barbara Perez, *The Gypsy and the State*, 2nd edn (Bristol, 1996).

Christopher Hibbert, *The English* (1987).

Christopher Hill, *The World Turned Upside Down* (1987).

Christopher Hill, *Society and Puritanism in Pre-Revolutionary England* (Penguin 1991).

Gertrude Himmelfarb, *The Idea of Poverty* (1985).

W. G. Hoskins, 'Harvest Fluctuations and English Economic History, 1480–1619', *Agricultural History Review, xii* (1964).

W. G. Hoskins, *Provincial England* (1965).

W. G. Hoskins, *The Age of Plunder, King Henry's England 1500–1547* (1976).

Bob Hudson, 'Unsettling the Unsettled', *Housing,* vol. 21, no. 10, October 1985,

Ann Hughes, *The Causes of the English Civil War* (1991)

C. H. Hull (ed.), *The Economic Writings of Sir William Petty together with the Observations upon the Bills of Mortality by John Graunt* (New York 1963).

Susan Hutson and Mark Liddiard, *Youth Homelessness* (1994).

Christopher Jenks and others (eds), *The Urban Underclass* (Washington, 1991).

David Jones, *Crime, Protest, Community and Police in Nineteenth Century Britain* (1982).

R. B. Jones, *Economic and Social History of England, 1770–1970* (1971).

W. K. Jordan, *Philanthropy in England, 1480–1660* (1959).

Michael B. Katz (ed.), *The 'Underclass' Debate* (Princeton, 1993).

J. Kent, 'Population Mobility and Alms', *Local Population Studies, no. 27* (1981).

Margaret K. Kohler, *Memories of Old Dorking* (Dorking 1977).

Peter Laslett, *The World We Have Lost – Further Explored* Cambridge 1983).

John Leach and John Wing, *Helping Destitute Men* (1980).

Leonard Leigh, 'Vagrancy and the Criminal Law' in Tim Cook, ed., *Vagrancy* (1979).

E. M. Leonard, *The Early History of English Poor Relief* (1965).

Ruth Lister (ed.), *Charles Murray and the Underclass* (1996).

C. Oman, *The Great Revolt of 1381* (1906).

David Owen, *English Philanthropy, 1660–1960* (1965).

W. T. MacCaffrey, *Exeter, 1540–1640* (Harvard 1958).

Glen Mathews, 'The Search for a Cure for Vagrancy in Worcestershire, 1870–1920', *Midland History*, 11/12 (1986/7).

Patrick McGill, *Children of the Dead End* (1915; 1980 edition).

Dorothy Marshall, *The English Poor in the Eighteenth Century* (1926).

Marcel Mauss, *The Gift* (1990).

Lawrence M. Mead, *Beyond Entitlement: the Social Obligations of Citizenship* (New York 1986).

Lawrence M. Mead, *From Welfare to Work* (1997).

B. R. Mitchell and P. Deane, *Abstract of British Historical Statistics* (1962).

Jeanne Moore and others, *The Faces of Homelessness in London* (1995).

J. S. Morrill, *Cheshire 1630–1660* (1974).

Charles Murray, 'The Emerging British Underclass' (1990).

Kathryn M. Neckerman, '"Underclass", Family Patterns', in Michael B. Katz (ed.), *The 'Underclass' Debate* (Princeton 1993).

Mark Neuman, 'Poor Law', in Sally Mitchell (ed.), *Victorian Britain* (1988).

C. Oppenheim, *Poverty: The Facts* (1990).

George Orwell, *Down and Out in Paris and London* (1989).

R. B. Outhwaite, *Inflation in Tudor and Early Stuart England* (1969).

D. M. Palliser, *The Age of Elizabeth* (1992).

Paul E. Peterson, 'The Urban Underclass and the Poverty Paradox' in C. Jenks and others (eds), *The Urban Underclass* (Washington 1991).

Frances F.Piven, *Regulating the Poor* (1972).

Plato, *The Republic* (Penguin 1987).

J. F. Pound, *Poverty and Vagrancy in Tudor England* (1986).

A. Redford, *Labour migration in England, 1800–50* (1926).

Melvin Richter, *The Politics of Conscience: T. H. Green and his Age* (1964).

Clayton Roberts and David Roberts, *A History of England Volume 1* (Englewood Cliffs, NJ, 1991).

M. Rooff, *A Hundred Years of Family Welfare* (1972).

Lionel Rose, *Rogues and Vagabonds* (1988).

M. E. Rose, *The English Poor Law, 1780–1930* (1971).

Peter H. Rossi, *Down and Out in America* (1989).

A. L. Rowse, *The England of Elizabeth* (1950).

Miri Rubin, 'The Poor' in Rosemary Horrox (ed.), *Fifteenth-Century Attitudes* (1994).

W. G. Runciman, *Relative Deprivation and Social Justice* (1966).

G. H. Sabine, *A History of Political Theory* (New York 1963)

Raphael Samuel, 'Comers and Goers' in H. J. Dyos and M. Wolff, *The Victorian City* (1976).

Karl de Schweinitz, *England's Road to Social Security,* New York (Perpetua edn, 1975).

G. B. Shaw, *Pygmalion* (Penguin, 1957).

David Sibley, *Outsiders in Urban Societies* (Oxford 1981).

Paul Slack, 'Vagrants and Vagrancy in England (1598–1664', *Economic History Review,* 2nd series, 27 (1974).

Paul Slack, *Poverty and Policy in Tudor and Stuart England* (1988).

Paul Slack, *The English Poor Law, 1531–1782* (1995).

W. J. Smart, *Christ and the Homeless Poor* (1938).

N. J. Smith, *Poverty in England, 1601–1936* (1972).

Peter N. Stearns, *European society in Upheaval* (1975).

Doris M. Stenton, *English Society in the Early Middle Ages* (1964). John Stewart, *Of No Fixed Abode* (1975).

John Stewart, *Of No Fixed Abode* (1975).

Philip Styles, 'The evolution of the Law of Settlement', *University of Birmingham Historical Journal, IX, no.1* (1963).

Barry Supple, *Commercial Crisis and Change in England 1600–1642* (1959).

E. Surtz and J. H. Hexter, *The Complete Works of St. Thomas More*, vol. 4 (Yale, 1965).

W. H. Syme, *Honour All Men* (1904).

R. H. Tawney, *The Agrarian Problem in the Sixteenth Century* (New York: Torchbook, 1967).

R. H. Tawney, *Religion and the Rise of Capitalism* (Pelican, 1966).

Joan Thirsk (ed.), *Agricultural History of England and Wales, IV (1500–1640)* (Cambridge 1967).

Lorraine Thompson, *An Act of Compromise* (1988).

Rosy Thornton, *The New Homeless* (1990).

Peter Townsend, *The International Analysis of Poverty* (1993).

G. M. Trevelyan, *English Social History* (1946).

Jill Vincent and others, *Homeless Single Men* (1995).

Rachel Vorspan, 'Vagrancy and the New Poor Law ...', *English History Review, 92* (1977).

Julia Wardhaugh, 'Homeless in Chinatown', *Sociology,* vol. 30, no. 4, November 1996.

Paul Q. Watchman and others, *Homelessness and the Law* (Glasgow 1983).

Sophie Watson, *Housing and Homelessness* (1986).

S. and B. Webb, *English Local Government: English Poor Law History part I, The Old Poor Law* (1927 edn).

Sidney and Beatrice Webb, *English Poor Law History* (1929; repr. 1963).

Sidney and Beatrice Webb, *History of English Local Government* (1929; repr. 1963).

Noel Whiteside, *Bad Times* (1991).

Tony Wilkinson, *Down and Out* (1981).

James A. Williamson, *The Tudor Age*, 3rd edn (1964).

Suzanne M. Wood, 'Camberwell Reception Centre ...', *Journal of Social Policy,* 5, 4 (1976), pp. 389–99.

Keith Wrightson, *English Society (1580–1680)* (1982).

E. A. Wrigley, 'A simple model of London's importance in changing English Society and Economy 1650–1750', in John Patten, *Pre-Industrial England* (Folkestone 1979).

E. A. Wrigley and R. S. Schofield, *The Population History of England, 1541–1871. A Reconstruction* (1981).

Index